MW00582259

ALL TO PIECES

DAVID GREENE

Unmentionables Series

BOOK TWO

This hardcover edition published March, 2019

ISBN-13: 978-0-9889462-8-6

Cover painting detail from *Lost on the Grand Banks* by Winslow Homer, 1885,
figures altered by Michael Banning

This is a work of fiction. Names, characters, places, and incidents are either the product of the author's imagination or are used fictitiously.

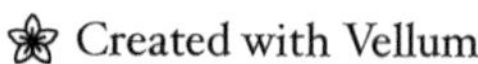

All to Pieces is a 19th-century phrase that means "completely, absolutely"

1

"THEY BOTH HAVE THE SOUP!"

"Young man!"

The elderly woman seated at the restaurant table wore a buckram-brim hat covered with chenille braid, crowned by periwinkle silk. As Cato approached, she untied the bow beneath her chin. Cato was dressed in a black waistcoat, white shirt, black bow tie, and a crisp white apron—a uniform meant to mimic the look of a waiter in a Parisian cafe.

"My sister and I"—the woman pointed across the table at her sibling—"have just arrived in Chicago this afternoon."

Cato nodded. "Excellent, madam. Where did you come from?"

"Cincinnati."

"How was your journey?"

"Most tiresome. The roads are terrible. There were so many interruptions." She threw up a gloved hand. "The war, you know. There were Confederate soldiers, then Union soldiers, so much confusion ...." Her voice trailed off.

Cato frowned. "I imagine it was difficult." Then he brightened. "But I hope you will enjoy your stay here at The Sherman House."

"I intend to do just that," the woman said. "Now then, I'm told that in this hotel every provision has been made for the convenience of ladies."

"Yes," Cato said, though his look betrayed his bewilderment. "Is there something in particular ....?"

"I hope that this restaurant contains a room d'toilette that is specially apportioned to the use of ladies."

"Yes," Cato said. "We do have a rest room for ladies." He smiled. "The finest that civilization can offer."

"Young man, how old are you?"

"I'm twenty-two, madam."

"Well then, I daresay you're far too young to know what civilization may or may not offer. Nevertheless, would you direct me to its location?"

"Madam, you'll find the ladies' room located just there." He pointed to the back of the room. "Through that passageway flanked by green drapery."

"Very good," she said. "I shall pay that room a visit in due time. Now, what have you on offer today?"

"Madam, we have oyster soup to start."

"I'll have that," the second woman said, before Cato could continue.

The first woman glanced at her sister with annoyance, then said, "I shall start with the soup as well. If you bring the soups, we'll decide on the rest later."

"Very good, ladies."

Cato hurried off to the kitchen. When he came back out he saw a well-dressed young man, not much older than himself, standing near the green drapery at the back of the room beneath the sign that read "Gentlemen."

The young man waved his hand in summons. Cato nodded and approached him.

"I'd like to speak to you," the man said. "If you have a moment."

"Yes, sir, how may I help you?"

The man took Cato's arm and pulled him back toward the Gentlemen's room. "In private," he said.

Cato resisted the man's pull. "I'm sorry, sir. The staff is not permitted to use the Gentlemen's rest room."

The man looked around. "Is there somewhere else we can go? I have something confidential to tell you. It concerns your friend."

"My friend?"

"I'm afraid I don't know his name. A few months ago he told me that he was Miss Holland's servant."

"Miss Holland?" Cato was confused. The only man in Chicago who'd ever been Miss Holland's servant was Jimmy. Miss Holland no longer regarded him as a servant, though he was legally still her father's slave. Jimmy lived with Cato and worked as a stevedore on the docks at the Chicago River.

"There's an alley behind the kitchen," Cato said. "We can talk there."

He led the stranger through the busy kitchen, past the aroma of roasting turkey and baking pot pies, and out a door into the alley.

"My name is Ames ... Walter Ames," the man began. "I work at D.B. Fisk, milliner. The shop is on Couch Place. Your friend came into our shop some months ago to buy a white ribbon for Miss Holland."

Cato had heard this story. He was silent a moment, then he said, "My name is Cato. Jimmy told me about his visit to you."

"Did he?" Mr. Ames seemed pleased by this. "Well, I remembered seeing him because he ... Jimmy ... is memorable in appearance." He looked earnestly at Cato, as if to convey some deeper meaning.

Cato nodded as though he understood what Mr. Ames meant, but in truth he wasn't at all sure.

"Back then," Mr. Ames continued, "I thought ... when Jimmy came in the shop ... I thought that, perhaps, he was in some kind of trouble. He was out of breath. He seemed agitated."

Jimmy had told Cato, months earlier, that he'd run into the hat shop to evade a gang of slave-catchers, and that, despite the awkward circumstances, he'd sensed something flirtatious in Mr. Ames's behavior, which had surprised him.

Cato decided to be candid. "He *was* in trouble, Mr. Ames. He was fleeing slave-catchers. They chased him right to the door of your shop."

Mr. Ames touched his hand to the side of his cheek. "Oh, then it's true." He reached out to take hold of Cato's arm. "I'm afraid they've got him!"

"Got him?"

"Yes," said Mr. Ames. "Just now. I was at the shop. I happened to be looking out the window. Those men, the slave-catchers—they ambushed him, Jimmy, right there on Couch Place, not thirty minutes ago. They had pistols. They forced him into a wagon. I'm sorry."

A look of dread spread across Cato's face. He couldn't speak.

"I didn't dare confront them," Ames continued. "They had weapons." He clasped his hands together. "But I recognized Jimmy, as I said, from our previous encounter. And I knew that he and you, that you and he ...." Mr. Ames stopped, unsure how to broach the delicate subject. "I've seen you both on the street together. And then I knew where to find you, since I've seen you here at the restaurant several times. You waited on me once."

Cato nodded in Mr. Ames's direction, but he was no longer seeing him. His mind reeled with a vision of the pistols aimed at Jimmy.

"I didn't know what else to do," Mr. Ames continued. "I thought of getting the police, but as I was unsure of your friend's status .... I mean his legal status." He raised his eyebrow meaningfully. "I thought the best I might do is come to you, to let you know."

"You were right, Mr. Ames, to come to me." Cato wobbled and took hold of Ames's shoulder to steady himself. "Where did they take him?"

"They forced him to lie down on the bottom of their wagon. Then they covered him with sacks—bags of feed, you know, for horses. And then they drove off. They went south on Wabash. I couldn't see them after that. I came here immediately."

"I must find them." Cato dropped to his knees. "How can this have happened?" He knelt for a moment, his hands covering his face. Then he lowered his hands and looked up and down the alley, as if he might see the wagon in question.

Ames helped Cato stand back up. "They'll probably take him back to the South," Ames said. "For the reward."

"Oh, no. That's not possible. There'll be no reward." Cato shook his head. "That's all done with now." He gestured wildly. "His owner, Dorothy Holland, she's here! It's all changed." His voice cracked. "There's no point in any of it!" There were tears on his cheeks.

"But they must think they can get money," Ames said. "That's what slave-catchers do."

Cato used his apron to wipe his eyes. He stared at Ames, trying to focus. "You say they put him in a wagon. What did the wagon look like?"

"It was plain—a plain wooden wagon."

"There must be something." Cato's mind raced. "There must be some way." He turned and leaned against the building. He rubbed his forehead as he thought. Then he looked back up. "You said they covered him with bags?"

"Yes. With feed bags. To hide him."

"Do you remember the feed bags? Did they have a label?"

Mr. Ames reached into his memory. "Yes." He closed his eyes, trying to picture it. "The bags had a name on them. They were from ... Pilkington."

"Pilkington," Cato repeated. He knew the name. "Pilkington

& Doyle! It's a boarding stable. It's a block from where we live. I must go there."

"Do you think they'll know these men?"

"They must!" Cato turned to go back in the restaurant. "Will you come with me, Mr. Ames?"

Ames nodded. "Yes, of course—if I can help."

Cato put his hand on the restaurant door, but didn't open it. "I have money. Gold coins. From a gentleman. A lot of money. I can give you a reward."

Ames shook his head. "No. You must not think of it." He looked at Cato kindly. "I am ...." His eyes went wide with meaning. "I am ... a friend."

Cato nodded. "I'll give the money to the kidnappers, then. That's all they want. I must find them." He opened the door to the kitchen and was blasted by the sound of dishes clattering as they dropped into a tub of running water. He turned back to Ames. "Wait for me," he said. Then he rushed into the room and called to the dishwasher.

"George!" he shouted. "I have to leave. Something's happened to Jimmy. You'll have to take my place!"

George came out from behind a sink. "You're leaving? What's happened?"

"I don't have time to tell you. Take over for me." He looked at the food already plated by the cooks. "There," he said, pointing. "That's for the two old ladies at table three. They both have the soup!" And with that, he tore off his apron, tossed it to George, and dashed out the door and into the street, where he took the arm of Mr. Walter Ames.

2

"GET A PRETTY SHINE ON HIM"

"Git up on that box."

Hogan pointed to an upturned crate that sat next to a wide barrel filled with water.

"Now, climb in there."

Jimmy was naked, except for the manacles around his wrists. He stepped down into the barrel and the water rose to his waist. His mind summoned up an image of Reverend Zeke. Every summer around the fourth of July, Zeke had stood waist-high in the cool water of Dyer Creek, where he'd baptized slaves who were new believers. Jimmy could still picture his sister Ella as Zeke cradled her chin with a handkerchief before lowering her into salvation. Ella had told him that night that her sins had been washed away, that she'd been reborn. Jimmy had rolled his eyes and laughed.

"Dunk down," Hogan commanded. "All the way!"

Jimmy took a deep breath and closed his eyes. He bent his knees as far as he could until he disappeared into the barrel. Water lapped around his chin, swirled around his nostrils, then drenched his hair. He shuddered.

Months earlier he'd nearly drowned in the Ohio River. But

he'd managed to climb up the embankment and drag himself onto Illinois soil. He, too, thought he'd been reborn—as a free man. But he wasn't. Not then. Not there.

Now he clenched his fists. One last bubble gurgled from his nose, then he rose like a shot, gasping for air, raising the manacles above his head. Water cascaded from his naked body.

"Git up out of that barrel."

Awkwardly, Jimmy climbed out of the barrel and back onto the crate.

"Now't you're all rinsed and pretty, let's see what we've got," Hogan said. "Come over here so I can get a look at you."

Mr. Hogan took a cigar from his breast pocket and a box of matches from his coat. When he lit the cigar, a copper Liberty Head penny affixed to his lapel flashed in the light of the match. Hogan was a Copperhead, which meant he was part of a faction of Northern Democrats who supported slavery. He was a self-appointed slave-catcher.

Hogan was the sort of man Mrs. MacMurrough had warned Jimmy to watch out for. Jimmy *had* watched out—as well as any man could. But then, as he was walking home from work, when he was half a block from the home he shared with Cato, Hogan and his thugs had ambushed him. They'd leapt out from an alleyway holding pistols and forced him into a wagon.

Now Jimmy stepped onto the ground, staring straight ahead as Hogan began to inspect him. Jimmy's hair had been transformed by the water into a collection of fuzzy locks of various lengths. His hair dripped like a mop. Hogan poked at it with a stubby finger, fiddling with the locks as if he were arranging them in a pattern. Satisfied, he began to hum as he ran his finger up and down Jimmy's chest, then across his shoulders, mumbling to himself, as though he were measuring Jimmy for a suit.

Hogan tilted his head from side to side, then bent down till his head was level with Jimmy's groin. He stared with a crude curiosity at Jimmy's genitals. He took a puff on his cigar. "Well, daze my eyes," he said, and blew out the smoke.

Jimmy felt an involuntary impulse to spit. But he swallowed it back.

Hogan stood up, spun Jimmy around, and inspected his back.

"Now, bless me. Look-a-there, Jonah." Hogan waved his cigar at Jimmy's back. "There's nary a scratch on the nigger's back ...." He looked down. "Nor a mark on his backside!" He snickered. "I do believe we've got us a fine obedient boy here, Jonah. What do you say? It appears to me he's never felt the lash."

Jonah was a short man who, though he was white, exhibited the tenuous tilt of a servant. He nodded, but kept his nose lowered to the ground and did not speak.

"Turn 'round," said Hogan.

Jimmy turned slowly. Earlier, Jonah had unclamped the manacles on his legs so that he could climb into the barrel. Jimmy wondered how far he might get if he knocked Jonah over and ran. In his mind's eye he could picture the pistol stuffed in Hogan's waistband. Hogan's other crony, Earl, leaned against a nearby tree with a rifle at his side and a wad of tobacco in his mouth, which he chewed from time to time in a thoughtful manner.

Jimmy didn't know where they'd brought him. He'd been fettered in the bottom of a wagon bed. They'd traveled southward for days. There'd been no commotion when they'd crossed into Confederate territory. Late one night, Hogan had thrown the bags of feed on top of him, then told him to keep quiet. But when Jimmy heard the wagon roll off the wooden deck of a ferry after they'd crossed the Ohio River, there was no other sound but the clop of the horses' hooves.

Jimmy wasn't surprised to hear they thought he was an obedient slave. It was a deception he'd worked to achieve. He'd given them the appearance of being obliging. But inside his thoughts were of escape.

"Scrub him up," Hogan ordered.

Jimmy opened his eyes. Jonah stepped forward with a bucket, a brush, and a bar of tallow soap.

"Lift up your arms," Hogan commanded.

As Jimmy raised his arms, Jonah sniffed at his armpits. He soaped and scrubbed them roughly, then worked his way up and down Jimmy's body. When he was done washing, Jonah climbed on the crate. He dipped the bucket in the barrel, then dumped the cold water onto Jimmy's head. He repeated this two times, until all traces of the soap were rinsed away.

"Now oil him good."

Jonah climbed down and produced a bottle of oil from his coat pocket. He poured some into his palm and rubbed it on Jimmy's shoulders. The rubbing felt oddly comforting. But Jimmy knew they were getting him cleaned up for auction.

"Get a pretty shine on him," said Hogan. "Especially on the legs. They like that."

As Jonah was oiling his calves, Jimmy's pulse began to race. "I could make it," he thought. He glanced around. He looked back at Earl, who stood idly chewing his tobacco by the tree. Behind Earl, puff-pink clouds floated in the blue sky, free to sail wherever the wind might take them.

3

"A CIGAR, YOU SAY"

Cato stood with Walter Ames in front of Pilkington & Doyle Livery.

"Mr. Ames, would you go inside and speak to them for me?" Cato asked.

Ames was puzzled. "But don't you want to?"

"Of course I do." Cato wrung his hands. "But I don't think I should." He swallowed. He looked around and saw no one nearby. "You see, I'm not an all-white person. I don't know how these men will reckon me."

Mr. Ames tilted his head. "What do you mean?"

"The fact is, Mr. Ames, I am ... was ... a slave. Like Jimmy." Cato pursed his lips. He wasn't sure how Ames would take this. "I was a house servant. That's how I know Jimmy. He was a field hand on a farm near the plantation owned by my father."

"Your father owns a plantation!"

"Yes. You see, my mother was a slave. One of his house-servants."

"So you mean he ... that is to say, your father ... "

"Yes," Cato said. "I'm afraid he forced himself on my mother."

Ames stared at Cato. "I must say, you *look* white." He studied Cato's face. "It's not easy to tell."

"Does it bother you?"

"Bother me? No ... not really." Ames shook his head. "I mean, why should it? I'm just surprised, that's all."

"My mother was light-skinned. I suppose that's why I look as I do. I reckon it's mostly my hair, and, perhaps ... my nose, that ...." Cato couldn't finish.

"Oh, but your face is ...." Ames tried to complete his thought, but he, too, couldn't finish. "Look, if you ask me, I think it was providence." He smiled broadly, then looked around to be sure no one was approaching. "What I mean is ... you're quite good-looking." Ames smiled, and colored a bit as he looked into Cato's eyes.

"You're too kind." Cato lowered his head. "Will you help me, by speaking to them?"

"I suppose I could." He looked up at the livery stable. "But the thing is ... I don't really know what to say to them."

"You could ask them if they remember any of the men you saw. Make up a story if you have to."

"A story?"

"Yes, to put them at ease, persuade them to tell you what they know. I don't think you should mention Jimmy or the guns."

"Oh, of course," Mr. Ames said. "I see."

"Do you have a watch?"

Mr. Ames put his hand in his pocket and brought out his watch.

"You could tell them you saw the man in the wagon drop it. Now you're trying to find him to return it. You recognized the name of the stable on his feed bags."

"Oh, yes." Mr. Ames dropped the watch back in his pocket. "Good idea. All right."

. . .

WHILE CATO WAITED on the corner, Ames entered the stable. The dank smell of hay and horse manure made him stop just inside the threshold. But he bucked up his shoulders and called out, "Hello?" Soon a dark-haired man in a leather apron appeared, holding a pitchfork.

"Yes, sir?" he said.

"Good day, sir. My name is Ames. I work at the millinery shop on Couch Place, D.B. Fisk."

The dark-haired man nodded, then set his pitchfork against a post, wiped his hand on his apron, and extended it. "Mr. Ames, I'm Mr. Doyle." He shook hands roughly.

"Mr. Doyle," said Ames politely.

"Now then, how can I help you?"

Ames cleared his throat. "This afternoon I saw a gentleman in the street below the window of my shop, arranging bags of feed in his wagon."

"Yes."

"As I was glancing at the gentleman, I happened to notice his watch fall from his pocket. The sun caught it—just so."

"I see."

"I suppose the fob must have broken. In any event, the gentleman didn't realize his watch had fallen. He got in his wagon and drove off. I rushed down the stairs to try to catch him, but I was too late."

"Ah."

Mr. Ames pulled his watch out of his pocket. "So I retrieved the watch, you see."

Mr. Doyle looked at the watch. "Yes, I see." He nodded. "A very fine watch."

"Yes. It's quite tasteful." Ames put the watch back in his pocket.

"But what is it you seek, Mr. Ames, here at the livery?" Doyle gestured vaguely at the horses and hay around him.

"Oh, yes. Well, I don't know this gentleman who lost the

watch, but I noticed that the bags he was arranging in his wagon ... they bore the name 'Pilkington' in red letters."

"Yes. Those are our bags."

"And so I thought perhaps my only chance of returning the watch to its owner would be to come speak to you."

"Mr. Ames, we sell many bags of feed, as you may imagine."

"Perhaps you'll recall the gentleman if I describe him."

"What'd he look like?"

"His overcoat was rather distinctive—that was the first thing I noticed. It was gray. And now that I think of it, it was rather like a Confederate coat. It was double-breasted, you know, with a turned-up collar."

"We've had no Confederate soldiers in here. You think he was a Reb?"

"Oh, dear, no." Ames brought his hand to his throat, then quickly put it back at his side. "No. It had no cuffs or stripes, no military insignia. As a matter of fact, it was rather plain and worn. I think it was .... Well, it was gray and long. That was the main thing."

Mr. Doyle did not register any sign of recognition.

Ames persisted. "Perhaps you might recall his hat. I'd call it a dustman's cap. You know, with a back flap. It was made of a rather coarse material. So I'd venture to say he was a working man."

"I've seen any number of fellows with such a cap." Mr. Doyle shook his head. "What did the man himself look like?"

"Oh, well, he was rather stout, perhaps a tad taller than I. I surmised that he was a sturdy man. He appeared to hoist the bags with little effort."

Doyle scrunched up his face as though deep in thought. But he was shaking his head from side to side, instead of up and down.

"And it surprised me, you see," Ames continued, "that he did all this hoisting whilst he had a cigar in his mouth."

Doyle's eyes lit up. "A cigar, you say."

"Yes. Well, the stub of one. I'm not sure if it was lit."

"Now then," Mr. Doyle said. "There was a man here yesterday that smoked a cigar. He kept it in his mouth the whole time he was here, even when he spoke."

"Yes. That sounds like him."

"He didn't have a cap on, though. And I don't recall anything of the man's coat, I'm afraid."

"Well, did he come with a wagon?"

"Oh, yes. He definitely had a wagon."

"Was it a plain wood wagon?"

"Very possibly," Doyle said. "As I think of it, I don't recall anything about it other than its being plain ... and wood, of course."

"Well, then! Did he have two companions?"

"Yes. As a matter of fact. There was a short fella and a taller one with him. They didn't speak, as I recall."

"Oh, I think that must be the man," Mr. Ames said. "He had two men with him, just as you say. Well, did you happen to get his name?"

"I got the name of the cigar-smoking man," Mr. Doyle said. "He told me his name was Hogan."

"Mr. Hogan?"

"Yes. And, as a matter of fact, he said he was about to go down to Kentucky."

"Kentucky!" Ames clutched awkwardly at his vest, then caught himself again. "Oh, dear. I hope he hasn't left already."

"He boarded his horses here, you know."

"Oh, did he?"

"Yes, well, we're a boarding stable."

"Just so."

"Mr. Hogan most likely bought all those bags of feed because he planned a journey."

"Oh, of course," Ames said. "Perhaps I'm too late."

"Could be," Mr. Doyle said.

"Do you have any idea where I could find him now?"

"He did mention that he was staying at a hotel ... at the Tremont House."

"The Tremont House! I suppose he must not have been a workman, then."

"That I can't say. I'd call him a rough sort of fellow. But you can't always judge a person by his looks," Doyle said.

"No."

"I mean," Doyle said, pointing toward Mr. Ames's pocket. "Consider his watch."

"That's right." Ames patted his pocket. "I must get this back to him."

"So, Mr. Ames," Doyle said slowly. "Is there anything else I can help you with?" He reached out to the handle of his pitchfork.

"No. I have nothing else. You've been very helpful, Mr. Doyle. Thank you."

"You're welcome," Doyle said, then turned and went back to his work.

WHEN MR. AMES returned to Cato and told him what he'd learned, Cato insisted that they go to the Tremont House right away. "I know the place. My father stayed there when he was in Chicago."

"I know it, too. It's a block from my shop."

"Will you come with me?"

Ames nodded. "But I don't think it's likely that this Hogan fellow would have taken your friend to the hotel."

"No. But maybe they'll know more about him. Maybe he left a forwarding address."

"It's possible."

"We must try," Cato said.

At the Tremont House, again Cato waited outside while Ames went in to inquire about Hogan. He used the same ruse, the story of the dropped pocket watch, to see what he could learn.

When Ames came back out, he was smiling. "I found out where he's from."

Cato stared at him. He could hardly stand still, waiting for Ames to continue. "Yes?"

"They were very kind. They looked him up in the register. When Mr. Hogan signed the register, he wrote his home town as Paducah, Kentucky."

"Did he leave a street address?"

"No. I'm afraid not. Just the city."

"Well, at least that's something." Cato considered what it meant. Finally he said, "Mr. Ames, you've been a great help."

"What will you do now?"

"What can I do? I ... I'll go to Paducah."

"Good heavens! All that way?"

"Yes. I have to find him. Jimmy means the world to me."

Ames nodded knowingly. "Well, I wish you luck." Then he added, "Please let me know what happens. D.B. Fisk. Second floor. I'm almost always there."

"Yes, Mr. Ames. I will."

Mr. Ames again took Cato's arm. This time he squeezed it. "I look forward to hearing from you." He gave Cato one last meaningful look, then he turned and left.

Cato stood still for a long time listening to the sound of horses and carts going past him in the street. He could hardly think how to proceed. But what choice was there? He would go to Kentucky. He had to find Jimmy. He couldn't rest until he had his arms around his lover again. His days as a waiter at The Sherman House were done. He headed back to his room on Washington Street to prepare for his journey.

4

"HERE WE HAVE A LIKELY NEGRO BOY"

Jimmy stood on a block, on a small platform that sat at one end of a room crowded with men. His captors had brought him into a granary marked by a small red flag that hung beside the front door. Beneath the flag was a piece of paper that read: "A likely Negro for sale at auction this day at ten o'clock."

The would-be buyers had the air and appearance of respectable-looking men. They sat in chairs scattered about the room. Jimmy had been outfitted by Mr. Hogan with a loincloth, which provided a small degree of modesty. Despite his circumstances, he stood up straight, with a sharp expression on his face. He was determined not to let anyone see the truth of how he felt.

He looked around the room. The buyers smoked and chatted quietly. Sitting among the men, waving her hand to swat away the smoky cloud that hung in the room, was an attractive, well-dressed woman. Her red hair hung in curls from beneath an emerald-green silk bonnet. She looked directly at Jimmy with surprising openness, a curious smile on her face. When he noticed her, he stared back at her. He sensed something immodest about her. The woman's hand rested on the arm of a gentleman who looked wealthier than the other men in the room. Where the other men wore caps, this man wore a top hat. Where the other men wore wool waistcoats, this gentleman's waistcoat was made of red silk.

Jimmy looked again at the red-haired woman. He couldn't tell if the man she was with was her husband or her father. He wondered what it would be like if he were sold to that man. Perhaps the woman might bring a softening effect to bear on his circumstances. But he didn't want to be bought by a wealthy man. All his life he'd been told it was the small farmers who made the most tolerable masters. The large plantations were often run by ruthless men who were cruel to their slaves—just as Cato's father had been.

As he thought of Cato, he conjured up a vision of his gentle lover sitting in the back of the room with a bag of gold coins in his lap. He didn't know where this apparition came from, yet he could picture him as plain as day. A tear formed in his eye, but he quickly shook it off, before anyone could see it. He wasn't sure how he'd do it, but he'd find a way to escape—or die trying.

The auctioneer climbed the steps that led to the top of the stage. He was a stout man. Color spread on his cheeks and over his face and neck from the exertion of his brief climb. However, when he spoke, it was evident that he'd gained his employment because of the forcefulness of his voice.

"Ladies and gentlemen," he called out. "Here we have a likely Negro boy who this day is no more than five and twenty years old. This strong buck is just over two yards tall. And, as you can see, he is sound in wind and limb."

The auctioneer now raised his finger to his mouth and tapped his lip as he gestured to Jonah, who'd climbed on the block to stand behind Jimmy. Jonah used his hands to pry open Jimmy's mouth, and the auctioneer continued.

"As you can see, gentlemen, this boy's teeth are good and

strong. And, you will note, all of them are present." He gestured again to Jonah, this time twirling his finger in a circle.

Jonah turned Jimmy around, which was awkward due the manacles holding his legs together. When Jimmy's back was turned to the buyers, the auctioneer continued.

"And ... now you will notice that this well-muscled but simple-minded boy has no scars from the lash. Indeed, there exists no blemish upon him that could mark him as anything other than an obedient buck. He's a fine, strong farmhand, gentlemen, known to be experienced in picking cotton, guiding a plow, shoeing a horse, mending a hoe. And, if I may say so, he can be seen to be of such a ripe age that we believe he has good prospects for increasing your stock through propagation."

The auctioneer smiled to acknowledge a smattering of chortling in the audience.

"Now, gentlemen, let the bidding commence at eight hundred dollars."

The auctioneer twirled his finger again, and Jonah turned Jimmy back to face the audience just as the auctioneer said, "All right, sir. I have a bid of eight hundred dollars from the gentleman in the second row in the gray coat. Do I hear nine-hundred?"

There was a brief silence, during which the auctioneer mopped his forehead with his handkerchief, then, seeing a hand raised before him, "Nine-hundred is bid by the gentleman in the third row in the brown coat. Do I hear one thousand?"

Again there was a pause. Jimmy glanced at the man in the brown coat, and then at the man in the gray coat. He couldn't reckon anything good or bad between the two of them.

"Feel free, gentlemen to look carefully at his teeth." Jonah pulled open Jimmy's mouth again, forcing him to look up at the ceiling.

"I have one thousand from the gentleman in the second row in the gray coat."

As he stared at the ceiling, Jimmy didn't know what to

think. He could hardly believe that men were still willing to pay such a sum of money to buy a slave—given the state of the war and the uncertainty that hung over the future of the South. But then, he supposed, they must be bidding in Confederate dollars ... and if Confederate dollars had value at all, they could be measured, if in no other way, by their ability to purchase a slave.

"One thousand dollars, gentlemen. Let us hear your bids. What say you?"

A voice called out, "One thousand two hundred."

Jonah let go of Jimmy's mouth, and Jimmy lowered his head. It was the man in the brown coat.

"Ah, gentlemen ..." the auctioneer said, raising his voice to a higher pitch as he gestured with his left hand, sweeping grandly from Jimmy's foot to his head. "An opportunity such as this is not so common as it once was. Do not miss your chance!"

Jimmy closed his eyes, and nervously jangled the manacles that bound his hands.

"I have one thousand two hundred. Do I hear more?"

For ten seconds not a word was spoken.

"One thousand two hundred going once."

The auctioneer raised his hand above him.

"One thousand two hundred going twice."

The auctioneer looked across the room, holding his hand precariously in the air above him.

A man stood up. "Two thousand dollars!"

Jimmy opened his eyes. The bid had come from the man in the red silk waistcoat. Having stood when he made his bid, the man now looked around the room, staring forcefully at his peers as if daring any of them to contradict him. His manner caused a hush to fall across the room. The woman with the red hair let go of his arm. She also turned in her chair to look at the others, with a satisfied smile.

Jimmy closed his eyes again.

"I have two thousand dollars," the auctioneer said, with no small measure of excitement. "From Mr. Crenshaw of Savannah,

Georgia." His eyes solemnly swept the room—but the faces before him were silent. "Two thousand, going once." He raised his hand high above him. "Two thousand, going twice." His hand hung ominously in the air. He held it there for as many seconds as he could stand, and then his hand came flying down. "Sold, to Mr. Samuel Crenshaw of Savannah, Georgia, for two thousand Jeff Davis dollars, good and true!"

Jimmy opened his eyes. They fell upon the woman with the red hair. She nodded at him. It was one short nod, as if to signal acknowledgment. And Jimmy, for a reason he could not explain, widened his eyes, clanked his manacled wrists together and nodded back.

5

"I'M IN DISGUISE"

Cato boarded an Illinois Central train at the Randolph Street Station. He hadn't bothered to change out of his waiter's uniform—he'd simply packed his satchel with clothes, and retrieved the purse of gold coins that he and Jimmy had received as a gift from his wealthy friend, the Quaker painter Erastus Hicks.

He'd decided to bring only some of that money with him. Before going to the station, he'd brought the rest of it to Jimmy's sister, Ella, for safe-keeping. But Ella hadn't wanted the responsibility, and insisted that Cato leave the money with Dorothy instead. Dorothy was Ella's former owner and the wife of Cato's white half-brother, William Askew. William had taken an oath of loyalty to the Union that forbade him to return to the South until after the war. In the meantime, William, Dorothy, and Ella were living together in Chicago. Cato trusted Dorothy to be able to keep the money safe, so he gave her the balance of the money he wasn't bringing on his journey.

He'd decided to bring sixty twenty-dollar gold coins with him—a total face value of twelve hundred dollars, more than half the money he'd received from Erastus. He wanted to have at least a thousand dollars to pay the kidnappers' ransom, plus another two hundred for travel expenses.

He knew that gold was worth a great deal in the South. A customer at the restaurant had boasted to him that in Richmond he'd been able to get sixty Confederate dollars for a dollar in gold. So Cato hoped he wouldn't have to spend it all. The train ticket to Cairo had cost him $11.90.

His plan was to take the train to Cairo, then transfer to a steamboat going east on the Ohio River to Paducah, Kentucky. There he hoped to pick up the trail of Mr. Hogan.

The train to Cairo was carrying troops, horses, guns, cannon, lumber, and a small number of civilian passengers. The railroad was paid a government rate to transport the troops; they economized by seating the soldiers on benches in freight cars. Regular passengers, like Cato, traveled in coach cars with comfortable seats and windows. Cato sat beside a window on a cushioned seat upholstered in green velvet. After he'd been seated a few minutes, a soldier came down the aisle and sat next to him.

The soldier introduced himself as Private Robinson of the seventy-fourth Indiana Infantry, Company C. He said he'd been assigned to guard the passengers during the journey; placing a soldier in each coach car was railroad policy. It was strictly a means of reassurance for the passengers, as there was really no chance of an attack while they were in the North.

As the train pulled onto the trestle that ran along the shore of Lake Michigan, Cato took stock of Private Robinson. He had intense blue eyes, dark brown hair, and a wisp of beard on his chin. He was most likely headed into battle in the South. He held a prayer book on his lap, which he began to read as the train left the station. Cato, who had previously spent a month attached to the Confederate army as his brother's servant, could imagine that Private Robinson's state of mind was as anxious as his own. The toll of dead and wounded on both sides was grim.

Cato had no idea how he was going to rescue Jimmy without being captured. The Fugitive Slave Act meant that anyone—anyone white—could legally seize him, then take him back to Cato's father. He was still his father's property. It wasn't just that it was legal for anyone to catch him—it was illegal to do otherwise. By law, he was a runaway. The act prescribed penalties for anyone who did not assist in his capture.

Most of the blacks in Chicago had been born free. If white Chicagoans ever wondered about Cato's race, they could choose to assume he was born a free man. But once he got back to the South, his circumstances wouldn't be the same. There were few free black men in the South. Everywhere, whites would regard him with suspicion. Anyone could stop him and question him. Nothing would protect him—not the law, not society, not common decency. His safety would depend on staying unnoticed, and on the chance of finding enlightened souls to assist him.

It would be a risk to let down his guard, even for a moment. He'd face the possibility of capture and re-enslavement, but also torture or even murder. He was well aware that more than a few white people had a particular aversion to the blending of races—and he was a living manifestation of what they saw as the corruption of white blood.

In light of this, Cato did his best to pass as white. Before leaving his rooms, he'd put on the same wig and hat he'd used when he'd traveled north from Tennessee. The wig was meant to conceal the tight curls of his hair and the hat was meant to obscure the wig. During his trip north, Dorothy had given him cover by pretending that she and Cato were married. Alone, he knew he was more vulnerable. He had no idea how convincing he was as a white man. He'd been encouraged that Walter Ames had mistaken him for white, even without his wig and hat.

It would only take someone looking at him in just the right way to uncover that he wasn't really white. As he looked out the window, he absentmindedly pulled on the strands of wig hair that fell below his hat. His intention was to allow the slightest bit of this hair to be seen, enough to look like wisps of straight brown hair, but not enough to be revealed as counterfeit. He knew it would be better for him to leave it alone, but he couldn't stop fussing with it.

A man in the seat in front of him was reading a newspaper. That gave him an idea. He'd look for a book to read as soon as he got a chance. Despite the fact that slaves were forbidden to learn to read, Cato had learned how from his friend Erastus Hicks. Since most slaves were illiterate, he knew that if he read a book on the train, it would add to the impression that he was white. It would also distract him and help pass the time.

When the train made a twenty-minute stop in Centralia, Illinois, he went to the bookshop across from the station. He bought a book, which on its illustrated cover bore the epic title *The Personal History, Adventures, Experience and Observations of David Copperfield the Younger of Blunderstone Rookery* by Charles Dickens. The book, which was printed in London, cost him half a dollar.

Back on board, he opened his novel, but then Private Robinson put down his prayer book to start a conversation. Despite his reassurances earlier that there was nothing to worry about, Private Robinson now spoke to him with a note of apprehension in his voice about what lay ahead.

"We're about to enter what they call 'the needle's eye.' There's 112 miles of single track from Centralia to Cairo. It's a bottleneck," he said. "We gotta protect it. It's our main route to Camp Defiance, which is at the southern tip of the state." He touched the butt of the pistol that was lodged in a strap on the front of his uniform. "We've got to keep this train moving. The lieutenant told me there's another train down at Cairo waiting to come north. That one has Reb prisoners. It's not safe to make 'em wait too long in Cairo." No sooner had he spoken then he looked chagrined. "Forget what I just said. I'm talking too much."

Cato nodded, then looked around. "Are there are a lot of soldiers on the train?"

"I ain't supposed to say," Robinson said. "Military secret, I think, but to tell you the truth, I don't know why the hell I ought or oughtn't say anything." Then he looked closely at Cato, as if he was noticing something about him for the first time. "That's a fetching coat and tie you've got on. How'd you come to stay out of the Army?"

Robinson's tone was one of simple curiosity, but Cato winced. He hadn't considered how he might explain his civilian status. He didn't have time to come up with an explanation, so he decided to tell the truth.

"I'm in disguise," he said. He pointed at his hat, as if that were evidence of his costume.

Robinson cocked his head. "You mean like a spy?"

Cato nodded, but he said, "I'm not supposed to say."

"Right," Robinson said. He seemed to take this at face value. After a moment, he asked, "Where're you from?"

"Chicago," Cato said. As he spoke, he realized he had to take care to hide any trace of Southern accent in his speech.

"Originally?"

"No, I ... I grew up on a farm." He decided to leave it at that.

"Me, too," Robinson said.

Cato wanted to shift the conversation away from himself. "Whereabouts?" he asked.

"In Fort Wayne."

Cato wasn't sure where that was. "Is Fort Wayne in Illinois?"

"Nope. Indiana. You don't know it?"

Cato shook his head.

Robinson looked past Cato out the window and pointed behind them. "It's three hundred miles northeast of here—just west of the Ohio border. My pappy has a farm outside of town. Hogs and wheat."

"We had cows and corn," Cato said. He hoped Robinson

wouldn't ask him about farming. All he knew about was cotton, and he'd learned that from Jimmy.

"So now you live in Chicago?"

Cato nodded. "How about you?"

"No siree," the soldier said. "You won't find me in the city. Too many people. But I was just there. I got leave to go to my Grand-pappy's funeral."

"Sorry to hear that."

"Now I'm headed back to rejoin my regiment."

The train began to slow down. "That's funny," Robinson said. "We oughtn't to stop yet." He leaned over Cato and raised the louvered sash of the window. His hip and the butt of his gun brushed Cato's chest as he leaned his head out the window. Cato's eyes fluttered. Private Robinson was a handsome man, whose uniform clung tightly to his body. Robinson stayed in that position, with his head out the window, brushing his body inadvertently against Cato's chest, for what seemed like a full minute.

"Dad blame it," Robinson said at last. "I can't see what's up ahead." He sat back in his seat and turned to Cato, saying, "I'm gonna go see what the problem is." He got up and went to the end of the car as the train came to a stop.

Cato looked out the window and saw Robinson jump off the train, then climb up the embankment. Robinson shouted something inaudible to someone in the distance, then dashed out of view toward the front of the train. A few moments later he came running back to their car, and was soon back in his seat.

He smiled at Cato. "One of your dad-blame cows," he said.

As soon as he spoke, the train began to move. After that, Robinson leaned back and closed his eyes. It looked as if he'd decided to take a nap. Cato stole a glance at his muscular thighs, then quietly took out his book and began to read.

Two hours later they arrived in Cairo. As Cato stood to leave, he extended his hand to the soldier. "Be careful, Private," he said. "Keep clear of those Rebs."

"I will," Robinson said, his blue eyes blinking. "You do the same."

CATO PLANNED to board a steamship in Cairo for Paducah. But first he wanted to find Mrs. MacMurrough. Jimmy had told him all about the old woman with the cat who lived on the banks of the Ohio River. She'd taken Jimmy into her home after he'd nearly drowned crossing the river. She'd hidden and nursed him while he recovered. Then, Mrs. MacMurrough and her friend, Mr. Mack, had helped him hop a freight car to Chicago. Since they were in the business of helping runaway slaves, Cato thought they might have information about men like Hogan who kidnapped slaves and returned them to the South.

He had so little to go on. He knew he couldn't simply show up in Paducah and expect to find Hogan. Even if Mrs. MacMurrough couldn't help him, he wanted to meet her. She was the only white person Jimmy had ever spoken of with affection. But he still had to determine where she lived.

6

"HIS EYES WERE ON FIRE"

Bonnie Crenshaw sat at her dressing table, brushing her hair. She gazed in the mirror at the reflection of her brother, Benjamin, who stood at the window across the room. Ben's hair was the same shade of red as hers. But in the window light, it was the auburn of his mustache and beard that stood out, like a cloud of cinnamon framing his face. He wore rust-brown plaid pants and a tawny copper and gold brocade vest that cinched at his waist.

"Where'd Pa put him?"

"In number four, with Little Joe, Pheby, and Uncle Isaac," she said.

"I don't know what Pa's thinking," Ben said. "He may as well have burned the money as waste it on another slave."

"The money don't signify to him."

"I don't see how that could be true."

"It's on account of how everything's changing." She gestured vaguely to indicate the calamity of the world outside. "Who knows what will happen. With things as they are, Pa may as well spend it now—while he can."

Ben frowned and stepped away from the window. "Spend it while he can?" The wooden part of Ben's left leg—the part below the knee—clopped on the floor. "What do you mean? You talk as if the 'Cause' is already lost. Do you mean to suggest that this was in vain?" He pointed down to his leg.

Bonnie reddened. "That's not what I meant." She looked away. "What I meant was, Pa's getting on in years. And God knows he has more money than we can ever use." She stopped brushing and turned to face her brother. "Besides, I reckon he did it for me."

"He bought the slave for you? Whatever for?"

"Because," she said. "I liked him."

"You liked the slave? Are you serious?"

She nodded.

"Oh, for God's sake."

"He's quite strong and ferocious-looking."

"And how could that possibly be of any use to you?" Ben took hold of the arm of the sofa near the window and lowered himself down onto it. "You already have two servants looking after you. You have Pheby to dress you. You have Little Joe to drive you around. What more do you need?"

"I need something to occupy me."

"Oh, dear God. I'm afraid to ask what that might mean."

"You should have seen him, Ben. They made him turn round and round. But his eyes were on fire. Like burning coals."

"You're worse than Aunt Hattie."

"Aunt Hattie is wanton and vulgar. I only refer to the quality of his energy. I know Negroes are like animals. But this one didn't seem domesticated. He stared at me."

"At you?"

"Yes. And it was quite bestial. He rattled his chains as if he might leap from the block and pounce on me."

"Why on earth did this behavior make you want Pa to buy him?"

"I knew right away that it would be ... propitious ... to break him in ... to civilize him."

"You think these slaves are like wild horses? That you can tame them?"

Her brother's question made Bonnie glance at a porcelain box on her vanity, which bore a miniature painting of a red horse rearing back on its hind legs. She loved that box. "Why not? They have all the same characteristics as wild horses. Think how useful he'll be once bridled and subdued."

"Useful for what?"

"Ah," she said. "That's my secret." She opened the porcelain box and took out a pin with which to fasten her hair.

"You and your silly games. There's a war on, you know. Do you have any idea what's going on in the world?"

"Of course I do. But there's nothing I can do about that."

Ben pursed his lips. "You could try to behave with dignity. This war is damn serious business. Why do you have to throw yourself into silly schemes?"

"I swear it's not a silly scheme. What I have in mind is serious." She put another pin in her hair. "Really, I only mean to perform a charitable task. I want to take a fellow who's innocent but rough, and polish him up. It's really a great opportunity for him."

Ben tapped the wood end of his leg on the carpet. "What if he doesn't care to be polished up?"

"Now, Benjamin. You have no intuition about these things. I do. The fellow is unblemished. He's already twenty-five years old, but he has no marks on him."

"So? What does that mean?"

"That means he's never been punished for any wrongdoing. He may be a wild horse. But he's never thrown a rider."

Ben snickered. "For all you know, he may've never had a rider."

"According to the bill of sale, he comes from a farm in North Carolina. He's quite muscled, which shows he's used to hard work. But for some reason he carries a chip on his shoulder. I shall cure him of that."

"How? Will you coddle him?"

Bonnie frowned. "And sap his vigor with indulgence? Indeed I shall not! You misunderstand my intention. I mean to maintain his strength. He'll have vigorous work. But I also plan to refine his sensibility."

"Do you?" Ben was curious. "What work will you have him do?"

"I haven't decided yet what tasks I'll set for him. For now, he's to work in the field. Later, I may find something special for him to do. But first, I must learn more of his temperament."

"I thought you said he was wild-eyed and chain-rattling."

"Well, yes. Such was his demeanor at the auction. But I believe he'll learn to behave differently with proper Christian guidance."

"And this guidance is to come from you?"

"Father says I may improve him as I see fit."

"God help the poor fellow."

"Now really, Ben. You must have some faith in me. I know what I'm about."

"Do you? Sometimes I wonder."

"You'll see." After a pause, she added, "He's quite good-looking, by the way."

"Is he? Well, I suppose I'll have to go and have a look at this brute. I've no doubt you're exaggerating."

"I am not!"

"I'll find out what Little Joe has to say about him. Joe's always forthright if you ask him anything straight out."

"Perhaps so." Bonnie inspected her fingernails, then said, "But Joe is short and timid. He'll probably want to keep clear of him. I think Uncle Isaac will want to, too, for that matter."

Ben smiled with amusement. "I don't think the slaves are afraid of one another."

"Well. I should think anyone would be wary of someone as imposing as Jacob."

"Jacob, eh?"

"Yes. That's his name. It says so on the bill of sale."

7

"I'VE NEVER HAD GOOD EYESIGHT"

All Cato knew was that Mrs. MacMurrough lived in a cottage by the river. He'd considered asking people in town if they knew her. Talking to anyone seemed risky. He trusted his instincts, but he didn't know if he was willing to risk everything on his intuition.

So he decided to keep to himself, bypass the town, and go straight to the bank of the river. If he made his way along the riverbank, he figured he'd be bound to pass Mrs. MacMurrough's cottage. Jimmy had described it to him: a brick chimney and several windows. The row of windows had made an impression on Jimmy, since the cabin Jimmy had lived in on the Holland farm had only one window.

Jimmy had also mentioned pink and white tulips in front of the cottage, and an arbor with a trellis that had been draped with a rose vine. But now that it was August, Cato knew the tulips would be gone and the vine would once again be out of bloom.

The part of Jimmy's description that Cato found most useful was its location. Jimmy had described it as being situated at the top of a path that wound up a hill. Jimmy had been particular about that: he'd said that Mrs. MacMurrough's cat had run up the path ahead of them—and Jimmy, who was still in shock from his fiasco in the river, had been unable to keep up. Cato would look for a cottage on a hill.

Walking along the river, it turned out, meant following the train tracks. He walked along the tracks, beside the levee, until they ended, then made his way along fields that followed the shore of the river. He knew that if he reached Camp Defiance, at the confluence of the Ohio and Mississippi rivers, he'd have gone too far.

Eventually, he saw a rise in the land ahead of him. He wasn't sure if he'd call it a hill. But when he got there, there was no cabin in sight. He kept going. The sun was setting. Soon it would be too dark to see anything at all.

But then, when he'd gone a quarter mile further, he saw another rise. As he approached, his heart beat faster. He could see a small rooftop at the top of the hill—and a brick chimney rising from the roof. He looked around and surveyed the riverbank. The river appeared to be a mile wide. He couldn't imagine how Jimmy had crossed it in a rowboat. He noticed a twig floating near the shore, which showed the current rushing southward.

He turned and saw the beginning of a path. "This must be it," he thought. Quietly, he made his way up the path. At the top he saw a cottage with a brick chimney, and a row of windows. There were no flowers, but there was an arbor.

He stood at the door and hesitated. He was sure this was the right place, but it occurred to him that Mrs. MacMurrough might not still be alive. It was possible someone else now lived here. He held his breath and knocked. After a moment, the door opened. He saw an old woman—with a cane. His face broke out in a smile.

"Land sakes," she said. "You startled me, son. I don't get but one or two visitors a year out this way."

"Sorry to disturb you, ma'am," he said. "I'm looking for Mrs. MacMurrough."

"Are you then? Well, bless me, lad, who else do you think I might be?" She looked at him more closely, squinting her eyes. "You wouldn't be the postman, would you? Last time I got a letter was May of 1860. 'Twas addressed to my dear departed husband, Patrick."

"No, ma'am," Cato said. "I'm a friend of someone you helped last spring."

"A friend, you say." She looked wary. "Of someone I helped?"

It occurred to Cato that Mrs. MacMurrough had taken quite a risk helping Jimmy and that she had no way of knowing if he was telling the truth about being a friend.

"Yes, ma'am. My friend's name is Jimmy."

"Jimmy, eh? Not sure as I recollect. What'd your friend look like?"

"His skin is quite dark," Cato said. "But he is uncommon good-looking."

"Oh, my goodness." Mrs. MacMurrough tapped the side of Cato's leg with the end of her cane. "Uncommon good-looking, you say? Well. Now, from what I can see, the same might be said of you. Stand back there a moment and let me have a gander at you."

Cato stepped back from under the shade of the door frame.

"Oh, yes," Mrs. MacMurrough said. "Quite handsome, you are! What's your name, son?"

"Cato."

"Are you now? Cato! Well ... I've heard all about you." She paused, then winked confidentially. "You're Jimmy's sweet friend, are you not?"

Cato nodded.

"Now what in heaven's name brings you to see me?" She was smiling, but then a dark look crossed her face. "Has something happened to him?"

Cato nodded.

Mrs. MacMurrough clutched her chest. "Oh, God help us." She looked around. "Come in. Come in, and tell me what's happened."

Cato stepped into the cabin. He saw a black cat sitting on a table.

"That's Donahue," Mrs. MacMurrough said. "He and Jimmy became fast friends." She sat in her rocking chair and pointed at a chair across from her. "Now, sit, sit. And tell me quick what's happened to Jimmy."

Cato sat. When he spoke, his voice squeaked like a child's. "He's been kidnapped."

Mrs. MacMurrough clasped her hands together. "Oh, no!"

"And I ... I don't know where he is." As he spoke these words, Cato could no longer hold back the tears he'd held inside for the past twelve hours. His eyes grew wet. "I've lost him!"

Mrs. MacMurrough pulled herself to her feet and came to Cato's side. She put her hand on his shoulder. "Oh, my poor boy. I'm so sorry. Your friend Jimmy is a good man, a good man." She patted his shoulder. "But when did this happen?"

"Today. This morning."

"What? Today! But where?"

"In Chicago."

"You mean to say you've come all the way down here from Chicago?"

"Yes, ma'am. I came on the train. It took me eight hours, plus another hour to find you. I didn't know who else to turn to. I found out about the man who took him. His name is Hogan."

"Oh, my goodness. But help me understand, son. Why did you come here, if this happened in Chicago?"

"Because the man, Hogan, was headed to Paducah. I've come down on the train. I knew how to find you because Jimmy once described your cabin and your location. I want to go to Paducah, but I don't know where to start to find Hogan. I was hoping there might be a chance you could help me."

"Oh, my boy. How could I help?"

"I thought, perhaps, seeing as how you helped Jimmy. Perhaps you might know something about men like Hogan. He's a Copperhead, I think."

Mrs. MacMurrough patted his shoulder again. "Oh, yes. I know all too well about those kinds of men." She walked back to her rocking chair and sat down heavily. Then she looked directly at Cato. Her eyes were sad. "I'm sorry, Cato. Truly, I am. But I don't know the first thing about a man named Hogan. I've known of a Copperhead or two. We have 'em here in this town. They're nasty men. Aye, and some women, too. But I don't know any of 'em by name." She shook her head. "Now what's a man with a fine Irish name like Hogan doing with the copper penny? Makes me ashamed, Cato. Truly. I'd rather have a Mr. Gardner or a Mr. Schmitt turn up a Copperhead than an Irishman."

Cato's face had collapsed the moment she said "I'm sorry." He looked at her with glassy eyes now, and tried to hold his head up. "I know what it is to feel that way," he said. "My father's name is Askew. In fact, I have English blood in me. But I sometimes feel shame for it."

"Indeed," Mrs. MacMurrough said. "The white race has much to answer for."

Cato nodded. But then he looked at his host with curiosity. "If you don't mind my asking, ma'am, how were you able to become so ... different ... from other folks? You're not like most white people."

"I suppose I'm not." Mrs. MacMurrough reached for a corn cob pipe that sat on the table beside her. She put it in her mouth, lit a match, and lit the pipe. She took a puff and rocked in her chair. Cato inhaled the smell of tobacco as it wafted in front of him.

After a few puffs, Mrs. MacMurrough said, "The funny thing is, I don't know what makes me the way I am. Maybe it's because of my eyesight. I've never had good eyesight, you know. I suppose you could say I feel people more than I see 'em.

When I meet a person, I pay more consideration to how the person feels than how he looks. But when other folks see someone, well, they see mainly a body. And right away what they see is whether the body is a man or woman, a white or a black, a person who's young or someone who's old. Only after they've got all that settled do they get around to letting their feelings have a say." She smiled at Cato. "Now you, you're a young man. I know you have no way to know it, but folks won't see you the same way when you get old."

"I'm not so sure if I will get old," Cato said. "I can't picture it."

Mrs. MacMurrough puffed her pipe. "Oh, my boy. You may not. You surely may not if you go to Paducah. It's not safe for you there. It's not safe for you anywhere in the South." She looked at him sharply. He was still wearing his hat. "I see you haven't removed your hat."

"Oh!" Cato quickly took off his hat. "I'm sorry. I forgot."

"Bless me. I understand why you wear it. It's the hair ... isn't it?"

"Yes." Cato touched his wig. "It's not my hair. It's a wig. I wear it as a disguise. I'm trying to pass for white."

"Would you mind taking it off? I mean the wig, as you call it."

Cato removed his wig and set it on the floor beside him.

"'Tis a shame, Cato, that you should have to hide your God-given hair. Tosh, you're six ways from handsome without that getup on." She smiled. "Now, come to think of it, perhaps my eyesight's not so bad after all. For I can see a good-looking fellow as plain as day when I want to." The cat jumped into her lap. "Ain't that right, Donahue?" She stroked his back. "Oh, and then how I do recall your Jimmy. Now there was a man that I could see, I'll tell you that. As fine a specimen of a man as ever I've laid eyes on. I had a good look at him in his skivvies, I did!" She chuckled. "Black as he was, I believe he went a shade of red when I eyed him then."

Cato smiled. And then, without warning, he began to cry again.

"Oh, dear. Oh, my child." She was up again on her feet in an instant and back at his side. "I'm sorry. Here I am gabbing away like a crazy old lady. Now, we have to think of what to do."

"Oh, Mrs. MacMurrough. What should I do? I don't know how I'll ever find him. And he must be so scared. I ..."

Mrs. MacMurrough put her hand on Cato's hair. "Now, now." She rubbed his head, and then his neck. "Our Jimmy's a strong lad. I don't just mean in body. He's strong of heart. I'd guess he's afraid, like as not—he'd be a fool not to be. But he's a brave lad. Think of what he did to get north in the first place."

"But he's all alone now."

"Aye. Aye. All by himself. 'Tis a terrible thing." She squeezed Cato's shoulder. "But, look now, he's not alone in his heart. You're in his heart. He told me so."

Cato turned to look up at her. "I know now," he said, "why Jimmy spoke of you as he did. You've shown us both such kindness."

"'Tis kindness you both deserve," she said. "I don't know why the world should have so little to give you. 'Tis a shame. 'Tis a shame on the human race."

"But what shall I do? I don't know how to find him."

"Well. I don't know." She stopped rubbing his shoulder. "I think you've got the right idea. If you could find this Irish good-for-nothing, Hogan." She shook her head. "Oh, but when I think of it—I don't like to think of you getting mixed up with a fellow like that. I'd hate to see you go down in the soup as well. Oh, dear, I don't know whether to tell you to go after him or tell you to stay put."

"I can't stay put."

"No," she said. "I reckon you can't. But, oh, my dear lad, you ... you must not fall prey to them, too. I don't know but I shan't sleep from now on with worry. When I think of it." She put out a hand and touched his arm. "Sometimes the world can be a weary place."

"You mustn't worry about me."

"Oh, no? And why is that? How will you protect yourself?"

"I can pass for white. I've done it before."

She eyed him, not without tenderness. "Aye. Perhaps," she said. "You are close. Close." She stepped back a foot and continued staring. "You're so close. But ..."

"Is it my hair?"

"Oh, well ... perhaps. But no ... the wig takes care of that."

"My nose?"

"Oh, bless you, lad. Yes ... perhaps. I don't know how you can change it, though."

"I'd thought, perhaps, makeup of some kind."

"Makeup!" She smiled. "Oh, dear, no. I don't think you should risk that." She stopped speaking as she continued to study him. "It would tell on you, I think."

"What then?"

"Well," she pinched her own nose. "There's only one thing for it. I don't suppose you have any spectacles."

"Spectacles?"

"Aye. I've a mind that spectacles would do two things. They'd sit on your nose, of course, and maybe cloak it ... just a little. But spectacles would also give you that air, you know. So much of the trick is in how you seem to be. 'Twould be good for you to have airs."

"You mean, so I can seem to be white."

"Well, aye. But I also mean it may make you seem ... well-off ... and wise and knowledgeable." She looked down at the floor, at the wig and hat that lay there. "And perhaps you could don a fine top hat, too. You know ... one like Mr. Lincoln wears. You'd look quite the gentleman in a top hat."

"I don't have any spectacles, Mrs." Cato looked downcast. "And I've never worn a top hat."

"No. And why would you? Nor can you wave your hand to

make 'em appear." She thought a moment. "Perhaps ... perhaps my friend Mr. Mack ..."

"Oh, yes. Jimmy told me all about him."

"Yes, well he may know how to get hold of some spectacles for you to wear. And he might know of a top hat. He was never one for airs himself, but he's got a habit of collecting things."

"Do you think he might know anything about Mr. Hogan?"

"Perhaps." She nodded. "Aye, come to think of it, Mack knows more about all that than I do. So it could be so. But you must not get your hopes up too much."

Mrs. MacMurrough stood and went to her bed, which sat next to the wall by the fireplace. She fluffed the pillow. "Now, back when Jimmy was here, he slept a while in this bed," she said. "And it did him good." She brushed her hands across the bedding, then patted it. "Come over here now and you do the same. Rest here tonight, my boy. In the morning I'll go and fetch Mr. Mack."

Cato stood. "That's very kind of you," he said. Then he looked around the cabin. "But where will you sleep?"

"Oh, well, I only sleep a little bit off and on. Take my word, son, I can sleep in that rocker as well as in a bed. In fact, on any given afternoon I'm just as likely to be fast asleep in the chair as not." She made her way to the rocker and sat down. Donahue quickly jumped up onto the chair with her. "Ain't that right, Donahue? Oh, yes, you like it when I sleep in the chair, 'cause then you can sleep all cozy in my lap."

Mrs. MacMurrough settled into her rocking chair and relit her pipe. Donahue curled himself in her lap. And Cato lay down on the bed. He was so drained that, despite his worry, as Jimmy had done in a similar situation, he fell fast asleep.

8

"WHAT DO YOU THINK YOU'RE DOIN' HERE?"

Jimmy walked in the dawn mist along a chalky road. The sun had finally risen high enough above the canopy of live oaks that lined the road to illuminate his path. It was the morning of his first full day on the Crenshaw plantation. Along with a dozen other slaves, he'd been dispatched to a cotton field. Jimmy was not surprised by this. Yesterday he'd noticed the field when he passed by it in the wagon that bore him from the auction house. The field was filled with cotton buds that had flared abundantly. He knew they were ripe for picking.

The night before, Little Joe had sat up with him, even though it would have been better to sleep. Joe gave him what he called the "lowdown" on the plantation's bygone times. The estate dated back to the colonial era. The land itself was situated along the banks of the Savannah River, fourteen miles north of the city of Savannah. Little Joe knew the distance well, because he was Bonnie Crenshaw's driver. Her trips to Savannah were frequent.

Taking advantage of the power of the river, the Crenshaws had built a sawmill in 1851 to cut lumber shipped downstream from South Carolina. In 1855 they also built a cider mill, to process apples brought down by wagon from the north Georgia mountains. The Crenshaws bottled and sold cider to markets in Savannah and Augusta. Most of the juice they made was suitable for a church picnic—but a few of the barrels were left to ferment. The hard cider, Little Joe confided, was mostly drunk by the family, or bottled and given as a gift to neighbors. But once a year, on Christmas, a jug of hard cider would be allowed to the slaves, as well.

From its earliest days, the Crenshaw plantation produced a succession of crops. On the northern end was a mulberry grove, where silkworms spun silk. In the swampier ground along the river were rice fields. Near the big house was a long row of vegetable gardens. On the rest of the land were cotton fields.

Because of Jimmy's experience picking cotton, he was placed in a cabin near the other slaves who worked the cotton fields. Those cabins were near the big house, which was on the highest point, overlooking the river.

The men walking beside Jimmy were all strangers to him, except one, a man called Poky. Poky was Little Joe's friend. He lived in the cabin next door, and had come around to visit Little Joe when Jimmy arrived. According to Little Joe, Poky's name was a joke. He was the fastest cotton picker on the estate. An ordinary man might pick about two hundred pounds a day. But Poky could easily pick twice that when he put his mind to it. Most days he held himself in check. He knew it did the other slaves no good for him to bring in so much more cotton than anyone else.

Poky had come up with a ploy to slow himself down. The slaves sang songs as they worked. At the end of each stanza, Poky would stop and raise both of his hands to the sky. He'd clasp his hands together, raise them above his head, drop to one knee and exclaim "Praise God!" or "Praise Jesus!" Then he'd shake his hands fervently for several beats.

The overseer, Eppley, had given Poky his nickname to goad

him into working faster. But Poky never took the bait. His back, which was full of scars, was the proof. Eppley whipped him whenever he brought in less than three hundred pounds of cotton. All the slaves knew Poky could avoid the whip, if he chose to. But he did what he did in order to take scrutiny off everyone else. As a result, all the slaves on Crenshaw Plantation treated Poky with the utmost respect.

When Jimmy was a boy, he'd been proud to pick more cotton than anyone on the Holland farm. In his youth he'd pursued it as a badge of honor. The Hollands, for their part, had honored him by sparing him from punishment. But whatever youthful solicitude he'd felt toward the Hollands had turned to antipathy by the time he became a man.

Privately, Jimmy thought he could match Poky pound for pound in picking speed. But he also knew that Eppley would gauge him in the future based on how much he brought in on the first day, so he resolved to keep his head down and slow his pace. He started by working at a painfully slow speed. The pace was so slow, he could barely stick to it. He was not surprised when, after fifteen minutes, Eppley came up to him.

"Boy, what do you think you're doin' here?" Eppley cried.

"Massa Eppley, I'm bein' real careful, so as to not break any branches," Jimmy said, in a voice as servile and dim-witted as he could manage. "I hate to break 'em."

Breaking a branch on a cotton plant was strictly forbidden, since the cotton would never bloom on any branch that was broken. Being careful, in this regard, was a reasonable explanation for going slow. But Eppley wasn't buying it.

"Now what kind of bunkum are you givin' me, boy," he said. "Massa Crenshaw paid good money for you on account of you're supposed to be 'bout the greatest cotton picker who ever lived—so he was told."

"Oh, no, sir," Jimmy said. "I don't know who might'a told him that, but he was surely mistaken. I'm no good at pickin' cotton, Massa Eppley. No, sir. I'm mostly good at plowin.'" Jimmy felt safe in establishing plowing as his best skill, since the speed with which the plowing took place had as much to do with the mule as with the slave who guided it. "At plowin' I'm about as good as any man. That must be what Massa Crenshaw heard. I can plow like the wind!" He looked up, beaming at Eppley.

"Well, we're not out here plowin' now, boy, and there won't be any plowin' for six months' time. So you'd better get good at pickin' cotton right quick," he said. He lifted his whip up in the air. "You see this, boy?"

"Oh, yes, sir, I see it." Jimmy lowered his head.

"Now how many pounds o' cotton you think a strong boy like you can pick?"

"Oh, I reckon a hundred pounds," Jimmy said. Then he looked at the plant he was next to. "At least that much. And nothin' broken!"

"That much, eh?"

"Oh, yes. At least that much!"

"That's hogwash!" Eppley spit. "Now look here, nigger. You'd best bring back nary less'n two hundred pounds today, or you'll be sorry you ever came down to this cotton field."

"Yes, Massa Eppley."

"Don't think I'm gonna be soft on you just because you're a hotshot Tar-heel boy. And don't think I don't know what you're trying to do. I've got my eye on you."

"Yes, sir."

"Now get back to work, and speed it up." With that, Eppley took his whip and struck it hard on Jimmy's thigh.

It was the first time in his life that Jimmy had felt the whip. He'd been brought up on a small family farm in Tennessee. His owners, the Hollands, had been forbearing masters. On the Holland farm, the slaves and masters were close-knit. Jimmy and his sister, Ella, and their mother, Wally, had been regarded as kith if not kin. He'd watched other slaves being whipped at the huge Askew plantation that sat next door to the Hollands' farm, but he'd come to imagine that he was insusceptible to such treatment himself. That was over now. He realized in an instant how vulnerable he was, how hopelessly trapped he was in his new predicament.

The lash startled him. He stumbled forward and yelped when the strap hit his leg. His eyes went wide with outrage. He could barely stop himself from turning on Eppley. Eppley wasn't a small man, but Jimmy was certain he could overpower him. As the pain rushed down his leg, his anger boiled up. He stretched out his fingers. He felt how easy it would be to put them around Eppley's throat. It would all be over in an instant.

Poky was watching him. A look of grave concern flashed on Poky's face. He shook his head. It was a quick jerk from side to side, but with a clear meaning that said "no"—as if he could read Jimmy's intentions.

Poky rushed over and patted Jimmy on the back. "We gonna step it up," Poky said. "Don't you worry, Massa Eppley, sir. We gonna get all this cotton picked right quick!" And with that he burst into song, "Way down to the river Jordan, where John baptized three ..." Poky raised his left hand and pointed up toward heaven while he picked with his right. All the other slaves joined in the song. "Roll, Jordan, roll!"

Jimmy looked around. He went back to picking. As the day wore by, he sped up. But he shook his head from time to time, as if he were saying "no" to someone unseen. He was sure now, more than ever, that there was no God.

As he thought of his predicament, as he let his mind touch on the memory of Cato, as he let his eyes fill with a picture of Cato's smiling face, he wondered if he would ever see his lover again. And every time Poky fell to his knees and cried "Praise Jesus!" Jimmy turned his head, looking away from the others, and spat into his cotton sack.

When the sun had set for the day, Jimmy made his way in the twilight to the gin-house, dragging a sack that weighed two hundred and ten pounds. He was covered in sweat. His bruised leg was sore. His biceps were bulging.

9

"WHAT AM I TO THINK WHEN I LAY IN BED AT NIGHT?"

When Cato opened his eyes, he saw that Mrs. MacMurrough was already awake. She sat in her rocking chair, smoking her corncob pipe. He stretched and sat up in bed.

"Ah, so you're awake now, are you?" Mrs. MacMurrough said.

Cato yawned. "How long was I asleep?" he asked.

"Well, let's see. I'd say you've been asleep a good nine hours," she replied. "And you've been quiet as a mouse. Not like that Jimmy. When Jimmy was here, he made such a racket. It scared Donahue, it did!"

Cato smiled. "Jimmy snores. It's terrible!"

"And now you'll be after something to eat, I should think." Mrs. MacMurrough stood up.

"OK," Cato said. "Thank you. But then we must hurry ... to get Mr. Mack. There isn't much time to track down Hogan."

"Ah, well ..." Mrs. MacMurrough used her cane to point to a spot on the far side of the room. "Look behind you," she said. "Mr. Mack is already here."

A white-haired man with a bright red face sat at the table on the other side of the room. His sleeves were rolled up and he wore a white napkin tied around his neck. He was chewing, but when Cato looked at him, he swallowed and smiled broadly, then set his knife and fork down on the table with a satisfied clink.

"And I've just finished some of Molly's griddle cakes," he said. Rising from the table, he unfastened the napkin from around his neck, walked over to Cato, and held out his hand. "Good morning, lad. I'm pleased to meet you. Though I wish it were under better circumstances."

Cato shook his hand. "Good morning to you, sir. I'm glad to meet you, too."

"Mrs. MacMurrough has told me about your troubles," said Mr. Mack. "I was sorry to hear about young Jimmy's misfortune."

"Do you think you can help us?"

"Well," he said. "Could be. I've an idea or two to discuss." He looked back at the table. "But you ought to have a bite to eat while we talk. We'll have to hurry if we're gonna catch up with that prick Hogan." He looked at Mrs. MacMurrough. "Excuse my language, Molly."

"Oh, Michael Mack, you'd think I was a virgin young girl."

"Do you know him?" Cato climbed out of bed.

"I know who he is. What's more, a friend of mine knows a thing or two about the bastard. But she's leaving this morning. So we'll have to be quick."

"She's leaving?"

"Aye, on the steamboat. If we hurry, you can go with her."

"You mean she's going to Paducah?"

"No, she's bound for Louisville. But you'll have time with her on the boat before you reach Paducah. She may know something that can help you." He pointed at the table. "But look, now, Mrs. MacMurrough has made some griddle cakes for you."

Mrs. MacMurrough went to the table and took a lid off a

plate that held the pancakes. "They're still fresh," she said. "Cooked not ten minutes ago."

Cato, with a sudden lift of spirits, jumped up and went to the table. Within a minute he was swallowing forkfuls of pancake. "Oh, my!" he said. "These are the best I ever had."

"Go on with ya," Mrs. MacMurrough said. "I dare say you're happy 'cause Mr. Mack has a lead."

"I'm happy because of Mr. Mack," Cato said. "And I'm happy because these pancakes are better than ... better than ...."

"Be careful now, boy," said Mr. Mack. "Whatever you say—it's going straight to Molly's head. Then I won't hear the end of it."

"Better than whiskey!" Cato exclaimed.

"What's this?" Mrs. MacMurrough said. "And how would a lad such as you know about a thing such as that?"

"A gentleman gave me some. Just to taste. Just once."

Mr. Mack raised his eyebrow. "Just once, eh?"

"Yes, and anyway, it's OK because he was a Quaker," Cato continued.

"Oh, well then," Mrs. MacMurrough said.

Mr. Mack took his watch out of his vest pocket. "All right, well, since we've settled that, we'd best be on our way. The steamboat leaves at nine o'clock and I told Mrs. Langdon that you'd meet her on board. It's seven o'clock already."

"Now, Michael," Mrs. MacMurrough said. "Don't you be forgetting your father's hat, nor your mother's frames."

"Ah, yes," Mr. Mack said. "I brought some of the things Mrs. MacMurrough wanted you to have." He went to a satchel that sat beside the door. From it he extracted a stovepipe hat and a small cloth case. He handed the top hat to Cato. "Here you are. Try this on for size. 'Tis a hat that belonged to my father. I dare say he had as big a head as you do, my boy."

Cato placed the hat on his head, but it sank down around his ears. "Oh, heck!" Cato frowned. "I don't think I can wear it."

"Now wait just a minute," Mrs. MacMurrough said. "You be on to forgettin' your wig."

"That's right!" Cato retrieved his wig from the floor. "Do you have a mirror?"

"Over there." Mrs. MacMurrough pointed to the mirror that hung on the wall beside the front door.

Cato put on the wig and arranged it. Then he placed the hat on top of the wig. This time it stayed firmly on his head. "It's perfect!" he said.

"Now, then," Mr. Mack said, as he removed a pair of glasses from the small cloth case and handed them to Cato. "These spectacles belonged to my mother. I don't know why I've kept 'em. The glass lenses fell out ages ago."

"You've kept 'em same as you keep everything," Mrs. MacMurrough said. "Because you're a pinchpenny who can't be bothered to throw anything away."

"Now then," Mr. Mack responded. "Be that as it may. I don't rightly know if you oughta wear 'em. If folks should notice there's no glass, they'll be wonderin' if you've gone barmy."

"Perhaps folks will think he's eccentric," Mrs. MacMurrough offered.

"Now, Molly, he's but a young man. I don't think he's had enough time to go eccentric. Look how long it took you."

"Michael Mack!"

"So for now," Mr. Mack said, "take these along and keep 'em in your pocket. Then talk to Mrs. Langdon about whether you ought to wear 'em. She'll know what to tell you. She's an expert on disguises and things."

"She is?"

"Yes, well, you see ..." Mr. Mack looked around the room.

"There's no one here but us, Michael," Mrs. MacMurrough said.

Mr. Mack continued, "Mrs. Langdon is what you might call a spy."

"A spy!" Cato's eyes went wide.

"Aye, lad, she is. Well, she's actually a detective for the Pinkerton detective agency in Chicago. But now I've learned—strictly confidential, mind you—that under secret orders from General McClellan, Pinkerton's agents are working in the South to gather information."

"A woman detective!"

"That's the beauty of it, son," Mr. Mack said. "She's a clever woman. And she's Southern to boot, so she can travel easily in the South. And then, too, she's a good-lookin' gal. Why, the men fall all over themselves hopin' to get close to her. Why, I myself ..."

"Now, Michael," Mrs. MacMurrough interrupted. "I think you'd best leave it at that. The point is, Cato, Mrs. Langdon is someone who may be able to help you find Mr. Hogan. She's someone who has her ear to the ground about a great many things."

"I've had occasion to work with Mrs. Langdon," Mr. Mack said with a degree of pride. "You could say I'm something of a secret agent as well."

"Really?"

"What Mr. Mack means," Mrs. MacMurrough said, "is that he, too, likes to go snooping about. He's about as nosy a man as ever did breathe."

"I make inquiries," Mr. Mack said. "Because I have to know what's what before I take fellows like your friend Jimmy in hand and show 'em how to safely get away."

"Aye," Mrs. MacMurrough said. "I suppose you could say he's as busy a busybody as you'll ever meet, but it's all in a good cause."

"Now, Molly," Mr. Mack said, glancing again at his watch. "It's gotten onto seven twenty, we'd best get started if we're to get to the dock by eight-thirty. I'll need to go on board to make sure that Cato and Mrs. Langdon are introduced."

"Shall I come with you?" Mrs. MacMurrough asked.

"I don't think we have time to bring you hobbling along with us."

"Oh, hobbling, is it? Well ... I suppose you're right."

Mrs. MacMurrough gathered up the things that Cato had brought with him, including his satchel and his original hat. She handed him both. "D'you think you can fit your old hat inside the satchel? It won't do for you to wear a top hat on your head and carry another hat in your hand."

"Maybe I should leave my old hat here," Cato said.

"I'd say take it with you, if you can fit it in," Mr. Mack said. "You never can tell what changes of appearance you'll need to make."

"So says Michael Mack, the spy," Mrs. MacMurrough said. "Well, I suppose he's right."

Cato managed to rearrange the contents of his satchel until he could stuff the hat inside it. He looked around the room. "I think I have everything," he said.

"Ah, now, here's the part I hate," Mrs. MacMurrough said. "I don't like to say good-bye. I've seen fine young lads like you go off, and then I never see them again. What am I to think when I lay in bed at night? You must keep yourself safe, Cato—so an old lady can get her sleep."

Cato took hold of Mrs. MacMurrough's hand. "I promise you, ma'am. I'll stay safe. I'll get Jimmy, and I'll bring him home."

"If fate should bring you back this way, you know where to find me." She threw her arms around Cato's neck, pulled him close, and kissed his forehead. "God's blessing be with you, lad. Remember what Scripture tells us, 'All things work together for good to them that love God.'"

"Romans 8 verse 28," Mr. Mack said.

"Bless me, Mr. Mack, so it is!" Mrs. MacMurrough exclaimed. "I don't know why I didn't think of it sooner." She dashed over to the bookshelves that sat along the wall of the cabin. Her head bobbed until she found the volume she was looking for. "Here's just the thing for you," she said. She pulled out a book, then handed it to Cato.

Cato looked at the book in his hand. "The Bible?"

"Aye, lad, this is what you need."

"Oh, but I can't take your Bible away from you."

"Tosh. Don't I have two besides this? And, what's more, they give 'em out for free over at the Methodist church."

Cato nodded. He said "Thank you" and began to open his satchel with the intent of putting it inside.

"No, no, lad," Mrs. MacMurrough said. "You must carry it at your side. It'll protect you, you see. Why, between your top hat and your spectacles and the Bible at your side, those scalawags won't dare lay a hand on you."

"I don't know, Mrs.," Cato said. "I fear if Jimmy saw me with a Bible in hand, he wouldn't speak to me."

"Jimmy!" Mrs. MacMurrough's eyes flashed. "What kind of nonsense is that? You think if Jimmy looked across the street and saw you standing there he'd give two hoots what sort of book was resting in your hand? Why, he'd be over to see you so quick he'd just as likely knock you over as not."

"But he's most opposed to religious things."

"Is he now?" Mrs. MacMurrough put a ferocious look on her face. "Well, you tell him that Mrs. MacMurrough herself gave you that Bible to carry for protection. Tell him if he doesn't like it he can come back here straightaway and duke it out directly with me. And you'd best warn him that I've set many a man bigger than him down on his knees in my day. Haven't I, Mr. Mack?"

"Aye," Mr. Mack said. "You don't want to get Molly riled up. That's for sure!"

At that moment, Donahue leapt from his perch on the top of the bookcase, onto the top of Cato's stovepipe hat, with the acrobatic grace that only a cat can accomplish. This feat was accompanied by an emphatic "Meow!"

Cato stood perfectly still, balancing his head so as not to cause the cat to fall off.

"Now then, what's this?" Mrs. MacMurrough's hands went up toward the cat, but reached only as high as Cato's ears. "I suppose you're king of the mountain, are ya?" she said, looking up at the cat.

"Donahue doesn't like it when you get excited, Molly," Mr. Mack said.

"Oh, did I upset you?" she said to the cat. "Or are you trying to hold young Cato down, to keep the lad from leaving us? I bet that's it." She looked at Mr. Mack. "Now fetch him off there, Michael."

Mr. Mack reached up and retrieved Donahue from the top of Cato's hat, then dropped him down to the floor. Donahue meowed again and jumped up onto the table.

"Oh, now," Mrs. MacMurrough said, her eyes growing moist. "You'd better hurry or you'll miss that boat. Go on now and hurry, afore I change my mind and jump on top of your hat myself."

Cato nodded. "I'll remember all that you've done for me ... and for Jimmy ... for both of us."

And with that, Cato and Mr. Mack left the cottage.

10

"THERE'S NO GOOD CHOICE"

At the Crenshaw plantation, Sunday afternoon was designated as the time for the slaves to attend to their personal chores: washing clothes, cleaning cabins, tending to their garden plots.

Jimmy's cabin had three other occupants: Little Joe, Pheby, and an old man everyone called Uncle Isaac. Since none of them were field hands, Jimmy had spent little time with any of them, except for Little Joe, who'd gone out of his way to stay up late with Jimmy to talk to him about the Crenshaws.

As a boy, Little Joe had played with Ben Crenshaw. He'd grown up to become the Crenshaws' driver. Pheby, in addition to attending to Bonnie Crenshaw, was the plantation laundress and seamstress. Uncle Isaac was too old to work the fields. Instead, he groomed and fed most of the horses, did light cultivation in the main garden, and was also in charge of the slaves' vegetable garden, which sat between cabins three and four.

After a while, Pheby left with the announcement that she had to go wash some clothes. Little Joe went off to work in the garden. Jimmy was left alone with Uncle Isaac, who sat on his bed whittling. He was working on a piece of driftwood that Jimmy assumed had come from the river.

"What's that gonna be?" Jimmy asked.

"Fishin' lure," Uncle Isaac replied. "Should get"—he paused while he held it out to study it—"about five lures outta this piece o' wood."

"Seems you know what you're doin.'"

"Yes." Uncle Isaac nodded. "If I don't know nothin' else, I do know how to make a fishin' lure."

"Have you been here a long time? At this plantation?"

"I have," he said. "As a matter of fact ... I've been here all my life." He smiled. "And as you can see, that's been a long time." He turned his head slightly backward. "I got the scars on my back to prove it."

Jimmy shook his head. "Damn white bastards."

Uncle Isaac raised his eyebrow. "What'd they do to you?"

"Took me. Sold me."

"That's what they do. It's a shame." Uncle Isaac shook his head. "I reckon you had to leave all your people behind?"

Jimmy nodded. "For the time being."

Isaac looked surprised. "Oh? How's that? You figurin' to go home again?"

"I am."

Isaac made a face. "How're you gonna do that?"

"I'm not sure. I just know I'm not gonna stay here."

"You fixin' to run away?"

"Why not?"

"Yeah, well ..." Isaac stopped whittling for a moment. "I ran away myself. Two times. A long time ago."

"Did they catch you?"

Isaac blinked. "I'm here, ain't I?"

"Yeah." Jimmy scowled. "Damn bastards."

"Anyway ... I was young once. I know how it is."

"Do you?"

"Of course I do, boy. What'd you think? You think I'm just a tired old nigger?"

Jimmy hung his head. "No, sir."

"Look," Uncle Isaac said. "I know you're hurtin.' But you know what? That's how it is. That's how it is and there's not much you can do that's gonna make it different."

"I'm sorry, Uncle," Jimmy said. "But I can't let it be."

Isaac's eyes softened. "Yeah. I know. I really do." He closed his eyes for a moment, then opened them again. "The trouble is, I don't like what I see when I see myself in your eyes."

Jimmy held up his hands. "I don't mean no disrespect. I just ... I just."

"You just don't wanna end up like me. I know."

"That's not what I meant."

Uncle Isaac started whittling again. Then he said, "The truth is, there ain't much good that can come from runnin'. But a man's gotta do what a man's gotta do." He looked at Jimmy. "You know, I suppose you're right to look at me the way you do. But it wasn't my fault I couldn't make it. I tried. But all I found out is, you're damned if you do, and damned if you don't. You're goddamn damned no matter what you do." It seemed as if his eyes had glazed over, but he managed to smile. "Excuse me for cussin.'"

Jimmy thought about what Isaac had endured. "It just makes me angry, is all," he said.

"I know," Isaac said. "But you got to be careful. Anger will eat your heart out. You've got to decide what to do. But there's no good choice." He shook his head. "No, sir. No good choice."

"No," Jimmy said. "There isn't."

Uncle Isaac stopped whittling and held up his first finished lure. "Remember, son, freedom might turn out to be just like this here." He pointed at the lure, and then he made a hook with his finger.

11

"YOU WANT ME TO BE A SPY?"

The steamboat to Louisville sat idling by the levee next to the stone-paved wharf. The boat was a handsome sight, sharp and trim, with a pair of tall chimneys and a giant paddle-box. The name of the ship, *The Cincinnati Queen,* was emblazoned in gilded letters on the side, with a cheerful swath of golden sun rays painted above it. The decks were fenced with clean white railings, and the Union flag flew brazenly from the jack-staff.

By pre-arrangement, Mrs. Langdon had told Mr. Mack to have Cato meet her on the port side of the ship—the side onto which cargo was loaded. She told him she'd wait on the hurricane deck, from which vantage point she'd have a favorable view of the levee. She further indicated that she'd be wearing a green Garibaldi dress with dropped shoulders and a bloused bodice with puffed sleeves, and that she'd be carrying a parasol. Mr. Mack had related these details to Cato during their walk to the wharf.

"What's a Garibaldi dress?" Cato asked.

"I haven't the faintest idea," Mr. Mack replied. "But I take great comfort in the fact that the dress will be green."

"I'll find her," Cato said.

Mr. Mack's face showed some doubt. "The ship's come down from Saint Looy," he said. He took out his pocket watch. "She won't leave here until 9 o'clock. I believe there's time enough for me to come on board. I'll make sure you find her."

"Is the boat going all the way to Cincinnati?" Cato asked.

"I believe it is," Mr. Mack said.

It was 8:35 by Mr. Mack's watch when he and Cato climbed on board. Cato spotted Mrs. Langdon first. "There she is!" He pointed at her. "In a green dress and a parasol."

Mr. Mack introduced Cato to Mrs. Langdon, who formally shook Cato's hand.

"A great pleasure to meet you." Her eyes sparkled. "I understand you're looking to find Mr. Horace Hogan."

"Yes, ma'am," Cato said. "He ... I have reason to believe that Mr. Hogan has kidnapped a friend of mine."

Mrs. Langdon nodded. "Your friend, I take it, was a runaway slave?"

Cato nodded hesitantly. "In a manner of speaking."

"And what about you?" Mrs. Langdon continued. "Are you a runaway, too?"

Cato looked around anxiously. There was no one close enough to overhear them. Even so, he was uncomfortable with Mrs. Langdon's directness.

"Don't worry, lad," Mr. Mack said. "You can trust Mrs. Langdon. It's best to tell the truth."

"Yes," Cato said. "We both are."

"Where, may I ask, did you run away from?"

"Tennessee," Cato said.

"Both of you?"

"Yes."

"Whereabouts in Tennessee?"

"My father's plantation is next to Jimmy's farm, which is owned by the Hollands. The nearest town is Jackson."

"Jackson." Mrs. Langdon nodded. "I see." She leaned closer,

looking intently at Cato. "You mention your father ... it explains to me something about how you look."

"Yes, ma'am."

"What is your father's name?"

"Askew. Augustus Askew," Cato replied, realizing how long it had been since he'd said his father's name.

"So you're an Askew then?"

"I am," Cato said.

"I take it your mother was a slave?"

"Indeed, ma'am."

"And your friend Jimmy, is he as light-skinned as you?"

"No, ma'am. He's quite dark."

"Well, Mr. Askew." Mrs. Langdon's look grew ominous. "I'm sorry to have to tell you that, despite the clarity of the law, it's likely that Mr. Hogan will not take your friend back to the Hollands' farm."

"No?"

"No," she continued. "Mr. Hogan finds it far more lucrative to catch runaways and bring them deep into the South, as far away as possible from wherever they actually came from."

"But why?"

"Because he believes, and I have no doubt he's right, that he can get a much higher price on the auction market than he can get as a reward for the recapture and return of a slave."

"You mean ..." Cato digested this. "You mean he's going to sell Jimmy to a stranger?"

"I'm afraid so," Mrs. Langdon said. She registered the look in Cato's eyes. "I'm sorry."

Cato didn't know what to say.

"If I may ask," she continued, "what sort of physical shape is your friend Jimmy in?"

"Oh, he's most fit," Cato said.

"Well, then, I'm afraid it's likely that Mr. Hogan will seek an owner who values heavy labor."

"Oh, no."

"There are half a dozen cities where Hogan might bring your friend to auction: Richmond, Charlotte, Charleston, Atlanta, Savannah, or Montgomery. He'll want to steer clear of Tennessee. But there's no telling which city he'll choose. Probably one of the five in the east."

"But how can I find him?" Cato's tone was forlorn.

Mrs. Langdon put her hand on Cato's arm and turned him until they were both facing away from the deck rail. "It's possible I may be able to find out something to help you," she said in a lowered voice. "I have a contact in Paducah who knows Hogan."

"Is it someone I can visit?"

"No. I don't think that would be a good idea," said Mrs. Langdon. "It would be too risky for you to try to see him on your own."

She stepped back to look at Cato from a fuller vantage. Cato was wearing his wig and top hat and a brown frock coat. He wore the glassless spectacles on his nose, and held his satchel in one hand and the Bible in the other. He looked, as much as anything, like a traveling parson.

"It's hard to know what to do with you," she said. "I don't know if it's better for you to pass as white, or for you to be more decidedly Negro."

"But why?"

"Well ..." She looked at Mr. Mack. "As I told Mr. Mack, I believe it's possible that I might be able to help you, if you, in turn, are willing to help me."

"Help you? But how?"

"I need someone to accompany me. I need someone who can gain the confidence of the local slaves in the places I'm going. The truth is, Cato, slaves are a good source of information for us." She leaned into Cato and spoke in a hushed voice. "The Confederates are easily duped. They think all the slaves around them are lighthearted, happy darkeys. They speak openly in front of them, saying things they'd never want the Union to know. Do you understand what I'm saying?"

"Yes, ma'am. But I ... I'm not sure what you'd want me to do."

"My hope is that you'll consider traveling with me, Mr. Askew, and acting as my servant. I've cultivated friendships with many important Southern families. In the homes that I visit, you'd be expected to fraternize with the slaves. It's from them that you would be able to learn important information."

"You want me to be a spy?" Cato didn't know whether to be excited or dismayed.

"Yes," Mrs. Langdon said. "I know it is a lot to ask of you. But it's rare for me to find someone as capable as you who's able to play this role. Mr. Mack tells me you know how to read and write."

"Yes, ma'am. I can read just about anything."

"Well, that's perfect. The only problem, frankly, is that you're so light you may have more trouble passing as a slave than passing as white. I'd need to you to act like one of those happy darkeys." She paused a moment. "How old are you, by the way?"

"I'm twenty-two."

"So young!"

"Never fear, he's a capable lad," Mr. Mack said.

Mrs. Langdon shook her head. "Be that as it may, it's a great deal of responsibility to take on at such an age. I'm nearly twice his age and even I can barely manage it."

Cato looked from Mrs. Langdon to Mr. Mack. "I'd like to help you," he said. "Truly I would. But, you see, I must find Jimmy. And I don't know if I dare wait any longer. If he's been sold away as you say ..."

"I'm offering quid pro quo," Mrs. Langdon said. "I'll help you if you help me. I'll make it my business to find out what Hogan's been up to. I'm willing to follow Jimmy's trail with you, if you, in return, will gather information for me."

"Oh. I see."

"And honestly, Mr. Askew, I think this is the best way for you to proceed. If you come with me as my servant you'll be much safer than you would be on your own. No one will ask you for papers. No one will wonder where you're going."

Just then the captain stepped out of the glass pilot house, which was close by, and lifted his hand as a signal. From down below on the boiler deck came the sound of grates opening on the furnace. Abruptly, a deckhand rang the big bell, which was right beside them, causing Mrs. Langdon to clasp her hands to her ears. A volume of black smoke tumbled out of the chimneys. Down on the levee, a man took up one end of the coil of rope that tied the vessel to the dock.

"Oh, good Lord," Mr. Mack exclaimed. "She's about to leave. I must go!"

"Yes," Mrs. Langdon said, gazing at the commotion on the levee. "You'd better hurry."

Just then a rush of pent-up steam wailed long and deep through the gauge-cocks, and the giant bell rang again.

"But what will you do, Cato?" Mr. Mack asked, as he turned to leave.

"Whatever it takes," Cato replied.

And with that, Mr. Mack scurried down the stairs to the gangplank and ran as fast as he could to get off the ship. Once he was safely off, he stood on the shore of the levee and waved his hat. "Take care of yourself!" he shouted.

"You too," Mrs. Langdon called, brandishing her parasol. "And Molly as well."

"Good-bye," Cato yelled. He put his hand on the top of his hat to hold it in place against the gathering breeze. "And thank you. Thank you!"

A deckhand leaned out over the end of the port bow to pull in the coil of rope that had been released from the mooring. There was a last-minute scramble on the gangplank for stragglers to get aboard and others to get ashore—with a great deal of yelling and even cursing.

The gangplank was withdrawn. Then a second great puff of black smoke issued up from the chimneys. The whistle blew; the signal bell rang; heat rose up from the boilers. And at last the giant paddle-wheel began to turn, grabbing hard upon the water until it was churning it to foam. *The Cincinnati Queen* moved quickly out into the channel of the Ohio River, bound for Kentucky ports of call.

12

"I REALLY DON'T WANNA SEE NO CRENSHAWS"

Throughout the South, Sunday was supposed to be the slaves' day of rest. But as often as not, the slaves had to spend most of the day doing personal chores. Having just arrived, Jimmy had no chores as yet. But he couldn't sit still in the cabin. He wanted time alone to think. He wanted to learn the lay of the land. Most of all, he wanted to plot his escape. He went outside and walked to the slaves' garden, where Little Joe was working.

He asked him, "Is there somewhere nearby I can go to be alone for a while?" Jimmy gestured at the area around the cabins. "I've gotta find a quiet place."

Joe leaned on his hoe, then scratched his forehead. "Quiet, eh? That does sound nice."

"Yes, and somewhere safe," he said. "You know, somewhere with no paddy rollers, no slave catchers, no overseers—nobody like that." Then he added, "And I really don't wanna see no Crenshaws, either."

Little Joe smiled. "Jacob, you must be dreamin' of somewhere in heaven." But then he grew thoughtful. "I tell you what. There's a place just out there." He turned to face the woods that lay a hundred yards behind the cabin. "Look at that opening." He pointed to a gap in the woods. "There's a path there. Do you see it?"

Jimmy nodded.

"Follow that path."

"Where does it go?"

"Just go on and walk it," Joe said. "You'll see where it goes."

So Jimmy followed the path, which began on the edge of the woods behind the cabin. It wound through the forest for a quarter-mile, then opened onto a meadow ringed by oak trees that were draped with moss. When he got to the meadow, he saw that he was alone—alone in a patch of privacy. It was just what he wanted. It felt like a secret retreat. He hadn't been alone, truly alone, in months. He'd never felt completely at ease in Chicago. There was too much bustle in the city. But he hadn't realized, until he sat himself down on a log at the edge of the meadow, how much he'd missed the country.

In western Tennessee, where he grew up, the landscape had been flat, the soil brown and arable. He'd spent many Sundays like this one, sitting on a fence, idly tossing rocks at hickory trees. Those Sunday afternoons had been his quietest moments, but also his most restless. Then, after he'd made his escape to Chicago, the familiar rural landscape of his youth had given way to muddy streets, grimy alleys, and a whirlwind of horses, carts, and passers-by. His Sunday afternoons were no longer spent in restless isolation, but in the arms of Cato in their unadorned room on Washington Street. He'd loved everything about his new life, except the city itself.

Then without warning he'd been snatched up and carried off to a place hundreds of miles distant. Nothing in Georgia looked right to him. The Georgia dirt looked strange. It was red and loamy. The air, too, felt different—humid and vaporous. He assumed that was because of the sea, which Little Joe had told him was nearby. He wondered if he could make use of the sea to get away.

He took stock of the meadow. It was filled with grasses. Spikes of brownish-purple flower-heads rose in clusters above the grass stems. Scattered about were pockets of sunflowers, mint, goldenrods, and milkweeds. In the woods, the air had been still. But now he watched as a draft of wind raced across the meadow. It blew up a flurry of milkweed filaments, then swept like an invisible hand, flitting across the goldenrod and the tall grass. The grass flower-heads bent effortlessly, then stood back up with just as much ease. He was mesmerized by the way the fronds of grass arched up and down in playful waves. It was a gentle display of give and take with the breeze.

Above the grass flew dozens of orange butterflies, white moths, and iridescent hummingbirds. They zipped and hovered and darted around the meadow. They chased one another, rushing in wild zigzags as if playing a game. Even as he felt pleasure in watching their lively freedom, he felt a counteracting sorrow. He was so far from having freedom in his life again, he wondered if it would've been better if he'd never tasted it at all.

When he'd asked Little Joe to suggest a place to go, he thought he wanted solitude. But in fact, it was his abysmal solitude that most pained him. He was alone. He was friendless. He found little comfort in the company of the Crenshaw slaves. Though they'd been kind to him, all he could see was how much they'd been beaten down. They'd been forced to wear slavery like a yoke, even in their private moments. Meekness had been ground into them. He could hear it in their speech, see it in their gestures. To him it felt as if they'd lost hope. He didn't blame them. But he could hardly bear to look at it.

For the thousandth time in his life he was astonished that men—white men—could be so inhuman. His surprise was due to a belief he rarely showed anyone else—a belief in goodness. It amazed him that such an improbable belief survived in him, even after fate continued to crush his soul. He didn't believe in God. How could he? But he did believe in something. It was hard for him to put into words what exactly he believed in. It was a kind of spirit. But it wasn't the specter of an old white man. It was a tender spirit, something good and kind. It was a friendly force. It was something that gamboled in the grass and swirled in the mossy trees. It pranced with the ants that hurried about his feet. When he caught sight of these things, he was filled with wonder. How could there be so much that was good in the world and yet so much that wasn't, both at the same time? Despite his ordeals, he believed there was something inherently good about life, something benevolent, even if he could only from time to time sense a spark of light in the darkness.

He understood that this seed inside him, this kernel of hope, the thing that kept him from despair, had been given to him by two souls—by Cato, his sweet-as-a-rabbit lover, and by Venus, his dog and greatest teacher. Grief over Venus's death had led him into Cato's arms. And in those moments he'd passed from one fulsome love to another.

How those moments had surprised him! It was as if he and Cato had both awakened at the same time. Their desire for each other stood alone, unparalleled. There'd been no model for them. Their lust had come like a force from another world. It filled them with a sexual longing for each other that was as extraordinary as it was abnormal. But how could any man find his own deepest self unnatural? Jimmy could not. In fact, he'd come to believe that the only normal, the only righteous part of his life, was his love for Cato.

It was this sexual desire that seemed so unnatural to the rest of the world that was the hallmark of his truest self. It was his sexual uniqueness that made him doubt the natural order. Its upside-down quality gave him hope that the world of slave-holders that he saw about him was not the natural world. He reasoned that if there was a world where men like him could love men like Cato, there must also be a world where there were no slaves; there must be a world where black men walked the streets in freedom; there must be a world where he and

Cato could live without fear. He'd learned as a boy to hope for such a world. He'd heard stories about the North. He'd placed all his hope in the North. And then the North—how it had betrayed him! Yet he couldn't let go of the dream that somewhere in this world that held darting hummingbirds and playful butterflies there must also be a world populated by men who were ... like Cato ... gentle, kind, and good.

And now, as he breathed the humid air, his mind turned back to the sea. Once before he'd used a boat to cross the Ohio River. Why couldn't he use one to travel along the shore and get away from the eyes of white men? Maybe he could learn to use a sail. He could row if he had to. He turned sideways on his log. He stretched his arms. He pretended there were oars in his hands. He pulled his arms back. He could feel his biceps enlarge as he drew against the water's resistance. His imaginary boat slid forward, gliding north, away from Georgia, away from the plantation, away from the whips and the cotton sacks, and back into the arms of his sweet gentle rabbit.

13

"YOU CAN HELP ME. AND I CAN HELP YOU."

The Cincinnati Queen hewed along the main channel of the Ohio River, puffing smoke and churning its wheel, as it made its way from Cairo, Illinois, toward Paducah, Kentucky.

"I think we'd better go down to the main deck," Mrs. Langdon said. "The breeze is too great up here. You'll never hold on to your hat."

Mrs. Langdon and Cato climbed the stairs down to the boiler deck and then down one more level to the main deck, where they found a pair of chairs that were well back from the deck rail, and sat. Even away from the railing the breeze was so strong that Cato had to remove his top hat and place it in his lap.

"I have questions about your proposal," Cato said. "You mentioned that you have friends in the South. Can you tell me where you plan to go?"

Mrs. Langdon studied Cato for a moment, then looked around to assure herself that they were alone. "How much do you know about the state of the war?"

"I know hardly anything at all," Cato admitted.

"Then ... I'd better bring you up to date. No matter what you decide to do, you need to know what's going on around you. Frankly, Mr. Askew, we're going right into the thick of it."

"In Kentucky?"

"Yes, Kentucky is very much in doubt. The rebels have taken Lexington and there's fighting going on all across the state. Alas, a great deal hangs in the balance. Right now, the Union controls Louisville and all of the Ohio River. But General Bragg is leading the Confederates up from the south. He wants to capture or destroy portions of the Louisville and Nashville railroad. That's a problem because the railroad has been the best way for the Union to get their boys down to the southern theater. Bragg's coming up from Tennessee even as I speak."

"What about Paducah? Do the Rebs control that?"

"No, and Paducah itself is safe for the time being. But once you venture south of the city, Mr. Askew, you'll soon cross enemy lines."

"Good gracious."

Mrs. Langdon looked around again. Despite no one being nearby, she shaded her mouth with her hand and spoke barely above a whisper. "My plan is to get off the boat at Louisville, then, if it's still running, I'll take the train to Elizabethtown—or as far as it goes. From there it's hard to say what I'll do. I'll be moving out of Union territory, so I'll have to take things as they come. I want to get to Chattanooga by and by. But before I do that, I want to find out what General Bragg is up to."

"Is he in command of all the Rebels?"

"In this part of the country, yes. General Bragg commands the entire Confederate Army of the Mississippi. I expect he wants to take over or destroy the railroad, then advance to Louisville and lay siege on the river. But we don't know for sure what he's up to. He's got battalions moving here and there. And, of course, the Union is on the move, too." She gave Cato a disapproving look, then pointed to his hat, which he held in his lap. "I wonder if you should put your hat back on your head."

"Right now?"

"Yes. I'm afraid that with your hat removed it's apparent that something's not right about your hair. The strands don't waft in the breeze in a natural way."

Cato put his hat back on his head. At the moment, the wind was calm. But he was aware that at any moment he'd have to hang on to the stovepipe hat to keep it from blowing off. He was wondering if he ought to switch back to his old bowler hat, which was much smaller.

"Do you ever smoke cigars?" she asked him.

"Me? Why, no!"

"I think if you're going to try to disguise yourself as white, it may help you do so if you add a cigar to your ... charade. But you'd have to actually smoke it, not just hold it in your hand."

"Where would I get a cigar?"

Mrs. Langdon huffed. "At a cigar store, of course. Look for any store with a wooden Indian in front."

"But I know nothing about cigars. What would I ask for?"

"Oh, well ... ask the man for a box of five-cent cigars—unless you've got extra money to spend. Then you might want to ask for Havanas. Those'll cost you ten cents apiece, but I'm told by gentlemen that they're much tastier."

Cato shrugged. "Ten-cent cigars would be a waste of money for me. I wouldn't know what's tasty."

"It's up to you. Now, I must warn you, in many locations in the South, Negroes aren't permitted to smoke cigars. It's a whipping offense. I believe that this custom works in your favor, though, with respect to the disguise. Do you see?"

"Yes, I understand," he said, though he didn't understand why she was coaching him in how to pass as white—since she'd proposed that he act as her servant. He wondered if she wanted him to be able to slip in and out of being black. "White folks only expect to see a white man smoking," he said.

"Exactly. Now if you smoke a cigar, you must always have great confidence. In fact, it would be a good idea if you always showed an air of confidence, no matter how you feel. You should do everything you do with an air of prerogative. That's what I do. And I have to pretend a great many things."

"What about finding Jimmy?"

"Ah, yes ... as I was saying before, I'm sure Mr. Hogan has set his sights on one of the big cities in the southeast. It's safer for him to do his business somewhere where he won't stand out. Truthfully, Mr. Askew, I believe there's little point for you to get off in Paducah. Of course, if you wish to, it's your decision. You will likely be safe there, as I've explained. But you won't be safe if you go out of the city. After that it would be dangerous for anyone, but most especially for a Negro disguised as white."

Cato considered this. He was tempted by Mrs. Langdon's quid pro quo offer. But he didn't want to lose any time on a side trip. "How long do you imagine you'll be ... spying ... in Kentucky before you go to Chattanooga?"

"It's hard to say."

"I would hate to be distracted from my search, Mrs. Langdon."

"I understand. But you must realize that it's going to take you a long time to find him, no matter what you do. There's no telling if Hogan will even use Jimmy's real name when he sells him. In fact, he most likely won't."

"But why not?"

"He won't want any of Jimmy's owners, I believe you said their name is Holland ...."

"Yes."

"He won't want any Hollands to come knocking on his door and claim Jimmy as their own property. There'd be no guarantee of any money in it for Hogan in that event."

"But the Hollands would never leave home. Not now. Not with the war going on."

"Well, that's as may be. You seem to be sure of it. But

Hogan won't want to take any risk he doesn't have to take. Who knows? He could encounter someone who's an acquaintance of the Hollands or someone from the town who merely knows of them. He might run across a soldier, a salesman, or any itinerant person. It's far safer for Hogan to create a counterfeit bill of sale for Jimmy with a false name."

"Then how will I ever find him?"

"You must follow Hogan's trail. If it leads to an auction, as I believe it will, then you'll have to find the name of anyone who bought a slave at the auction and track each of those buyers down."

Despite Mrs. Langdon's admonition, Cato took off his hat, and held it once again in his lap. He didn't see how he could do all those things. And yet, he couldn't imagine going back to Chicago without Jimmy. If he tried to imagine his life without Jimmy, all he could see was that his life would have no meaning. There was nothing for him to do but persevere. But how should he proceed? He wished he could ask Jimmy for advice.

Mrs. Langdon looked at Cato and frowned. "Mr. Askew, I must tell you that I am not an abolitionist."

"What?" Cato could not follow this sudden turn in Mrs. Langdon's chain of thought.

"I thought it my duty to inform you of this."

"What do you mean? Are you saying that you support slavery?"

"I do."

"But why?" Cato was astonished that someone in her position, who risked her own life to be a Union spy in the south, would hold such a belief.

"Well, I suppose you may as well ask me why men eat animals. I suppose from the animals' point of view, it must not seem tolerable. And yet, I think you'll agree that it is obvious that this is what God has intended us to do."

Cato nearly stood and walked away. He wasn't sure if he could discuss something as elemental as this in his current emotional state. But when he considered where he would rush off to and what he would do as an alternative, he couldn't envision anything. To buy time, he put his hat back on his head. He tapped his fingers on his lap. Then he looked Mrs. Langdon squarely in the eyes, and in a tone that seemed to him to be a complicated combination of gentle and angry, he spoke. "Madam, are you suggesting that I am merely an animal?"

Mrs. Langdon snorted and rapped her parasol on the wooden deck. "You? No, not you. Of course not. You, after all, are half-white. You aren't like the others. But no doubt it is difficult for you to see this."

Now Cato did stand. "Yes," he said. "I cannot see this at all."

"Now I've offended you."

"What did you expect?"

"I only wished to have it clear for the sake of being honest with you. I hope you will not take it personally."

"Not take it personally? How could I not? Do you have any idea what ... ?" He broke off talking. He felt as if there was no point in even attempting a discussion.

"Please sit down, Mr. Askew." She pointed with her parasol at the chair from which he'd risen. "What does it matter about this particular point? I have no intention of returning you to slavery. Nor do I have an intention of returning your friend to slavery. On the contrary, I have offered to help you find him—and perhaps you will both then be able to escape bondage." She shrugged. "I have no objection to that outcome. In the grand scheme of things it seems perfectly acceptable to me."

"I see." Now there was more than a little bitterness in Cato's voice. He saw that her support for slavery was flexible when it suited her purposes.

"So the point is, I will help you. I have selfish reasons to do so. I am being honest with you about everything. I hope that you will appreciate this so that you can trust what I tell you. And what I am telling you is that you need my help. You won't succeed on your own."

Cato, who had remained standing, now sat down again. "Why do you want *my* help so much?"

"Because I have learned that you will be in a position to learn what I cannot learn myself. It's as simple as that. The only thing is, you must walk on both sides of the dilemma into which you were born."

"You mean I have to use my black blood to help my white blood?"

"In a manner of speaking."

"How ironic. I think that I may say so. I think that I may say how sorry I am that you should be forced to call upon an animal to give you assistance, when you'd prefer to have it for your supper in accordance with God's plan."

"Now you're being rude, Mr. Askew."

"Am I?"

"I think you've let yourself get carried away with emotion and it's clouding your judgment. You must consider what is the best way to reach your objective."

"I don't understand you. I trusted you more before you confessed your belief in slavery."

"That's not logical, Mr. Askew. Honesty should always be grounds for trust."

"But what is your purpose? Why are you doing this work? Why are you spying for the Union? I can tell from your accent that you're Southern-born."

"Yes. I'm a Southerner. I'm proud to be that. But I'm also a patriot. I believe in the Union. I believe in the United States. I am not one of those dreamy idealists who thinks it's possible for the South to succeed on its own. They are fools. The South by itself has nothing—no industry, no capital, no banks, no allies, no established government, not even a real army. It has no future in the world! I have my eyes wide open, Mr. Askew. There is no outcome for this war other than a Union victory. And the sooner it happens the better it will be for all concerned."

"So you would betray your own people? And you expect me to trust you?"

"Have you been listening to what I've said? I have the best interests of my people at heart. I'm doing what I think is right. It's not easy to do what I do. You must not try to dissuade me. Have you no sense of self-interest?"

"You and I are not alike, madam," was all that Cato could say.

"No." She shook her head. "We are not. And yet, why should that be an impediment to our working together? You can help me. And I can help you."

Cato stood up again. "I'm going back to the upper deck. I need time to think about what I will do."

"Very well."

"I must warn you: I'll most likely get off in Paducah. If I do, you may take that as a sign that I have decided to continue on my own."

"Suit yourself." She nodded. "But if you decide otherwise, you'll find me down here." She looked around and spotted the door to the interior cabin. "I'll be in the main cabin."

And with that they both stood. Mrs. Langdon walked to the main cabin, and Cato walked to the stairs to climb to the upper deck.

14

"YOU ARE A CURIOSITY"

"Jacob?"

Jimmy turned around with a start. There in the bright sun of the meadow, not ten yards away from him, stood a man in brown plaid pants—a white man—with a peg leg and a cane. Jimmy stood up from his log so quickly that he lost his balance. He fell back onto the log for a moment, then awkwardly stood back up again.

"I didn't mean to startle you," the man said. "It appeared as if you were trying to row that log across the meadow."

Looking against the sun, Jimmy narrowed his eyes, but tried not to squint. He didn't know what to say. He couldn't imagine what kind of expression was on his face. He said, "Good day." Then he stepped away from the log and turned to walk back toward the opening in the woods.

"You don't need to leave," the man said. "I just wanted to meet you. Little Joe said you might be out here in the meadow."

Jimmy hesitated, then turned around to face the man. He was annoyed. Why had Little Joe revealed his whereabouts?

"I'm Ben Crenshaw," the man said, as he walked closer, eyeing Jimmy with a mix of concentration and wariness. "I believe you've already met my father, Samuel, and my sister, Bonnie."

Jimmy cocked his head. He had no idea what this was leading to. He thought that the man was actually going to reach out to shake his hand.

But the man, Ben, stopped walking when he was five feet away. Then he stood staring.

Jimmy watched Ben's eyes as they looked him up and down. Like the men in the auction house—Ben was sizing him up. Yet there was something odd about his appraisal. His eyes lingered. Then he nodded, a short quick nod that reminded Jimmy of the way his sister Bonnie had nodded when she'd looked directly at him at the end of the auction.

Ben turned his head to look around the meadow. "It's beautiful here, isn't it?"

Jimmy was confused. He wasn't sure how to handle the man's tone, which was unexpected. He looked vaguely at the meadow, then said, "Yes, sir."

Ben smiled, as if he was heartened to finally hear Jimmy's voice. "Well, Jacob, I imagine you were hoping to have a quiet moment alone. I'm sorry to have disturbed you."

The man's demeanor was disorienting. Jimmy still didn't know what to say. He decided to use a cordial tone. "It's not that I'm disturbed, massa. I just didn't expect to see anyone out here."

Jimmy didn't correct Ben Crenshaw's understanding of his name. He'd decided to play along with Hogan's deceit about his name being Jacob—and about his having come from North Carolina. Hogan's goal was to legitimize the illegal sale. Jimmy's was to protect his anonymity. He didn't want anyone on the Crenshaw plantation to know his real identity. It was a way to keep his true self from being possessed. It was also a way to protect himself when he made his getaway. When he escaped they'd be on the lookout for a slave named Jacob from North Carolina instead of Jimmy from Tennessee.

Ben Crenshaw continued to scrutinize him. Then he glanced around at the meadow and said, “I don’t know why no one comes out this way anymore.” He looked back at Jimmy. “I used to come here all the time when I was a boy. It’s peaceful.” He seemed for a moment to be lost in a private memory. Then he raised an eyebrow. “I understand you come from North Carolina.”

Jimmy nodded.

“It’s quite pretty up there.”

Jimmy hesitated. He wondered if the man was trying to trick him. Perhaps he was testing him to see how accurately he knew North Carolina. Jimmy had never been there. But one of the slaves who’d raised him, Juba Jake, had lived in North Carolina for several years after he was first brought over from Africa. Jimmy knew if he had to, he could recount one of Jake’s stories. But he was afraid to go out on a limb. So he said simply, “It’s considerable hot in the summer.” He knew that wasn’t much of an answer. So he added, “But the winter’s altogether fine.” He hoped that would be enough.

“I’m afraid you’ll find it’s quite hot here in the summer as well,” Ben said. Then he went quiet and began to blink. He seemed to be feeling as awkward as Jimmy was. Finally he said, “But we, too, have a fine winter.”

Jimmy nodded. He didn’t say what he thought, which was that he had no plans to experience the winter in Savannah.

Ben took another step closer. And now Jimmy could smell him. The man was suffused with a scent. It was an unexpected smell, spicy and sweet. Ben seemed to be sniffing at Jimmy, too. Jimmy could see his nostrils flare. “My sister told me you were rather ferocious. But I don’t see it.”

Jimmy lowered his head. He was convinced, now, that Ben Crenshaw was playing a game with him—but he didn’t know what the game was. After a silence that felt too long, he said simply, “No, sir.”

"No," Ben repeated, with a satisfied smile. "But you are a curiosity."

Jimmy cocked his head, but kept it lowered. He wouldn't be baited.

"How come they sold you ... back in North Carolina?"

The question caught Jimmy by surprise. The first thing that popped into his mind was the story that Reverend Zeke had told at a Sunday sermon when he was a boy, about a woman named Sara from the Askew plantation who had stolen food. Augustus Askew had sold her child to punish her. He seized on this. "It was on account of my mother," he said slowly. "She stole some food."

"Your mother stole food," Ben repeated what he'd just heard. "And they sold *you*?" He seemed skeptical.

"Yes, sir," Jimmy said. "It was to punish her."

"Oh," Ben said, as he understood. "I see." He was clearly embarrassed. "Well, that's a pity for you. It seems you did nothing wrong."

"No, sir."

"I'm told that you have no marks."

"Marks?"

"From the whip."

"Oh ... no, sir." Then he remembered Eppley's lash from yesterday. "Just a small scratch."

"A scratch?"

"Yes, sir. On my leg."

Jimmy regretted mentioning it the moment he finished speaking. He ought to have kept Ben Crenshaw believing he had no marks or bruises, and that it was because he was obedient, which was the illusion he wanted to create.

"I see," Ben said. Then he took a step backward and lifted his cane up as though it was a pointing stick. "Let me see your back."

"My back?"

"Yes," Ben said. "I've never seen a slave your age with no

marks."

"You want me to take off my shirt?"

"Yes."

Jimmy unbuttoned his shirt with hesitation. He saw that Ben was watching him closely again, with a degree of scrutiny that was like that of the men in the auction house. When he had removed his shirt, he held it at his side.

Ben Crenshaw walked around him. Without warning, he put his hand on the back of Jimmy's neck, then pressed his palm into it. He ran his palm from the base of Jimmy's neck down to the bottom of his waist, cupping the skin as he went, coming to rest just above the waist of his pants. Jimmy stood frozen. He was acutely aware, once again, of the spicy, sweet smell of the man who was touching him. He held his breath.

Ben removed his hand and walked back around to face Jimmy again. "Let me see your leg," he said.

"My leg?"

"Yes. Show me the scratch."

"Oh." Jimmy bent down and tried to pull up the cuff of his pants to reveal the bruise that Eppley had inflicted on the back of his thigh. But he couldn't get the fabric to stretch sufficiently to allow it to be pulled up high enough.

Ben watched him struggle with the pants leg. "You'd better take those off," he said.

Jimmy stood back up. His calf muscles trembled. He had an apprehensive feeling about what was happening. He undid the belt of his pants. He turned slightly, and took them off. Then he stood back up. He was wearing only his underwear.

Ben Crenshaw looked him up and down. Then he walked around and stood behind Jimmy again. He touched his hand on the back of Jimmy's thigh. "Oh, I see," he said. "It's just here." He ran his finger down the bruise. "Who did this?"

"Massa Eppley," Jimmy said.

"Why?"

Jimmy hesitated. "I was picking cotton," he said. "He wished me to hurry it up."

"I see," Ben said. "And did you?"

"Yes, sir."

Ben gently slapped Jimmy's buttock, which caused Jimmy to start. He took a step forward and turned his head to the side. Ben then walked back around to face Jimmy. He stood still for a moment, gazing thoughtfully at Jimmy's chest. He put his hand out, as if he were going to touch his chest, but his hand came to rest on Jimmy's shoulder. "Well," he said. "You must be careful. I think it's best if you keep yourself unmarked."

"Yes, massa."

"My sister has hopes for you in that regard."

"Yes, sir," Jimmy said. But he wondered what Bonnie's hopes could possibly be. Did she want his unmarked body as a testament to his obedience? He tried to think of a way to bring this discussion to an end. But he couldn't. "Me, too," he said. "I hope to stay unmarked."

Ben nodded. "I'm glad to hear that." He took a final look at Jimmy's torso. "You may put those back on now." He pointed at Jimmy's shirt and pants with his cane.

"Yes, massa." Jimmy quickly put his pants and then his shirt back on.

Ben watched him without moving. "You know, you're a good-looking fellow," he said.

Jimmy stood motionless. He didn't speak.

"Let's keep it that way, all right? You must mind what Eppley says."

Jimmy nodded. "Yes, sir." He looked around for an excuse to get away. He looked longingly at the opening in the woods where the path that led back to the cabin was located. He said, "May I go now, massa?"

"Go?"

Jimmy hung his head and tried to look as anxious as possible. “Yes, massa. I told Uncle Isaac I’d help him in our garden with some ... some hoeing, this afternoon.”

“Hoeing?”

“Yes, sir. We’ve got to till it, I reckon. Weeds comin’ up.”

Ben narrowed his eyes. “Very well,” he said.

Jimmy turned and started to walk away.

“Wait a minute.” Ben hobbled back up to him. He put his hand in his vest pocket and took out a coin. “Here,” he said. “Take this.”

Jimmy stopped. He looked at the coin in Ben’s extended hand. “What’s it for?” he asked.

“Give it to Pheby. Tell her I want her to make you new pants. She’ll need this when she next goes into town for cloth,” he said. “And have her get material for a new shirt, too. Those clothes you’re wearing don’t fit you very well.”

Jimmy took the coin. “Yes, sir.” He knew that Pheby sometimes accompanied Little Joe and Bonnie Crenshaw on shopping trips to Savannah. But Jimmy didn’t understand why Ben was giving him the money and these instructions instead of giving them directly to Pheby.

“Be sure to have her take your measurements. Tell her she must be careful to get the fit right.”

Jimmy nodded. He turned and began again to walk toward the cabin.

But before he’d taken five steps, Ben called out to him. “I lost it in the war, you know.”

Jimmy stopped. Once again, he reluctantly turned around.

“My leg. I lost it defending Charleston at James Island. I was in E Company, Chatham Volunteers, forty-seventh Georgia Volunteer infantry.”

Jimmy took a deep breath. He had to force himself to say something he didn’t feel. “I’m sorry to hear about your leg, Massa Ben.” He said it as if he hadn’t previously noticed that there was a peg where Ben ought to have had a shoe.

“I just wanted you to know.”

Not knowing what to say, Jimmy waggled his head. “Yes, massa.”

Then Jimmy turned and moved away from the meadow as quickly as he could. He made it to the woods without looking back. Then he walked straight to his cabin, found Uncle Isaac, and asked him if it would be alright for him to hoe the garden.

15

"I DON'T WANT ANY STAMPS"

Cato shook with anger. For the first time he thought he might hate white people as much as Jimmy did. He knew it was odd that it should have taken him so long to come to this feeling. After all, his own mother had been raped by his father. He'd grown up in the shadow of a father who'd rejected and disowned him. He'd witnessed untold cruelties inflicted upon those who, like him, were held in bondage. He'd felt the scorn of white people throughout his life. And yet, it was Mrs. Langdon's boast about having her eyes open that had opened his. As far as she was concerned, he was nothing more than an animal—or rather, half an animal. It was so absurd he wanted to laugh, but instead he spit. He spit hard, and in that moment he could feel Jimmy's spirit fill him with energy.

The wind gusted. He was tired of holding the top hat down on his head. He took it off and glanced around. No one was looking at him. He walked to the railing, leaned over, and flipped the hat out into the water. The hat sailed above the Ohio River, caught an updraft that blew it out toward the middle of the river, and landed in the water top-side down, where it bobbed momentarily like a black buoy in the gray water, then began to float away. *The Cincinnati Queen* was traveling upstream. The hat drifted with the current in the other direction. Then it began to pitch, until finally it listed to the side. Within a minute it filled with water. Then it sank into the river, leaving no trace. A weight lifted from him.

He walked back to the middle of the deck, then stepped into a passageway between the pilot house and the great bell. He glanced around, bent down, and pulled the wig off his head. He thought about going back to the railing so he could throw it overboard, too. But instead, he stuffed it into his satchel. He took his derby hat out and placed it on his head, pressing it down tight against his own hair, where it felt snug and secure. There was only one way he was going to proceed from now on. He was going to prevail by dint of his self-confidence. He wasn't going to cower. Let them see his hair. Let them see his nose. He would take one piece of advice from Mrs. Langdon. He could act with prerogative, and he was going to let the world see it. Jimmy had once called him a rabbit. But no more!

He stepped back out to the deck rail just as the great bell rang. He looked into the pilot house. The pilot was spinning the wheel starboard. More bells rang below him on the boiler deck. Smoke began to puff in short spurts from the chimney. The giant paddlewheel slowed momentarily as the ship keeled toward the shore. Cato looked across the deck rail. He saw the port of Paducah, Kentucky coming into view.

Ten minutes later he was walking down the plank to the shore. When he arrived on the dock he turned to look up. Mrs. Langdon stood on the main deck, watching him. He lifted his derby to her. She rapped the bottom of her parasol once on the floor of the deck, then turned and walked away and out of his life.

Cato strode past the steamship depot and out into the town. He found himself on a main thoroughfare. Stores lined both sides of the street—which had raised wooden sidewalks. Cato picked the right side and began to walk; his boots clomped loudly on the wooden planks, but he held his head high. After fifteen minutes of walking he finally saw what he was looking for. He went into a store, in front of which a wooden Indian stood sentinel.

The words "Cigars and Tobacco—G. Harrison, Proprietor" were painted in ornate gold letters on the store's front window. Inside was a narrow room with a glass-topped oak counter that displayed colorfully labeled boxes of cigars and smaller metallic boxes of snuff. There were spittoons on the floor at both ends of the counter. Behind the counter was a long dark-wood cabinet with open shelves on top that displayed clay jars, each stenciled with the name of a flavor of pipe tobacco: rum, brandy, bourbon, apple, cherry, and vanilla. The whole store was fragrant with the sweet, earthy smell of tobacco.

The man behind the counter looked up. He was an older man with a dignified bearing and a long beard that was gray at the ends. Cato hesitated for a moment, waiting to see if the man objected to his presence in any way. When the man peered over his spectacles and smiled, Cato asked, "Are you Mr. Harrison?"

"I am, sir. How may I help you?"

"Mr. Harrison, I'd like to see a box of Havanas, if you have them."

"Yes, of course," the man said. "Any particular brand?"

"What's the best you have?"

"Well, sir, I'd say the Partagas if you like 'em strong, or the La Coronas if you'd rather have 'em a tad milder. Now, of course, we do have nice American cigars, too—from good Kentucky tobacco."

"No offense to the Commonwealth," Cato said. "But I prefer something Cuban. How about La Corona?"

"Yes, sir. I have a box of twenty-five La Corona Cremas. They're quite exceptional."

"How much do they cost?"

"That box is three dollars, sir."

"Three dollars!"

"Yes, sir. I'm afraid the price reflects the times. The war, you know."

Cato took one of the twenty-dollar gold coins from his purse and held it aloft where the man could see it.

"Do you have change for this Double Eagle?"

The proprietor's eyes widened at the sight of this coin. "Well, sir ... not what you would call coin change. I have excellent postage stamps. Everyone accepts them around here. They're as good as cash money."

"I don't want any stamps."

"Of course. Of course. I was thinking ... if you're traveling south, I have come into possession of a few, uh, Confederate notes ... perhaps ..."

"No, sir. No." Cato shook his head forcefully. "I will not take notes."

"Well, sir, perhaps instead of change you might like to consider a box of the Portages as well. They're said to be the best in the world. You may want to stock up. The prices are apt to go even higher, if I may say so."

"No, I shouldn't want anything that strong. And I only want one box. Let me have a look at the box of Cremas." Cato put his twenty-dollar coin back in his purse and took out a quarter-eagle coin that was worth two dollars and fifty cents. He was beginning to realize that the large denomination coins he carried were going to be difficult to manage.

Mr. Harrison removed a box of La Corona cigars from a shelf in the counter case below him, opened it, and held it out for Cato to inspect. "The finest tobacco, sir. And quite fresh. They just came in last week."

Cato leaned over and sniffed the aroma wafting from the box, which, mild or not, was rich and earthy, mixed with a slight smell of cedar from the box itself. "Excellent!" he said. He looked around. "And what of matches?"

"Oh, well, sir, for a keen man such as yourself, I have something special." He went to a drawer in the cabinet behind him and pulled out a box. "These are Swedish matches ...." He set the box on the counter. "You see, sir ..." He opened the box. "Safety matches. They're made with red phosphorus, not white. These are the safest matches made by man, absolutely guaranteed not to ignite on their own—and no smell, you see." He held them up for Cato to sniff. "They come from Lundström."

"Swedish, you say?"

"Yes, sir."

"I'm afraid to ask their cost."

"Well ... as I said, the times being what they are, and these coming all the way from Europe ... their cost is half a dollar."

"Half a dollar!"

"Yes, sir. But if you buy 'em now with the cigars they'll only cost you two bits. You get fifty matches in the box, which ought to last you quite a spell."

"Very well." He handed Mr. Harrison his quarter eagle and a dollar coin, a total of three dollars and fifty cents. The proprietor went to a locked cash drawer, took a key that was chained to his belt, and opened it up. He dropped the coins in and removed a silver quarter. Then he paused. He seemed hesitant to part with the quarter. "Are you sure you don't want to have postage? It's what everyone is using now."

"No, thank you. A silver quarter would suit me best."

"Yes, sir." Mr. Harrison reluctantly handed Cato the quarter. Then he wrapped up the cigar box in paper and handed Cato this and the box of matches.

"By the way, Mr. Harrison," Cato said. "Do you know my friend, Mr. Hogan? He's fond of cigars. I'd like to buy him a gift. But I don't recollect what brand he prefers."

The shopkeeper's eyes lit up at the prospect of another sale. He scratched his chin. "Mr. Horace Hogan?"

"Yes," Cato said. "That's the man. He drives a wagon. He's often here in Paducah."

"Well ... I haven't seen Horace Hogan for more'n a week. He came in here to buy cigars ... oh, maybe 10 days ago."

"I see."

"He told me he was about to go up to Chicago. He said he had to pick up a shipment of some kind. If you ask me, it's not a good time to take a trip of any sort, what with the fightin' and skirmishin' all over the place."

"So you don't think he's in town?"

"Whether he's here, I couldn't say." He thought a moment. "It seems to me you ought to ask at Gleason's stable." The shopkeeper turned and pointed. "See there? It's just across the street. Horace generally stops in at Gleason's before he leaves town."

"I'll go see them," Cato said.

"As to what Hogan likes, I can tell you what kind of cigars he gets. Mostly he buys the nickel cigars ... but, if I may suggest it, I'm sure he'd prefer to smoke Havanas—that is, if you wish to make him a gift."

"Well, in that case I'll be sure to wrap up a few of these La Cremas for him. He should like that."

The shopkeeper was visibly disappointed, but said, "I'm sure he will."

Cato considered whether he could get any additional information. He had no idea if Hogan lived in Paducah, or had relatives in town. But if he started down the wrong path, the shopkeeper might become suspicious. So he said, simply, "Thank you."

"Now then," Mr. Harrison continued, "if I see Mr. Hogan, shall I tell him you were asking after him, Mr. ... ?"

"Askew," Cato said before he had a chance to think. "But I'd rather it be a surprise," he added. "I mean about the Havanas."

"Oh, certainly." The shopkeeper eyed him. "May I ask, sir? Are you, perhaps, European?"

Cato swallowed and wrinkled his forehead as if the question

required consideration. He tried to think how to answer. "Why, yes," he said at last. "How did you know?"

"Well, I thought to myself, the gentleman looks like a Spaniard."

"Do I?"

"I would say so, sir." Mr. Harrison nodded knowingly. Then he added, "Excuse me for saying it, but you don't talk like one."

"No," Cato said. "That's true. I never did." He smiled as he thought about how to continue. Then he said, "I was born in Spain. But my mother brought me here as a baby. I've lived here all my life, and I've only ever spoken English. If you must know, I don't speak a word of Spanish."

"Do tell!"

"Yes. And so, good day to you, sir."

"Good day!"

And with that, Cato discovered the virtues of a Spanish lineage. He decided that from now on he would find a way to mention his Spanish ancestry to anyone who looked at him crosswise. "I could even give myself a Spanish name," he thought. Offhand, the only Spanish name he knew was Velazquez. It was the name of a famous painter, which he knew because his friend Erastus had told him the names, histories, and methods of the painters he most admired.

Cato left the cigar shop and walked across the street toward the livery stable, considering whether or not he should attempt a Spanish accent when he introduced himself as Mr. Velazquez.

16

"IT'S ABOUT HOW THE WORLD IS SHAPED"

Jimmy gradually increased his pace in the field. He went from two hundred and ten pounds of cotton a day to two hundred and twenty, then up to two hundred and thirty. He knew he could pick more, but two hundred and thirty was as high as he was willing to go. For the time being it was good enough. Mr. Eppley had taken to striding beside him from time to time to brandish his whip, grunt, and make a show of watching him. But he'd said nothing threatening to Jimmy ever since Ben Crenshaw's visit to the meadow. Jimmy could only assume that Eppley's forbearance was due to Ben Crenshaw's instructions.

He had seen Ben Crenshaw only once since their encounter in the meadow. One afternoon Crenshaw rode past the cotton field on a handsome brown horse. He rode in such a way that only his good leg could be seen from the field, and it was outfitted with a long black boot. He wore cream-colored riding pants, a bright red waistcoat, and a shiny black top hat. Jimmy wondered how his wooden leg was fixed in the stirrup on the other side of the horse. But if Crenshaw was in any way unsteady, it didn't show. He loped along slowly, holding the reins in one hand and a riding crop in the other, barely bobbing in the saddle.

As Jimmy watched, he saw Crenshaw turn to glance toward the field of slaves only once. But in that glance Ben Crenshaw had clearly looked for and fixed his gaze upon Jimmy. Then he'd lifted his crop, tapped it on the horse's flank, and trotted out of sight.

A few days later, after sundown, Jimmy talked to Uncle Isaac, who told him that he'd heard through Little Joe that Bonnie Crenshaw had that very day taken Pheby shopping for cloth for Jimmy's new clothes. And indeed, when Little Joe came in that night he told Jimmy that he'd been instructed to take his measurements. He pulled out a long ribbon of tape and stretched it around Jimmy's chest. He made marks on the tape with a pencil and told Jimmy what he knew about the cloth they'd purchased.

"Missus Crenshaw was quite particular about that cloth. I don't know what you've done to make 'em carry on so, but they're set on dressing you up good and fancy."

Jimmy shrugged. "I don't know either," he said. But that wasn't entirely true. He suspected it had something to do with the unspoken desire that had led Ben Crenshaw to run his hand down Jimmy's back.

"It doesn't make sense," Little Joe continued. "They can't expect you to wear those fancy clothes out in the field. Maybe they're fixin' to move you into the house. Have you ever worked in the house before?"

"Once or twice. But hardly ever."

"Then I guess you'll have to learn right quick."

"Learn what?"

"Oh, you've gotta be able to act proper. You've gotta do everything just so and step into the proper spot at the right moment. You've gotta be just like a shadow. You've gotta always know what they want. But man, you've gotta never get in the way. I can teach you. The trouble is, I'm not sure what job they're fixin' to give you."

"Who's working in the house now?"

"Right now there's Pheby, who takes care of Missus Bonnie. Jane's the cook and her husband, Toby, is the butler. Becky's the maid. She cleans and dusts. I reckon that's everyone, except for me. I take care of Massa Crenshaw and, of course, I tend the horses and do all the driving and any errands in town."

"Who looks after Massa Ben?" Jimmy asked.

Little Joe shook his head. "No one. Not anymore," he said gravely. "We did have a slave here named Elijah. He looked after Massa Ben most all his life. When Massa Ben went off to the Army, he took Elijah with him. Then when Massa Ben went into the battle, he got shot in the leg—so they sent Elijah out to carry Massa Ben off the field. But the Yankees kept right on shooting and a bullet caught Elijah in the stomach."

"The Yankees shot a slave?"

"They did—they shot him in the stomach. But he kept going anyway. He picked up Massa Ben and carried him back to camp. But then, after he laid Massa Ben down at the camp, he fell over and—well, he was hit real bad, and the next day he ... he died, quick as that. Massa Ben was most broken up about it. He and Elijah were close."

Jimmy's eyes went wide, but he said nothing.

Little Joe continued. "After that—after they took off his leg —they brought Massa Ben home. During that time, he stayed in his bed in the house and he didn't speak a word to anybody for a whole month. And since then, Massa Ben won't let anyone else help him. I guess he doesn't want anyone to see him like that. I mean with his leg and all. He dresses himself nowadays."

"I'm sorry to hear about Elijah."

Little Joe hung his head for a moment. Then he said, "Elijah was a nice man—a gentle man, always polite, always smiling. Never did nobody no harm. And then to get shot like that." Little Joe shook his head.

"I saw Massa Ben on a horse the other day," Jimmy said. "How's it he's able to do that, get on a horse—with no leg?"

"I help him get up there. He climbs up with his good leg, then throws the other one over t'other side. I fasten the wooden end into the stirrup with twine. Then when he comes back, I untie it and help him get down again. He's steady, once he's in the saddle."

"I guess it wouldn't be good if he fell off."

"Off Mabel?" Little Joe laughed. "She'd sooner die than let Massa Ben fall off. Mabel's solid—like a boat on the calm water." He mimicked a smooth line with the palm of his hand.

"Where does he ride to?"

"Nowhere in particular," said Little Joe. "He just likes to ride. He takes the air. That's what he calls it."

A FEW DAYS LATER, Jimmy was presented by Pheby with his new clothes. "Here you go, Jacob," Pheby said. "Now you put these on right quick. They want to see you up at the house. They're waitin' for you there."

"Waiting for what?"

Pheby wrinkled her nose. "I have no idea," she said. "But go around back of the cabin and put these on, then let me see how they fit you before you go. They'll be wanting to see how well I did with the fit." She'd brought a basket with her, which she held up for Jimmy to see. "I've got a needle and thread in case I need to fix 'em."

Jimmy went behind the cabin and put on the new pants, which were made of a cream-colored heavy cloth that reminded him of the riding breeches worn by Ben Crenshaw. Jimmy's pants had a fitted waist with gussets on the side that he could tie to cinch them tight. They had a buttoned drop-down flap in front. They fit as snug as any pants he'd ever worn. But when he put on the white cotton shirt, which fit him in the chest and shoulders, he found that the sleeves were too long. As soon as he came back in the cabin, Pheby frowned.

"Oh, now what did Little Joe do with that tape on your arms? He must have stretched it clear down to your fingertips."

"I can roll up the sleeves."

"Oh, no," Pheby said. "Hold your arm out here so I can see it."

Jimmy held out his arm and Pheby pinched the cloth at his wrist to mark it.

"Now take that shirt off and give it here. I can fix those sleeves in two shakes."

Jimmy took off the shirt and sat on the floor while Pheby got busy with scissors and needle and thread. Twenty minutes later, when she'd finished her alterations, Jimmy put the shirt on, buttoned it, tucked it in his pants, and stood before her.

"There now," she said. "You look handsome! Those clothes fit you good, if I do say so myself."

"I never wore clothes that fit me so well as this," Jimmy said. "How'd you get these ruffles in this shirt?" He fluffed the white ruffles up near his chest.

"I have my ways," Pheby said. "Now turn around for a minute," she commanded.

Jimmy turned and Pheby appraised his backside. "Mm-hmm," she said. "They fit you just like I thought. You see, I know how you be shaped, boy!" She was pleased.

"And how do you know that?"

"Oh, I have my ways." She winked. "Don't you worry about that!" She blushed. "Now you'd better get over there and see what those white folks want." Then she looked at him sternly. "And don't you be goin' out to no cotton field wearin' my clothes!"

"No, ma'am."

When Jimmy arrived at the house he knew to go in at the back door, which led into the kitchen. Inside, a woman was chopping carrots. Jimmy assumed it was Jane, the cook. She was a tall, thin woman who was about the age of Jimmy's mother. She exhibited an air of propriety about the room in which she worked.

Jimmy introduced himself. Jane nodded with an amused look. "I know all about you, Jacob." She came around from behind the table in order to get a better view of him. "I see you're wearin' Pheby's clothes."

"Yes, ma'am."

"Pheby did good. You're lookin' just fine."

"Thank you." The kitchen was much larger than the kitchen in the Hollands' house, where Jimmy had grown up. There were two fireplaces, one at each end of the room. A giant kettle was simmering over the fire nearest him. Jimmy stepped over to it. "What's in the kettle?"

"Beef stew."

Jimmy leaned over the pot and sniffed. "It smells good."

"Tell Pheby to come by later with her big bowl. Tell her I'm talkin' 'bout the big yella bowl she keeps in her sewing room."

"I'll tell her."

"Y'all can have some of this stew once the Crenshaws are done with it."

"Won't they notice?"

"Nope."

"They let you do that?"

"I'm not supposed to make extra. But they don't pay me no mind. Not about that leastways. Not today. Today's the day when Little Joe brings in the new supplies for the week. So today's when no one looks to see what's left over from last week. Anyway, they won't notice it. The Crenshaws have plenty. And about this, they don't much care." She dumped the carrots into the pot. "Don't get me wrong. It's not because they're kind and generous. They're not. It's because they're lazy and they don't notice. If they did, I'd pay for it."

Jimmy looked at her dubiously. He wasn't sure if he ought to add any insights of his own. After a moment, he said, "The Crenshaws don't seem as bad as some."

"Humph," Jane said. "Don't let them fool you." She wagged a finger. "They're just like all the others. Sometimes they blow hot. Sometimes they blow cold. Right now, you're on their good side. But you best look at Poky's back before you make up your mind on the Crenshaws."

"I've seen Poky's back," Jimmy said. "That's from Eppley."

"Eppley! And what's he? He's the arm of the Crenshaws," Jane said. "They pretend he ain't, but Poky's back comes straight from them."

Jimmy nodded. "You're right. But I hate Eppley worse."

"Honey, don't nobody like Eppley. Eppley is the loneliest man in this whole place." Jane smiled. "That's how he gets punished."

"Lonely?" Jimmy made a face. "What kind of punishment is that?"

"Take my word for it. He's lonely. He a drunkard. He miserable. That's how life works," Jane said. "At least, sometimes. At any rate, he a miserable man with a miserable job." She put her cutting knife down hard on the table. "Now you best get goin'. They's waitin' on you in the library."

"Where's that?"

Jane wiped her hands on a towel. "I'll take you."

Jane led Jimmy out of the kitchen and down a hall. She opened a door, stepped into the library, and announced, "Here's Jacob."

Jimmy entered the library, where he saw Bonnie Crenshaw seated behind a small table on which a large atlas was open. Ben sat in a wingback chair facing the fireplace. He was facing away from the door, but a cane was hooked over the arm of the chair, so Jimmy knew it was him.

Bonnie Crenshaw rose from her seat. "Jacob. Come in," she said. She came around from behind the table and took Jimmy by the hand. "Come, let us go by the fireplace so my brother can see how you look." She led him to the fireplace, where she left him standing by himself as she stepped back to stand beside the chair where her brother sat.

Ben Crenshaw took hold of his cane and seemed, for a moment, as if he was going to stand. But as his gaze fell upon Jimmy, he let himself sink back into the chair. Jimmy tried to read the expression on his face, but his stare was so intense that it was impossible to look at him directly. Jimmy lowered his head. He studied the Persian carpet on the floor. Even though he was fully dressed, he felt the same as he'd felt on the auction block. He could feel the eyes of his owners upon him. It was as if they'd never seen a slave in their library before.

"What do you think?" Bonnie said.

"The material you chose is just right," Ben said. "And Pheby's never done better."

"I think she was inspired," Bonnie said.

"Indeed," Ben said. "I almost don't recognize him. It's astonishing, when you think about it."

"Just wait," Bonnie said. "We've only begun. Soon you'll think he's beyond compare."

"So I take it you've decided what you want to have him do?"

Bonnie nodded. "Yes. I'm going to start by teaching him geography."

"I see," Ben said. "A visual introduction to learning."

"We'll begin with the atlas."

"Yes. The atlas is a good place to start."

"And then reading." She turned to Jimmy and raised her voice. "You don't know how to read, do you, Jacob?"

"No, ma'am."

"Well, I'm going to teach you. What do you think about that?"

Jimmy wasn't sure how to answer her. He didn't understand why the Crenshaws wanted him to know how to read. It was against all the norms of their society. It was against the law, in fact. He knew he was the object of some scheme hatched between the

Crenshaw siblings. They'd been talking about him as if he weren't there—as if he were a witless fool. Well, that was fine. He'd been acting the fool; that was how he wanted them to think of him. But he was intrigued by the idea of learning how to read.

Cato had always wanted to teach him. They'd never had enough time to pursue it, but Jimmy had always imagined that someday he'd be able to read. How proud Cato would be! And Jimmy could learn. He knew he could. It was only the white man's game to pretend that slaves couldn't or shouldn't know how to read.

But then he wondered—if he learned to read, might that mean he could also learn to write? If he could write, he could find a way to write to Cato. If he could get a letter to Cato to let him know where he was, it would mean everything.

He was excited, but on his face he showed confusion. "If I may ask, ma'am. What do you mean for me to learn? You want me to learn both readin' and writin'?"

Bonnie smiled. "We want you to learn everything, Jacob. But you must not say anything to anyone else. It will have to be kept secret. What we have in mind to do is not customary—or even legal, strictly speaking. But we Crenshaws are governed by a higher law. And, well, we want to use you as part of an experiment."

"What kind of experiment?" he asked. He shook his head. "I'm afraid I don't understand."

"We want to see if we can elevate you to a higher level of civilization."

He wanted to ask her why, but he simply blinked and said nothing. He couldn't react without further thought. This new offer from the Crenshaws made him unsure what he should do. Up until this moment, he'd wanted nothing more than to escape. But he did want to learn to read. Now it seemed he could—but only if he stayed around long enough to learn how. Would he really be willing to delay his escape while he sat day after day in the Crenshaws' library? There was no one he could talk to about any of it. All he could do was blink again.

"Do you feel you might be able to make something better of yourself?" Bonnie asked.

"Something better?"

"Yes, Jacob. Do you think you can become something better than you've been?"

"I've done all my work, ma'am. I've brought in more than two hundred pounds a day."

Now Ben Crenshaw spoke. "No, Jacob," he said. "Your work is fine. We're not talking about your work in the field. It's not about that."

"It's about transforming your soul," Bonnie said.

Jimmy's eyebrow went up. "My soul?"

"Yes. You believe in God, I suppose," Ben said.

Jimmy hesitated. He didn't know how to answer that question except honestly. He reasoned that any other answer would lead to a tangle of deceptions that would make it more complicated for him to maintain the deceptions he'd already undertaken. "I've not had reason to do so, Massa," he said.

Both Ben and Bonnie looked at him with surprise.

"Really?" Ben said.

"Well," Bonnie said. "That makes it all the more interesting."

"Why not?" Ben asked. "Why don't you believe in God?"

Jimmy looked at them one at a time. Part of him wanted to shout his answer. Part of him wanted to jump out and grab them both. But he kept his composure. He replied to Ben, "I don't know much, massa. I'm just a poor slave."

"I think you know more than you admit," Bonnie said. "I can see it in your eyes."

Jimmy blinked and lowered his eyes again.

"I'm afraid they give you away," Ben said.

Jimmy turned his head to the side.

"You see, Jacob," Bonnie said. "We can see your potential. We have faith in you. You must learn to have faith in yourself."

"Yes, ma'am."

"For today, we're going to start with a lesson in geography. Do you know what that is?"

Jimmy knew something about it, but he shook his head no.

"It's about how the world is shaped—the land, the sea, the very earth itself," Bonnie said.

"It's all laid out in maps," Ben said.

"You've seen a map, haven't you?" asked Bonnie.

"No, ma'am."

"Well. Come over here to the table and I'll show you what they look like and how they work."

She moved to the table where the giant atlas lay open. She indicated the pages. "You see," she said. "This is a picture of the state of Georgia." She pointed at a spot on the map. "And this is Savannah, where we are."

Jimmy stared at the map. He made a show of confusion on his face, but inside he felt a welling clarity.

"This large blue area is the Atlantic Ocean, you see? And here is the Savannah River. You see this smaller blue line? It empties right into the sea. That represents the river." She turned the page and there was a map that showed a large portion of the east coast. "Do you understand?"

Jimmy understood what she was explaining. He understood it so well that his heart began to race. In front of him he saw clearly that all that nearby water meant it was possible to escape by boat. "Yes, I understand." He put his finger on the river near Savannah. "This is us."

"That's right," Bonnie said.

"Seems to me if you had a boat you could sail right into the ocean," Jimmy observed.

"Of course," Ben said. "And I do have a boat. I have a fine little sailboat, the *Wentworth*."

Jimmy's eyes lit up. "Have you sailed to the ocean?"

"Many times," Ben said. "The ocean's not far away, Jacob," he added.

"It's been a long time, Ben, since you've gone that far out in the *Wentworth,*" Bonnie said.

"Not since the war began. It's too dangerous now. The Union Army's got a blockade near Port Royal, just forty miles from here."

"What's a blockade?" Jimmy asked.

"It's a squadron of ships," Bonnie said. "Of course they're Yankee ships. And there's no telling who they might fire on."

"Too bad you can't sail it anymore," Jimmy said. "I wish I knew how to sail." Jimmy realized he might be pressing his luck to lay bare his thoughts. But he was counting on the fact that the Crenshaws didn't credit him with much ambition.

"Now what would you want to go sailing for?" Bonnie asked.

Jimmy shrugged. He thought for a moment about how to explain himself. He remembered all too well his struggle to cross the Ohio River in a rowboat. "I saw a man in a rowboat once," he began. He shook his head gravely. "That poor man couldn't make the boat go the way he wanted it to. He was moving the oars this way and that. I thought it was too bad he didn't have a sailboat. I reckon it would have been more pleasant to let the wind carry him along in the water."

"It's a very fine thing to do," Ben agreed. He had taken his cane and gotten out of the chair. He came to stand beside his sister. "But a man has to know how to sail, Jacob. Sailing pits a man's will against the will of the wind. A man might want to go east. But the wind may want to blow west, or north, or south. And many's the time it won't blow at all. Your rowboat man could very well have had it worse in a sailboat."

"How do you make a sailboat go the way you want to go, then?" Jimmy asked.

"A sailor uses the sails, the keel, and the rudder together. It takes practice and knowledge."

"I see." Jimmy nodded. "The sails, the keel, and the rudder."

Now Ben pointed to the map. "Many's the time I've sailed up to here." He indicated with his finger. "This is South Carolina. And above that is your previous home, North Carolina." He pushed his finger onto the page and slid it back to South Carolina. "This is Charleston."

"Where you were hurt," Jimmy said.

A tender look washed over Ben Crenshaw's eyes. "Yes," he said. "At James Island. You can't really see it on this map. They don't have enough space on the page to show everything."

"But they show all the important things," Bonnie said. "A map is a representation of the earth. It shows how everything is laid out: the land, the rivers, the ocean. Do you understand?"

Jimmy wrinkled his forehead. He nodded tentatively. But his eyes had lost their glaze. He was staring intently at the map. "I understand," he said.

"Excellent!" she exclaimed. "I believe we'll have you reading in no time."

Jimmy was sure that was true. He vowed to himself that he would learn to read as quickly as he could. And he would find a way to study the maps at every opportunity.

Even now, staring at the little line of blue that ran past Savannah to the Atlantic, he saw that he could easily begin his journey on a boat in the nearby river and it would take him right to the ocean. "It empties into the sea," Bonnie had said.

In a boat it would be easy—so easy that with nothing more than the current he could float away. He'd float away from the cotton field, float away from Eppley, float away from the Crenshaws, and glide away from bondage, out into a sea of freedom.

17

"WHAT ABOUT A HORSE?"

When Cato pushed open the heavy oak door at the entrance to Gleason's stables, he was surprised by the smell. It wasn't that he didn't expect the smell of horses, he just hadn't expected it to be as strong as it was—like a strong cigar, he thought. Holding the wrapped box of La Cremas in one hand and his satchel in the other, he closed the door and stood inside waiting for someone to greet him. As he waited, he noticed a horse whose stall was near the entrance. The horse stood with his head drooped down, looking rather dejected.

The horse was dark-skinned, almost the same color as Jimmy. He had a cream-colored triangle running from his forehead partway down his nose. His mane was thick and black. His eyes were a soft golden-brown color, like pieces of amber.

Cato set his satchel on the ground. He stepped over to the stall and held his hand out in the horse's direction—an offering. The horse smelled him, then looked at him directly. The horse blinked. Experience had taught Cato that horses could recognize a smile. So he smiled. He wondered if this horse knew how to smile as well. As if to answer his question, the horse raised the sides of his mouth in what could only be called a silly grin.

Something about this exchange made Cato feel a rush of warmth.

He thought about his situation. He was alone in a strange town. He didn't know anyone in Paducah. He'd lost Jimmy and didn't know if he'd ever find him again. He was himself a runaway slave. At any moment he might be captured. At any moment he might be whisked off to an unknown fate. He was pretending to be white. He was pretending to be confident. He was pretending to be an ordinary man going about his ordinary business. But he wasn't. And he knew that if he let the charade drop, even for a moment, it might be fatal.

But now he stood in front of a fellow creature who—it seemed—had smiled at him. The horse was a stranger, and could have no conception of the cares that weighed on his mind. Yet the horse could hardly be without cares of his own. For a moment, Cato tried to imagine the world through the horse's eyes. What would it mean to see a strange man? How would it feel to see that strange man smile at him?

The horse nudged his hand, sniffing more intensely. Cato stepped in closer. He stroked the horse's back. The horse lifted his neck, alert and wide-eyed. It felt to Cato as if both man and horse needed a friend. But Cato could no more imagine what cares weighed on the horse than the horse could imagine those that weighed on him. What he could imagine, and what he assumed the horse could imagine as well, was that it was a good thing to smile. It was a good thing to let a feeling of warmth come between two creatures.

Cato took this feeling to heart. He leaned closer, put his arm around the horse's neck and kissed him just below his ear. The horse made a sound—a gurgling sound in the back of his throat. "Good boy," Cato said. He stroked the horse's head with a tender caress. "Thank you," he whispered into his ear.

Cato knew it wasn't likely that he'd find Hogan in Paducah. If he found out where Hogan had gone, he'd have to follow his trail further—probably into the South. He knew he couldn't count on taking trains or steamboats. The war had made it impossible to rely on public transportation. It occurred to him that the best way to follow Hogan would be to travel the same way that Hogan himself was traveling. If Hogan was using a horse and wagon, Cato could travel with a horse and buggy.

He was at a livery stable. He'd brought money for Jimmy's ransom, but also for travel expenses. Now he thought it might be a good idea to spend a portion of it. He decided to ask Gleason about buying a horse and buggy. As he was thinking these thoughts, a man came in through the front door. The man wiped his hands on his apron and said, "Good morning, sir. May I help you?"

"Are you Mr. Gleason?"

"Yes, sir. What can I do for you?"

"Mr. Gleason, I'm Mr. Velasquez. I have two requests. First, I'd like to know if you have a horse and buggy that I might purchase. Second, I'd like to know if you can tell me the whereabouts of my friend, Mr. Horace Hogan. I understand from Mr. Harrison at the cigar shop across the street that Mr. Hogan may have stopped in to see you before he left town. I bought Horace some La Crema cigars, but now it seems he left town before I could give them to him."

"Well, sir, as to the second question, I can tell you that Horace was here yesterday. He boarded his team with me the night before last. He came back to get them and left here yesterday morning."

"Did he say where he was headed?"

"He said he was going to Georgia. He had a delivery to make down there."

"Did he say where in Georgia?"

"No, sir. I'm afraid he didn't. I only know he was going to Georgia because he asked me if I could recommend a livery in Chattanooga."

"Chattanooga?"

"Yes, he said he was going to pass through Chattanooga on

his way to Georgia. He told me he already had a place to board his team in other spots along his route, but he didn't know a livery in Chattanooga."

"So did you have a recommendation?"

"Yes, sir. I told him to try Carlson's stable."

"I see. Is that a good stable?"

"Yes. I can vouch for Carlson. He runs a fine stable."

"Thank you."

"I'm afraid, however, that with respect to selling you a buggy, Mr. Velasquez, my options are limited."

"I don't require much."

"The only carriage I have for sale at the moment is a one-seat buggy. It has no top."

"I don't mind that. What about a horse?"

"I have several nice horses."

Cato pointed to the horse he'd petted in the stall. "What about that one?"

"Oscar? Oh, well ... I'm afraid Oscar might not be the best choice, sir. Not if you want him to pull a buggy."

"Why's that?"

"Oscar is used to being a riding horse. He's one of my best saddle horses. He's never been in a harness."

"But he could pull a buggy if he were harnessed, couldn't he?"

Gleason scratched his head. "I'm sure he could. But I don't know how well he'd take to it."

"It must be as easy to pull a buggy as to carry a man on his back," Cato said. "I would think it might even be easier."

"Perhaps. But in my experience, animals don't reason like that, sir. They only know what they're used to."

"While I was waiting just now," Cato said, "I spent some time getting to know Oscar. The fact is, I've taken a fancy to him."

"I see," Mr. Gleason said. But his look was questioning.

"Do you think you could try hitching him up?" Cato looked at Oscar and smiled at him again. "Perhaps he won't object."

"Well ..." Mr. Gleason seemed unsure about how to proceed. "Perhaps we should discuss the cost first."

"Yes, by all means."

"The carriage I have to sell is a one-seat buggy, which, as I said, has no top. However, it was made right here in Kentucky. It's a very good quality for a carriage of its sort. Seeing as there's no top, it would only cost you $35. But as for a horse like Oscar —well, as I mentioned, he's one of my best saddle horses. I'm afraid I'd have to charge $50 for him."

"Fifty?"

"Yes, sir. For the horse and the saddle. He has his own saddle. He's a fine animal."

"I'm sure he is. Those prices are agreeable to me."

Mr. Gleason looked surprised, as if he'd expected some bargaining to take place. But then a look of concern crossed his brow. "What form of payment do you have in mind?" he asked.

Cato opened his satchel. He took out his purse and removed four twenty-dollar gold coins. He held them out. "I'd be willing to give you eighty dollars in gold coins," he said. "For the buggy, horse, and saddle, and three weeks' worth of feed."

"Ah," Mr. Gleason said, his eyes widening at the sight of the gold coins. "I'll accept your offer, sir." Then he looked at the stall. "That is to say, if Oscar is willing."

"Let's see if he is," Cato said.

An hour later, Cato gave Mr. Gleason his money and the deal was done. Gleason had allowed Oscar time to sniff the buggy, in order get used to it before he put on the harness. Then he'd instructed Cato to feed Oscar a treat from the back of the buggy, so he'd regard it in a favorable light. When the harness was first put on, Oscar had hesitated—looking back dubiously at the large, rolling thing stuck behind him—but then when he'd finally pulled forward he'd seemed satisfied with the relative ease of the weight of it. Mr. Gleason was surprised at how quickly Oscar had taken to his new role. “I wouldn’t have guessed,” he said.

The sun was setting. Cato walked to a hotel that Mr. Gleason recommended. He planned to go back to the livery in the morning, when Mr. Gleason promised to have Oscar fed and ready to go, and Oscar’s saddle and his bags of feed loaded in the slot that was built behind the seat for the purpose of transporting baggage.

In the morning Cato would begin his journey to Chattanooga. There he would visit Carlson’s stable.

18

"DON'T YOU WANNA LOOK GOOD?"

Jimmy's life began to follow a routine. From sunup till noon he spent his time in the library with Bonnie Crenshaw, who gave him lessons in reading, arithmetic, manners, and morals. For the reading lessons, Bonnie prepared pieces of paper, each bearing a word for him to learn. She'd begun by teaching him the words for colors: red, yellow, green, blue, purple—each word spelled out in ink with its color painted on a square above it. Then she'd moved on to teaching him the words for numbers, from one to ten. Each sheet had the word, the number itself, and a series of hash marks designed as a visual aid to counting. Eventually, Jimmy was expected to select two or three sheets at random and calculate their sum.

All of this was easy for Jimmy to accomplish. What was more difficult for him was to portray an arc of gradually diminishing dim-wittedness. Early on, he decided there was little point in trying to keep up the illusion that he was an irredeemable simpleton. Bonnie Crenshaw was determined to educate him. And while he wasn't certain of her motives, he couldn't think of a reason why he shouldn't go along with her project. He understood the advantages of knowing how to read.

On the one hand, he wanted nothing more than to escape at the earliest opportunity. On the other hand, he thought it would be wise to delay his escape until he'd learned to read well enough to be able to do something useful with the skill. His desire to get back to Cato as soon as he could was countered by a vision of how proud and impressed Cato would be if he returned with a degree of skill in reading that could compare to Cato's own ability.

At the same time, it was growing progressively more difficult for him to reconcile his habitual feelings about white people with the way the Crenshaws were treating him. Their treatment of him seemed, on the surface, to be kind and solicitous. He didn't know how to respond to it. He was happy enough to be relieved of manual toil each morning, but he didn't like how it made him look to the other Crenshaw slaves. Even though he hoped to be leaving as soon as possible, he felt uncomfortable with the outsider role his relationship with the Crenshaws had put him in.

In the beginning, the other slaves had welcomed him. But, starting with the making of his fancy clothes, some of them had come to resent the fact that he was given special treatment. He was granted privileges that, to their way of thinking, he hardly deserved. Everyone was at a loss to understand why it was happening. Jimmy himself could not explain it—which only made him more suspicious.

Little Joe, Uncle Isaac, and Jane's husband, Toby, were the most resentful. They'd begun to treat him with a degree of disdain. Pheby, Jane, and Poky reacted in a more restrained manner. Perhaps they realized he couldn't be blamed for what was happening to him. Pheby, in particular, took the time to try to help him understand the Crenshaws' behavior.

One morning Pheby asked Jimmy to come see her in the sewing room before his visit to the library. The sewing room was reached from a short hall off the kitchen. It was a well-appointed room with a fine wood table and a comfortable wingback chair. It also had its own fireplace and a large window that looked out onto the flower garden. Jimmy imagined that the room must have been designed for use by Bonnie Crenshaw—though he guessed that it was Pheby who did most of the actual sewing there.

When Jimmy opened the door, he found Pheby sitting in the wingback chair, looking out the window. She was pleased to see him. "There you are," she said. "I just finished making you a waistcoat—the newest addition to your fancy wardrobe." She handed him the brown wool vest and asked him to put it on and button it up. He did so, then stood before her while she inspected the fit. She ran a finger beneath the fabric, all around his waist.

"Not bad," she said. "But I've got to take it in a little—here in the back." She latched her finger onto the fabric at the back of his waist and wiggled it to indicate where it was loose. "I made the vest wider than the waist of your pants—to leave room for your shirt. But that shirt fits you so tight, I guess I left too much extra room."

"Why do you want it all to fit so exact?" Jimmy asked.

"Why not? Don't you wanna look good?"

"Not that good."

Pheby put a thread in her mouth to wet it, then stuck it into the eye of the needle. "Too late," she said. "It'll only take a minute to fix this and then you'll be ready to go."

"I still don't understand," Jimmy said. "Why do you think they want me to have these clothes? I can't wear them in the field. The only time I put them on is when I'm getting lessons."

Pheby shrugged.

"And why are they giving me lessons anyway?" Jimmy asked. He had his own suspicions about the Crenshaws' motives, but he wondered what Pheby thought they were. He also wanted to be sure Pheby understood that he didn't have any kind of formal arrangement with them.

Pheby took the waistcoat and laid it on her lap. She began to pinch and pull, adjusting the fabric. "As far as I can see," she said, "Missus Bonnie's got the idea she can make you her special pet. Ever since she was a little girl she's been living in a dream world. I can tell you this: she never had friends of her own. When she was little, she tried to pretend we were her friends."

"The slaves?"

"Yes." Pheby nodded. "It was just make-believe for her playtime. The rest of the time, she'd look the other way."

"But why me?" Jimmy asked. "Why would she want to make a pet out of me?"

"I overheard her talk about how you're like a wild beast she can tame."

"Me? A wild beast?" Jimmy rolled his eyes. "I haven't done anything wild around her—at least not yet."

"It's not because of what you've done." Pheby had her head bowed as she concentrated on her sewing. She looked up at Jimmy. "I think it's all in her mind," she said. "But something's got her all heated up."

"Heated up? About what?"

Pheby finished her alteration. "Here, put this on." She handed him the vest. He put it on and buttoned it up. She ran her finger around the back of the waist and nodded. "Fits good," she said. "Now, I don't want to make you blush, Jacob. Let me just say that you've got a certain, uh, quality that might make a woman get heated up."

"I do?"

"Yes, fool, you do ... and don't you pretend you don't know what I'm talkin' about. I've seen you strut your stuff around here."

"What?" Jimmy pretended to be taken aback. "I haven't strut any stuff."

"Yeah, well ... maybe," Pheby said. "Maybe you just can't

help it. But if I were you I'd be careful. These white folks don't think twice about doing whatever they feel like doing with you."

"What should I do?"

"Just don't let her get the idea ...." Pheby grasped to find the right word. "Let her get the idea you want her, you know, like the way a man might want her."

"I don't." Jimmy was aghast. "I swear to you. I don't want anything like that. Nothing like what you're talkin' about."

"She's a good-lookin' woman."

"So?"

"So ... you're a man. Sometimes nature takes its course."

"What? No! That ain't gonna happen!" He paused while the implications sank in. "Damn, Pheby, why'd you say a thing like that out loud? You know how fast they'd string me up ... if they even thought I was lookin' at her that way."

"Don't worry. Can't nobody hear us."

"So you say." Jimmy looked around. "Besides which ... you know," he said, "I'm not like that."

"Stand up," Pheby commanded. "I want to check the shoulder." Jimmy stood. Pheby asked, "What you be like, then?"

"I don't want a white woman, Pheby. No ma'am. No way. Not now. Not ever."

Pheby latched her fingers under the shoulder of the waistcoat and tugged. "Hmm. It's good. This is all done now."

"I've already got a sweetheart," Jimmy said.

"You do?"

"Yes. I do. Back home. And I don't want anyone else. I swear it."

"I believe you," Pheby said. "But you got to watch yourself with the Missus."

"I will," Jimmy said. "Believe me. I will."

Pheby sat down. She wiped her hands on her apron, then tilted her head. "And also, Jacob .... You'd best keep an eye on her brother, too."

"What?"

"The same thing's goin' on with him—the same as her."

"What're you talkin' about?"

Pheby threw up her hands. "Well ... I suppose it ain't nothin' you'd know about."

"Pheby," Jimmy said, "I don't understand." Though Jimmy did understand, only too well.

Pheby lowered her hands onto her head. "Massa Ben ... he's, well, different."

"Different how?"

"Didn't Little Joe tell you about Elijah?"

Jimmy nodded.

"Well, he probably didn't tell you that Massa Ben liked Elijah in a certain way." She wrinkled her nose. "The way he liked him wasn't in the regular way of things."

"You mean he liked him ... that way?"

Pheby nodded. "And to tell the truth, Elijah wasn't opposed to it neither."

"Ben and Elijah?"

"Like two peas in a pod."

"I reckon Massa Ben must have been sad," Jimmy said, "when Elijah got killed trying to save him." It was painful for Jimmy to imagine a black man dying for a white man.

"Elijah ... he loved Massa Ben," Pheby said plainly. "There ain't no other way to put it."

Jimmy didn't see how a slave could love someone who owned him—not like that. It made him wonder what kind of man Elijah had been. "What was he like?"

"Elijah?"

"Yeah."

"Oh, he was pretty. Like you. And he was sweet. Everybody liked him. He could charm the tail off a dog. And he was especially sweet when Massa Ben was around. Of course Massa Ben's a mighty fine-lookin' man, just like his sister's a mighty fine-lookin' woman."

"So what am I supposed to do?"

"About Ben? Just keep clear of him. That's all I can say. Keep clear of both of them."

"I don't see how I can."

Pheby shook her head. "I don't suppose you can."

"You know, this is all your fault," Jimmy said.

"What'd I do?"

"You made these damn clothes look too good. See here." He walked back and forth in front of her. "It's these clothes that make me strut. I used to walk like a normal man."

Pheby nodded. "You're right. I should've made you some ugly clothes. I'm sorry. Boy, you know what? I'm as bad as they are. I couldn't help it either. You just got them strong legs ... and them big arms ... and that pretty face ... and Lord only knows what else you got situated underneath all them clothes."

"Pheby, aren't you a married woman?"

"I am."

"Then don't you start flirtin' with me, too. I've got trouble enough."

"You're right. I'm sorry."

"I'd better go over to the library. They'll be waitin' for me."

"Yes. You go. But it's only Missus Bonnie who's in there today. You won't see Massa Ben this morning."

"Why not?"

"He went out riding this morning. Little Joe saddled him up."

"So he's just riding around again?" Jimmy asked.

"I expect so. He just likes to ...."

"Take the air," they both said at the same time—and then they both laughed.

"I reckon he doesn't go out in his sailboat anymore," Jimmy said.

Pheby looked confused. "What're you talkin' about?"

"I heard Massa Ben has a sailboat."

"He does," Pheby said. "And you're right, he ain't gone out in that boat for a long time. Not that I know of."

"Not since he lost his leg, I reckon," Jimmy said.

"I suppose that's right," Pheby said.

"So where's the boat at?" Jimmy asked.

"Don't ask me," Pheby said. "Little Joe or Uncle Isaac might know. I never saw it. I reckon it's somewhere by the river. Why do you want to know?"

"I just wonder what a sailboat looks like."

"Oh, is that it? You're just curious?"

"That's right." Jimmy smiled mischievously. "I'm curious."

"Hmmm," Pheby said doubtfully. "Well, Missus Bonnie's gonna be curious about where you are if you don't get in there right quick."

"I'm going right now," Jimmy said.

WHEN JIMMY ENTERED THE LIBRARY, Bonnie instructed him to stand in front of the fireplace so she could inspect his new waistcoat. Like Pheby, she ran her fingers around the waist. "Excellent," she said.

"Pheby had to take it in," Jimmy said. "That's why I'm late."

"She has a good eye," Bonnie said.

"Can I ask you something, missus?"

"Yes, if it's not impertinent."

"Why did you pick me to teach all these things to?"

"As I told you," Bonnie said. "I see your potential."

"You think I'm different from the others?"

"Well ... yes and no. You have a spirit ... just like a wild horse. And it interests me ... to see if that spirit can be harnessed."

"Missus Crenshaw," Jimmy began. "I can't agree with you. My spirit is not wild. And I'm not a horse."

Bonnie laughed. "No. Of course not. That's why it's all the more interesting." She walked around Jimmy again, this time simply eyeing him without touching his waist. "But that was a good answer. Tell me, Jacob. Do you have a sweetheart?"

Jimmy stood silent, staring at the carpet.

After a moment, Bonnie asked, "Why do you say nothing?"

"Because I don't like to talk about it," he replied. He lifted his head. "But since you ask—yes, Missus, I do. I've got a sweetheart. But I had to leave my sweetheart behind when I came here."

"So she's still in North Carolina?"

Jimmy rubbed his chin. "Truthfully, I don't know."

"And you have no sweetheart here at our plantation."

"No, ma'am," he said. "And ... truly ... I don't want one."

"Why not?"

"Because I love the sweetheart I left behind."

"Well, Jacob, that's very loyal of you. And, if I may say so, rather unlike most men ... not to mention most Negroes."

"I don't see why that should be so," Jimmy said. "As I see it, if you're in love, you've got to be loyal. Even a dog knows that."

"Ha. Even a dog? What a thing to say!"

"Yes, ma'am."

"Now you see, this is why you were chosen," Bonnie said. "You have civilized impulses despite your provenance."

"My what?"

"Your origin."

"Oh."

"And you make a good point. Dogs are quite loyal—though they're hardly civilized, if you ask me."

"They're the best creatures in this world," Jimmy said.

"Why do you say that?"

He didn't want to talk about his dog with Bonnie Crenshaw. But he couldn't let her comment about dogs being uncivilized pass. "Because, when I was coming up, my dog was my closest friend ... and teacher."

"Your teacher!"

"Yes. She—Venus—made the most of everything .... She

never let anything make her sad ... at least not for more than a few moments."

"What happened to her?"

"She died." Jimmy took a breath. Then he added, "She was old. She had a good life."

"Well, then," Bonnie said. "I think this is excellent advice: 'Make the most of everything.' We must tell Ben this is your philosophy."

"No ..." Jimmy shook his head. "I can't say it is. I'm not so high-minded as Venus. And, well, for some things, there's really no way to make the most of them."

"What things?"

He spoke quickly, to stop himself from saying something else. What he wanted to say was "things like slavery." But instead he said, "Things like being sold away from your mama." It wasn't true that he'd been sold from his mama, but he knew she'd be sympathetic to it.

"Ah, well." Bonnie considered this. "But look at the opportunity you've gained as a consequence of that. Isn't that a way to make the most of it?"

Jimmy sighed before he replied. The sigh was for show. "I'm trying, Missus. Truly." And he did, in fact, agree with her. He *would* make the most of it. Though the opportunity he looked forward to was the one that would take him away from her forever.

19

"GIDDY-UP"

Cato lay in his hotel bed, unable to sleep. He was ruminating about what would be the safest route from Paducah, Kentucky, to Chattanooga, Tennessee. His options had dwindled during the months since he and Dorothy had traveled north from Tennessee. Back then the Confederates had retreated south to Mississippi, which had left Kentucky and most of Tennessee under Union control. Earlier in the year they'd been able to travel freely in Kentucky. But during the five months since then, the Confederate Army had advanced from Mississippi up to Chattanooga, and were now laying siege to Kentucky.

Cato wouldn't be able to get from Paducah to Chattanooga without crossing the tracks of the Louisville and Nashville railroad, which bisected Kentucky. He knew from Mrs. Langdon that during their siege of Kentucky the Confederates hoped to capture or destroy as much of the railroad as they could. But without knowing how far they'd advanced, Cato didn't know how far south in Kentucky he dared to travel.

He wanted to go all the way to Bowling Green, in the southern part of the state. Five months earlier, he and Dorothy had met Walter McNish in Bowling Green. Mr. McNish had helped Cato and Dorothy by acting as an intermediary. He'd relayed letters between them and his friend and fellow Quaker, Erastus Hicks. Mr. McNish had done this by carrying their letters back and forth between the Confederate postal system in Clarksville, Tennessee, and the Union postal system in Bowling Green, Kentucky, where he lived.

Cato hoped Mr. McNish would help him again. But traveling as far south as Bowling Green was risky. He'd be safer, he thought, if he went no further than Cave City, a town to the north. Mr. McNish had accompanied Cato and Dorothy from Cave City to Mammoth Cave back in April. He'd taken them on a private tour. Cato reasoned that if there were too many Confederates nearby, he could hide inside Mammoth Cave, which had many chambers and passageways that would make it easy to stay hidden.

When he got to the livery that morning, Cato asked Mr. Gleason what he thought was the best route to Cave City.

"Well, sir," he said, "I'd follow the Ohio River north and east. That'll be the easiest way to cross the Tennessee and Cumberland rivers. Keep on till you get to Salem. That's a thirty-four-mile trip from here." Mr. Gleason advised that after stopping in Salem he should also stop in Fredonia, Madisonville, Greenville, Morgantown, and Brownsville along his route. "From Brownsville you'll have to ride over the top of Mammoth Cave. It's another twenty miles from Brownsville to Cave City. You could be there in a week if Oscar keeps up a good pace."

"I'd better write all that down," Cato said. "Do you have pen and paper I can use?"

"I do," Mr. Gleason said.

After writing down the directions, he shook hands with Mr. Gleason, who asked, "Now one more thing, son, do you have a firearm?"

"A gun?" Cato shook his head. "No. Do you think I need one?"

"Where you're going I think you ought to be able to defend yourself. If I were you I'd stop at Fred Hummel's gun shop at Fourth and Broadway."

Cato took Mr. Gleason's advice. Half an hour later he visited the gun shop, where he gave Mr. Hummel twenty-five dollars for a Colt Navy .36-caliber handgun. Cato had never fired a gun. He had no idea what he'd do with one. But having it at his feet in the buggy made him feel safer.

After stopping at the gun shop, he set off on the road out of town. Two hours later he passed Fort Anderson, where he crossed the Tennessee River on a ferry boat. Two hours after that, he crossed the Cumberland River on another ferry. On each of the ferries, he stood beside Oscar, holding his reins to keep him steady on the boat. He petted his neck while Oscar alternated between staring with great curiosity at the water and tucking his nose shyly under Cato's arm.

While he was passing the Union forts, Cato felt safe from the Confederates. But after crossing the Cumberland River he'd begun to travel away from the Ohio River. From that point onward he and Oscar were inevitably moving closer to the Confederate Army.

At Fort Smith he came across a group of Negro soldiers on patrol. They were Union soldiers dressed in blue. Forty minutes later he passed a field where slaves were working under an overseer. This change in situation came hard and fast. The farther he traveled from the Ohio River, the farther away he got from the free states. He was heading straight into slave territory.

Oscar, who was unaware of these matters, trotted with a steady and stately gait. He pulled the buggy with a jauntiness that seemed like pride. For the most part, Oscar focused on the road in front of him. Cato had decided not to put blinders on him. As a result, he glanced sideways from time to time, with curiosity about the passing landscape. Cato wondered if this was the farthest from home Oscar had ever traveled.

The sun was still an hour from setting when Cato drove into

the town of Salem, where he found a livery to board Oscar. He stayed in the stable long enough to see Oscar start his supper, then he left to find a hotel.

Although he'd encountered white people that day, no one had challenged him or looked at him with suspicion. But he still thought he ought to do more to enhance his disguise. So when he left the livery, he stopped in an alley to practice smoking one of his La Corona cigars. After his first puff he doubled over, coughing uncontrollably. The smoke made him nauseated. He decided he'd have to avoid inhaling. The best he could do was to hold the cigar between his teeth and let it burn while he breathed from the side of his mouth. He imagined how Jimmy would laugh if he could see him. He had no doubt Jimmy would smoke a cigar without a problem.

After that, he walked down the street with the cigar clenched in his mouth, wearing the spectacles and bowler hat, clutching his satchel in one hand and, following Mrs. MacMurrough's advice, the Methodist Bible in the other. He wasn't sure what he looked like, but he was sure he didn't look like a slave.

At the front desk of the Salem Hotel he set down his satchel, took the cigar from his mouth, stubbed it out in an ashtray, then made a point of carefully removing a gold coin from his purse, which had the desired effect of putting the clerk in a respectful mood. He registered as Mr. Velasquez of Chicago, Illinois.

The journey the next day from Salem to Fredonia was, as Mr. Gleason had foretold, a short one. He arrived in Fredonia in the early afternoon. Oscar seemed disappointed to find himself in a stable again so quickly. Cato whispered in his ear, "Rest up good, boy. We've got a long ways to go tomorrow." The drive east from Fredonia to Madisonville, at thirty-five miles, would be the longest leg of their journey. Cato knew that the risk of encountering Rebel soldiers grew larger as he drove deeper into Kentucky.

But the trip the next day from Fredonia to Madisonville on

Beulah Road proved to be quiet. There were times when Oscar cantered along so briskly and the weather was so fine that Cato hummed a tune as if he were simply on a pleasant journey through pretty countryside. Had he known nothing about the current state of the war, he might have enjoyed himself. Oscar, for his part, behaved as though it was all lovely. Cato was certain Oscar had never before been this far from home. He trotted along in a happy rhythm as if it were a marvelous adventure.

As the miles went by, Cato thought about how much his experience of life from moment to moment was shaped by worries about what might happen next. Oscar, by contrast, trotted along fully immersed in what was unfolding around him at any given moment. He didn't worry what might be around the next bend in the road. Cato wondered if human beings were wise to worry or foolish for doing so.

He decided it was better to worry. If Oscar had any idea of what they might be riding toward, Cato thought, he wouldn't be so jolly. He'd probably choose a different path. On his own, he could just as easily trot north—away from all danger—as go deeper into Kentucky toward the Rebel Army. Unlike Cato, Oscar had no personal reason to put himself in harm's way.

As he thought of this, Cato began to imagine himself in Oscar's place. Out loud, he asked, "What am I doing?" He glanced at the passing landscape and said again, even louder, "What *am* I doing?" He pulled back lightly on the reins as he gently called to Oscar, "Whoa, boy. Whoa!"

Oscar slowed and stopped. Cato wasn't sure if he should continue. His musings had driven home the fact that he was putting Oscar at risk for something that by rights should be his risk alone. He sat still on the seat. Then he dropped his head between his legs. After a minute, he raised his head and looked around. He'd come to a stop in the middle of the road. There was no one coming from behind him; nor was anyone coming toward him.

He'd never owned a horse before. He'd never felt the weight of the responsibility he'd suddenly begun to feel. He knew, of course, that cavalries rode horses into battle. They did so without hesitation—even though some of the horses were bound to be wounded or die in the fighting. Teamsters drove horses under the whip with no more worry for the horses' anguish than slave drivers worried about the anguish of their slaves.

Perhaps the cavalry rider believed that his horse wanted to defeat the enemy as much as he did. Or perhaps the cavalryman simply had a deep faith in the horse's loyalty. Even though Cato had only known Oscar a few days, he could already feel the horse's loyalty. He could tell that Oscar would go wherever he led him.

Cato got out of the buggy. The realization of how vulnerable to danger Oscar would be in the deep South came over him with such force that he didn't even take the time to pull to the side of the road. He went to stand beside Oscar. He stroked his forehead and told him, "I don't want you to get hurt, boy." Cato thought that Oscar could sense the emotion coming from Cato —but was unsure of what to make of it. He blinked.

Cato looked out at the field where they'd stopped. It was filled with rows of watermelons, cantaloupes, and pumpkins. Beyond the field he saw another field, bordered by a fence, where five cows idled. The cows looked back at him with mild curiosity. He looked up and down the road once again. It was still empty. He considered his situation. He couldn't realistically turn back, despite the danger. And he couldn't realistically proceed without Oscar. He really had no choice, except to acknowledge to himself and to Oscar what he was forced to do.

He whispered to Oscar, "I'll do all I can to keep you out of harm's way." Oscar looked Cato in the eye and tilted his head, as if trying to understand.

Back in Paducah, Mr. Gleason had proffered to sell Cato a whip. But he'd declined to buy it. After their trial run around town, he'd decided that he wanted to control Oscar with nothing more than his voice. Now he got back in the buggy and called out, "Giddy-up."

Oscar, when he heard the command, looked back at Cato, and tilted his head once again. Then he turned forward and—with a start—he took off at a fair clip, prancing down the road in a bounding gait. Despite the pace, they didn't reach Madisonville until half an hour after sunset. The dusk light was just enough to guide them into town. But when he'd settled into a stall at the local livery it was clear that Oscar was exhausted.

Once more, Cato stayed by Oscar's side until the stable gave him food to eat. And once again, Cato left to find an alley where he could light up a cigar. This time, as he walked down the street seeking a hotel, he ventured a few billowy puffs on his cigar when no one was looking. He found he could tolerate the smoke with a few quick coughs.

In the distance, he noticed a white man walking in his direction. The man, dressed in a long wool coat, was walking straight toward him. From a distance, Cato couldn't tell if he was wearing a uniform, but it was decidedly gray—and there was a gun strapped to the man's hips.

Cato had stored his own gun in his satchel. He thought about moving it into his pocket, where he'd be able to reach it more easily. But there wasn't enough time to do that now, not without the stranger seeing what he was doing. As the man approached, he saw a smirk on the man's face.

Cato made an abrupt turn. He walked into the nearest building, a general store, to get out of the stranger's path. He strode into the shop with as much confidence as he could muster. Nevertheless, moments later the stranger followed him into the store. Cato noticed, then, a silver badge on the man's gray coat.

Cato felt the best thing to do was to be polite. He took the cigar out of his mouth and flicked it. "Good evening, sir," he said.

"I'm Sheriff Hobbs," the man began. "What's your business here, boy? Where're you from?"

Cato blinked at the man's use of the word "boy." It was spoken in a different tone than the tone he'd heard up until now from the white men he'd met. "I'm Mr. Velasquez," Cato said. "I'm from Chicago." Cato put the cigar back in his mouth and took a puff.

"Velasquez, eh?" The sheriff scratched his chin. "What kind of name is that?"

Cato took the cigar from his mouth and held it nonchalantly at his side. "It's Spanish, Sheriff," he said, with a smile forced onto his face. "Though I was born in Chicago, my ancestors are from Spain."

"Is that so?"

"Yes, sir."

"Have you got your papers?"

Cato wrinkled his forehead to show his confusion. "Papers?!" He paused for a moment. As his mind reeled, he remembered Mrs. Langdon's dictum to show confidence no matter what he felt. He snorted, then breathed out heavily. He colored his voice with indignation. "Papers of what sort?"

"Look here, boy. I know every man in this town," Sheriff Hobbs said. "Ain't nobody here who owns a Spanish boy."

"I don't doubt you, sir," Cato said reasonably. He made a show of letting his temper cool. "I'm not from around here and I certainly don't have an owner or any papers. Why would I?"

"Are you saying you're a white man?"

Cato closed his eyes, then opened them, to show his forbearance. "Really, sir. What else would I be?" he asked.

Sheriff Hobbs stepped closer and looked him straight in the face. "You don't look all that white to me."

Cato locked eyes with the sheriff, and with a tone of growing impatience, he said, "I can only assume that you've never met someone of my ancestry."

"Perhaps," said Hobbs, but his face was screwed up with

doubt. Then he cocked his head. "You talk fancy. I'll give you that."

Cato blinked, then nodded, and then smiled in a grudging way. "Look, Sheriff, I understand your vigilance, but I'm just passing through town. In fact, I'm looking for a hotel. Perhaps you can suggest one for me."

"Passing through to where?"

"I'm going to Bowling Green."

"Is that so?" He looked around the store. "I don't understand," he said. "If you're looking for a hotel, what're you doing in the general store?"

Cato looked around the store. He saw the man at the counter who reminded him of the man in the cigar store. "I stopped here to obtain postage from that gentleman there," Cato said. "I have a letter to post."

"You read and write, do you?"

"Yes, Sheriff. I can assure you we have excellent schools in Chicago."

"Where's this letter you speak of?"

Cato sighed audibly. "I haven't written it, as yet."

"Is that so? Who're you gonna write to?"

"If you must know, I need to send correspondence to my business partner in Chicago, Mr. Pilkington."

"Your business partner?"

"Yes, sir." Cato stared at the Sheriff, now—his eyes intense. "We own a livery in Chicago: Pilkington and Velasquez. Perhaps you've seen one of our labels on a bag of feed. We sell quite a few of those."

"I ain't," said Hobbs. After a moment, the Sheriff shook his head. "Very well, Mister, I reckon you must be who you say you are." After a long moment, he let his expression soften. "Look here, Velasquez. We don't get many strangers in this town, leastways not any Spanish ones. I have to keep track of who's coming and going. You understand."

"Of course."

"And seeing as how we sometimes get niggers tryin' to run north, well ..."

"We all must do our job," Cato said. "You can't be too careful. As for me, my business takes me south. Now, Sheriff, can you suggest a hotel?"

"There just one hotel in town," he said. "If you keep goin' the way you were goin' you'll come to it just down the street."

"Much obliged, Sheriff," Cato said. And he turned and walked up to the counter. He took a shiny quarter from his pocket. "I'd like to purchase two-bits worth of postage," he said to the clerk.

The clerk nodded—took the quarter, then reached into a cash drawer, from which he extracted a variety of stamps. "Here you are, sir."

Cato dropped the stamps nonchalantly in his pocket. He turned and walked past Sheriff Hobbs, to whom he nodded. Then he walked out of the store as steadily as he could manage. He continued his way down the street to the hotel, wobbling only slightly. As he went he thought of the many novels from his father's library that he'd read in secret. The novels had given him the vocabulary—the fancy words—he needed to save himself. He thought it fitting that words from made-up stories had saved him when he made up his own story. But the more he reflected on his audacity, the more unnerved he felt about what had just happened.

At the hotel's front desk, he registered. The clerk gave him a key. He went up to his room on the second floor. He entered the room and walked to the bureau on the far wall. The bureau held a wash basin. Into the basin, Cato threw up.

20

"THE CROWN OF LIFE"

Most of the apples used in the Crenshaws' cider mill came by wagon from the north Georgia mountains. But the slaves also had two apple trees of their own —planted in their garden. Since it was September, the slaves' trees were full of fruit. One Sunday afternoon, Poky and Uncle Isaac carried two baskets of apples they'd picked from their trees to the Crenshaw cider mill. Inside the mill, the smells were a mixture of sweetness from the apple juice and dankness from the mill's dark brown timbers, which over the years had grown clammy with evaporated stickiness.

For a moment, Poky and Isaac stood in silence. They looked around to make sure there was no one in the mill but Lewis, the slave who managed it. The only sound they heard was the rumbling of the timbers that were turned by the water wheel. Finally, Poky spoke. "We've come to balance the accounts," he said.

Poky and Isaac each handed Lewis a basket of apples. Two baskets of apples could produce a full jug of fermented cider. In exchange, Lewis gave Poky half a jug of hard cider; later, Lewis would take the other half-jug for himself. Despite the fairness of these transactions, they never informed the Crenshaws of their system.

Poky and Isaac took their liquor to a spot behind a row of bushes that grew along the river. The bushes gave them privacy. They sat on a pair of flat rocks on the riverside. It was in this spot, on such occasions, that they came to discuss matters of consequence regarding life on the plantation.

"Poky, I hate to say it, but our boy Jacob is headed for a world of trouble," Isaac began.

"Is he?"

"Pheby told me what's been going on in the big house. The boy goes up there every morning."

"To do what?"

"She says Massa Ben and Missus Bonnie dress him up in those fancy clothes, then they parade him around the library like a freak of nature." Isaac shook his head.

"What's he supposed to be doin' there?"

"Pheby says they've got him learnin' things."

"Learnin'? About what?"

"As near as she can make out, they're teachin' him geography."

"Geography?" Poky raised his eyebrow.

"Yeah, you know—such as has to do with maps and landmarks."

"I wonder what that's about?"

"Could be they're teachin' him how to survey the land," Isaac guessed.

"What for?" Poky asked. "The Crenshaws already know where the plantation begins and ends."

"That's true," Isaac said. "And if they needed a survey, they'd hire someone from Savannah. Why teach it to Jacob?"

"I reckon,"Poky said, "that he doesn't know what to do."

"There's not much he can do," Isaac said.

"After his lessons," Poky continued, "he changes clothes, then he comes out to the field. Eppley won't lay a hand on him with the whip, but he makes sure he can't get too much water. And then yesterday Eppley tripped him with that doggone stick of his. And what could the boy do?"

"Nothin,'" Isaac said.

"Nothin' but mutter and keep pickin' the cotton," Poky agreed. He poured Isaac a generous cup of the cider, then poured one for himself. He raised his cup. "Here's to your health."

"And to yours, Poky."

They both sipped.

"Yes," Poky said, "Lewis makes some good stuff."

"You're right about that," Isaac said. "And you know what? It's just what I need."

"You and me both."

"So just between us," Isaac said. "The boy told me he's fixin' to run away."

Poky raised his eyebrows. "He is?"

Isaac shook his head ominously. "I don't know if he'll live to see the end of that day."

Poky wagged a finger. "Can't no one know at sunrise how a day's going to end."

"Ain't that the truth," Isaac said. He looked up at the sun, which was low in the sky and partly obscured by clouds that glowed pink and orange in the light.

Poky took a drink. "Here's to the end of this day, which—so far—has been mighty fine."

"I'll drink to that!" Isaac said, raising his cup.

The two men sat in silence for a moment. They watched the sun as it set. They listened to the current of the river and to the growing chorus of cicadas.

"When do you think Jacob's gonna make his move?" Poky asked.

"Beats me," Isaac said. "He's gotta get a plan first. Right now, he's got no plan—all he's got is talk."

"Have you told him how hard runnin' is?"

"I've tried. But you know what it's like. He's young. He thinks he's special. He thinks the rest of us broke down before he got here. He thinks we've all given up."

"Well?" Poky asked. "Is he wrong?"

Uncle Isaac shook his head. "No." He took a long drink of cider, then wiped his brow. "But what can we do? There ain't nothin' to do."

"You're right about that." Poky took a long drink as well. He raised his cup. "Ain't nothin' to do, but wait for the hereafter."

"Pffft," Isaac said. "I wish I could believe that."

"There's a balm in Gilead," Poky said. "I know it."

"You think so?"

"There's got to be."

"Well, maybe," Isaac said. "But while we're waitin' on Gilead, at least we've got cider in Georgia."

"Yes, sir!" Poky said. Then he scratched his chin. "I wonder if there'll be cider in heaven, too?"

Isaac shook his head. "Sometimes I think it's all a joke."

"A joke?" Poky was confused.

"Yeah ... and the joke's on us."

"No, man."

"What could possibly be the reason?" Isaac asked. "Why should it be like this? Why should we live on this earth as slaves. Why should we be the one's pickin' cotton from sunup to sundown? Why should we get nothin' but a few scraps of food. And why should we get whipped for no reason, and only get a few hours a week to ourselves. Why, Poky? Why would God make the world like that?"

Poky shook his head. "I don't know," he said. "The Good Book tells us ... 'Blessed be the one who perseveres under trial.'"

"Well, we sure do got the trial, that's for damn sure."

Poky nodded. "Then it says, 'And having stood the test, that person will receive the crown of life.' James, chapter one verse twelve. A preacher taught me that when I was ten. I put it to memory."

"The crown of life!"

"Yes, sir," Poky said. "The crown of life."

They each took a measured drink of cider.

"And what about the white folks?" Isaac asked. "What're they gonna receive?"

"You reap what you sow, Isaac. Book of Galatians. God cannot be mocked!"

"Oh, yes! Do not mock God!" Isaac lifted his cup. "I'm gonna finish this drink!" And he began to tilt his cup to his mouth.

But Poky beat him to it. He quickly drained his cup, then stood up. "And the time will come, Isaac." Poky raised up his hand. "You'll see. The white folks are gonna reap. Oh, yes, I do believe they're gonna pay for what they do."

"You think so, Poky?"

"You can't hide from the Lord." Poky shook his fist. "No, sir, sinner. You can't hide!"

"Let them rot in hell's fires," Isaac said. "Fire and damnation!"

"Whatsoever you sow ... that shall you reap!"

Now Isaac stood up. He looked around. Satisfied that no one else could see or hear him, he raised his voice. "When the time comes, Poky, I'm gonna help that boy. I'm gonna help him run away."

"For sure?"

"Yes, sir. I'm gonna do it. I swear by God. And I'm gonna run right with him!"

"Oh, Lord ... Isaac!"

"I'm gonna get free, Poky. I'm gonna get free if it's the last thing I do."

Poky clasped him on the shoulder. "You know what, Uncle? I'm gonna be right there with you!"

21

"WE CAN HIDE HERE FOR DAYS"

It took Cato three days to reach Brownsville, Kentucky, on the western edge of Mammoth Cave. Those three days passed without incident. No one in Greenville or Morgantown, the cities where he'd spent the past two nights, had questioned his presence. In fact, it had been eerily quiet in Morgantown. The hotel clerk told him that the Union Army was nearby. He overheard another hotel guest say that the Confederate Army was already in Bowling Green, just twenty-four miles south. No one knew where the fighting would break out, but it seemed inevitable that a great battle was brewing.

Cato renewed his decision to go to Cave City to wait. Everyone expected the Confederates to advance north from Bowling Green toward Louisville. Cato thought he could find a place to hide in the cave until the Confederates passed. Then he'd continue to Bowling Green after they left. In Bowling Green he planned to visit Walter McNish, who had so generously helped him earlier in the year. It was McNish who'd given him a tour of Mammoth Cave, and it was from that experience that he knew there were many places inside it to hide. His biggest challenge would be to keep from getting lost.

Mr. Gleason had told him he'd have to travel south and then east, directly over the cave, to get to Cave City. As soon as he set out from Brownsville, he was wary. It occurred to him that he might encounter the Confederate Army at any moment. No amount of fancy speaking was going to save him if that happened—nor would the pistol in his satchel.

He decided that if he saw or heard anyone coming, anyone at all, he'd immediately hide. His biggest concern was where—it was one thing for him to hide, and another entirely to hide Oscar and the buggy as well.

He decided he'd drive the buggy off the road at the first sign of trouble. He'd drive into the nearest clearing and leave the buggy there. Then he'd saddle Oscar and ride him far into the woods. Then, he thought, maybe he'd find an entrance to the cave in the woods. Mr. McNish had told him there were untold ways in and out of the cave—for it was truly mammoth.

It wasn't much of a plan. He didn't know how much warning he'd have. There were sure to be bends in the road that he couldn't see around. And he knew that even if he had plenty of warning, he couldn't count on quickly finding a clearing to hide the buggy. He decided he'd just abandon the buggy on the side of the road if he had to. He could ride Oscar all the way to Cave City if it came to it.

He had Oscar proceed at a slower than usual trot, held the rein with one hand and shaded his eyes with the other, so he could see as far into the distance as possible. At one point, when he came around a bend, he heard a rumbling sound. He immediately panicked, thinking it must be the sound of the Confederate cavalry. But then he saw a flash of lightning, and he realized the rumbling had been thunder.

"Just what we need," he called to Oscar. "How do you feel about getting wet?"

Oscar kept trotting forward, unperturbed by the thunder.

Cato peered into the distance. He could see that rain showers were coming straight toward them. "Maybe the rain'll keep the Army from traveling today," he thought. So he kept going, but nudged Oscar to trot a little faster.

Within half an hour, the rain overtook them. The storm came hard and fierce, with lightning, thunder, and wind. After two minutes of being pounded by rain, Oscar turned his head to look back at Cato, as if to ask if he really should keep going.

Cato looked for an opening in the woods. Eventually, he saw a clearing. He stopped, climbed out of the buggy, then took Oscar by the reins and led him into the clearing. Once the buggy was out of sight of the road, he considered what to do. Rain was pouring in sheets. Cato was soaked. He didn't think it wise to just stand in the pouring rain.

He went into the compartment at the back of the buggy and took out the saddle. He put it on Oscar, who looked at him with confusion. "Don't worry, boy," Cato said. "We're gonna look for shelter." He undid Oscar from his harness to the buggy, then led him away along a small path.

The fact that there was a path at all seemed like a miracle. It made Cato wonder if he was on private land. "Maybe there's a house up ahead," he said to Oscar. He pictured a house and a barn where he and Oscar could take refuge. It would be a risk to approach a stranger. But he'd experienced kindness from strangers before, and he had to believe it was possible he could do so again.

As they walked along, however, the path grew more and more faint, until soon it disappeared. Cato looked around. They were deep in the woods. Twenty yards to his right, the land sloped steeply upward, covered by an outcropping of rocks. The rocks zigzagged up the hill.

The rain was pouring. Cato thought maybe he could find somewhere in the rocks to keep dry. He led Oscar through the trees toward the outcrop. As he got closer, he noticed a dark space just to the right of the largest rock. When he got close to it, he realized it was a gradient drop off into a pit. The ground sloped down gradually behind the large rock.

The slope of the pit was like a ramp. When he got to the top, he could see that it led into a large opening. "It's a mouth to the cave!" he said to Oscar.

The opening was so big that not only could he pass through it, Oscar could, too. He led Oscar down the ramp and up to the gaping hole. With some trepidation, he stepped into the dark opening. He immediately felt a breeze, and smelled a dank odor.

He turned and led Oscar back up the ramp, then tied him to a nearby tree. "Wait here, boy," he said. "I've got to go get the lantern. I'll be right back."

As he started to walk away, Oscar whinnied. Cato went back to him. "Don't worry. I won't leave you here." He took some of the oats he kept in his pocket and gave them to Oscar to eat. Then he turned and began to walk away again. Again, Oscar whinnied. But this time Cato steeled himself. The rain was blowing sideways from the wind. He put his head down and kept going. He walked as fast as he could back to the buggy, and from the buggy's back compartment he took out his lantern. Then he dug into his satchel, took out his box of matches, and put them in his pocket. Then he grabbed the satchel and ran as fast as he could back along the path toward the cave.

When he got back, Oscar was shaking. Cato didn't know if it was from the rain or from cold or from fear of being abandoned. He stroked Oscar's mane, untied him, and led him down the ramp toward the opening to the cave. There he took out a match and lit the lantern.

He peered inside. He saw an immense space—and it was completely empty. Cato led Oscar into a cavern that looked like a gigantic room. "This is perfect," he said. "We can hide here for days."

Once they were safely inside the cave, he opened his satchel, took out a towel, and dried Oscar off. After a few minutes, Oscar calmed down. But he was still wary. Cato thought it must feel strange to the horse to be standing under the earth.

Cato looked around. The room stretched out into the darkness, beyond the farthest reach of the lantern's light. "I wonder how big this place is," he said. "You know what, Oscar? Someday they'll have to call this Cato's Cave, since I discovered it."

Oscar didn't react to that one way or another.

Cato noticed, then, how silent it was—so hushed that his breaths sounded loud. He set the lantern on the cave floor so he could cup his hands around his mouth. He tilted his head up and called out at the top of his voice, "Cato's Cave!" The sound of his words reverberated in the distance, until the final faint echo was supplanted by a rumble from the cave's entrance, where thunder boomed in from the storm outside. Then there was silence, again, mixed with the faint sound of rain from the mouth of the cave and something that sounded like the gurgle of a stream.

Cato wondered if there might be an underground stream. Holding the handle of the lantern between his teeth, he climbed onto Oscar's saddle. Oscar turned his head to give Cato an uncertain look. "I want to explore my cave, Oscar. I just want to ride around a little. Don't worry. We won't go too far."

He nudged Oscar in the side and the horse began to walk hesitantly. They headed toward the cavern wall on their left, from where Cato could hear the sound of water. As they came closer, Cato saw a glint of water in the lantern's light. It flowed from an incrusted basin down into an underground stream that ran along the edge of the wall, where it wove between pillars of stalactites and stalagmites. Oscar approached the stream and leaned his head down in order to take a drink. But Cato pulled him back with the rein, fearing the underground water might be foul.

Then he turned Oscar back toward the center of the cavern. He held the lantern high in the air. He was straining to see how far into the distance he could see, when something on the cave floor caught his eye.

He looked down to see the coiled body of a snake. The snake lifted its tail and rattled. At the same time, it raised its head and darted its tongue. Oscar saw the snake, too. He neighed, then reared back, throwing Cato from his back. Cato fell hard onto the cave floor, where he hit his head on a rock. Everything went dark.

22

"IT AIN'T GONNA HAPPEN"

On the same afternoon that Poky and Uncle Isaac got drunk on cider, Jimmy returned to the meadow he'd visited on his first Sunday at the plantation. He'd made a habit of coming to the meadow every Sunday when his chores were done. It was the only time he had to himself, and the meadow had become his refuge. There he stood apart from his life, in a space he'd begun to regard as hallowed.

He always sat on the same log—the one he'd been sitting on when he first saw Ben Crenshaw. But after his first visit, he sat facing the path, so that no one could come up on him by surprise. He didn't want anyone to encroach on his private experience. Ben Crenshaw hadn't followed him to the meadow since that first time.

Despite this, he often thought about Ben while he was in the meadow. He knew Pheby was right to warn him about Ben's intentions. He'd felt those intentions when Ben had run his hand down his back during his inspection.

He'd heard stories about slave-owning men who lusted after their slave women. Cato himself had been conceived from such a lust. But until his encounter with Ben, he hadn't considered that a slaveowner might lust after a male slave. As he thought about it, though, he became convinced that it must be more common than he'd realized. His relationship with Cato had taught him that the world pretended that certain things were not true, when, in fact, they were.

Some slave women were known to take advantage of their sexuality to gain privileges—even freedom—by exploiting their sexual relationships with their masters. Now he found himself in a situation that felt similar. The Crenshaws were offering him advantages he hadn't asked for. He wondered if his lessons in the library were being offered because of their sexual interest in him. He thought he detected an element of desire in the way they looked at him. But he didn't know how to respond.

They each had their little flaws—flaws about which they were clearly insecure. But to Jimmy, these insecurities were a point in their favor. It didn't matter to him that Bonnie had no friends or that Ben was missing part of his leg. If anything, her friendlessness and his disfigurement made Jimmy more sympathetic to them.

He knew that Bonnie Crenshaw was attractive in ways that most men admired. She dressed stylishly. She was feminine. She was classically beautiful—with smooth skin and symmetrical features. She was refined in her bearing, but also delicate, even fragile. And even though women had no role in his sexual desires, he found her polished appearance and refined demeanor appealing. He sometimes wondered what it would be like to be her—which was not something he wondered about with most white people.

Ben Crenshaw, like his sister, was attractive in unusual ways. His appeal was due in part to hair that was a striking shade of red. His locks were often tousled in a way that added brashness to his serious disposition.

His face, too, had a distinctive coloring. When he stood in any soft light, the contours of his facial features were partly shaded by the shadow of whiskers on his chin and above his lips, and partly aglow due to the pale blush of his cheeks, which also emphasized the contrast between the paleness of his skin and the blueness of his eyes.

For a man who didn't perform much physical labor, his body was surprisingly well-shaped. He was lithely muscular on top, and, as Jimmy had especially noticed, voluptuously supple from behind. Most of all, he had a pleasantness and a gentleness of manner, which were both qualities Jimmy found agreeable in men.

But none of these things was enough to alter the fundamental dynamic. Ben Crenshaw was white. He considered himself to be Jimmy's owner. It was a bridge that could never be crossed. Jimmy was confident there was no possibility that his own sexual impulses, however independently they might want to manifest themselves, could break through this fundamental personal taboo. To reassure himself of this, he pictured Ben Crenshaw in his mind's eye. He tilted his head back. He let his mind play with the image. He licked his upper lip with his tongue. He let his imagination call up a prurient image of Ben's body. He sighed. He pictured how well-shaped Ben looked in those tight riding breeches. But after a moment, he shook his head. He muttered, "Don't worry, Cato. It ain't gonna happen."

Those words settled the matter in Jimmy's mind. Whatever it was that Ben Crenshaw could offer, he wasn't able to give Jimmy what he wanted most, which was to return to Cato.

23

"YOU WERE CLEAN PASSED OUT"

Cato was on his back with his eyes closed when he sniffed a musky odor. He opened his eyes. Above him he saw the wet canvas roof of a tent, which accounted for the damp smell. When he looked around, he found he was lying on a cot. He was alone, except for a soldier who sat on a cot nearby. The soldier, dressed in the double-breasted blue coat of the Union Army, stared at him with intense, pale-blue eyes. One of his hands rested on a wooden board on his lap that held a sheet of paper. He held a pencil in his other hand. The soldier smiled and said, "Well, you're awake! Howdy."

Cato blinked. "You?"

"Yes." The soldier smiled. "It's me. Surprised to see me?"

The man across from Cato was Private Robinson of the seventy-fourth Indiana Infantry, Company C—the soldier he'd sat next to on the train to Cairo.

"Yes, I ..." Cato looked around again. "Where are we?"

"We're in a tent in a camp of the Union Army called Camp Woods. We're just outside Munfordville, Kentucky. Our regiment scout, Joe Bird, found you. You were laid out on the floor of a cave five miles from here. You were clean passed out."

Cato was astonished. "How did he find me?"

"Joe was on a scouting run. That's his job—lookin' for Rebs. But Joe never travels on the road. It'd be too easy to spot him. He likes to sneak through the woods. So there he was, sneaking along in the woods, when he came across an empty buggy—with a horse standing unharnessed right next to it. As soon as Joe got there, the dad-blamed horse started to jump up and down, making all kinds of commotion. Joe tried to calm him, but the horse kept nudgin' him, like he wanted to go somewhere. Joe's a Shawnee, so he can just about talk to horses. He knew somethin' was wrong. So he let the horse lead him—and darn if the horse didn't lead him to the cave where he found you. If it hadn't been for that horse, Joe would have never found you."

Cato looked at the entrance to the tent in a panic. "Where is he?"

"Who? Joe?"

"No, I mean Oscar—my horse."

"Oh, Oscar. Well, your friend Oscar's quartered downstream alongside the Green River. Right about now I expect he's havin' a drink and some chow with the rest of the cavalry horses in camp. Your buggy's down there, too."

"Is he OK?"

Private Robinson nodded. "Yep—fine as a fiddle. But I reckon he was thirsty. He was pullin' the buggy when they brought you in on a stretcher. As soon as Joe unhitched him, Joe said he went straight for the stream. I saw him. He's a fine horse. Smart, too."

Cato laid himself back on the cot and closed his eyes. "He saved my life!" Then he opened his eyes and sat up. He looked around. "Is this your tent?"

"You could say it's mine—in a manner of speaking. It's where I'm billeted, along with fourteen other soldier boys."

"How'd I end up here?"

"As it happened, I was walking by right when Joe and

another fella brought you into camp on a stretcher. I recognized you right off—so I said, 'I know that man.' And before you could say 'Jack Robinson,' Joe brought you here to my tent. Joe said he couldn't bring you to the medical tent on account of you're not in the Army. I reckon he didn't know where else to put you." He pointed to the bag on the ground. "We brought your satchel, too."

"Thank you." Cato opened the satchel and reached inside, looking for his purse.

"Everything should be just like you left it," Private Robinson said. "Nobody's opened your bag, far as I know."

Cato found his purse, which felt no less heavy with coins than the last time he'd held it. He saw that everything else in the satchel was where he expected it as well. "Everything looks OK," he said.

"Good," the soldier said. Then he smiled. "I'm Jack Robinson—same as the fella in the old saying—only I'm not so quick as the fella they were talking about."

"Thanks for helping me, Jack."

"I'm glad I could be some help." The soldier's pale-blue eyes lit up. "I'm afraid I never got your name on the train."

"My name's Cato—Cato Askew."

Jack Robinson reached out and shook Cato's hand. After a moment he said, "I was surprised to see you here. The last time I saw you, as I recall, you were about to do some spyin'. But you never said where. How'd you end up in a cave down here?"

"I was on my way to Cave City. But I got caught in a rainstorm. My horse and I took shelter in the cave."

"You and the horse? It must've been a big cave."

"The inside was so big I rode Oscar around—just the same as if we were outside."

"Imagine that! But what happened?"

"I was riding Oscar. But I was also trying to see how big the cavern was, so I was looking as far as I could into the back of the cave. I wasn't looking down. But then something moved on the cave floor and caught my eye. I looked down and saw a rattlesnake. Oscar reared. I fell off. And then ... well ... that's all I remember."

"Joe said he found a snake crushed to death right next to you. He thought the snake must have bit you. But I reckon your horse stomped it before it could get you."

"I'm sure he did."

Jack smiled. "Hooray for Oscar!"

"Right now, Oscar's my best friend."

"How's your head?"

Cato put his hand on the back of his head. "Tolerable—except in the back. It still hurts there."

Jack set his board and pencil down on his cot and stepped over to Cato's cot. "Let me see," he said. He sat down next to Cato and used his hand to part Cato's hair, probing it to find the injury. "Oh, I see it," he said. "There's a lump here."

Cato was startled by Jack's touch on the tender spot. "Ouch."

"Sorry."

Cato pointed at the board and paper on the cot across from him. "What's that you were doing?"

"I was just making a drawing."

"Drawing what?"

"It's a sketch. I draw just about everybody. I've sketched all the fellas around here at one time or another. This time I was drawing you. I would have asked you, but you were asleep. I hope you don't mind."

Cato took this in. "No. I don't mind," he said. "I've been an artist's model before," he said with some pride.

"I can't rightly call myself an artist." Jack shrugged. "It's just a pastime."

"Can I see the sketch?"

Jack hesitated. Then he said, "Oh ... I reckon that's only fair. But it's not really finished yet." He stood and fetched the board and his paper. He showed it to Cato, who stared at it for a while before he spoke.

"I think it's good," Cato said.

"Really? Good, how?"

"Well, you don't make me look ugly."

"Ha!" Jack's eyes twinkled. "So that's what counts, is it? That part was easy." He raised his eyebrows with a meaningful look. "I'd be a liar if I made you look ugly."

"Well, I like it. I like how with just a few lines you show what I look like ... that takes skill. I mean, anybody would know it was me."

"Yeah, well. I go slow. One line at a time. To say the truth, I spend more time looking than drawing."

Cato stared at the sketch some more. "It's well done. It really is." The drawing made him think of Erastus. "A friend of mine is an artist. I was the model for a painting he made of Jesus getting his feet washed by Martha."

"How about that! Which artist was it?"

"His name is Erastus Hicks. I don't reckon you'd have heard of him."

"No." Jack Robinson shook his head. "But that don't mean much. I know a few of the old masters like Michelangelo and Raphael and such—but that's it. And I only know that much from a book in the library back in Indiana."

"Erastus is a Quaker. He lives in Philadelphia now."

"I see." Jack scratched his head. "So he ... what ... he painted you as Jesus?"

"Yes."

Jack nodded. "I can see that. You've got sort of a glow about you. I noticed it right off."

"A glow?"

"Well ... I don't know. Your skin ... it, uh ... kind of glows."

Cato laughed. "I reckon that must come from my papa. Or maybe it's from my mama. I'm not sure."

"How's that?"

"My skin's a mix of colors."

"Well, anyway," Jack said. "It's like how in pictures of Jesus he's got a halo that makes him glow."

"There's no halo on me." Cato smiled. "Far from it." He was aware, as he had been on the train, of the body warmth emanating from Jack's uniformed leg, which was almost touching his own as they sat together on the cot. He glanced down at the soldier's muscular thighs, just as he'd done on the train. He swallowed.

As if Jack could sense Cato's eyes on him, he abruptly stood up and went to the entrance of the tent. He looked out, and then called back. "Hooray! It finally stopped raining," he said.

Cato stood up. "Well, in that case," he said. "Would you take me to see Oscar? I want to make sure he's all right."

"I sure will," Jack said. "Come on." He put his arm around Cato's shoulder. "We'll need to walk down the river a ways. You think you can make it?"

Cato nodded. "I'm fine."

"All right then." Jack smiled and stared at him once more with his intense pale eyes.

24

"BLOW LOUDER, LOUDER"

As the sun began to set on Sunday afternoon, Jimmy left the meadow. He arrived back at the cabin just as Pheby was leaving.

"Where're you going at this hour?" he asked her. "It's gonna be dark soon."

"Not far—just up to the house. I got chores to do." She was carrying a basket of yarn and knitting needles.

"Are you making me more clothes?" Jimmy smiled.

Pheby rolled her eyes. "Boy, ain't you got enough clothes?"

"Not like the ones you make."

"Well, at the moment, I'm about to make Missus Bonnie a coverlet. But I gotta get this yarn rolled up first."

"Why go to the big house, if it's just for that?"

"Like you said, it's gonna be dark soon. I need proper light to see what I'm doin.' I ain't gonna waste none of our oil or candles here. So I'm fixin' to use a lamp in the sewing room up there."

Jimmy nodded.

"Now, if you want to be a gentleman, you could come up there with me and help me."

"Help you how? I don't know how to knit."

"You don't have to knit. All you have to do is help me roll." She pointed at the yarn in her basket. "I got to take all this yarn and roll it up in a ball."

"What for?"

"On account of that's how it's done. If you don't roll it, it gets all tangled up when you knit." She made a tangling gesture with her finger. "It's easier to do when I've got someone to help me."

"Maybe," he said. "What do I have to do?"

"You just gotta hold this skein of yarn between your hands while I roll it up."

"That's it?" Jimmy figured he could manage that. He rubbed his chin. "OK."

When they got to the sewing room, Pheby lit the lamp and sat in the wingback chair. Jimmy sat on the footstool. She showed him how to stretch the skein of yarn between his two hands and hold it while she slowly pulled it and rolled it into a ball.

"Did you spin this yarn?" Jimmy asked.

Pheby pointed at the spinning wheel that sat in the corner of the room. "Right over there."

Jimmy turned to look at the spinning wheel, then turned back to look at the skein of looped yarn in his hands. A puzzled look came over his face. "How come you didn't just spin it into a ball in the first place?"

Pheby laughed. "Boy, you don't know nothin' about spinnin' yarn. When it comes off the wheel you gotta wrap it up in loops twixt the wood rods so it won't fall all over everywhere. It doesn't just fall off there in a ball all nice and easy like that."

Jimmy shook his head. "It seems to me it'd be just as easy to find a way to roll it as to loop it," he said.

Pheby narrowed her eyes. "You want me to teach you how to use the spinning wheel? 'Cause I'll show you how."

"No, ma'am."

"Then you keep quiet while I roll."

"All right."

"Now, I didn't mention it earlier, but I got something to tell you."

"Oh? About what?"

"Missus Bonnie told that me she and Massa Ben are gonna drive to Savannah tomorrow. So there won't be no lesson for you tomorrow morning." Pheby smiled. "It looks like you gonna have to work all day tomorrow, just like everybody else."

Jimmy shrugged. "I don't mind," he said. "I'm no loafer. I hate sitting in there every morning. I'm bored with it."

"Oh, so you bored?"

"Hell, yeah. That's why I got plans."

"Plans? What kind of plans?"

"I'm fixin' to absquatulate."

"You say what?"

"It means skedaddle, disappear."

"Did they teach you that word?"

"No. I already knew that word. We used to say it back home."

"So you fixin' to run off?"

Jimmy nodded. "That's why it's better for me to spend time in the field. That way I can get the lay of things."

Pheby shook her head. "If you run away, you gonna take a mighty big risk. You know what they'll do if they catch you?"

"I know." Jimmy looked out the window. It was now completely dark. "But I don't care. One of these days, I'm gonna do it. I got to!"

"You fixin' to get back to your sweetheart?"

Jimmy nodded. "Yeah ... I've been gone too long."

Pheby frowned. "Uh-huh. Well ... you'd better talk to me before you absquatch or whatever it is you gonna do. Don't just up and disappear on me one day."

"Don't worry," Jimmy said. "I won't go without saying good-bye."

"I suppose you must miss her pretty bad."

Jimmy nodded again. "Considerable."

"And I suppose she misses you, too."

"Absolutely."

"Well, all I can say is, you be careful. You hear me? Anywhere you run around here you gonna run into them Rebel soldiers."

Jimmy nodded.

"They're ornery and they've got guns."

"I'll be careful."

"And besides that, there's all kind of scalawags and no-account cracker ruffians and rotten hoodlums and Lord only knows what else you gonna find when you run out of here."

"I won't find nobody like that. I'm not goin' that way."

"What way you goin' then?"

"I'm going by the sea."

"By the sea! How you gonna do that?"

"In a boat."

Pheby dropped the ball of yarn in her lap and made a face. "A boat! That's crazy."

"Why do you say that?"

"You expect to row a boat all the way up to Philadelphia or New York or wherever?"

"I don't have to row that far. All I gotta do is row out to a Union ship."

"What ship?"

"One of the ships they've got in a blockade."

"Who told you that?"

"Massa Ben."

"Oh, is Massa Ben helpin' you plan to vamoose?"

"He doesn't know anything about it. He just told me about the blockade when I asked him why he doesn't take his boat out anymore."

"So I guess you been schemin' for a while then?"

"Since I got here."

"And where you gonna get a boat from?"

"I'm gonna borrow it from Massa Ben! Like I said, he's got a sailboat—but he doesn't ever use it."

"So you a sailor?"

"No. But I'm gonna learn it."

"From who?"

"I can't say just yet." Jimmy thought for a moment. "Maybe I'll learn it from a book."

"A book!" Pheby shook her head and began to pull the yarn harder, rapidly rolling it onto her ball. "I don't see how you gonna learn sailin' from readin' a book. All I can see is how you either gonna get drowned—or if you lucky you might get eaten by a shark first—or else you gonna get shot out of the water by a Yankee gunboat—or you gonna get captured by the secesh patrol boats, and then they gonna drag your big behind back to the Crenshaws—and then Eppley's gonna see to it that you can't ever walk again, let alone row a boat."

"Are you finished?"

Pheby made a stern face. "Yes."

"You gotta have faith, Pheby."

"Oh, I got faith. I got faith in them paddy rollers and them gunboats and them constables. And they ain't gonna take kindly to no boy like you sailin' no boat down no river."

"Ain't nobody gonna see me. I'm gonna steal the boat and go at night."

"You think it's safe at night? That's just when them paddy rollers get to work. You know they out in them woods all night long—and they just itchin' to catch a fool that looks like he's runnin' away."

"I don't think they watch the river. It's too dark out there."

Pheby shook her head again. "You think nobody's ever thought how one of us might take a boat down the river? Sure 'nuf, them good ol' boys'll be sittin' in a skiff down by the mouth of the river—and they ain't there waitin' to catch no fish."

"You might be right." Jimmy nodded. "But I gotta take my chances."

"Look here, Jacob. You better think about what you gonna run into. Talk to Little Joe. He knows more about it than me. He hears what folks say down in Savannah. He's got friends down there."

"I will. I'll talk to him."

"You do that."

THE NEXT DAY, Jimmy arose with the other slaves—before the roosters had awakened. In harvest season, slaves had to be in the field and ready to work by the first light of dawn. They couldn't leave until the last light of dusk had disappeared. To Jimmy, it felt like the middle of the night. He walked in the dark with the other slaves to a field below the big house that was bounded by the railroad tracks that ran across the southern end of the plantation.

The weather had been unrelentingly hot and humid. But a thunderstorm in the middle of the night had swept away the humidity, making the air noticeably cooler and drier. Jimmy was glad to be outdoors instead of in the library. He could tell it was going to be a pleasant autumn day. He'd never been one to sit in a chair inside a house on a beautiful day.

Eppley instructed the slaves to pick in the field nearest the sawmill. Then, without explanation, he mounted his horse and rode off down the road. This was something he did on occasion. Since he was often gone during these absences for more than an hour at a time, some of the slaves thought he must be carrying on a dalliance with a woman. There was a woman of ill repute named Sarah who lived nearby. Whatever the reason, Eppley's absence raised the slaves' spirits.

Even though Eppley was gone, the slaves couldn't slow their work. They were judged at the end of the day by the weight of the cotton they'd picked. Jimmy always worked at a slower pace than he was capable of. That meant that when Eppley was gone, he could slow down or even stop for a while, and still make up his weight before the day was over.

So as soon as Eppley was out of sight, Jimmy stopped working. He saw and smelled something that transported him back to his childhood in Tennessee--blue wood-smoke curling from the chimney on the roof of the sawmill. Someone was burning hickory wood inside. It reminded him of the hickory smell from the smokehouse on the farm where he grew up.

This recollection left Jimmy in a dreamy state. All around him, the world was waking up—and he, too, felt as if he was waking from a bad dream. He stood idle for a moment, listening to the peaceful sound of the flowing river and the languid creak of the water wheel as it turned beside the mill.

Not far from the field, he saw a small herd of sheep. The sheep were nestled in a swath of fenced land just beyond the railroad tracks. As the light from the rising sun fell along the swath, Jimmy saw the ram, with his prominent curled horns, stand, look around, then begin to graze. The sheep, one by one, stood and did the same. As each animal stood up, it woke an assortment of flies and gnats, which took up the task of buzzing about each unshorn animal's wool.

In the distance, Jimmy heard roosters crow in the barnyard near the big house. Then he heard the rumble of an approaching train. The train blew its whistle in three short, high-pitched blasts: toot, toot, toot. This began a conversation. The roosters echoed the train horn with a peal of triple calls: *caw, caw, caaaaw.* The train engineer leaned out the window as he passed the barnyard, and let off a long, steamy whistle that rose in a crescendo, peaked in the middle, then faded mournfully. The roosters erupted in a chorus of cries. Again the trainman tooted three times. The roosters cawed indignantly in response. Finally, the trainman clanged his bell. At this the roosters and the hens flew around in a flurry of squawking and beating feathers.

And then, to add to the commotion, a steamboat came around the river bend sounding its whistle, which, unlike the train's whistle, was deep and low, with a long decay. The boat was loaded with rough lumber for the sawmill. As it approached the mill, it reversed its paddlewheel, churning up the water while backing and filling and slowly maneuvering itself to turn toward the dock, where raw lumber was piled on the far side of the mill.

At the sound of the steamboat whistle, a flock of orioles flew up from the trees that lined the river, filling the sky with black and orange flapping wings. And then, at last, when all the cawing and whistling and crowing and frothing of water had ended, Poky began to sing. His deep baritone voice filled the air with "Blow dat trumpet, Gabriel." Poky kicked his feet and swung his arms as he chanted: "Blow louder, louder; and I hope dat trump might blow me home, to the new Jerusalem." Then everyone up and down the row clapped their hands and joined the song.

Jimmy was so entranced that he, too, joined in. He lifted his hands to the sky and raised his voice on the phrase, "I hope dat trump might blow me home." The song matched his thoughts perfectly. With his hands waving, he scanned the riverside near the sawmill for Ben Crenshaw's sailboat, which, he reasoned, was probably moored somewhere within the plantation boundaries. He didn't see a boat, but the beauty of the moment allowed him to picture it. In his mind's eye he saw himself sailing down the river, holding the rudder, then gliding out to the ocean, where he tacked north and climbed away at last from the land of cotton.

25

"BEEN SAVIN' THAT A LONG TIME"

Oscar opened his mouth in what seemed to Cato like a goofy smile.

Cato stroked the horse's mane. "You saved me, boy," he said. "Do you know that?"

"I think he knows it," Jack said. "He's got his mouth open because he's waitin' for a reward."

Cato looked Oscar in the eye. "Is that it? You want a treat?"

"How about this?" Jack reached into his pocket and pulled out an apple. "It's ripe—and sweet. I know because I just ate one."

Cato smiled at Jack, then turned to the horse. "Oscar, this is my friend, Jack Robinson. And as you can see, he's a thoughtful man."

Oscar glanced at Jack, then fixed his eyes on the red fruit in Jack's hand.

"It's comin' right up, Oscar my friend," Jack said. He pulled a pocket knife from his vest pocket, cut off a slice of the apple and brought it up to Oscar's mouth. Oscar instantly grabbed the slice in his teeth, and chomped.

"Where'd you get that apple?" Cato asked.

"From a tree downriver, back closer to the camp." He admired the apple in his hand. "There's plenty left if you want a slice."

"I believe I would," Cato said.

Jack cut off a slice and handed it to Cato, then another that he handed to Oscar, then a third that he ate himself.

"It tastes good," Cato said. "I wonder if that tree is from Johnny Appleseed."

"Who's that?"

"Someone I heard about from my friend Erastus," Cato said. "Johnny Appleseed went around the country and planted apple trees everywhere he went."

"Everywhere?"

"Yep."

"How about that?"

"Erastus told me a person's got to plant seeds wherever he goes."

Jack looked at the core of the apple left in his hand. "Well, I reckon there's a few seeds in here."

"Then let's plant them," Cato said. He pointed to a spot where there was open ground. "How about over by that bush."

Jack nodded. "OK. If you say so." He walked over to the spot, knelt, and started to scoop the soil out with his fingers. When the hole was big enough, he dropped the apple core into it, then covered it with dirt. "How's that?"

"I reckon that's all it takes," Cato said. "Of course, I think my friend Erastus meant the apple seeds were like a symbol."

"A symbol of what?"

"Like spreading seeds of kindness ... or seeds of understanding."

"Oh, I see," Jack said. "Is that what you do? Spread seeds of kindness?"

"I try to," Cato said.

"I reckon I ought to, too."

Cato smiled. "You just did. Look what you did for Oscar."

"Well, but that's 'cause I love horses." Jack put his hand on Cato's shoulder.

"I never knew it till I met Oscar," Cato said, "but I love horses, too."

They looked at each other, and there was a moment of awkward silence as each tried to discern the meaning of the other's look.

Jack looked up at the sky. "It's getting dark. We'd best get back to camp."

"Lead the way," Cato said.

WHEN THEY ARRIVED BACK at Jack's tent, Cato asked a question that had been on his mind since he'd found out where he was. "Where do you reckon I should sleep tonight?"

"Oh, about that," Jack said, looking around. "I expect you're gonna have to make do with my cot." He pointed. "It's the one they put you on this afternoon." He ran a hand through his hair. "Tain't nowhere else that I know of. All the other cots in my tent are taken."

"Then where will you sleep?"

"Me?" Jack scrunched his forehead. "I reckon I'll have to sleep on the same cot. I reckon we're gonna have to share it."

"Oh." Cato was surprised.

"Do you mind?"

"No. That's fine," Cato said. "Truly, it's kind of you." He walked over to the cot and sized it up. "But how are we gonna manage—it's kind of small for two, isn't it?"

"That depends," Jack said. "I mean, well ... you're kind of skinny. And I'm not too big. We'll just have to scrunch up, I guess. Is that all right with you?"

"I suppose so. I just ..."

"What?"

"I don't like to put you out so much."

"You won't. Anyway," Jack said, "I sleep like a dog. My head goes down, my eyes go closed, and then just like that—I'm asleep."

"I suppose we can manage," Cato said.

"It's just for tonight, right?" Jack said. "I expect you'll be goin' on your way tomorrow."

"I reckon so."

THAT NIGHT, Jack and Cato sat outside the tent talking. Without saying so, they were waiting until the other soldiers had settled into their cots. They kept talking until everyone inside the tent seemed to be asleep, then they went inside. Cato sat on one end of the cot while Jack sat on the other.

"OK, now," Jack said. "Let's get some shut-eye." He stood and carefully took off his uniform—folding each garment in a neat pile under the cot, until he was wearing only his underwear. Then he took off his undershirt, and folded it, too. He left his underpants on.

Cato imitated him, removing his garments, folding them, placing them under the cot. He, too, left his underpants on. He stood facing Jack awkwardly. He was embarrassed to let Jack see his back, which bore the scars of a severe whipping given to him by his father as punishment for learning how to read.

Jack got into the cot first, and scooted as far over as he could to one side. "Come on and get in now," he said. "You must be tuckered out after the day you've had."

"I am," Cato said. He climbed in, and quickly turned on his side. If Jack got a glimpse of the scars on his back, he said nothing.

Cato nestled against Jack, who immediately pulled up the blanket, then wrapped his right arm around Cato's chest. "How's that?" Jack whispered. "I don't know where else to put my arm."

Cato was surprised by the feel of Jack's arm. But he said, "It's OK."

"Have you got enough room?"

Cato nodded. "But I feel like I'm in the way."

"Don't worry about it." Jack shimmied around in the cot. "It's snug, but, hey, it's chilly out and you're nice and warm. So relax, for Pete's sake, and get some sleep."

"OK," Cato whispered. He let his body go still. He felt the warmth of Jack's skin. He stayed dead-still for a long time. He felt as if he was half asleep, half awake—never completely letting go of his awareness. But then, without realizing it, he fell asleep. And in the distraction of the dream world, his body slid along Jack's.

In response, Jack's body slid back.

Instantly, Cato sprang awake. He opened his eyes. It was still the middle of the night. From the cots all around him came the sounds of the other men snoring. But Cato could tell by the nature of the breathing coming from behind him that Jack was awake, too. There could be no doubt about it.

Cato tentatively slid his body again. He pressed his butt ever so slightly against Jack's groin. Immediately, he felt a subtle, swelling pressure from Jack's penis, which began to push against the thin layers of white cotton that held it in. A small sound escaped from the back of Cato's throat, which he tried to cover by masking it with a sound like a snore.

But then, Jack's hand, still wrapped across Cato's chest, moved, almost imperceptibly. One of his fingers slid along the smooth surface of Cato's chest. Jack's finger glided with infinitesimal care across Cato's skin until—after a heart-stopping hesitation—it touched delicately on Cato's right nipple. Cato tried to not react. But another soft moan escaped from the back of his throat, even as he tried to swallow it.

This time Cato didn't pretend to snore. He felt a terrible conflict. His only goal in life was to get back to Jimmy, to get back to his lover. But here he was—without foresight or plan. Against all odds, he found himself lying in bed, half-naked, wrapped in the arms of a handsome Union soldier, a sweet man whose breath wafted against his neck in fast, short breaths that were fertile with desire. The muscular bicep at the top of Jack's arm pressed into Cato's shoulder as Jack's finger continued to glide across the curves of Cato's chest. Cato stopped breathing and lay utterly still.

When Cato stopped breathing, Jack's finger also stopped moving, and he, too, held his breath. It was a full stop—a complete hesitation. After a long moment of silence, he whispered into Cato's ear, "Is this all right?"

Cato didn't know what to say. He couldn't control how his body reacted. The feel of Jack Robinson's swollen cock pressing against the cleft of his ass aroused him. He couldn't will it otherwise. If there was a switch that would stop the titillation coursing through him, some noble part of him tried to press that switch, but the switch didn't respond. His body had its own mind. He didn't have time to consider the situation rationally. He couldn't weigh what it might mean, how it might affect his future. His rational mind was pushed back into a corner where he couldn't hear it, as if it were muffled by a pillow. In its place, erotic force pulsed through his body.

He was filled with lust so strong it made him arch his foot. He thought it must be the strongest force in the world. He thought, "Why is it so?" And then, even though it was dark, even though Jack could barely see him, he nodded slightly. And he whispered, "Yes."

Instantly, Cato shifted his hips. He let them thrust ever so slightly, as he moved his buttocks to wrap around the probe behind him—an enfolding movement that felt as inexorable as the movement of the heavens. The mounds of his ass slid sensually like a sheath, until they enveloped the bumped-out shape in Jack Robinson's underwear.

And then, Jack's cock expanded. Apparently it had only been at half-furl. But now it unrolled rapidly, and the force of its extension jolted Cato. It grew bigger than he'd imagined possible. And all at once, Cato turned his body around in the cot so he could look at it.

In a series of swift, deft moves, Cato maneuvered his hands beneath the sheet that covered them. He slid out of his underwear, then lifted the sheet just high enough to make his throbbing penis visible for Jack to see. Jack, in response, pulled down his own underwear, then kicked it off the end of his feet. He joined Cato in holding the sheet slightly aloft, so that they could each look under and see the nakedness of the other. They watched as their cocks touched together beneath the tent of the sheet, then bounced off each other in a throbbing spasm.

The room was dark. The only light came from the opening of the tent, from the moonlight outside. But it was enough light for each to look the other in the face—and to see each other's eyes. Jack's pale blue eyes were electric, as they darted back and forth. He seemed to be trying to understand, trying to take in what was happening. He moved his hand to let the cotton sheet float down to cover their nudity.

Instinctively, then, each of their hands beneath the sheet found the location of the other's cock. But then they both stopped. Silent, once again, they took the measure of the moment, and—at the same time—they both seemed to remember where they were. They both tilted their heads. Each tuned his ears to try to determine if anyone else in the room was awake, if anyone else could notice what they were doing.

Satisfied that no one else was awake, they quietly pushed the middle of their bodies apart, so that they had enough room to caress each other's cocks. Cato wrapped his fingers around the arched end of Jack's cock, which stretched damp and naked out of its foreskin. Fluid oozed from the slit of Jack's penis onto Cato's finger—and Cato slid its lubrication around Jack's cock head as if his finger was a tongue. Jack's eyes rolled back in his head for a moment. And he smiled: a big, goofy smile of delight.

Then, all at once his face grew serious, and as if by pre-arrangement, they abruptly pushed their lips together at the same time. It happened with such suddenness that it was like a gasp for air. Then, with equal abruptness, in reaction to the sound this made, they each tried once again to keep quiet, even though the breath and heat coming from both of them felt immutable. Gradually, they bowed their bodies outward so they could keep their lips pressed tightly together even as they made space to stroke each other.

The kissing sent an electric current reeling through their bodies, intensifying their erections. The pressing together of their lips also muffled the sounds that threatened to escape and expose them—making it seem like they could hear their slurping and smacking only inside their heads. They were lost inside their own private shared space.

Cato's tongue pushed in, reaching to find the back of Jack's throat. And in doing so, Cato felt as if he was traveling deep into Jack Robinson's head. He was awestruck by the significance of this act. He'd never been with anyone but Jimmy. It was all still so new and unexpected for him. It was especially astonishing for him to have his tongue inside the mouth of a white man—even if that white man didn't fully realize Cato's race. He thought that Jack Robinson either hadn't noticed his race, or didn't care about it, or both. Somehow, this lack of notice had a liberating effect, as if it freed Cato from a superficial cloak that he invariably wore.

But if Jack was unaware of their racial difference, Cato was not. In fact, he was acutely aware that Jack was white—that his skin was smooth and pale, that his eyes were luminously blue, that his hair was silky and soft, that his nose was angular and sleek as it nudged against his own. Cato was transported in his imagination like a traveler in a foreign land, where he beheld the grandeur of the Caucasian. He wanted to memorize every second of it. He was certain that having his tongue inside Jack's mouth was a moment outside all the other moments of his life—that he'd likely never have a passport to visit this country again. And so he took it all in: the sensations, the vision, the fragrant, exotic smells of the pale Yankee boy from Indiana whose cock, he realized, was spurting out a stream of sticky fluid into his hand in a rhythmic pulse that was escalating.

And just as Cato realized that Jack was ejaculating, he felt himself fall, like a man falling off a cliff, with such unnerving force that he wanted to cry out. He desperately exhaled into the muffled hollow of Jack's mouth. He didn't think he could keep quiet. He felt that his body would surely explode. Spasms began to shake his balls, and his hips began to shake, and then streams of cum began to erupt from his penis. Jack quickly put his hand across Cato's mouth—and pressed as hard as he could, for they both realized that the sound that would have otherwise come from Cato's mouth would have awakened the entire seventy-fourth Indiana Infantry, Company C.

Cato was so full of sperm that it seemed like a full minute before his body stopped spasming. His white, sticky ejaculate shot all over Jack Robinson's chest and shoulders and even stuck to the bottom of the wispy brown whiskers at the bottom of Jack's chin.

Jack shook his head, rolled his eyes, then grinned with delight. "What a shot!" he whispered.

Cato looked down at his own chest, which was also covered with cum. "What about you?" he asked quietly. "You must've been savin' that for a while."

"Been savin' that a long time," Jack said.

"Me, too."

They both looked around the room. Miraculously, no one seemed to be awake. Jack retrieved his undershirt from beneath the cot, wiped Cato's chest, and then wiped his own.

"You remember when I first met you, on the train?" Jack whispered.

Cato nodded.

"I sat down next to you on purpose."

"You did?"

"I was walkin' up the aisle lookin' for an empty seat. When I saw you with an open seat I jumped right in it."

"Really?"

"And the whole time you were readin' that book, I was tryin' to sneak a look at you sideways."

"Me, too," Cato said. "I was looking at your legs. And then when you leaned past me to look out the window, I almost rose up in my seat."

"I let my body rub against your chest."

"I remember," Cato said. "It made me catch my breath."

"I had to get off the train right quick, then," Jack said. "Before I embarrassed myself on account of my hard-on."

"I thought you had to go get that cow."

"Well, that, too."

"Do you think it was fate?" Cato asked. "What are the chances?"

"I never imagined you'd feel the same way as me. But I was drawn to sit down next to you."

"I think we must have a special instinct. It must've been an intuition that let us find each other," Cato said.

"And now what?" Jack asked. "I'm going off to war and you're going off to Cave City."

"We might not see each other again," Cato said.

"Dad blame it. I hate that," Jack said. "But who knows? Maybe we'll meet again."

"Maybe," Cato said. He was silent for a moment. "Whatever happens," he whispered, "I'll never forget you."

Jack nodded solemnly. "Nor I, you."

They nuzzled their heads together, then returned to their former positions in the cot. Jack once again wrapped his arm firmly across Cato's chest. After a few minutes of quiet breathing, they each drifted off to sleep.

26

"I NEVER HEARD ANYTHING SO BEAUTIFUL"

After Bonnie and Ben Crenshaw returned from their visit to Savannah, they sent word to Jimmy through Pheby that he would be expected in the library after breakfast the next morning. This was understood to mean after the Crenshaws had finished their breakfast, which meant at eight in the morning—two hours later than the time the slaves began their work in the field. Jimmy wasn't expected to work in the field before his lessons. Nevertheless, he got up with the other slaves.

Most mornings, he spent the two hours before he was due in the library helping Uncle Isaac with his chores. But on the morning after the Crenshaws' Savannah trip, he offered to help Pheby instead—thinking she might have more yarn to roll. Pheby did want his help, but not to roll yarn. She'd been instructed to make a yellow dress for Bonnie Crenshaw.

"I'm about to make some dye," she told Jimmy. "You could help me with that."

"That sounds like a lot of work," Jimmy said.

"It ain't hardly any work at all. All you have to do is haul some water up from the well, bring it to the kitchen, and pour it into a big pot I hung over the fireplace." She handed him a large jug. "Without messin' up your clothes."

He took the jug. "How many jugs do you need?"

"About five."

After Jimmy brought the first jug of water into the kitchen, he peeked inside the pot over the fireplace to see what was inside it. "There's nothin' in there," he said.

"Not yet," she said. "Go ahead and pour that first jug of water in there. I'm gonna put flowers in there next."

"What flowers?"

"Wait here," Pheby said. She went outside and came back in with a basket. "You see? These are goldenrod flowers. I picked 'em yesterday. Now all I gotta to do is simmer 'em in hot water —then I'm gonna get yellow dye."

"That sounds easy."

"There's nothin' to it," Pheby said.

As Jimmy was toting in the third jug of water, on his way past the front door he heard music coming from the front parlor. Someone inside was playing the piano.

"What's that music?" he asked Pheby when he got to the kitchen.

"That's Massa Ben. Most days before breakfast, he plays the piano."

"What's he playing?"

Pheby shrugged. "You gonna have to ask him."

"All right. I'll do that," he said.

The next time Jimmy came from the well, instead of going in through the back door as he was supposed to do, he climbed the steps to the verandah and entered the house through the front door. Inside, he stopped in the vestibule next to the front parlor—and listened. The music sounded like the kind of music Cato had told him about. Cato had once heard a man play Chopin in the Askews' parlor back in Tennessee, and he'd never forgotten it.

It hadn't occurred to Jimmy that Ben Crenshaw might play

the piano. As he stood listening, he had to agree with Cato, the music sounded like it came from heaven.

Just then the music stopped. Ben, who'd been hidden from sight behind the open case of the piano, abruptly stood up. He held onto the side of the piano to keep his balance, and looked straight at Jimmy.

"Jacob!"

"'Excuse me, Massa Ben. I was bringing this water jug to the kitchen for Pheby. I heard you playing ... and ... I just stopped to listen for a minute."

Ben stepped to the side of the piano. He was wearing the copper and gold brocade vest that Jimmy had seen before. But his white cotton shirt was untucked at the waist, as if he hadn't finished dressing. His red hair, as usual, was tousled and glinting in the sun that streamed through the window behind him. He moved his hand along the edge of the piano to steady himself. "Do you like music?" he asked.

"I never heard it before ... I mean, not that kind of music," Jimmy said. "I mean ... not music played like that on a piano."

"What did you think of it?"

"Massa Ben ... it sounded like something that angels might play up in heaven."

Ben smiled broadly. "That was Beethoven. His sonata in C-sharp minor. It's called the 'Moonlight Sonata.'"

Jimmy tilted his head. Then he asked, "How'd you learn to play like that?"

"Practice, Jacob. Lots of practice."

Jimmy nodded, then turned to leave. "I'm sorry I interrupted you."

"Don't be," Ben said. "It's nice to have an audience. Why don't you stay?" He ran his hand through his hair, then haphazardly tucked in his shirt. "Stay a few moments. I'll play you the whole piece."

Jimmy looked back toward the kitchen, but then he said, "All right."

Ben pointed at the jug in Jimmy's hand. "Leave that jug in the hall, then come in and have a seat."

Jimmy put down the jug and stepped into the parlor. He didn't feel comfortable taking a seat in any of the upholstered chairs. So he sat on the floor. Ben smiled at this, then sat again at the piano bench. He played the "Moonlight Sonata" from the beginning. He played it poignantly—swaying slightly on the bench as he moved his hands delicately across the keyboard. His head bobbed in synch with the cadence of the notes, causing his red curls to bounce up and down on his forehead. His face showed him to be lost in concentration and full of emotion.

Jimmy listened in rapt attention as he watched Ben's face. Eventually, the music moved him so much that he couldn't bear to keep his eyes open. He closed his eyes and bowed his head. When the piece was finished, he raised his head and opened his eyes. Ben looked at him expectantly.

Jimmy was silent for a long time. Finally he said, "I never heard anything so beautiful."

Ben's eyes welled up at this complement. "Thank you," he said. "That means a great deal to me."

Jimmy looked around the room—at the beautiful mahogany furniture, at the elegant piano, at the russet-colored mums on the table, at the thick green and pale pink oriental carpet on which he sat. The contrast between the luxury in which Ben Crenshaw lived and the austerity of the slaves quarters was considerable. It was a moment of insight that might have made him angry. But in this moment, having just tasted the aesthetic pleasure of Ben's privileged life, he was more startled than angry. He was startled to suddenly comprehend the enormity of beauty missing from his own life. Barring a miracle, he thought it unlikely he'd ever again have an experience like this.

"What are you thinking?" Ben asked.

"About how different your life is from mine," Jimmy said.

Ben blinked. He wasn't sure how to respond. After a

moment, he said, "Yes, I'm afraid it is."

Jimmy stood, then walked to the piano. He looked at the keyboard. "Could I try it?"

Ben nodded.

Jimmy put his finger above a key, then struck a note. He smiled awkwardly, reacting to the sharpness of the sound as if he'd been pinched. He played another note. But this time he held his finger on the key longer. He listened attentively while the sound slowly died away. But then he shook his head. "I don't understand how you make all those notes sound the way you do," he said.

"Here," Ben said. "Let me show you." He took hold of Jimmy's hand. "Hold out your index finger." Jimmy complied while Ben used Jimmy's finger to strike a series of notes. "This melody we're playing is called 'Twinkle, Twinkle, Little Star,'" he said. "It's an English lullaby."

After Ben finished speaking, he sat still on the bench. He stared at the keyboard, saying nothing. Jimmy was keenly aware that, even though he'd finished the tune, Ben continued to hold his hand. Jimmy gently pulled his hand away. Ben looked up at this. "You could learn to play," he said.

Jimmy shook his head. "I don't think so."

"All it would take is time," Ben said. "And someone to teach you."

"Perhaps," Jimmy said. He smiled. "I do have nimble fingers." He thought of how deftly he could pick cotton. "But it wouldn't be right for me to learn to play. I don't have a piano."

"May I see your hand again?" Without waiting for an answer, Ben took hold of Jimmy's hand and inspected it. "You have long fingers," he said. Slowly, he ran his finger up and down the length of Jimmy's finger. "That helps." Then he flexed the fingers on his own hand and added, "Mine are long, too."

Jimmy glanced at the fingers that held his own, then gently withdrew his hand from Ben's touch once again. "I'd best get back to Pheby," he said.

Ben stood and again held the edge of the piano to steady himself. He looked into Jimmy's eyes. "I know you must think I'm spoiled," he said. "You must think I have everything I could want." He paused, glanced around the room. "And I do. I know I do. I have all this." He gestured vaguely with his free hand. "But Jacob, I don't have the one thing I want most."

Jimmy didn't speak. He lowered his head, feeling uncertain about where this would lead.

"I once had what I wanted most. I had love," he said. "And it was the greatest blessing of my life. But then ... I lost it ... in the war."

Jimmy nodded slightly.

"And since my loss, I've been without any kind of loving touch." He put his hand on Jimmy's shoulder. "Looking at your fingers made me think of it. Men find it so difficult to touch."

Jimmy looked away, but otherwise didn't move.

"And, of course, it's especially difficult for a man who's disfigured to be without love." He bowed his head. "I know I'm a source of revulsion and distaste to others."

Now Jimmy looked up. "Massa Ben ... I doubt most folks care much about your leg. Everyone knows about the war."

"That's kind of you to say, Jacob." He squeezed Jimmy's shoulder. "But it shames me, truly, to be missing a limb .... It's a vile deformity. No one wants a man with an unsound body."

Jimmy shook his head. "But you're sound in every other way."

"Speak truthfully, Jacob. Do you cringe to look at me?"

Jimmy chose his words carefully. "I have no cause to feel that way. I ..." He broke off, reddening.

Now Ben pulled his hand from Jimmy's shoulder. "I'm sorry. I know I'm embarrassing you. It's just that you've always seemed to me like an understanding sort of fellow—and kind—like someone I could talk to. You see, I can't talk to my father or my sister. Not about anything so personal."

Jimmy wagged his head, flushed again.

"But you seem to be someone who's like me in certain ways. I mean, except, of course, that I'm rather appalling to look at, whereas you ... well ... I do believe some folks might declare you the epitome of male beauty. I mean, that's what my sister thinks." He laughed awkwardly, then reached out and ran his fingers across the top of Jimmy's hair and down the back of his head in a gesture that strained to be casual.

Jimmy tilted his head—as if doing so might cause Ben's hand to slide off it. "I'm nobody special, Massa Ben."

"But don't you see?" Ben squeezed the back of his neck. "You are special. This is the very thing Bonnie and I hope to reveal to the world. We want others to see what we see in you."

"I don't think that has as much to do with me as it has to do with you," Jimmy said. "I don't think I can be what you and Missus Bonnie want me to be."

"But you must try, won't you please, Jacob?" He squeezed Jimmy's neck again, then finally took his hand away. "And you must try not to think ill of us for wanting this."

Jimmy nodded. He looked again in the direction of the doorway, back toward the kitchen. "I'm afraid Pheby's gonna be powerful vexed if I don't get that water to her soon. She's fixin' to make dye for a yellow dress."

"Ah."

"I don't want to mess it up for her."

"Yes. Certainly. You should go."

Jimmy began to leave. But then he turned back. He wasn't sure why; he knew it would be better if he said nothing more. But—filled by a tender impulse—he wavered for a moment, then spoke. "Thank you for showing me how to play those notes."

"Of course."

Having expressed this degree of tenderness, he added, "And ... the way you play the piano ... it's beautiful. I won't forget it."

Ben stepped forward, as if he was going to reply—but

before he could do so, Jimmy hurried from the room and rushed back to the kitchen.

JIMMY HAD NO SOONER FINISHED EXPLAINING to Pheby what had delayed him than it came time for him to go to the library for his daily lesson. But when he arrived in the library, only Bonnie was there, looking somewhat agitated.

"I'm afraid my brother won't be joining us today," she said. "He's not feeling well."

Jimmy looked surprised.

"From time to time my brother suffers from ... I suppose you might call them spells ... dark moods. I believe they come to him as a result of things that happened to him while he was fighting in the war."

"I reckon he has memories about losing his leg."

"Yes," Bonnie said. "But you see, he had other losses. It wasn't just his leg. In some ways the other losses were the more ruinous for him. So you see, you must always be kind to him."

Jimmy nodded, but said nothing.

"However, you must also maintain proper decorum at all times. My brother is not skilled at knowing what others think or feel. I'm afraid in your case he might misconstrue certain kindnesses as being something more than they are." She looked at Jimmy to see if he was following her. "Do you understand?"

Jimmy was fairly sure that he understood. But he didn't want her to know he did. He shook his head. "No, ma'am."

"I'm just saying ... be nice to him ... but not too ... well, intimate."

"You want me to be nice ... but not too nice?"

"Yes." She nodded. "That's more or less right." She moved to the atlas table. "You see, he's not like other men. He has certain ideas—about intimacy—that are ... I guess the best word for it is—'confused.'"

Jimmy could see how much Bonnie was struggling to explain

without saying directly what she meant. He decided to give her some help that would steer her away from himself. He said, "Pheby told me Massa Ben lost a slave, Elijah, in the war."

"Yes, indeed he did." Bonnie's face showed she was startled by this change in the direction of the conversation. But she quickly recovered. "Poor Elijah. He was much loved ...." She paused a moment, then added, "By all of us. It was a terrible tragedy."

"Is that the reason for Massa Ben's dark moods?"

"Well ... yes ... partly." She hesitated again before continuing. "And you see, it doesn't help matters that you remind him ... indeed, you remind us all ... of Elijah, in certain ways."

"Me?"

"Yes. I'm afraid it's not easy to explain. It has partly to do with how you look. Elijah was quite handsome. But also partly to do with another quality Elijah had. He was ... I'm not sure how to put it ... sensitive ... in certain ways. You, of course, are more than that. But you do have a sympathetic manner, at least from time to time. I'm afraid my brother interprets that as a sign of amenability. I don't know how else to explain it."

"What does he think I'm sympathetic to?"

"To the trials of life, I suppose."

Jimmy shook this off. "Most folks think I'm pretty tough," he said.

"Yes, that was my impression when I first saw you ... but since then I've come to know you better. You're not so very tough, are you?"

"More than you think."

Bonnie smiled. "Perhaps that is just the impression you like to give."

After that, they went on with their lesson. But Jimmy found it impossible to concentrate. All he could think about was that he had to do something about Ben Crenshaw. He still had no idea what that should be.

27

"HIS EYES ARE SO BLUE!"

Before Cato left Camp Woods the next day, Jack Robinson introduced him to Joe Bird, the Shawnee man who'd rescued him from the cave. Joe's skin was similar in color to Cato's skin, but his thick black hair had none of the curliness of Cato's. He wore it straight and parted in the middle. His demeanor was so gentle that he radiated serenity—yet his eyes were dark and piercing, with an intensity that made it clear he was not a passive man. He wore buckskin leggings attached to his moccasins, forming a kind of boot. The soft moccasins made no sound when he approached, and Cato easily understood how such a man could scout the woods unseen.

Cato thanked him for what he'd done. Joe, in turn, said it was all due to Oscar.

"The horse showed great bravery," he said. "To kill the snake."

Cato, Jack, and Joe all turned their attention to Oscar, petting him. Joe leaned into Oscar's ear and whispered, "You are not colorful, strong one, but you are full of courage."

When it came time for Cato to bid farewell to Jack, they stood staring at each other sheepishly. Cato felt he couldn't display the full measure of emotion he felt—not in front of Joe. He assumed Jack felt constrained in the same way. And so, after an awkward hesitation, they settled on clasping their hands on each other's forearms. They held their hands together as long as they dared, gazing into each other's eyes the whole time, reliving the moments of intimacy they'd shared the night before. Cato's eyes fluttered just as they had when Jack leaned over him to look out the window on the train.

"You have your drawing of me," Cato said. "I wish I had something to remember you by."

"How about this?"

And then, to his surprise, Jack leaned in and kissed him straight on the lips. Cato could not suppress a surprised squeal —even as his eyes darted from side to side, looking at Jack's brilliant blue eyes, and trying to ascertain how closely Joe was watching them.

Cato was filled with a complex emotion. He was ashamed—and yet he was also ashamed of being ashamed. He couldn't control the paradox of what he felt. Finally, his chagrin at being ashamed overwhelmed the shame itself, and in an impulsive burst of affection he put his hand around Jack's neck, pulled him closer, and pressed them both deeper into the kiss. Putting out of his mind what Joe might think, Cato thrust his tongue into Jack's mouth.

Jack, to his credit, didn't hesitate to respond in kind. He, too, put a hand behind Cato's head, and stroked his hair, while hugging him with the other arm, until it felt like there were no boundaries between them. Cato felt Jack's hand slide down his back and land on his butt. But then Cato knew he couldn't bear to continue—not without more, not under these circumstances —and so he abruptly pushed himself away.

When they looked up, it was evident that Joe had been watching them. He tilted his head, and raised an eyebrow, as if he was observing a strange phenomenon. But then he scratched his chin, smiled, and said, "You do not look alike, but I think you must be brothers."

"Yes," Jack said. "We are much like brothers."

Joe nodded. "Close."

"Very close," Jack said.

"Joe," Cato said, "I'd like to go. Will you take me to my buggy?"

"Yes, if you're ready. Lead your horse and follow me."

Cato went to Oscar, took his reins, and began to lead him away. When they were twenty yards along, Cato turned and shouted back to Jack, "Farewell, Private."

"Keep clear of them Rebs!" Jack yelled in reply.

JOE GUIDED the way out of camp, walking in front of Cato. But when they got to the edge of the camp, he dropped back and walked at Cato's side. As Joe drew near, Cato became aware of his scent, which was earth-like, a pleasant woody dampness. Cato had been struck by how gracefully Joe moved through the physical world. He was tall and muscular, but his light-footedness and measured way of walking gave him an ethereal quality, as if he floated when he walked.

"Jack told me your journey will take you to Cave City," Joe said.

"I'm going there just till the Rebs pass. Then I'm going to Bowling Green."

"I hid your buggy behind a pair of tall hemlocks. Only men with keen eyes will see it there." He paused and added with a deadpan expression. "So it should be safe."

Cato smiled at the innuendo. "How far is it?"

"It's half an hour's walk."

"Thank you. You've been very kind to me."

Joe's forehead furrowed. "I've been watching the Confederate Army. They're marching under orders from General Chalmers. They haven't reached Cave City yet. But they will soon. So you must be careful. Jack said that when they come to Munfordville, there'll be a battle."

"What do the Rebs want with Munfordville?" Cato asked.

"It's where the railroad crosses the Green River. That bridge is one of the largest bridges in Kentucky. Both the Rebs and the Union want to control it."

"I see," Cato said. "So you'll warn Jack and the others if the Rebs come?"

"Yes," Joe said. "That's my mission."

"You don't wear a uniform. Are you a soldier?"

"No—but I bring the Union Army military information about the Confederate Army."

"That sounds dangerous."

"Perhaps." Joe shrugged. "But don't worry. No one ever sees me."

Cato smiled. "I believe it." Then he added, "I've been wondering ... why did you hide my buggy?"

"Jack thought you might lose it if the Rebs came before you left the camp. So I moved it."

Cato was pleased to know that Joe and Jack had discussed his safety. He wondered how close they were. "Do you know Jack well?"

Joe shook his head. "I haven't known him long. He arrived at the camp three days ago. He told me he had just returned from Chicago."

"Yes," Cato said. "I met him on the train from Chicago to Cairo."

Joe cocked his head. "So you just met him as well?"

"Yes—last week."

"I'm puzzled." Joe wrinkled his forehead. "Your fondness for each other is peculiar."

He wasn't sure how to respond to this comment. The only thing he could think to do was to explain it by way of Jack's upbringing. He said, "Jack comes from Indiana. He's very sweet-natured."

Joe frowned.

"Why do you make that face?" Cato asked.

"The word 'Indiana.' I find it strange how white people have named their states. They know that 'Indiana' means 'land of Indians.' But it seems they do not know that the entire country is the land of Indians."

"You're right," Cato admitted. Then he asked, "Don't other states have Indian names too?"

"Yes," Joe said. "But I don't think white people even know the meaning of those names. 'Illinois' means 'tribe of superior men.' 'Kansas' means 'people of the south wind.' 'Oklahoma' means 'red people.' But the whites in these states do not honor the native people."

"No," Cato said. "I suppose that's true." Then he added, "They don't honor the Negro people either."

Joe nodded. They walked on for a while, then Joe asked, "Did you mean that men in Indiana kiss each other?"

"No," Cato said. "That's not what I meant. I suppose I meant that his family must be naturally affectionate."

"Shawnee men do not kiss each other on the lips," Joe said. He spoke without judgment in his voice. "But as you see, I'm often surprised by how white men behave."

"Me, too," Cato said.

Joe looked fixedly at him. "That's what I thought. You're not white, are you?"

"Well ... I'm partly white," Cato said.

Joe's eyes softened. "I noticed the tan color of your skin, but I didn't know exactly what it meant."

"My father's white. My mother was not. Most of my life I was a slave."

Joe stopped walking. He turned and put his hand on Cato's shoulder. "You were a slave—and yet you wish to keep going south. Why do you take this risk?"

"I'm looking for someone—I'm looking for a friend who was kidnapped."

"Why would someone kidnap your friend?"

"My friend is dark-skinned. He was snatched in Chicago by men with guns—to be sold back into slavery."

"I'm sorry."

"I miss him. I'm very close to him."

Joe cocked his head again. "Close, like with Jack?"

"Closer," Cato said—and he raised his eyebrows meaningfully. "After Bowling Green, I'm going on to Chattanooga. I have reason to believe that the men who took my friend stopped at Carlson's stable in Chattanooga. That's the only clue I have to go on. I hope someone at Carlson's can tell me where they took my friend after that."

Joe was silent for a while as he digested this. Then he continued walking. Finally, he asked, "May I tell you a confidence?"

"Of course."

"I think I would also like to be as a brother ..." He swallowed hard. "... to Jack Robinson."

Cato said nothing as he pondered Joe's meaning. The only explanation he could think of was that Joe's inclinations in matters of intimacy might be the same as his and Jack's and Jimmy's. When Cato and Jimmy first met, it had surprised Cato to discover that there was another man in the world who was attracted to men. But now Cato had met two such men, in Jimmy and Jack. It did not seem impossible that Joe Bird might make it three. He'd begun to feel that an invisible hand had been guiding him to these encounters. Or perhaps he'd been guided toward these chance meetings by his own impulses.

He wondered if he might be ascribing his own feelings to a man who'd been raised in a culture very different from his own. For the Shawnee, the notion of being like a brother might have another meaning. So he was cautious in how he responded. He said, "Do you mean you want to be close with Jack?"

"Yes." Joe nodded. "I would like that—but he doesn't feel the same about me as he does about you."

Cato's face showed his surprise. "How do you know?"

"Because he has never kissed me on the lips."

"Oh," Cato said. Then he laughed.

"Why do you laugh?"

"Well ... I think if what you want is for Jack to kiss you, you should tell him."

"That is not right." Joe scowled. "How can one ask a man such a thing?"

"I'm sure Jack won't be offended if you tell him you want to be his brother."

Joe's eyes, which had been so intense, suddenly looked like the eyes of a puppy. "Because of his sweet nature?"

"Not just because of that. Did you ever think he might feel the same way about you?"

"No." Joe shook his head gravely. "I don't think so."

"Why?"

Joe walked for several paces, staring at the ground. He seemed hesitant to speak. But finally he said, "Jack is very handsome."

"Yes," Cato agreed. "And what does that matter? You're handsome, too."

"But I'm Shawnee."

"So what? I'm sure Jack doesn't care about such things. I'm not white. That didn't matter to him."

"But you're very light-skinned. Perhaps he didn't realize your race," Joe said.

"If he didn't know," Cato said, "it's because he doesn't care about such things."

"I hope that's true," Joe said.

"I'd bet Jack feels the same way about everyone," Cato said. "Regardless of race."

Joe tilted his head. "As for me," he said, "I do not hold a bad opinion of any race. I think it is good that men are not all the same. My people say it is not necessary for eagles to be crows."

"Yes," Cato agreed. "Some men are different." He assumed

Joe was talking about race. But then he wondered if he might have meant something else. He looked searchingly at Joe. "So are you the same as other men?"

Joe again stopped walking and looked at the ground. When he finally looked up at Cato, his eyes were plaintive. He said, "The Great Spirit did not make me the same as other men."

Cato reached out and touched Joe's arm. "I understand. I am not the same either."

Joe's eyes fluttered nervously. "I've never been able to speak about this."

Cato smiled. He understood the excitement of finding a kindred soul. He put his arm around Joe's shoulder. "Let's keep walking," he said. "You can tell me anything."

They walked for several minutes before Joe, with sudden animation, said, "Since I met Jack Robinson, I have dreamed about him. And I've wondered what it is he dreams of."

Cato said, "I understand."

"You see, I like him so much. I cannot stop thinking about him."

After a moment, Cato said, "You should tell him. I think he would want to know this. Jack is not the same as other men either."

"Truly?" Joe was buoyed by this. "But he does not seem different at all. He seems so ordinary."

Cato nodded. "It was a surprise to me, too."

"You mean he is two-spirit?"

"Yes," Cato said.

"Oh, Cato. I can hardly look into his eyes. His eyes are so blue!"

"Yes," Cato said, laughing again. "He's beautiful."

Joe smiled broadly. His face, with its pronounced cheekbones, had until then exhibited an imperial and serious air. But now he showed the face of a boy. It was clear he was eager to express his feelings.

"Oh," Joe said. "And his legs!"

Cato giggled. "Which you can see, because he wears such a tight uniform."

"Yes!" Joe said. "It clings to him. It's flattering, I think."

"But he does not realize any of this," Cato said. "Which is what makes him so fetching. Because he doesn't know his own beauty."

"No," Joe said. "He does not."

"And so," Cato said. "You must tell him how you feel. I'm sure he won't mind if you tell him."

"But what can I say?"

"Just what you said to me—that you wonder what he dreams at night."

"Yes ... but ... that is not the part that is difficult."

"Tell him what you think about his eyes."

"Really?"

"Yes. Then he'll know you like him in the way that I like him."

Joe wrinkled his forehead. "You say you like him the way that I do, yet you don't seem bothered by how I feel."

"I'm not. I like Jack, but I care about my friend who was kidnapped much more."

"So you won't mind if I tell Jack how I feel?"

"No. I think you should."

"But what if he's offended?"

"How could he be? He'll be flattered. And if he likes you in the way that you like him, he'll find a way to let you know."

"But what if he doesn't like me that way?"

"Then he'll let you know that, too. But he'll be kind."

Joe shook his head. "If he doesn't like me, I'll have to spend my life alone."

Cato suppressed the urge to roll his eyes. He'd never thought of himself as being experienced with men, but compared to Joe he really was. "You shouldn't put so much weight on his feelings. He's only one man."

Joe again shook his head. He said earnestly, "Desire has rooted in my heart. I cannot pull out the roots without injury."

Cato rubbed Joe's shoulder. "I understand," he said. "But there are other men besides Jack."

"Have you met such men?"

"All my life I've been guided toward like-minded people—as if by chance. Look at us. Did we really meet by chance? I've been wondering if there is something that guides us."

"The Great Spirit."

"The Great Spirit would not want you to be alone."

"How can you know that?" Joe said. "Some men are alone. Even ordinary men are alone—and I am not ordinary."

"No." Cato shook his head. "You are not ordinary. All the more reason I think you will find someone special. But you cannot know where or when you'll find him. It could be anyone. It might not be Jack."

"But Jack is the one who's entered my dreams. Why should it not be him?"

"Because Jack is a soldier. The war is on. It might not be easy for you to be together."

"What does it matter if it's easy?" Joe asked. "You should know this. You have told me that you and your friend are slaves. You have told me that your friend has been kidnapped. You have told me that you are going south to find him—even in all this danger—even with all these white people who would stop you if they knew the truth. You do not choose easy!"

"You're right," Cato said. "I just mean you can't know what to expect. You might meet someone besides Jack. You said you've only just met him."

"How long did you know your friend, before you ... uh ... before you ..."

"Before we kissed?"

Joe nodded.

"Many months. Almost a year."

Joe's eyes were wide with curiosity. "How did it happen?"

"It happened when his dog died. My friend was very sad—and he came to see me that night. And we went to a spot hidden in the woods. And I sat next to him to comfort him." Cato could remember the moment as if it were yesterday. "And then something happened between us. It came without either of us speaking. It was as if we both just knew. And we got very ... stimulated ... all at once."

"What's your friend's name?"

"Jimmy."

"I suppose he's strong and good-looking."

"Mighty strong," Cato said. "And mighty good-looking. I miss him. Being with Jack only made me miss him more. I can't explain it. What happened between Jack and me was just by chance. It wasn't like that with Jimmy. He means the world to me."

"I'm sorry you lost him. It's terrible what white men do to others."

"I don't know if I'll ever find him." As he said this, Cato put his head in his hands.

Now it was Joe who rubbed Cato's shoulder. "You're my friend, Cato. I've never had such a friend. I think you're right. You and I didn't meet by chance."

Cato looked up. "Then you feel it, too?"

Joe turned to look at Oscar, who throughout their conversation had been walking steadily behind them, even though Cato had long since dropped the reins. "I think the Great Spirit acted through the horse. Animals are in harmony with Spirit. Much more than men. Oscar guided me to you."

Cato looked around at Oscar, then stepped back to take hold of his reins. "Yes ... Oscar has guided me, as well."

"I think Oscar will guide you to Jimmy, too," Joe said. "The Great Spirit will show him the way."

"Do you think so?"

Joe nodded.

"I hope you're right. I don't want to live my life without him."

"I'm jealous," Joe said. "I wish I had a love like that."

"Don't give up hope. "After a moment, Cato added, "You're right about us being friends. I've never had a friend like you, either."

"Perhaps we are like brothers, then," Joe said.

Cato smiled. "Yes ... but ... not like ... like ... "

"Like brothers who kiss?"

"Well ..." Cato shrugged.

"It's all right that it is so, Cato. You're a comely man, but it is Jack Robinson who's in my heart."

"As Jimmy is in mine."

"So we really will be like brothers, then."

"Yes."

They continued walking without speaking. As they approached the spot where he'd hidden the buggy, Joe abruptly stopped walking and put his hand out to stop Cato and Oscar from walking as well.

"Wait!" he said.

"What's wrong?"

Joe cocked his head. "I heard something." He looked back at Oscar. "Quickly," he said. "Bring the horse and follow me now into the woods."

Joe led them into the woods. Then he said, "Wait here. Someone is coming. I must go and see who it is. I'll return as soon as I can." And with that he headed deeper into the woods, walking quickly, but crouching to lower his height. He made barely any sound as he went. After a few minutes, he came back. "There are Rebel soldiers ahead."

Cato flinched. "A lot of them?"

"No," Joe said. "It is only a few men. They're clearing trees."

"What? Why?"

"They do this to make way for the Army. It means they're

about to advance. I must go back to the camp and warn the others." He pointed. "Your buggy is just ahead. Come quickly."

When they got to the buggy, Joe quickly helped Cato harness Oscar, then he stood back while Cato climbed into the driver's seat. "I'll remember your advice, Cato," Joe said. "And I'll tell Jack Robinson how I feel."

"Jack will be a lucky man," Cato said. Cato raised his hands to urge Oscar forward, but before he departed he asked, "Do you think we'll meet again?"

Joe pointed up with his finger. "That is not for us to know." Then he added, "But I hope that we do."

"Me, too," Cato said. He touched his hand to his mouth and blew a kiss to Joe. And with that he and Oscar headed south, and back into a world of unknown dangers.

28

"WHY'D HE HAVE TO GO AND DO A THING LIKE THAT?"

Over the next two weeks, Jimmy continued his search for Ben Crenshaw's sailboat, but he found no boat of any kind. He asked Pheby, Poky, and Little Joe about the boat. They all believed it was moored somewhere along the river—but none of them knew where.

Then one Sunday afternoon, when Isaac was working in the garden, Jimmy asked him, "Do you know anything about Massa Ben's boat?"

"You mean that sailboat?"

"Yes. The *Wentworth,* he calls it."

"He had to loan it out—on account of he lost a bet."

"A bet?"

"Yeah. Do you believe that?"

"Then where is it?"

Isaac was digging out potatoes with a small spade. "It's a long story," he said. He stopped to lean on the spade handle while he explained. "Downriver a ways is Mulberry Grove plantation—owned by a man named Winkler. Winkler's got a married daughter who lives in Savannah. Every season Winkler likes to send his daughter a gift of some duck and quail by boat.

He boasted to Massa Ben that his slaves could row those dead birds down the river so fast that they'd still be warm when they got there. Massa Ben said that couldn't be true. He said it might be true if the birds were to go down the river in the *Wentworth*. That's when Winkler decided he wanted to have a race between his oarsmen in his rowboats and Massa Ben in the *Wentworth*. Massa Ben agreed, so they bet on it. Massa Ben wagered the *Wentworth* as a one-year loan if he lost. I guess those Mulberry Grove boys were as fast as Winkler claimed they were. They won and the sailboat lost. So now the sailboat's down there at Mulberry Grove on loan for a year."

"Why'd he have to go and do a thing like that?" Jimmy shook his head. "Wagering a boat on a race? That man's got nothin' but dumb pride."

Isaac lifted the spade and shoved it into the ground again. "Massa Ben said it was bad luck. He said the wind died down just when he was about to win. I reckon you can't count on the wind."

"When is the boat coming back?"

"The race was last summer. So Winkler's still got it for another half a year at least."

"Damn it!" Jimmy pounded his hands together.

"How come you care so much about that boat?" Isaac asked.

Jimmy didn't see the harm in telling Uncle Isaac about his plan. He figured he might very well need Isaac's help at some point. He said, "I told you I'm fixin' to run away."

"Yeah, so?"

"So I need that boat for my plan."

"What plan?"

"I'm fixin' to sail out of here."

"Sail?" Uncle Isaac stopped digging and raised his eyebrows. "Sail to where? New York City?"

"No, not that far. All I've got to do is reach the Union boats. The Yankees have boats right off the coast of Savannah. They've got a blockade."

"Says who?"

"Says Ben Crenshaw."

"Yankees, huh?"

"That's right. And if you reach those boats, according to Little Joe, the Yankees'll take you in."

"They'll take you in? And then what?"

"And then you're free!"

"Just like that?" Uncle Isaac was skeptical.

"Near as I can tell."

Uncle Isaac tilted his head. "You're sayin' that's all there is to it?"

"Yep."

"All right. Let's say it's like you say." Uncle Isaac rested one hand on the spade handle and scratched his chin with the other. "You got to know how to sail if you want to do something like that. You know anythin' about sailin'?"

"No."

"Well, then, how're you gonna sail?"

"I'm gonna learn," Jimmy said.

Uncle Isaac grimaced. "It don't matter anyway—cause there ain't gonna be no sailboat for another six months."

"I can't wait that long," Jimmy said.

Uncle Isaac returned to digging. "Well ... I reckon if those Winkler slaves can row like the dickens, maybe you could get one of 'em to row you out of here."

Jimmy held up his hand. "I don't want any help from them."

"No? So you're gonna do it all on your own?"

Jimmy nodded.

"I see. How come you don't want help? Seems to me it ain't only Massa Ben's got pride."

"It's not because of pride," Jimmy said. "It's on account of it's too dangerous. I don't want anybody to get in trouble."

"Yeah, well ... supposin' somebody was to say he wants to help you—trouble or no."

"Somebody like who?"

"Somebody like me."

"You? Why would you do that?"

"'Cause you're a pain to have around. I'd be happy to see you finally go back to where you come from." Isaac's eyes twinkled.

"What?"

"Look here, Jacob. How come you gotta think like that? Can't a body want to help you just because it's what one man does for another?"

"Sorry." Jimmy hung his head. "I'm not used to anyone looking out for me. Most of my life I've had to look out for myself."

"Yeah, well, the way I figure—when you looking out for somebody else, you looking out for yourself, too." Uncle Isaac rubbed his hands together. "You know, I might like to row out of here myself. And two can row faster than one."

Jimmy looked doubtful. "You mean that? You'd come with me?"

"Sure."

"Even with you bein'—you know—old?"

"Look here! That's the main reason I want to get out of this place. If I don't get out of here now, I never will. And besides, just because I'm old doesn't mean I'm lily-livered or weak-kneed." He glanced down at the holes he'd dug in the garden. "Speaking of which, why don't you bend down here and help me pull out some of these tubers?"

Jimmy knelt and did as he was asked. Then he wondered, "Where can we get a boat?"

Uncle Isaac got down on his knees as well. "If we're talkin' about a rowboat—there's a rowboat sitting down by the mill."

"How can that be? I've been looking for boats. I never saw a boat by the mill."

"That's 'cause you can't see it."

"Why not?"

"You know how part of the mill sticks out over the water?"

Jimmy nodded.

"They keep the boat hidden underneath there. They slid it under the mill and tied it up so you can't see it."

Jimmy's eyes lit up. "So we could go and grab that boat any time we want?"

"Most likely."

"That's all I needed to know."

"Now, listen here, son, don't you go tryin' to do anything on your own. You're gonna need two to row fast ... and besides, I've already been downriver, so I know what to expect."

"You've been downriver on a boat?"

"Oh, yes! I've rowed boatloads of this and boatloads of that downriver for the Crenshaws at one time or another: cotton, rice, cider, you name it. Me and Poky usually go together."

"So what's it like down there?"

"Well ... you got islands in the river, and of course if you go too far you're gonna find paddy-rollers watching the channel. I suppose you're gonna find Reb soldiers on guard now, too. When we go, we've always got to have a pass."

"How about at night? Did you ever go at night?"

"Nuh-uh—just during the day." Uncle Isaac thought for a moment, then he added, "There was a time it was foggy. I reckon that fog was as close as I came to going at night. The fog made it mighty risky. It was so bad you couldn't see the shore or the channel."

"But if there was fog that would mean the paddy-rollers and Rebs couldn't see us either, right?"

"Maybe."

Jimmy grinned. "I think a foggy night would be a perfect time to go."

"Maybe. But like I say, you take a chance. A body could row straight into the paddy-rollers real easy—or straight into the ground, for that matter."

"So what? We won't be going fast. If we run aground, we'll just heave 'er out and keep goin.'"

Once again, Isaac said, "Maybe."

"Look here, if you don't want to go ..."

"I'm not sayin' that. I'm just sayin' we're gonna have to be careful, and have a plan for when something goes wrong. Last time I ran away, it seemed as if everything went wrong." Isaac stood and picked up the spade again. Then he turned back to Jimmy and said, "I'll tell you this—two heads are better 'n one —especially when you gotta make quick decisions."

Jimmy nodded. "OK, then, when should we do it?"

Uncle Isaac pursed his lips. "See, that's just it. You want to go quick. That won't do. I gotta give it some thought. There's a lot to ponder. We've got to decide what to bring, what not to bring, when to go, how far to go, what to do when we get there. Also ..." He paused and looked around. "It'll mean saying good-bye to everyone here. I'm gonna have to think on it some."

"OK," Jimmy said. "But don't take too long. It's already been too long that I've been away from home."

"I know, son." Uncle Isaac thrust the spade in the ground again. "You're young and rarin' to go. But for now, you be patient. I'm gonna see about gettin' you back to your people. But I wanna be sure you get there safe and sound."

Despite Jimmy's impatience, he knew it was smart to take time to plan his escape. The Crenshaws had just begun to teach him how to write. If he knew how to write, he thought, he'd be able to write to Dorothy Holland in Chicago, who, in turn, would know how to reach Cato. When he lay in bed at night, he realized that finding a way to communicate with Cato was just as important as escaping. Maybe more so.

Whenever Jimmy tried to imagine what Cato was doing during his absence, he always came to the same conclusion: he assumed that Cato was doing all he could to find him. But what he was actually doing, Jimmy couldn't guess. He hoped that whatever it was, he wasn't putting himself in danger. He worried that the longer he was gone, the more risks Cato might take. That, as much as anything else, made him eager to make his escape as soon as he could.

"OK, Uncle," he said. "You tell me when you're ready."

"Don't worry. I will," Isaac said.

Jimmy pulled several underdeveloped potatoes from the ground and held them up to inspect them. "These are kind of scraggly."

"Put 'em back," Isaac said. "They ain't ready yet."

Jimmy did as he was told. Then he asked, "You know anyone who can write a letter?"

"You mean someone besides the Crenshaws or Eppley?"

"I need someone I can trust."

"Well, there's a black preacher named Andrew at a plantation downriver who knows how to read. I know that 'cause he reads from the Bible every Sunday. He holds services in a barn down there. Folks come from all around to hear him. Years ago, I used to go down there on Sundays. But I haven't been in a long time."

Jimmy didn't like the idea of a preacher, but he could hardly be choosy. "OK, but can he write?"

"I think so." Uncle Isaac scratched his head. "Don't readin' and writin' go together?"

"Not necessarily," Jimmy said. "They've been teachin' me to read, but I only just started to learn how to write."

"Who do you want to write to?"

Jimmy looked up at Isaac, who was still standing and leaning on the spade. "My sweetheart," he said.

"Oh, I see." Isaac kneeled down to help Jimmy replant the young potatoes. "I suppose you want to let her know how you 'bout to come flyin' back into her arms right quick."

Jimmy smiled. "More or less."

"I suppose she's real pretty."

"Absolutely," Jimmy said.

"Uh-huh, it's no wonder you're rarin' to go." Isaac's face suggested he was picturing a lurid reunion between Jimmy and his sweetheart.

"So then," Jimmy said. "How can I find this preacher?"

"That's easy," Isaac said. "All you got to do is go down to that barn where he preaches on Sunday morning."

"Where's it at?"

"It's downriver four or five miles. Not far."

"Will you take me there?"

"I reckon. But first we'll need to get passes. It used to be, they'd always give me one when I asked—seein' as how it was for church. But I don't know how they're gonna feel about you. They're gonna wonder why you got religious all of a sudden."

"I'll tell them I want to see what it's all about. I'll tell them I asked you to take me. That's just about the truth anyway."

"I suppose that'll do."

"Can we go next Sunday?"

Uncle Isaac laughed. "Boy, you're just chompin' at the bit to write that gal, huh? Well, I don't blame you. All right. We'll go next Sunday morning—if the Crenshaws give you a pass."

29

"TO KEEP HIS SOUL INTACT"

Following Joe Bird's advice, Cato didn't wait for the Confederate Army to show up. Instead of going to Cave City, he made his way directly to Mammoth Cave. He hid the buggy, then brought Oscar down to the same spot in the cave where he and Dorothy had visited with Walter McNish earlier in the year. The next morning he led Oscar out of the cave and back up to the road. Everywhere he looked he saw ruts and damage—the aftermath of trampling feet, horses' hooves, and wagon wheels. It was clear that the Confederates had passed. He decided he would hitch up the buggy and set out immediately for Bowling Green to get advice from Walter McNish, before he continued to follow Hogan's trail in Chattanooga.

After traveling all day in a southwest direction along the Louisville Road, they arrived just after dusk in Bowling Green. Cato found a stable to board Oscar, then checked in at the Marshall House hotel, where he, Dorothy, and Jimmy's brother and sister, Sammy and Ella, had stayed on their journey to meet Jimmy in Chicago the previous spring. It was there that they'd first met Walter McNish, who regularly took guests of the hotel on tours to Mammoth Cave. When Cato inquired at the front desk about contacting Mr. McNish for a tour, the clerk gave him directions to his house, which was nearby.

The next morning, Cato drove to the McNish residence. When he knocked on the door, it was Mrs. McNish who answered. In the spring, because they'd been traveling incognito, Dorothy and Cato had introduced themselves to Mrs. McNish as Mr. and Mrs. Fitzwilliam Dawson. That had been Cato's first experience passing as white. Later, Dorothy told Walter McNish their true names—but Cato didn't know if Mr. McNish had ever told their real names to his wife. So he again introduced himself as Fitzwilliam Dawson and reminded her that they'd met the previous April. Mrs. McNish remembered him and asked about his wife.

Cato decided not to explain that Dorothy was actually married to his brother. Instead, he merely said that she was in Chicago. "She's well," he added. Then he shuffled on the doorstep and asked, "I wonder if I might have an audience with Mr. McNish?"

"Yes, of course. Do come in. I'm quite sure my husband will be glad to see you," she said. She pointed to a room off the entry foyer. "Make yourself at home in the parlor while I fetch him." She left to get her husband.

When Walter McNish entered the parlor, he rushed to shake Cato's hand. "It's very nice to see you, my boy. But I didn't expect to see you here in the South again!"

"I didn't expect to return so soon," Cato replied.

Mr. McNish could tell from Cato's anxious state that something was wrong. "Come, sit down," he said. "And tell me what has happened."

Cato spent the next half hour relaying his story. He began with Hogan's kidnapping of Jimmy from Chicago. He told of his train ride to Cairo and his meeting with Mrs. MacMurrough, and of his subsequent encounter with the Union spy, Mrs. Langdon, on the steamboat from Cairo to Paducah. He told how he'd fallen off his horse while sheltering from a storm in a cave—and how he'd been knocked unconscious, and then rescued. Without giving all the details, he recounted his stay with the Union Army at Munfordville while he recovered. He then mentioned how two nights before he'd hidden overnight in Mammoth Cave while the Confederate Army marched past Cave City on their way to Munfordville.

"There were many bats in the cave," Cato said. "They frightened my horse."

"Ah, yes. You're lucky the soldiers didn't come into the cave—bat droppings are used for gunpowder. They're worth a dollar a pound, I'm told. But I suppose the Rebs were in too great a hurry to bother with the bats this time."

They spoke about their mutual friend Erastus Hicks. Mr. McNish and Erastus Hicks were old friends. Both men were Quakers, which was why Erastus had trusted Mr. McNish to serve as an intermediary to ferry confidential letters between himself and Dorothy and Cato.

Cato told Mr. McNish that Erastus had given him a generous gift before leaving Chicago for Philadelphia—and that he was prepared to buy Jimmy back from Mr. Hogan if Mr. Hogan could be found.

"But now so much time has passed," Cato said. "I think Jimmy's probably already been sold. But I'm determined to find him."

"And Dorothy?" Mr. McNish asked. "Is she still in Chicago?"

"Yes," Cato said. "She's living in Chicago with my brother, William. They were married, you know. But William took an oath of loyalty to the Union, so they're unable to return to the South until after the war."

"What a state the world has come to," Mr. McNish said.

"No one seems to know what to expect next."

"Indeed."

"Can I still send a letter to Dorothy from here without fear of Confederate censorship?"

"I doubt it," Mr. McNish said. "One day the U.S. post office is closed and a Confederate post office is opened. The next week, the Confederate office closes and the U.S. office opens. Then it goes back the other way. It changes so quickly, you cannot rely on sending a letter north."

"That's what I feared," Cato said.

"But—as it happens, I'm going on a journey to Philadelphia in a week's time."

"To see Erastus?" Cato's voice rose with enthusiasm.

"The main purpose of my journey is to attend a meeting of the Society of Friends. In June, I was part of a delegation that called on President Lincoln. We made an appeal to him for emancipation. Unfortunately, he rejected our proposal. He said since he cannot even enforce the Constitution in the South, he doubted that a decree of emancipation would be any more effective." Mr. McNish threw up his hands to show his exasperation. "Now the members of my delegation are meeting again in Philadelphia to decide what to do next. We still hope he may be persuaded."

"I see."

"Of course, I expect to visit Erastus while I'm there. You may be sure of that. I'd also be happy to carry a letter for you. A letter mailed from Philadelphia should reach Dorothy in Chicago without obstruction."

"That would be wonderful," Cato said. "Could you also bring a letter from me to Erastus? It's almost every day that I've wished I could ask him for advice."

"I saw Erastus when I was there in June, of course. He mentioned how fond he'd become of you—and of your friend Jimmy. Erastus may be able to advise you, but I'm afraid I don't know what to suggest you do about finding Jimmy. It's such a difficult situation, since you don't know where he is."

"My last hope lies with Carlson's stable in Chattanooga," Cato said. "I was able to trace Hogan's movements to Gleason's stable in Paducah, Kentucky. Mr. Gleason told me that Hogan was headed to Chattanooga and that he'd referred Hogan to Carlson's stable. If Hogan stopped there, Mr. Carlson may be able to tell me where he went next."

"I certainly hope so," Mr. McNish said. "I'm an optimist by nature, Cato. I always believe goodness will prevail."

"Even now? With the war?"

"Well, I should think now is when we most need goodness. I don't know anyone, man or woman, who hasn't had their world turned upside down by this war. And to think they're fighting over an institution as abhorrent as slavery! It goes to show you how surprisingly different the hearts of men can be. But I believe light will always outshine the darkness, my boy. How can it not? There've been many dark days behind us, and I fear there will be such days ahead of us, too. But these are the times that call for faith. You must have faith, Cato. Only faith can assist you."

Cato had been sitting on the parlor sofa. Now he stood up. "You're right, Mr. McNish. The fact that I've managed to get as far as I have these past several weeks has shown me that. Erastus always taught me to turn my attention away from trouble and to put it on all that is good." He stepped to the parlor window to look out at Oscar, who was tied to a post in front of the house. "The horse I met has been one of the good things to come out of this situation. Truly, Mr. McNish, the love I've felt from my horse, Oscar, has kept me going."

"Erastus is right. This is what matters most in life. We must always look for good." McNish joined Cato at the window, gazing at the horse outside. "It's easy to let evil get the best of us. But it can never conquer goodness—not really. I don't want to suggest that you might not find your friend. But even if you can't find him right away, it's good that you have friendship—even that of a horse. Hold on to that. You can't know how long it will be until you find Jimmy or he finds you."

Cato turned away from the window. "I hadn't thought about Jimmy finding me," he said.

"Why not? It's possible, is it not?"

"How could he? I myself don't know where I'll end up from day to day."

"And yet, don't you imagine he's as determined as you are to achieve the same outcome?"

"Yes. I think he must be."

"And if you both are reaching for the same goal, does that not double the odds of success?"

"Yes. I suppose it must."

"Then keep your thoughts on that goal—and think, my boy, of the happiness that will be yours when you achieve it. What could be more wonderful than to find that which is lost? If life were only ever smooth and easy, I daresay we might have trouble discovering happiness."

Cato smiled. "You sound like Erastus."

"Well, he and I feel much the same about these things."

"It's like being with him again. It's been a long time since I was in the presence of a man who raises my hope for the world."

"I'm glad to know it," Mr. McNish said. "I only wish I were as good as Erastus at backing up my words with actions." McNish paused and looked at Cato hesitantly. Then he said, "You know, he's been out in the battlefield again."

"As a nurse?"

"Yes. He volunteered once before, you know. He served as long as he could. Then he quit for a while. 'To keep his soul intact,' as he put it. After that he went to Chicago, where, as you know, he met his friend, Mr. Frazza. But although he was happy with Mr. Frazza in Philadelphia, he felt he couldn't stand by without having another try at caring for the wounded." He paused. "And ... well ... I must tell you, Cato, that he was himself wounded. In the Second Battle of Bull Run at Manassas in Virginia."

"What?" Cato came up quickly to McNish and put out his hand, which McNish grabbed hold of. "Is he badly hurt?"

"Steady, boy. He's going to be all right. But I'm afraid ... well, the hard part is, due to his injury, it appears he won't be able to paint again. He's lost the use of his hand."

"No!" Cato squeezed McNish's arm, then stumbled to the sofa, collapsed onto it, and buried his head in his hands. After a few moments, he looked up and asked, "Why? Why should it be so? It would have been better if he'd lost his leg. But to lose painting? That's what he lives for!"

"Yes." McNish nodded sadly. "It has been a terrible blow. And I fear he ... he's been sorely dispirited by it. His friend Frazza has tried to comfort him. But it's been hard for Erastus to face this loss. And, I must tell you, it's given me much pain as well, Cato. I cannot bear to see anyone I love suffer. From the moment I saw you I was loath to tell you what had happened. But I think it is better that you know—especially since you're planning to write to him. You've been one of the great lights in his life, you know. As if you were his own son."

"Yes," Cato said. "I must write to him. I must remind him of everything he's taught me."

"I think it would do him a world of good," McNish said. "If he could hear good news from you."

"If only I could go with you. I would so like to see him. I would give anything to be able to help him in his recovery."

"Well, of course, I'd be happy to have you come with me."

Cato screwed up his face. "I can't go with you now." He shook his head violently. "I can't delay my search for Jimmy."

"No," McNish agreed. "I daresay you cannot. Nor would Erastus want you to. He puts much store in your happiness with Jimmy. The best thing you could do for him, in fact, is to find your friend—and then write to him all about your happiness when you do."

"But what about now? I must write to him now."

"Perhaps," McNish said. "But perhaps not." McNish sat down on the sofa next to Cato. "I've been trying to decide what I think is the best course. I know how important the truth is,

Cato. And yet, I fear that if Erastus hears about your trouble, it will drive him deeper into despair. He is a strong man. But even strong men cannot withstand repeated blows."

"But then, if you see him, surely you'll have to tell him what's happened to Jimmy."

"Yes, maybe. But if I see him I will be able to better judge how strong he is. If he's doing poorly, I may choose to delay telling him."

"Yes. I think you're right. It might be better to wait. I could write to him after I've found Jimmy."

"And then, perhaps, you'd also be able to visit him on your way back to Chicago. That would be the greatest tonic of all." McNish hesitated, then added, "You know, the last painting Erastus made before his injury was a painting of you. He said it was done from a sketch he made of you in Chicago."

"Yes," Cato said. "I remember the sketch."

"He told me the painting was a bit scandalous in certain aspects. He said it wasn't meant for the eyes of others. But then I reminded him that I studied anatomy with him at the university—and that I was hardly a delicate soul. So he showed it to me."

Cato was slightly embarrassed. But he asked, "What did you think of it?"

"It was an excellent likeness. I see that now, as I look at you. I have no doubt he'll want to share it with you when you visit."

"But how can I visit him if I don't find Jimmy?" Cato asked.

McNish took hold of Cato's arm and looked him in the eye. "That would be all the more reason to visit him. If the worst happens, my boy, you and Erastus will need to give each other strength."

By the time Cato had left, he'd decided to give Mr. McNish a letter to Dorothy but not a letter to Erastus. Having made that decision, since it was too late in the day to start for Chattanooga, he set about the task of writing to Dorothy. There was so much to tell her—but he didn't know how to put everything he felt into words. Dorothy was his best friend. She knew how close he was to Erastus. She loved Erastus herself. He had to tell her what had happened to their friend. She also knew how much he loved Jimmy. So he was sure she'd understand why he couldn't visit Erastus until he'd found Jimmy.

By visiting Mr. McNish, he'd lost a day in his pursuit of Jimmy's kidnapper. But after days of being on the road alone, he'd needed to talk with someone who knew the people he loved. Dorothy would understand that. So would Jimmy. Cato was certain that no one would ever love him as much as Jimmy loved him. Jimmy had once been willing to give up their relationship—and his own happiness—for Cato's sake. And as he recalled that, Cato's heart swelled with new determination. He would do anything, anything he could, to find his lover again.

30

"MY LIFE IS NOTHING BUT EMPTINESS!"

It was on the Saturday night before Jimmy's planned visit to meet the preacher Andrew that Little Joe came into the cabin and told Jimmy that he was wanted in the big house. "You better get up there right quick," Joe said. "Massa Ben says he needs your help."

"Help with what?"

Joe shrugged. "I don't know. He just told me to fetch you to help him."

"Am I supposed to put on my fancy clothes?"

"He didn't say," Joe said. "I doubt it. Just go as you are. He seemed in a hurry about it, whatever it is."

So Jimmy went as he was, dressed in his work clothes. He was tired and dirty, and resented being called in for some new task. When he arrived at the big house, he asked Jane the cook where he could find Ben.

"As far as I know," she said, "he's up in his room."

"His bedroom?"

Jane nodded. "Why? What do you want with him?"

"It's what he wants with me," Jimmy said. "He's called for me, and I have no idea why."

"Well, go up the stairs. His room is at the top of the stairs on the right."

"Where's Bonnie?"

"She's in her room—at the other end of the hall. The old massa's room is in between the two of 'em—but he's not home. He's gone down to the city."

"It seems Massa Crenshaw is hardly ever here," Jimmy said. "I've only seen him once since I got here."

"He's never here on weekends. He's got some gal down in the city. I don't know why he don't just bring her up here. He acts like his wife is still alive and he has to keep it all a secret."

"Maybe Missus Bonnie wouldn't approve," Jimmy said.

"You're right about that. She wouldn't. Neither would Massa Ben," Jane said. "But if they had any sense, they'd let him get on with his life. I reckon they both know what's what. Their father goes to Savannah every weekend. What do they think he's doin' down there? Conducting business? Ain't no business needs him to go down there every Saturday."

"Do you have any idea why Massa Ben wants to see me?"

"Nothin' good, I can tell you that." She gave Jimmy a strange look. "He's in one of them moods."

"You mean one of his dark moods? I heard about them."

"Yup, dark as I've seen. And what's more, he's been drinkin.' He was out riding right up till sunset. Then he came hobbling back in the house. He was clomping around in the foyer, so I went out there to see what he needed. But he just waved me away. Then he stomped into the parlor to pour himself a glass of whiskey. He drank it down fast, then sat himself at the piano and commenced to playin' that Swanee River song like a hot-blooded fool, like he was angry. Then he just quit playin' all of a sudden and got up. I watched him go up the stairs. The man had to hold onto the railing just to walk straight."

Jimmy nodded. "If I don't come down soon, would you come and knock on the door?"

"And say what?"

"Just make up some excuse."

Jane scowled. "Oh, I reckon I could do that."

"Thank you," Jimmy said. Then he left and made his way up the stairs carrying a candle. At the top, he knocked on Ben's door.

"Come in." Ben's voice was muffled.

Jimmy walked in. The room was dimly lit by an array of candles that sat on a bureau near the bed. Ben Crenshaw was sitting on the bed, in the process of taking off his boot. When he got it off, he tossed it against the wall.

"Jacob," he said. "Come in. I need your help."

Jimmy stepped closer. "What help do you need, massa?" His voice was wary.

"I hurt my knee getting off my horse," Ben said. "Unfortunately it was my good knee. I usually get undressed by myself. But the way my knee hurts, I can't bend well enough to do it. I need you to help me."

"You want me to help you undress?" Jimmy said this as if he was surprised, but he wasn't. He told himself to keep calm.

"Yes," he said. "Who else?"

Jimmy said, "What should I do?"

"Start by helping me with my shirt. Put down your candle and come and pull the sleeves off my shoulders. I've already unbuttoned it."

Jimmy set his candle on the bureau and stepped closer. He knew Ben could remove the shirt himself. He'd hurt his knee, not his arms. Jimmy was tempted to remark on this, but he held his tongue. He carefully slid the shirt off Ben's shoulders, pulled off each sleeve, then stepped back, holding the shirt awkwardly. Ben wore no undershirt.

Jimmy found himself staring at Ben's bare chest. He was startled by how white Ben's skin appeared. The whiteness was thrown into relief by the line of dark red hair running from his chest down to his navel and on to his waist.

"Now then," Ben said. "Put the shirt over there on that chair."

Jimmy did as directed.

"Now fetch my cane. It's by the chair. I need to stand up to get out of these pants."

Jimmy brought him his cane and helped him stand up.

Once he was standing, Ben indicated his pants. "Now, I've got to take these off." His forehead furrowed. "Hold me steady, while I let them down. Then I'll sit back on the bed so you can pull them free."

Jimmy nodded and wrapped his hand around Ben's torso to hold him steady.

Ben dropped his cane and used both hands to undo his belt. He let his pants fall to his knees, then sat back on the bed and extended his legs. Jimmy stepped around and pulled off both legs of the pants. Ben was left wearing only his underwear.

Ben said, "Now help me up again." Jimmy extended his arm. Ben grabbed it and stood up. Once he was standing, he said, "I need help with these, too." He indicated his underwear.

Jimmy's jaw clenched. "Are you fixin' to take those off?"

"Of course." Ben nodded. "That's how I sleep."

Jimmy grimaced. He wasn't prepared to see Ben naked. But he nodded his head anyway. "You want to do it the same way?"

"Yes, but I won't be comfortable unless you take off your shirt and pants first," Ben said.

"Me?" Jimmy was startled. "You want me to take off my clothes?" He took a step backward. "What for?"

"It won't be so embarrassing for me if I'm not the only one standing here naked."

"You don't need to be embarrassed," Jimmy said. "It's nothin' I haven't seen before."

Ben gave Jimmy a lopsided grin, then he blinked several times, as if he was thinking about what to say. "But I *would* be embarrassed," he said at last. "Besides, I want to see if you've kept yourself free of marks."

"Massa, I can tell you for sure, I haven't had any marks since the last time you looked."

"Show me," Ben commanded.

Jimmy didn't move. He wasn't sure what to do. Considering the punishments he'd seen other slaves receive for disobedience, he knew what he was risking if he refused. He was afraid of where Ben was headed. But he quickly decided he ought to wait to see how far Ben would take things--before he risked punishment.

"Go on and see for yourself," Jimmy mumbled in annoyance. He removed his shirt, then undid his belt and took off his pants, until he, too, was wearing only his underwear. He looked back toward the door. He wondered if enough time had passed for Jane to come knocking.

Ben made no attempt to disguise his fascination with Jimmy's body. He looked at him just as he'd done that first day in the meadow. His eyes traveled up and down. "Turn round," he said.

As he'd done in the meadow, Jimmy turned around.

"You're right," Ben said. "You're still as pure as ever." Just as he'd done in the meadow, he ran his hand down Jimmy's back. "Your skin is so smooth. It's remarkable." He let his hand come to rest on the top of Jimmy's buttock. "You know, my skin is just as smooth as yours in some places, but furry in others." He took a step backward, turning slightly, until he was facing Jimmy. "You can feel it, if you like."

Jimmy found himself looking at the body of the man in front of him—at his unexpectedly broad shoulders, at the gently curving mounds of his chest, which, though not muscled by labor, were supple, and downy with auburn hair. He gazed at the small hard dots of his nipples, at the lithe, arched curve of his lower back, at his milky skin. He'd never touched a white man in an intimate way. Despite himself, he felt a surge of curiosity.

He didn't know why it should be so. His sister, Ella, would

never understand. He knew the difference between himself and Ella had to do with his being a man. Being a man, he thought, made him susceptible to purely physical desire.

He resented the Crenshaws, but he was not indifferent to Ben Crenshaw's body. It didn't matter that Ben was white. Ben Crenshaw was, despite everything, a sweet-smelling red-haired man whose face was uncommonly beautiful, whose eyes were green and soft, and whose aristocratic physique was elegantly comely. When he glimpsed the man's well-shaped buttocks, Jimmy couldn't stop himself from taking a sharp breath, as the image sprang into his mind of plunging himself into the cleft.

Even so, he remained as still as he could. His nostrils widened slightly in response to a whiff of Ben's scent. He closed his eyes. He tried to control the images in his mind, which were pulling him toward desire. In the same instant, he recoiled. He was not, not under any circumstances, going to show Ben Crenshaw an iota of desire. Yet, he couldn't think how to control it. When his eyes opened, they fell upon Ben Crenshaw's groin, where he saw the undeniable swelling of Ben's penis.

Ben, too, was staring at Jimmy's groin. He was breathing heavily—and Jimmy could smell the alcohol on his breath. Jimmy turned sideways, hoping to shield his crotch from view, while he tried to rapidly fill his mind with unerotic images. He pictured Eppley—confident of the repugnant overseer's power to thwart desire. But it was no use. He couldn't hold on to Eppley's image, and meanwhile Ben moved his hand from Jimmy's back to his chest, and touched his nipple. The feel of Ben's fingers flitting across his nipple made Jimmy cry out. He realized that what came out of him was the exact sound Cato made when Jimmy touched him that way.

"Please, stop," he cried. "You cannot do this."

"Come now, Jacob," Ben said. "You must know it would break my heart to stop."

Jimmy glanced down at himself to verify what he feared. A trace of elongation had begun in his own underwear. "Please," he said. "It's not because I feel nothing. You can see that for yourself. But my body is not in line with my heart. Please, massa. Please. Don't go any further."

Ben's head lolled to the side—and he lurched forward, as if he was losing his balance. He looked into Jimmy's eyes. "Jacob," he said. "My God, you seem about to cry."

Jimmy turned his face away.

"What's wrong?" Ben knit his brows. "I don't understand. I thought you liked me. You told me, even with my leg, you said I wasn't appalling." He tried again with his lopsided smile. "Doesn't this feel good?" His hand moved again across Jimmy's nipple.

"Please don't!" Jimmy's eyes glistened as he returned Ben's gaze. "You don't understand," Jimmy said. "My heart is already taken. I don't want to dishonor the person who is the most important person in my life."

Ben pounced on Jimmy's use of the genderless pronoun. "Is this person a man?" he asked, an ache in his voice.

Jimmy's eyes darted from side to side, searching Ben's face as he tried to decide what to say. He didn't know if it was better or worse to acknowledge the truth. But it didn't matter. He was overcome with the feeling that it was no longer possible to pretend. He said in a quiet voice, "Yes."

"Oh. Oh." Ben's eyes flashed, then blinked. Perspiration shone on his brow. He suddenly seemed on the verge of madness. "I knew I was right. I knew what I felt was not misplaced." He stepped back slightly, and once again surveyed Jimmy from head to toe. "Oh, Jacob, Jacob, you're so beautiful. Don't you know how much I want you? I have never seen a man as beautiful as you! Can you not show me a little affection?"

"If you're an honorable man," Jimmy said, "you'll stop."

"But why? I can see it with my eyes. You desire me, too." He pointed at Jimmy's groin. "Can't I just touch it?" He reached out his hand.

"No!" Jimmy shook his head and took a step backward.

"Please!" he shouted. "Please don't touch it. I don't want to do this."

"And look," Ben said. "Look at what you've done to me." He pulled his underwear down, letting his erection spring out. "You see?"

Jimmy turned his head. "I don't want to see it," he said.

"I ... I ... I am your master, am I not?"

"What does it matter?" Jimmy said, his eyes still averted.

"Why?" Ben shouted. His voice cracked with agony. "Why can't you be kind to me?"

"I'm sorry," Jimmy said. He looked directly into Ben's eyes, avoiding any view of what was below. He made his voice as soft and sympathetic as he could. "I'm sorry, I know what you want, but it can't come from me."

"Can't I just kiss you? Just once?"

"No." Jimmy's voice was choked with emotion. "Massa, you can't command a man to love you."

"I ... I know that, but ... am I no longer to know love?"

"Pheby told me about Elijah," Jimmy said. "Elijah must have loved you."

"Yes! Oh, Jacob. If only you'd known him."

"But I'm not Elijah," Jimmy said. "I can't be Elijah. I can't be what you want me to be. It's not in my power. This situation between you and me—it's not right. It won't make you or me happy."

"It's because of my deformity," Ben said. "Isn't it?"

"It's not that. It's what I told you. Don't you understand? I love another man." Jimmy continued to stare into Ben Crenshaw's eyes, his own eyes now full of compassion. "I know what it's like to be unable to have what you want. I really do." He reached out and stroked Ben's hair. The feel of its silky softness shocked him. "But I don't want to do this with you. My heart is taken. Truly, Ben, I'm sorry."

Jimmy was aware that he'd omitted the word "Massa," that he'd simply said "Ben." It could have been a sign of disrespect.

It could have made Ben angry. But it did just the opposite. All Ben's defenses melted.

As the weight of what Jimmy had said sank in, Ben sighed. "Oh, damn, damn. I can't do it either. Not if you don't want it. It's no good without that." A tear formed in his right eye, then dropped quickly down his cheek. "Oh, Jacob, my life is nothing but emptiness!" He pulled his underwear back up to cover himself. His face was red with embarrassment. Then he turned and pushed Jimmy away. "Just go!" he shouted. As Jimmy quickly dressed, Ben yelled "Leave me!" and then, with a moan, fell back on the bed.

And with that Jimmy left.

31

"I MYSELF AM A TEACHER"

It was dark outside the Marshall House when Cato finally finished composing his letter to Dorothy. This is what he wrote:

Dear Mrs. Askew,

My dear Dorothy, there is much to tell you about what has happened to me since I left you to pursue Jimmy's trail. But in this letter I will endeavor to tell you mainly of the matters that bear upon my future plans. The rest I will recount to you when we see each other again, which I hope will be soon. I miss you and my brother sorely.

You'll be pleased to hear that I am currently at the Marshall House in Bowling Green, Kentucky, where I have visited with our friend Mr. McNish. It has meant a great deal to me to find myself, once again, in the presence of a compassionate Quaker. Like our friend Erastus, Mr. McNish is a man of estimable character and gentle kindness.

Alas, Mr. McNish has told me of a grave misfortune that has befallen Erastus, who, in keeping with his generous and noble heart, ventured last month, once more, to attend a battlefield in Virginia as a nurse. I am sorry to say that in this fight at Bull Run in Manassas, Virginia, Erastus was wounded. Though his injury was not lethal, I fear it may nonetheless prove deadly for Erastus's soul, for he has lost the use of his right hand entirely, and thus is no longer able to paint.

Because of this calamity, I will endeavor to visit Erastus in Philadelphia before I return to Chicago. However, at this moment I do not know what to predict regarding the future of my journey. Thus far, I have been able to trace Mr. Hogan, the man I told you about, the man who kidnapped Jimmy, to Chattanooga, Tennessee. I will go there tomorrow to call in at Carlson's stable, which was recommended to Mr. Hogan as a stable for his horses.

I wish I could tell you where I will go after that, but I will not know until I see Carlson—and once I'm in Chattanooga, I'll no longer be able to write to you, since the postal service to the North has been suspended. This letter, as you will have surmised, is to be mailed to you by Mr. McNish from Philadelphia. Mr. McNish is going there to attend a meeting of the Society of Friends, who are working for our emancipation—and he will, of course, also visit Erastus.

Mr. McNish has suggested that we should refrain from informing Erastus of what has happened to Jimmy. He says Erastus has fallen into a despairing mood and he fears that knowledge of our misfortune would come as an added blow that might be more than Erastus can bear. Therefore, he wishes to spare Erastus the burden of knowing what I am doing at this time.

Nevertheless, because of the uncertainty of where I will go next, I can only suggest that if a considerable time has passed and you've had no further communication from me, you should write Erastus—for I will make every effort to visit him, whether or not I'm able to find Jimmy.

I wish I could give you a more assured account of my future. But know that I will do my best to find Jimmy and to visit Erastus. Once I have secured their well-being, I hope to return quickly to Chicago to be reunited with you, William and Ella. Please tell Ella that I will do everything in my power to bring her brother back home.

Your devoted friend,
Cato Askew
Tuesday, September 16, 1862

The next morning, Cato handed this letter over to Mr. McNish, bade him farewell, then set off on his journey to Chattanooga. It took more than a week to reach the southeastern tip of Tennessee. He stopped first in Franklin, Kentucky. Then he went on to make overnight stops in Gallatin, Lebanon, Murfreesboro, Manchester, Tracy City, and Jasper, all towns in Tennessee, before he finally arrived in the city of Chattanooga eight days after departing from Bowling Green.

Most of his journey was deep inside Confederate-held territory. He'd seen Confederate flags, both the older "Stars and Bars" and some of the newer "Battle Flags," in each of the towns south of Gallatin. He'd also driven, without incident, past scattered groups of Confederate soldiers. Throughout the journey he'd kept to himself. He'd spoken only to the stable attendants with whom he left Oscar each night, and to the clerks at the hotels where he lodged. When he greeted these clerks and attendants, he continued to make a point of smoking a cigar, brandishing a gold coin, and introducing himself with a Spanish surname. He'd stopped carrying his Bible to these encounters—though he did take it out each night to read a passage or two and to remind himself of Mrs. MacMurrough's kindness.

It was on the morning of the ninth day after leaving Walter McNish that Cato finally visited Carlson's stable. Unlike Gleason's place, the Carlson stable had no heavy door at the entrance. Instead it had a pair of half doors that swung like the entrance to a saloon. Inside it was filled with the same pungent smell of horses, but Cato had become so accustomed to the smell that he barely noticed it.

He asked to see Mr. Carlson. The man that met him at the stable entrance told him, "There is no Mr. Carlson here. He's gone to fight in the Army."

"Then may I speak to the owner of this establishment?" Cato asked.

"You're speakin' to him," the man said. "My name is Johnson. I bought the place from Carlson just before the war began. What can I do for you?"

"Mr. Johnson, I'm looking for a man named Hogan, Mr. Horace Hogan. I have reason to believe he may have come here with his team several weeks ago."

"Hmm," Mr. Johnson said. "You say he came with his team?"

"Yes. I believe he had one or more men with him, and a wagon with his horses. One of the men with him would have been a Negro."

"Oh, yes," Mr. Johnson said. "That fellow—I recollect he came in here just as I was closing one night. He was quite a coarse fellow, as I recall. He swore a lot, which I'm not used to. I'm a Christian, you know."

"Yes," Cato said, "that sounds like him. I'm not surprised to learn that Mr. Hogan uses crude language at times. He's a rough fellow."

Mr. Johnson stroked his chin. "So what do you want with him then?"

"Mr. Hogan captured a runaway slave in Chicago. I hope to find him so that he might return my property to me."

"You mean that darkie he had with him is yours?"

"Yes," Cato said. "He belongs to me!" He said this with some emotion. Then he amended the statement by saying, "Well ... he belongs to my father, actually, but I have been sent to find Mr. Hogan and to retrieve our property." He indicated his satchel. "I'm prepared to reimburse Mr. Hogan for any expenses he's incurred in this undertaking."

"Well," Mr. Johnson said. "All I can tell you is that Hogan said he was fixin' to sell the darkie at auction."

"What?"

"Yessir. I remember it distinctly. He asked me about auction houses, which I know little about. But I told him he best go to Atlanta or Savannah to inquire about selling a darkie. As you know, the situation ain't settled here in Tennessee. The thing is, Hogan made out like the darkie belonged to him."

"That's outrageous," Cato said. "If he sells Jimmy, Mr. Hogan will have stolen our property."

Mr. Johnson's shoulders rose, then fell. "I had no idea," he said. "We get all sorts comin' through here. You never can tell who's honest and who isn't."

"Do you know which city he went to?"

"He went to Savannah—of that I'm sure. He asked me how far Savannah was from Atlanta. I told him Atlanta is 120 miles from here, and Savannah is another 250 miles beyond that. To which he said, 'Good, then I'll go there.' I remember thinking it was a strange thing to say. It sounded as if he wanted to go as far away as he could. I s'pose it makes sense, now that I know what he was up to. I reckon he wanted to get far enough to finish his deed before you could catch up with him."

Cato grimaced. "He's a scoundrel! He needs to be brought to justice. Mr. Hogan would not only rob me but also the poor fellow who buys from him what isn't his to sell." Cato rolled his head around as if he had a crick in his neck. "How long will it take me to get to Savannah?"

"I reckon it'd take ten or twelve days to get all the way to Savannah by horse," Mr. Johnson said. "Seems to me it's a long way to go without knowing exactly where this Hogan fella's gone to."

"I have no choice, Mr. Johnson. I'm bound by honor to retrieve what is mine."

"Naturally." Mr. Johnson rubbed his forehead as though contemplating the dilemma. Then his eyes lit up. "You know, you could go quicker if you took the train," he said. "That is—if that train's runnin' from here to Atlanta. Can't rightly know these days. But I know for a fact you can take a train from Atlanta to Savannah, if that's where you're headed. Those gosh-darn Yanks ain't got that far—at least, not yet."

Cato considered this, but then dismissed it. "It's a good idea, but I can't leave my horse."

"Why not? I can look after your horse right here," said Mr. Johnson. "I'd give you a real good rate under the circumstances."

"I'm sure you would, Mr. Johnson. But I prefer to rely on my own conveyance—even if it takes longer. I fear it's too perilous, in these times, to rely on other means of travel."

"Suit yourself," Mr. Johnson said.

"One more thing, Mr. Johnson," Cato said. "I'm going to Savannah. But I have no reason to go through Atlanta. Are there other ways to go?" Cato thought the throngs of people in Atlanta might slow him down. He was also wary of finding a throng of Confederate soldiers gathered in the city.

"Well, let's see ...." Mr. Johnson scratched the side of his cheek. "I s'pose if you want to steer clear of Atlanta, you could go by way of Athens and Sparta. That's what I call the Greek route in Georgia."

"How long would that take?"

"I reckon it's five days or so from here to Athens, maybe two more to Sparta, then maybe four or five days from there to Savannah. That's as near as I can figure."

AND SO CATO elected to take the Greek route through Georgia. He traveled by buggy with Oscar from Chattanooga to Athens. Throughout his journey he wished he could travel as fast as the train. The terrain was growing more rugged the farther south he traveled, and with each mile he could discern a growing racial enmity.

More than ever, he was mindful of the fact that he was a slave pretending to be white. The white people he encountered appeared to have been hardened by the war. It was as if they felt aggrieved by the consequences of slavery, as if it was those they'd enslaved who bore the real responsibility for the malevolence of the Yankees. Or perhaps they sensed a growing audaciousness in the slaves themselves. Both the white and black populations knew that the Union Army gladly freed the slaves anywhere they captured territory. To Cato it felt like a powder keg. He could only guess what would happen if the Union conquered Georgia.

He'd also come to believe that, as Mrs. Langdon had told him, what mattered most to his deception was his bearing—his attitude. As long as he behaved in a manner consistent with the unquestioned privilege of being white, he would be perceived, without question, as white. His audacity succeeded because it was so presumptuous. He was confident he'd continue to succeed as long as he didn't falter in his display of a superior demeanor.

When he arrived in Athens, he saw that they had a train depot and he reconsidered the advantages of taking the train. Traveling by buggy to Savannah would take him another six or seven days. On the train, by contrast, he could make the trip in a single day. He'd been traveling more than a month since Jimmy was taken. From that day forward he'd agonized over Jimmy's despair at having been resold into slavery. He wanted nothing more than to reach him as quickly as he could. But the thought of leaving Oscar behind made him sick. And he believed what he'd said to Mr. Johnson—taking the train would bring new perils. For one thing, he'd have to find another means of travel when he reached Savannah. He'd also have to find another way to transport Jimmy when he found him. Traveling with Jimmy on a Confederate train was out of the question.

And so, he journeyed on with Oscar from Athens. On the second day, he expected to reach Sparta, Georgia. But that morning he'd been unable to rouse anyone at the stable where he'd placed Oscar the night before. The building had remained locked with Oscar inside until the owner finally showed up at ten a.m. claiming he'd had to go and get a tooth pulled. And so Cato got off to a late start—so much so that by the time he was approaching Sparta, the sun was near to setting.

Since it was near the autumnal equinox, the dusk would fade quickly. He slowed down, straining to see signs of the town, which he believed to be close. He could just make out something headed toward him. What he saw sent a shiver down his spine: three men on horseback, and a fourth driving a wagon. He knew at once that they were slave-catchers.

It was too late for him to try to hide. So he resolved to greet them and express as much confidence as he could muster. When he was ten yards from the men, he stopped the buggy and called out, "Good evening, gentlemen."

All four men were much older than Cato. He knew that all the eligible young men had to enlist in the Army—and so it fell to older men, and to any men rejected by the Army, to patrol for runaway slaves. All of the men on horseback carried whips, which were prominently displayed in their saddle holsters. Cato immediately sensed their belligerence.

One of the men on horseback rode up close to him and said, "What have we here?"

"You have a tired traveler," Cato quickly replied, trying to maintain a cordial but slightly irritated tone. "I've been on the road all day."

"Is that so?"

Cato simply nodded.

"Where you headed?"

"To Sparta."

"Oh, I see," the man said. He smiled and looked around at his cronies, then turned back to Cato. "What business have you got in Sparta?"

"I'm only stopping there on my journey. I plan to take

lodging in Sparta for the night. Tomorrow I'll continue my journey to Savannah."

"Savannah?" The man repeated it as though it was a dirty word.

"Yes. I have property to attend to there."

"Is that right?"

Cato nodded. He was growing increasingly wary. He thought briefly of his gun, which was back in his satchel, but he realized how useless it would be even if he could reach it. All four men were armed with rifles. His only option was to continue to pretend to be confident.

The man looked Cato up and down. "That surprises me," he said. He was frowning. "I'd say you look mighty young to have property in Savannah." He turned around and looked at one of the other men on horseback. "What do you think, Bill?"

The man who'd been addressed as Bill rode up beside Cato. Bill asked, "How come you ain't in the Army?"

Cato furrowed his brow. He knew something about the laws of conscription in the South. He'd discussed them with his brother, William, before William had enlisted. He knew that certain occupations were exempted from the draft, including railroad workers, miners, druggists, and teachers. "As you may know, gentlemen, some are exempt from the military draft."

"Like who?" Bill made a show of scratching his head.

"Well, railroad men, for one, are exempt from service, and so are miners and druggists ... and teachers. There are several others as well."

"Is that right?"

Cato nodded.

"So what're you supposed to be?"

Cato seized on the occupation he felt most able to pass himself off as. "Me? I myself am a teacher." But as he spoke, Cato knew from the look on the other men's faces that he'd made a grievous mistake.

"Oh, is that so!" Bill said with a laugh. "A teacher. Well, a teacher!" He looked around at his friends. "Seems we got us a teacher here, boys."

The third man on horseback drew his horse close to the buggy, and looked at Cato dubiously. "Well then, little teacher, what can you teach us?"

Cato decided to try expressing exasperation. "Really, gentlemen. As much as I'd like to stay and converse with you—it's late. The sun has set. I must really be on my way to Sparta." Even as he spoke, Cato was stunned to realize how badly words were failing him. His confidence was melting rapidly. Jimmy fondly called him his "rabbit" and, despite himself, he now drew up a picture of what he must look like to these men—a scared young weakling with a voice that cracked when he spoke.

"Oh, must you really," the third man said. "Well, ain't that too bad."

"What's this little teacher look like to you, Pete?" Bill asked.

"Can't rightly say," Pete said. "He's a pretty little thing, though, ain't he?"

All three men laughed.

"Oh, yes," Bill said. "He's pretty as a picture. But you know something? I can't put my finger on it. There's somethin' about this boy that don't look quite right."

"No," Pete agreed. "Somethin' don't look right to me, either."

"But I can't say exactly what it is," Bill said. "What d'you think, Pete?"

"If you ask me, he looks like a colored man," Pete said. "He's kinda yallow around the edges."

"Now, Pete," Bill said. "Are you sure? Seems to me, he's just too pretty to be a colored man."

"That could be, Bill. But I do believe the little man's got some colored blood in him," Pete said. "See here, how coarse his hair is?" He flicked his hand at Cato's hair.

"Naw." Bill shook his head. "I don't think that's it," he said.

"No?" Pete seemed surprised.

"Naw. Pete, I really don't think that's it."

"You don't say? Then what is it?"

"I tell you what, Pete, I think what we got here is a Nancy-boy."

"Oh, Bill! A Nancy? What a thing to say! But now that you mention it, he does look mighty tender."

Cato felt himself redden—and at the same time, he knew how unhelpful it was for any color to be added to his complexion. He didn't know what to do. His hands were still on Oscar's reins, but to drive the buggy forward he'd have to swerve around the wagon blocking his path. He turned to look back toward his satchel in the rear compartment, thinking again of the gun inside, but he was too frightened to move. His began to shake so much that he had to drop the reins, before Oscar misinterpreted his intentions.

The third man on horseback came up to the buggy to take a look. "I think maybe you're both right," he said. "I think what we got here is both a nigger and a Nancy-boy."

Pete held up his hand. "Now, Sam. Don't forget. He's a teacher."

"Oh, yes," Bill said. "A teacher. I almost forgot." He looked around at the other men, grinning. "See, that way he didn't have to go and hurt his pretty little self in the Army."

"No," Pete said. "We couldn't have that. Not for a pretty little teacher." All four men snickered.

In a panic, Cato picked up the reins and tried to signal Oscar to pull forward and sharply to the right. But before the buggy had moved two yards, the man called Sam drew a pistol from the holster on his waist and pointed it at Cato. "Where you think you're goin'?"

Cato stopped immediately.

Pete came around and put his hand on the side of the buggy. He dismounted and held firmly onto the side of the buggy. "Get down out of there, nigger," he commanded.

Trembling, Cato climbed down from the buggy.

"Unharness that horse, Bill," Pete said. "We'll leave the buggy here. It ain't worth nothin' anyway. But I do believe we can make use of that horse. You unhitch him, Bill, and I'll tie him to the back of mine so I can bring him to town."

"Get in the wagon," Sam said to Cato. He indicated the wagon with his pistol. Cato moved slowly toward the wagon.

"Hurry it up," Pete said.

Cato tried to climb in the wagon, but his arms trembled so much he couldn't pull himself up. The man in the wagon grunted, climbed down, picked Cato up, and heaved him up and over the side of the wagon.

Meanwhile, Bill pulled his horse alongside Oscar, to unhitch the harness that held Oscar to the buggy. As soon as he was unharnessed, Oscar whinnied and took several steps away. "Better grab him, Pete," Bill said. "Damn horse is feisty!"

Pete took several steps toward Oscar, in an attempt to grab hold of his reins. But before he could, Oscar snorted and reared back. When he came down, he kicked Pete with his front leg—Pete fell hard to the ground. Oscar reared again and neighed even louder. This time, when his feet came back to the ground, he turned and took off running. He galloped into the field, away from the road.

"For God's sake," Bill said. "Do something, Pete. That horse is getting away."

Now Pete stood up and dusted himself off. "Did you see that? Damn horse nearly killed me."

Pete took his pistol out of his holster. He turned and aimed it at Oscar, who by then was twenty-five yards away. He fired. In the distance, Oscar cried out. He stopped and shook his head, as if he was trying to shake something off. Then he turned around, his nostrils flaring.

"You got him," Sam yelled.

Cato shouted, "Oscar!" then immediately cupped his hand over his mouth. The last thing he wanted was for Oscar to come back toward the man with the pistol. He stood up in the wagon, waved his hands, and cried out, "Run!"

Oscar looked back briefly at the men in the road, but then he turned again, and ran toward a thicket.

"Oh, for Christ's sake," Bill said. "Now he's getting away into the woods."

Sam waved his arm dismissively. "Let's don't worry about the horse," he said. "We can come back and catch the horse in the morning. Right now we oughta get this nigger over to the sheriff." He pointed at Cato in the wagon. "So we can get the reward."

"You know something?" Bill said. "I bet a nigger like that'll fetch a good reward." He turned to his companion. "Don't you think so, Pete?"

"Maybe," Pete muttered. "Let's see what he's got in the back." He climbed into the buggy and opened the storage compartment behind the seat. "Why, looky here." He pulled out Cato's bag. "The boy's got himself some fine luggage." He held up Cato's satchel.

"See what's in it," Bill said.

Pete poked around in the satchel. "Oh my goodness," he said. "You won't believe what I found." He drew Cato's pistol out of the satchel. "Damned thing's got a gun!"

"Oh, my," Bill said. "The little man ought not to carry a big old gun like that. He could hurt his little self."

Pete continued to dig in the satchel. "What have we here?" He pulled Cato's purse out of the bag, opened it, and assessed its contents. "Well, I'll be a son of a bitch!" he yelled. "You really ain't gonna believe this one." He waved the purse in the air. "The nigger's carrying a purse full of gold coins."

"What?" Bill cried. "You got to be joshin' us."

"No, sir. I ain't. See for yourself," Pete said. He handed the purse to Bill, who opened it and looked inside.

"Well, don't that beat all," Bill said. He turned to the others.

"Look here, fellas—looks like we're rich!" He, too, waved the purse in the air.

"Give it here," Pete said. "I'll put it in my coat pocket. Ain't no reason for the sheriff to know about this."

Bill handed the purse back to Pete, who carried it over to his horse, where a coat was tied to his saddle. He put the purse into the pocket of his coat. Then he took Cato's pistol and stuffed it back in the satchel. "We'll take this satchel with us as evidence, pistol and all. That'll give the sheriff something to work with."

"You better tie him up first, Bobby," Bill said to the man driving the wagon. "I mean, since we're gonna leave that gun in his bag."

Bobby climbed into the wagon, dug into a corner of it, and came up with a length of rope. He used the rope to tie Cato's hands behind his back. Meanwhile, Pete brought the satchel to the wagon and laid it firmly into the wagon bed, at the opposite end from where Cato was seated. Then the whole entourage turned around and headed back toward Sparta.

Cato turned to look at the woods. He saw Oscar, three hundred yards away, peering through the trees, watching them go. Even from that distance, Cato saw the blood dripping down Oscar's neck. Cato glanced up at the night sky through the film of his tears. A constellation of stars swirled above him. All he could think was that they looked so very far away. He was powerless to help Oscar, and powerless to help himself. He sank back into the wagon, bowed his head, and whispered to himself in a voice so quiet and desperate that only he could hear it, "Oh, Jimmy. What should I do?"

32

"MY NAME IS JIMMY"

On Sunday morning, Jimmy and Uncle Isaac left before sunrise to begin their journey downriver to the plantation where Andrew preached. As Uncle Isaac had predicted, the Crenshaws were surprised by Jimmy's request for a pass—in part because he'd never asked for one before, but also because they remembered quite well when he'd told them he had no reason to believe in God. But they accepted at face value his claim that he now wanted to see what he could learn from a preacher. The fact that Uncle Isaac would accompany him on the journey assured them of the trip's legitimacy.

The road to Mulberry Grove plantation was not close to the river, which disappointed Jimmy, who'd hoped to learn more about the river's shape. It took them just over an hour to get there. When they arrived, Jimmy roughly counted about forty other slaves gathered in the barn where Andrew preached.

"Are all these people from this plantation?" he asked.

"I reckon 'bout half are," Uncle Isaac said. "The rest of 'em come from somewhere's nearby like we did."

Jimmy noted the presence of three upturned pots in the barn, vessels that were meant to "catch the sound"—symbolically if nothing else—of anything the preacher might say that would upset the masters. In Jimmy's youth, Reverend Zeke had not only avoided words that might have upset his masters, he'd advocated a philosophy of turning the other cheek—a viewpoint that had enraged Jimmy as a boy and provoked his estrangement from religion.

Like Reverend Zeke, Andrew was a free black man who chose to stay in the South to spread the word of God among the slaves. Unlike Reverend Zeke, a large man who waved a white handkerchief up and down to illustrate his points, Andrew was a small man, who used no props but brought his words home with a booming voice, despite his age. His face was dark but his hair was as white as the robe he wore. He sermonized with great ardor, as Zeke had done, about the coming glory of heaven—and the ever-present degradation of sin. He bounced on his feet, shook his arms, waved his finger, and performed all such manner of theatrics as he could devise to exhort his congregation to have faith in the Lord, however difficult the circumstances might seem.

Jimmy was as enraged by these entreaties as he'd always been. He couldn't stand the idea of a deity who demanded that black men patiently put up with white men as a condition for reaping happiness after death. What kind of God could be that cruel? What was the point of such a test? It made no sense to him. It was, he believed, just a way to appease—to let the evil go unchallenged.

He listened to Andrew's sermon and quietly seethed. But he kept his emotions in check for the sake of his goal, which was to obtain Andrew's help in writing to Cato. Jimmy considered that Cato, for his part, would likely find Andrew's religious zeal agreeable—in no small part because of the influence of Cato's Quaker friend, the painter Erastus Hicks, who spoke, sentimentally, in Jimmy's view, of a light within each person.

Jimmy had never seen anything even resembling a light in men like Hogan or Eppley or any of the myriad others who practiced cruelty as if it were merely an asset to be exploited. Despite this, Cato, under the painter's influence, had adopted what Jimmy believed was an irrational belief in the goodness of men. This was an irritation to Jimmy, but it was also, in its own way, an allurement. Cato's faith in humanity provided a means for Jimmy to indirectly experience faith and hope, which, despite his skepticism, were postulations he found comforting to entertain at arm's length. But these credulous beliefs also elicited in Jimmy a passionately protective instinct. Cato's innocence and naiveté, he feared, made him vulnerable. And even now, although it was Jimmy who was enslaved in a faraway place, he was more worried about the actions Cato might undertake than he was about the risks of the schemes he'd planned for himself. He, at least, did not suffer from injudicious optimism.

He was pragmatic. He considered that the best way to approach Andrew would be to act as much like Cato as he could manage. And so, when he came up to the preacher after the sermon, he began with a compliment.

"That was a spirited speech, sir," he told Andrew. "Uncle Isaac, here"—he pointed to Isaac, who stood beside him—"told me we'd hear a rousing message today, and he was right."

"Thank you," Andrew said with a slight bow. He looked at Isaac. "It's been a long time, Isaac."

"Yes, Reverend. Been a few years, I reckon."

"Indeed. It's nice to see you again."

"We came down from Crenshaw plantation," Jimmy said.

"How is life up that way these days?"

Isaac answered. "Oh, it's 'bout the same as always, Andrew, work and sleep and get half a mouthful to eat. You know how it is."

Andrew nodded. "Yes. I do." Then he looked at Jimmy. "I don't believe we've met before."

"No, Reverend," Jimmy said. "This is my first time here." He reached out to shake Andrew's hand. Jimmy had already decided that the best way to engage Andrew's sympathy was to tell him the truth about his situation, despite the fact that no one at Crenshaw plantation knew his real story. "My name is ... Jacob, or at least that's what the Crenshaws think it is."

Andrew looked puzzled. "I don't follow. Jacob isn't your real name?"

"No, sir. My name is Jimmy."

Now Isaac spoke, "Boy, what you talkin' 'bout?"

"It's true," Jimmy said to Isaac. "My name really is Jimmy. I just haven't wanted to let on about it."

"Why not?" Andrew asked.

"'Cause up until a month or so ago I was livin' as a free man up in Chicago. Then a scalawag copperhead named Hogan caught me off guard, kidnapped me, trussed me up, carried me all the way down here to Georgia, and made out that I belonged to him so he could sell me at auction. Sam Crenshaw bought me, and I've been here ever since."

Isaac looked aghast. "You tellin' the truth?"

Jimmy nodded.

"How come you never said nothin' about it?" Isaac asked.

Jimmy shrugged. "I didn't think it would do any good. And I reckoned if I was to ever run away to get back to my people, I'd rather have the paddy rollers lookin' for Jacob from North Carolina than lookin' for Jimmy from Chicago."

"Why are you tellin' us now, then?" Isaac asked.

"Because I want you and the reverend here to understand why I've got to write a letter, why I've got to let my people know what's happened to me."

Andrew raised an eyebrow, as he began to surmise the point of their meeting. "So I suppose, Jimmy, that you're lookin' to have me write a letter for you."

Jimmy nodded. "Yes, Reverend. It would mean the world to me and to my family."

"Well ..." Andrew paused. He looked at Isaac. "I believe Isaac here can tell you that there generally ain't much good that comes from running away. But I also know that that what I say won't stop a man from tryin'. I don't think it's a good idea. But I know from experience that what I think doesn't matter much, once a man gets the idea in his mind."

"You're right," Jimmy said. "I'm afraid it won't matter. I'm set on going home, Reverend. And there's nothing you'd say that would stop me. Not now. I've lost too much time already."

Isaac decided to chime in with some further information. "You see, Andrew, the boy's got a sweetheart back home. And I can tell you, he's about as sick as a puppy to get back to that gal."

"Oh, I see," Andrew said. "So is that who you want to write to?"

"Yes," Jimmy lied. "Her name is Dorothy. She lives in Chicago, which—as I mentioned—is where this Hogan fellow grabbed me. But I'm planning to meet her in Philadelphia."

"Philadelphia!" Andrew shook his head with evident confusion. "Philadelphia's a long ways from here."

"Is that where you're headed?" Isaac asked. "I thought you were fixin' to get to one of them Yankee boats."

"The Yankee boats are just the beginning," Jimmy said. "I mean to go north after that. As near as I can tell from looking at the Crenshaws' map, Philadelphia's the first place along the way that I'm gonna feel safe enough to get out."

"So you reckon the Yankees are just gonna carry you up there and set you down in Philadelphia?" Isaac asked.

"Why not?" Jimmy asked. "They've got no cause to keep me on a boat."

"What if you don't make it as far as Philadelphia?" Andrew asked.

"I look at it like this," Jimmy said. "If I make it to Philadelphia, it'll be a gift from God. If I don't make it—if they catch me or kill me—then it won't matter. But if you write this letter for me, at least I'll go to my fate knowin' I had the chance to tell my loved ones where I've been."

"But if the paddy rollers or the Reb soldiers was to catch you," Andrew said, "it wouldn't be good for you to have a letter in your pocket. As you know, they don't look kindly on those who read and write."

"I don't care," Jimmy said. "I'm willing to take that risk."

"Look here," Andrew said. "I've got a friend—someone who's traveling up to Washington City next week. He's someone I can trust. I can ask him to mail a letter for you. He won't know who it's from."

"Does that mean you'll write it?"

"It's against my better judgment," Andrew said. "But I'll do it as a favor to Isaac. He did me a kindness some time ago, and I'd be glad to repay it."

Isaac nodded. "That's good of you, Andrew. But you don't owe me nothin.'"

"Thank you, Reverend," Jimmy said.

"I've got one condition," Andrew said.

"What's that?" Jimmy was suddenly wary.

"I want you to pray with me, Jimmy. I want to pray for your safety and for the safety of those you love."

Jimmy didn't miss a beat. "Certainly, Reverend," he said. "Why not?"

Jimmy, Isaac, and Andrew held hands, while Andrew prayed. Andrew's earnestness made Jimmy realize—as if for the first time—just how big a risk he was about to take. And so he was humble, and grateful for the blessing, however little store he put in it.

Afterward, Jimmy dictated his letter to Andrew. He'd spent many days composing it in his mind. This is what Jimmy dictated and what Andrew transcribed:

Dear Miss Askew,

By the time this letter reaches you, I hope to have arrived safely in Philadelphia, having escaped the bonds of slavery on Crenshaw plantation in Savannah, Georgia.

Since my kidnapping on the streets of Chicago, I have thought considerably about where to go, should I once again obtain my freedom. I have decided it would be safer for me, and those who want to be with me, to find a less perilous location in which to meet than Chicago.

For now, I've decided to entrust myself to our friend Erastus Hicks in Philadelphia until such time as my loved ones in Chicago may join me.

I realize the prospect of a journey from Chicago to Philadelphia will be a great inconvenience. But I do not feel safe returning to Chicago, even for a brief visit. Those who claim to own me here in Savannah may resort to extraordinary means to get me back here again—for they have grown attached to me in an inordinate way.

I would rather defend myself against recapture under the protection of Mr. Hicks than rely on the hand of fate in Chicago. I am certain that Mr. Hicks will be able to vouch for my safety.

You may endeavor, then, to contact me through Mr. Hicks to let me know what to expect. I ask that you also inform my brother Cato and my sister Ella of these circumstances as soon as you are able.

Your loving friend,
Jimmy Holland

Upon hearing the letter, both Andrew and Isaac looked confused. Jimmy's text did not offer the platitudes of affection that they thought befitting a letter from a man to his sweetheart. Nor could they understand why, exactly, Jimmy did not want to go directly to the city where his beloved lived. In short, they were alive to the fact that some hidden meaning was betokened by Jimmy's peculiar explanations, but they were too polite to question him about it.

Instead they asked him about his friend in Philadelphia.

"Who's this Erastus Hicks?" was Isaac's first question.

"He's a painter. I met him when I was a slave in Tennessee."

Andrew was confused. "I thought you said you come from Chicago."

"I ran away to Chicago with Dorothy and my sister Ella and my brother Cato earlier this year. But we were all slaves in Tennessee. One day Erastus Hicks came to Tennessee to find work. Our master hired him to paint a portrait. While he was with us, he taught my brother Cato to read. After we escaped, he came up to Chicago to help us. After that he went back to his home in Philadelphia."

"How come a white man helped you like that?" Isaac asked.

"Because he's a Quaker," Jimmy said. "And he's very fond of my brother."

"He sounds like a decent man," Andrew observed.

Jimmy pursed his lips. "He's all right. I don't care for some of the things he's done. But I know he'll help me—for my brother's sake."

When the letter was duly written, Jimmy signed his name at the end of it, and sealed it in an envelope. He handed it over to Andrew, who promised to give it to his friend to take north to Washington City for mailing.

Jimmy wanted to be sure that none of the Crenshaws learned of the letter's existence. He didn't want the other slaves to know about it either. To this end he had Uncle Isaac swear to secrecy.

33

"WHAT'S ALL THAT NOISE ABOUT?"

Cato awoke in a jail cell in the sheriff's office in Sparta, Georgia. His attempts the night before to talk his way out of the charges against him had failed. As the slave patrollers had predicted, they were able to make good use of Cato's gun. They told the sheriff that Cato had drawn a gun on them as soon as they stopped him in the course of performing their sworn duties. This meant, in their telling, that he must be a runaway—since no innocent man would have attacked them without provocation.

Cato tried to tell the facts of what had happened. But he was too humiliated to recount truthfully the way in which the paddy rollers had mocked him as a teacher and called him a Nancy-boy. Instead, he tried to reuse the ploy that had worked for him earlier in his journey. He told the sheriff he was of Spanish descent, and that he was from Chicago, and that the patrollers had stolen his money.

But although the sheriff was more reasonable than the patrollers, he was skeptical that a man of Cato's youth and uncertain lineage would be carrying such a large quantity of gold coins. He decided to confine Cato in the jail while he attempted to determine whether or not any local slave owners might come forth to claim Cato as their property. To do otherwise, and then to discover that he'd freed a runaway, would be the sheriff's undoing.

The sheriff was a tall, thick-set man. When Cato awoke the next morning, he told Cato that he hadn't liked being kept up late. He complained that he'd not gotten enough sleep. As evidence of this, an hour later he dozed off while sitting at his desk, a few yards from where Cato sat in his cell.

Since he'd been confined, Cato had surveyed his surroundings—wondering if there was any way he could escape. But the jail cell doors were made of thick iron bars and locked with a key that was kept in the sheriff's desk drawer.

Cato sat on a cot in his cell in a state of abject misery. Not only was he in danger of being returned to slavery, he'd lost Oscar and all his money. He pictured that moment when Pete fired his gun at Oscar—and pounded his fist into the wall. He had to escape. He had to find Oscar, and see how badly he was hurt.

Oscar had done what he could to escape. But Cato was certain he'd been wounded. And Cato could only imagine that the patrollers were right in their assertion that they could round him up easily. Where could a horse hide? How could he hide if he was wounded?

Cato felt guilty—guilty for having brought the horse into such dangerous circumstances, and guilty for having failed to keep him safe. Over and over he obsessed about his decision to call himself a teacher. That decision had come at a moment when, in retrospect, he believed the encounter could have gone either way. But the pride he'd put in his voice with the word "teacher" had rankled the men. And now he blamed his own pride for Oscar's fate.

As if things weren't bad enough, he suddenly became aware that he smelled smoke. He climbed up on his cot and peered out the cell window. There he saw a building on fire, no more than two hundred yards away. The building looked like a barn.

For a moment, he wondered if he should do or say anything. The sheriff was asleep. The barn was far enough away that the jail didn't seem in imminent danger. And yet, he also saw that no one seemed to be alert to the presence of the fire. He scanned the area. There was no one to be seen. And as he looked more closely, he could see that there were other buildings near enough to the barn to be in danger of catching fire as well.

It was with a sigh that he stepped off the cot, went to the cell door, and shook it. He yelled, "Sheriff! Sheriff!" But yelling it twice did not arouse his sleeping jail-keeper. So he rattled the cell door again, then looked around to see if there was anything else he could use to get the sheriff's attention. He spotted the tin cup that sat in a corner, which he'd been given to use as a water cup the night before.

He took the cup and used it to bang on the cell door. This time the sheriff awoke—but he was not happy about it. "Damn it! What the hell's wrong with you?" he shouted. "What's all that noise about?"

"Sheriff, there's a building on fire outside. I think it's a barn."

"What?"

"It's on fire, and it's burning fast. And no one's out there. No one's trying to put it out."

The sheriff stood up and went to the window on his side of the cell door and looked out. "For Christ's sake," he said. "How'd that happen?" He frowned at Cato, as if Cato was somehow responsible for the fire.

"I didn't see it start," Cato said. "I just smelled the smoke."

The sheriff left the office, and a few minutes later Cato heard him calling out to various people. Then, after a while, he saw the sheriff and three other men gather around the perimeter of the barn. Cato watched as they began a frantic search for water and buckets.

As Cato was watching, he heard a sound behind him. He whirled around, startled. A fierce-looking man stood in front of him, on the other side of the jail cell. Cato stepped backward in shock. He tottered and fell backward onto his cot. He sat on the cot and stared in disbelief. The man before him was dressed in leggings and a buckskin shirt. He had a swatch of red paint smeared in a zigzag line on his forehead. A tall black feather rose from a band around his forehead. It was Joe Bird.

"Bezon!" Joe said.

"What?" Cato was dumbfounded by Joe's presence.

"It means 'Howdy' in Shawnee," Joe said. He put his hand on the bars of the cell door. "I've come to get you out of here."

"But how? Where did you come from?"

"There's no time to explain," Joe said. "Where's the key?"

"He keeps it in that desk drawer on an iron ring." Cato pointed at the desk. "But then he locked the drawer. And now he's out there fighting that fire." He pointed out the window. "Did you see it?"

"Yes, I saw it," Joe smiled mischievously. "I started it. Which drawer?"

"The drawer's on the right side of the desk. It's either the middle one or the lower one—I couldn't tell for sure."

Joe extracted a knife from a sheath on his waistband. Within a few moments he'd pried open the drawers of the desk. He rummaged in them until he found the large iron key ring and carried it back to the cell door. There were three keys on the ring. The second one opened the cell door.

Cato embraced Joe. Then he stepped back. "You started the fire?"

Joe nodded.

"What for?"

"So I could get you out of here."

"But how did you ever find me?"

Joe shook his head. "There's no time to talk," he said. "Come on. We have to get away. You'll have to follow me. Be as quiet as you can."

"Where are we going?" Cato asked. He could hardly believe what was happening. It was as if an angel had come down from heaven to save him.

Joe put his finger up to his mouth. "Just follow me. I'll tell you everything when we're safe." Joe went to the door and peeked out. He held up his hand. "Wait!" he said.

Cato crouched behind Joe. He could see that there were now seven men near the burning barn. They'd gathered around a well at a nearby house. One man was drawing water from the well in a bucket. The other men formed a line from the well, spreading out in succession toward the barn, passing the buckets of water from one man to the next. All the men faced the barn, except the man at the end, who, after throwing water on the fire, turned to run the empty bucket back to the well. Joe waited until that man reached the well, then he stepped out from the doorway of the sheriff's office. Cato followed.

Joe walked slowly and deliberately around the side of the office, until they were on the opposite side of the building from the men fighting the fire. Then he nodded toward the building next to the sheriff's office, which was a bank. He walked slowly and steadily to the far side of the bank. Then he did the same with each building in succession until they'd put five buildings between themselves and the sheriff's office.

At that point, Joe removed his headband. He carefully placed the band and its feather in a pouch he carried. "It sticks up too much," he explained. Then he looked around and nodded toward a fenced pasture that began twenty yards away. "Let's move out to that field," he said.

When they got to the wooden fence, they climbed over it.

"You see that bale of hay?" Joe indicated a pile of hay ten yards away.

Cato nodded.

"We'll each grab a handful of that hay. Then we'll carry it to the cows at the other end of the pasture." He pointed to a group of three cows at the far end of the field. "Walk slow and natural," he said. "Act as if we're gonna feed the cows." The cows were near a patch of woods. "We can run over to the trees from there."

Joe and Cato carried the hay to the cows, who looked up at them with some surprise when they dropped it in front of them. Cato looked back toward the town. It was evident that no one had noticed their actions. Instead, he saw a crowd swarming around the barn. The flames had been put out. But there was still quite a lot of smoke.

"Let's go," Joe said.

They walked from the cows to the thicket of trees. Cato's legs wobbled all the way. He was still shaken from all that had happened. He was certain that at any moment the slave patrollers would lurch out from behind a nearby tree.

Once they were safely out of view, Joe took stock of their surroundings. His eyes darted quickly, taking it all in. He leaned down and pulled a couple of leaves off a plant growing on the forest floor. He sniffed the leaves. "Wild ginger," he said with some satisfaction. "It likes to grow in the shade." He handed the leaves to Cato. "Here. You can make a mild tea from this. It's good for digestion."

Cato couldn't believe how calmly Joe acted—as if they were merely on an expedition to collect herbs. He had to repress an urge to laugh. Instead, he solemnly smelled the wild ginger and nodded, then put the leaves in his pocket. He had noticed in Kentucky how observant Joe was of the natural world. He seemed to scrutinize everything with the curiosity of a child.

Joe went on to inspect a tree at the edge of the thicket. "This is an old tree," he said, touching the tree's trunk. "You should sit down and lean against it. It will comfort you."

Cato had no reason to argue with that. He sat next to the

tree, leaned his head against it, and closed his eyes. Whether or not it came from the tree, he had to admit he felt relief.

Joe remained standing. "We shouldn't stay here too long," he said. "The sheriff will go back to his office soon and find that you're gone. We need to get as far away as we can before that happens." He took an orange out of his pocket and handed it to Cato. "Here," he said. "It was in the desk drawer above the one with the key ring. I reckoned you'd be hungry."

Cato realized he was. "Thank you." He eagerly peeled it and removed a wedge, then handed it to Joe, who popped it in his mouth. "Just tell me one thing," Cato said. "How did you know where to find me?"

"It's a long story." Joe paced in a circle, keeping his eye on the field beyond the thicket. "Mainly, I tracked you."

"All the way from Kentucky?"

"All the way," Joe said. "You told me in Kentucky that you were headed to Carlson's stable in Chattanooga. So when I decided to look for you, that's where I went."

"Did you talk to Carlson?"

"I talked to Johnson. He said he bought the place from Carlson."

"Oh, that's right."

"Johnson told me about this Greek route that he came up with. He said he reckoned you'd take that route to Savannah, so that's the route I followed. I was about to catch up to you. I knew how far behind you I was because of Oscar's dung."

"You recognized Oscar's dung?" Cato seemed incredulous.

"Of course. All animals have distinctive droppings."

"My poor Oscar. I think he must be badly hurt. We have to find him."

Joe held up his hand and continued, "Last night I was only half a day behind you. But then this morning I found your buggy on the road outside town. I could see something bad had happened. There was a lot of Oscar's dung on the ground nearby, and many footprints from his hooves. His footprints led off the road and into the field."

"Oh, Joe." Cato shook his head. "It was terrible. A band of slave patrollers waylaid me. They made me get out of the buggy. Then one of them untied Oscar. You should have seen it—Oscar reared up and kicked him and knocked him down. Then he turned right around and ran into the field. But when the man got up, he was so angry he took out his pistol and shot him."

Joe nodded. "Yes, I know. I followed Oscar's footprints. I found him in the woods this morning, before I came to find you."

"Really? You found him?"

"Yes."

Cato leapt to his feet. "Thank God!" He grabbed Joe's arm. "How bad is he hurt?"

"Don't worry. He'll be fine. The bullet hit part of his ear—mostly on the tip. I tied a piece of cloth around his ear, which he didn't like too much. But I put some sprigs of yarrow on the cloth, which will help his wound scab and heal."

Cato leaned in and kissed Joe on the cheek. "I can hardly believe you did all this. I think you saved my life." He hugged Joe hard. "How can I thank you?"

Joe blushed. "You don't need to."

Cato looked back toward town. There was no one in the field near them. "Let's hurry," he said. "I need to see Oscar."

Joe verified that no one was watching them, then took Cato by the hand. "All right," he said. "Follow me."

As they walked, Cato could not hide his curiosity. "Joe, why did you follow me all this way into Georgia?"

"Because I was worried about you."

"But why did you leave Kentucky in the first place. Why did you leave Jack?"

"I had to," Joe said. "After I left you I went back to Camp Wood to warn Jack and the others. But I couldn't give them enough warning before the Confederate Army arrived. The Rebs surrounded the camp. The Union commander told us there were more than 25,000 Rebs. He talked to the Confederate general before any fighting started."

"Oh, God," Cato said. "It must have been a terrible battle."

Joe shook his head. "They didn't even fight. Since the Union commander knew he was outnumbered, he decided to surrender. After that, the Rebs took all the Union soldiers prisoner, including Jack."

Cato stopped walking. He said, "That's bad news." After taking a moment to absorb the news, he asked, "But how'd you get away?"

"Before they surrendered, Jack said since I wasn't actually a Union soldier, I ought to take one of the horses from Camp Wood so I could get away. He said there wasn't any point in letting the Rebs get all their horses. So that's what I did. I took a horse and I snuck away."

"And you came after me?"

"Yes. I was worried about you. There wasn't anything I could do about Jack. So I thought I ought to come and help you find your kidnapped friend." Joe tugged on Cato's hand to pull him forward. "This morning, when I saw your buggy by the side of the road, it wasn't hard to guess that someone had taken you. I knew it must have been slave patrollers."

"How could you know that?"

"Because ... well ... Cato, you do very nearly look white. But I don't think you look as white as you think you look."

Cato had to admit he was right. "The paddy rollers said I was colored around the edges."

Joe nodded. "I figured they'd take you into town. So that's where I went. I snuck around to the back of the jail. I peeked in the window—and there you were, sitting on a cot."

"And then you decided to start a fire?"

Joe shrugged. "Don't worry. I made sure no one was in the barn. And it rained last night, so the barn was damp. I knew the wood wouldn't burn too fast. I figured they'd be able to put out the fire pretty quick."

They began walking again. Cato squinted at Joe's face. "Why do you have red paint on your forehead. Is that war paint?"

Joe nodded and touched his forehead. "I put it on because I knew I'd have to move quickly. The lightning bolt gives me power and speed. The red color gives me strength. It makes me look fierce, don't you think?" He made a menacing face to demonstrate. Then he smiled. "White men are easily frightened."

"And the feather?"

"I wore that to make sure that even from a distance men could see that I'm a brave. White men think if they see one brave, there's more hiding behind him."

"But you did this all by yourself?"

"Yes. Well ... me and my new horse." Joe beamed. "You should see him. He's very beautiful. Almost as beautiful as Jack!"

"But where is he?"

"He's with Oscar. I tied them both up in the woods." Joe leaned around a tree and looked back toward the town. "We need to walk faster. They've got the fire out. The sheriff will be looking for you soon."

"Just tell me one more thing," Cato said. "Did you talk to Jack? Did you tell him how you feel?"

Joe nodded.

"And what happened?"

A huge grin spread across Joe's face. And there was nothing more he needed to say.

34

"FROM YOUR SEECRIT FRIEND"

The week that followed Jimmy's visit to Reverend Andrew was the busiest week he'd experienced on the Crenshaw plantation. Since the crops were at peak harvest, there was a great deal of work to do. And Mr. Eppley had been made to understand that there was particular urgency about completing it.

Eppley, whose mood was jumpy to begin with, responded to this imperative by growing ill-tempered, which did nothing to further his goals, since his bad attitude was much more likely to impede the slaves' performance than to advance it.

Eppley's practice in the field was to march up and down the rows in a dogged fashion, nagging the slaves. During his patrol he kept his eye out for any offense that might provide an excuse for punishment, however dubious the infraction might be.

One afternoon, in the course of his promenade, he came upon Jimmy, who was standing in such a way as to be blocking his path. Eppley might well have stepped around Jimmy and allowed him to get on with his work without interruption. But Eppley fancied that liberal use of the whip on his part was key to getting the work completed. Since he'd been forbidden by

Ben Crenshaw to use his whip on Jimmy—a constraint that defied his overseeing methodology—he chose instead to slam into Jimmy, knocking him headlong onto the ground. This unexpected assault took Jimmy by surprise, since he'd been deep in concentration on his task and hadn't noticed Eppley's approach.

Once Jimmy was down, Eppley kicked him, both in the torso and on his legs. Eppley was mindful of Jimmy's headstrong nature. He had a sadist's instinct about what degree of abasement would provoke Jimmy's insubordination, which would then set the stage for even more advanced punishments. What Eppley didn't know was that Jimmy was determined not to let anything spoil his upcoming plans. He'd decided he'd do nothing to incur any punishment or restriction on the eve of his escape. And so he simply lay still, taking each blow without any sign of retaliation.

Eppley was dumbfounded. He looked around, wondering if there was some external circumstance that would explain Jimmy's unexpected submissiveness. Seeing none, he drew out his whip. He found himself on the verge of defying Ben Crenshaw's prohibition, so vexed that his arm was shaking. He didn't like to be bamboozled. He was certain that Jimmy was pulling some trick on him. It was only when he followed his own logic that it dawned on him that Jimmy's scheme was to force him to use the whip, knowing that if he did so the overseer would bring castigation from the Crenshaws upon himself.

This wicked calculation on Jimmy's part was something Eppley could not countenance. But he decided to bide his time. He determined it would be better to wait until there was an opportunity for retribution that would be worthy of Jimmy's chicanery.

"You'll not trick me that way," he shouted, cackling at his own cleverness. Then he spat on Jimmy. "Git up and git back to work."

Jimmy could see that Eppley had gone out of his mind. He

didn't wish to enrage him any further, so he quietly stood and continued his work, saying nothing, despite the considerable pain in his legs and side.

Eppley harrumphed, and spat again. Then he resumed his conspicuous parade up and down the rows.

Eppley continued his bizarre and unpredictable behavior all week, but Jimmy remained calm in the face of each of Eppley's indignities. By the end of the week, though, Jimmy was exhausted mentally and bodily, and he was more determined than ever to escape from the Crenshaw plantation as soon as he could.

Jimmy's morning sessions in the library did little to counterbalance the indignations Eppley had incited during the preceding afternoons. Ben Crenshaw spoke each morning in a tone that seemed both melancholy and imploring about the importance of his instruction. Bonnie Crenshaw, likewise, extolled the virtues of her tutelage, oblivious to Jimmy's state of mind. Jimmy found it difficult to concentrate on his lessons, since he was both physically weary and inwardly distracted.

As he went through the motions of each lesson, he felt as though his spirit stood outside his body, impatiently watching the proceedings. He nodded and shook his head. He answered when called upon. But in his imagination he was already rowing down the Savannah River.

He was also pondering how he would say goodbye to the other slaves, especially Pheby, who didn't know about his imminent plans. She'd made it clear to him how difficult his departure would be for her. As he'd grown to know her, he'd found Pheby to be very like his sister, Ella. Except that with Pheby, he found himself more freely able to express his feelings, since she knew so little about who he was. If anything, she'd formed preconceptions about him based on Ben's slave Elijah. Her descriptions of Elijah were clearly meant to convey to Jimmy how much she thought he and Elijah were alike. And, although he'd never known the man, he felt that Elijah's avowed affection for Ben was a precedent that warranted some forbearance toward Ben on his part.

He was surprised, then, to discover that there were moments when he felt twinges of pity for the Crenshaws. Despite their condescension, he was not indifferent to their efforts on behalf of his advancement. He was aware that they saw themselves from the vantage point of their peers. He could see how from that perspective they were generous and kind-hearted. But he also knew that they couldn't see themselves from the point of view of their slaves. Had they been able to, he thought, they'd know they were not nearly generous or kind enough—not while slaves were being whipped to enrich their coffers.

Ben Crenshaw, in particular, was a quandary. Jimmy had conflicting emotions about him. He was attracted to his body, but he also felt disgust for his presumptuousness. And this mixture of desire and disgust confused him. Ben Crenshaw was guilty of an arrogance shared by many slave holders. He presumed that owning Jimmy gave him the right to be intimate with him.

Despite this, Jimmy's strongest feeling about Ben Crenshaw was commiserative. He knew what it was like to be in the grip of desires that were shunned by the world. He'd also learned over the past few months what it felt like to lose a beloved.

Cato, however, was not dead. And Jimmy was determined that he would either find his way back to Cato or die trying.

So on Sunday afternoon he began the steps that would lead him to one outcome or the other. He began by talking to Uncle Isaac. Earlier, he'd agreed to bring Isaac with him. Since then, he'd begun to worry that Isaac would slow him down more than he would help him along. But Isaac was so desperate to seize what he saw as his last chance, Jimmy couldn't leave him behind. He could easily imagine how desperate he would be himself, if he'd been living in the conditions that Isaac had endured for more than sixty years.

"Are you ready to do this?" he asked Isaac.

"I've been ready to do this for most of my life, son. And if it don't work out this time, I reckon I'll never have another chance. I'm ready to pack my bag."

"The last time I ran away it was in Tennessee," Jimmy said. "I took along a little bit of food and a little bit of money. Before long, I wished I'd brought more food. We ought to talk to Jane and see what she can do for us in the way of food."

"I can do that," Isaac offered.

"You got any money?"

"No." Isaac shrugged. "Where would I get money from?"

"Maybe Pheby will give us some."

"That gal will give you anything you ask, if she's got it. Just don't let Little Joe know."

"All right," Jimmy said. "I'll ask her."

"And I'm pretty sure I can put my hands on some apples," Isaac added.

"That's good," Jimmy said. "They're easy to carry."

"Which reminds me," Isaac said. "I had a talk with Poky some days ago. He wants to go with us."

"What?" Jimmy threw up his hands in disbelief. "You told him?"

"Of course I did! I can't leave here without lettin' my people know I'm goin,'" Isaac said. "What'd you expect?"

"Look here," Jimmy said. "I don't begrudge anyone the chance of getting away. But we can't take everybody with us. It's gonna be hard enough even with only two of us."

"Poky ain't everybody. He's just one more. And he knows the way down the river better 'n I do. And you know how strong he is. If you want someone to help row, he's the best man for it."

Jimmy couldn't deny that. And he could see from Isaac's expression that if he said no to Poky, Isaac would be devastated.

"Is he ready to go? Can he go on Wednesday night?"

"Why not?" Isaac said. "I don't reckon he's got any other plans that would get in the way."

Jimmy rubbed his forehead as he considered what to say. Finally, he said, "All right, Poky can come. But that's all. We can't take no one else."

"Ain't no one else figurin' to come," Isaac said.

"Fine," Jimmy said. "You tell Poky to meet us by the sawmill at midnight on Wednesday. We got to make sure to wait until everybody else on this plantation is asleep—especially Eppley. Eppley's the one I worry about most. His house is right by the sawmill. He can look straight out his window and see what we're up to."

"Not only that," Isaac said. "Little Joe says the man don't sleep too good unless he's passed out from drinkin.' And lately, according to Little Joe, he's been off the bottle on account of this harvest. Joe thinks that's why he's been so out-of-sorts."

"Well, maybe we should make sure he gets something to drink on Wednesday night," Jimmy said. "Something that'll knock him out good."

"I suppose we could leave a jug of hard cider on his porch. Or maybe two!"

"Won't he think that's suspicious?"

"I don't reckon Eppley troubles himself too much with thinkin,'" Isaac said.

"Can you get a jug of hard cider by Wednesday?"

"Poky can get one from Lewis."

"Good. Then ask Poky to sneak a jug onto Eppley's porch on Wednesday."

"I'll do that," Isaac said.

"Let me get something to write with," Jimmy said. "I'm gonna give you a note I want Poky to put on the jug."

Jimmy went into the cabin. Next to where he slept, he kept the rough knapsack he'd made to hold supplies to bring along on his escape, which included a pen and several sheets of paper that he'd lifted from Bonnie Crenshaw's writing desk in the library. The Crenshaws had already taught him how to write a few words. He tore off a strip of the paper and on it he wrote: "From your seecrit friend." He was certain of the spelling of "from," "your," and "friend," which were all words he'd learned. But he had to guess how to spell "seecrit" by sounding it out. The note, he figured, would make sure that Eppley understood the cider was meant for him. He brought it back to Isaac. "Have Poky tie this note onto the jug before he leaves it on Eppley's porch."

"What's it say?"

"It tells Eppley the cider is from his secret friend."

"How's that?" Isaac asked. "Eppley don't have no friends."

"He does, too," Jimmy said. "What about that gal he goes off to visit every few days?"

"I suppose."

"Do you think he'll drink it right away?" Jimmy asked.

Isaac smiled slyly. "I've known that man twenty years. If he don't, it'll be the first time."

Jimmy nodded. Then he asked, "When was the last time you had a look at that rowboat?"

"Poky and I used it two weeks ago. Crenshaw sent us down to Mulberry Grove plantation with a load of cider. The overseer there sent us back up with a load of rice."

"Where are the oars kept?"

"Inside the mill. Right by the door."

"But the mill is locked at night, isn't it?"

"Yes. But that's because Lewis locks it. I can ask him to leave it unlocked on Wednesday night."

Jimmy thought for a moment. "No. That'll get him in trouble. They'll wonder why he left it unlocked the same night we ran off." Jimmy thought some more. "I have another idea," he said. "Ask Lewis to sneak the oars down to the rowboat on Wednesday before he locks the mill. He can hide them in the boat. Then he can leave the mill locked. That way he can say one of us must've taken the oars earlier when he wasn't looking."

"Why don't I do just that?" Isaac asked. "I can go over to the mill tomorrow to see Lewis. Then when he's not looking, I can take the oars out and hide 'em in the boat. That leaves Lewis out of it."

"But what if he notices they're missing?"

"He won't say nothin'. I know him. He likes to keep to himself. That's how he stays out of trouble."

Jimmy sighed. He saw it as a risk. But he thought it would be safer not to let Lewis know about their plans. The fewer people who knew, the better. Jimmy didn't want anyone to know where he was going. He didn't want to worry about slave catchers chasing after him in Philadelphia. "All right," he said. "But wait until Wednesday to get the oars. The less time they're missing, the less likely anyone'll notice."

Isaac nodded.

"I'm gonna let Pheby and Little Joe know we're leaving," Jimmy said. "But I don't want them or anyone else to know where we're going. If anyone figures out where we're headed, the Crenshaws could send up people to catch us. It'll be easier to keep it secret if nobody knows."

"All right."

And with that Jimmy and Isaac had their plans set to escape on Wednesday night. Jimmy spent Sunday night brooding about all the things that could go wrong. He decided to wait until the last minute on Wednesday to tell Pheby and Little Joe about their plans. He wanted to be sure that Pheby, in particular, had no time to try to talk him out of it.

35

"DON'T YOU BELIEVE IN JUSTICE?"

Cato and Joe arrived at the spot where Joe had tied up the horses to find them waiting patiently. Cato immediately inspected Oscar's ear, which was healing nicely. Oscar could barely hold still during this inspection. He nuzzled Cato relentlessly. Cato laughed and hugged him in return, filled with relief. Then he stepped back to inspect Joe's new horse. The horse had a distinctive chestnut coat, topped by a white mane and a solid streak of white from his forehead down to the tip of his nose.

"He's a beautiful horse," Cato said. "Does he have a name?"

Joe nodded. "I've given him a name. I don't know what he was called before. But I know he likes the name I've given him."

"What do you call him?"

"Nice."

Cato laughed. "Nice? That's it? What kind of name is that?"

Joe folded his arms across his chest. "What do you mean? Nice is a nice name."

"But why?"

"Because he is nice—a nice horse, in every way."

Cato laughed. "OK, Nice, it's nice to meet you." He stroked

the horse's neck. "You have pretty eyes."

"I told you he was pretty," Joe said. The he turned to Oscar. "I'm sorry, Oscar. Don't be jealous."

"I think Oscar is probably more hungry than jealous," Cato said. "Both of them must be hungry."

"Yes," Joe said. "We must find food for them."

"If my buggy is still where they left it, I have food in there—and a saddle. The patrollers didn't take the oats or the saddle. They took my satchel. Then when they found my money, they forgot about everything else."

"They took all your money?"

"Yes. It was in a purse. The one named Pete took it. He put it in his coat pocket."

Joe made a sour face. "That's not right. We must get it back from them."

"Get it back? How?"

"Leave that to me," Joe said. "Meanwhile, we should go to the buggy and see if the food is still there. "It will be fastest if we ride the horses." He looked at Oscar, whose saddle was missing. "I can ride Oscar bareback, if you ride Nice."

"Will Nice let me?"

"Of course! Nice is nice to everyone," Joe said. "Aren't you, boy?"

They easily found the buggy, which was still on the side of the road. Inside the back compartment, they found both the saddle and the feed. After the horses had eaten, Joe said, "I think we should leave the buggy here. It will be easier for us to travel together on horseback."

"Travel where?"

"To find your friend," Joe said. "And to punish the man who kidnapped him."

"You want to come with me to find Jimmy?"

"Of course," Joe said. "I have to help you. I don't think you're going to be able to do these things properly on your own."

"Why's that?"

"Because, for one thing, you don't know how to walk quietly. I've been thinking about calling you 'Lalawethika.'"

"Lala—what? What does that mean?"

"It's a Shawnee name. It means 'He makes a loud noise.'"

Cato rolled his eyes. "I'm not that bad!"

"Yes," Joe said. "You are. This is how you sound in the woods." Joe proceeded to stomp around on the leaves by the side of the road, making little whoops and bouncing his head.

Cato laughed.

"It will be better when I teach you how to walk softly. Before we go to find your friend, we need to go get your money back from the men who stole it. And to do that, we need to take them by surprise. We can't do that with the way you walk."

Cato was skeptical. "Wouldn't it be safer to just keep going and look for Jimmy?"

Joe shrugged. "It might be. But you don't have any money. Where are you going to stay? I think you are used to staying in hotels, no? That's what you told me in Kentucky."

Cato nodded.

"And besides, it's the right thing to do. We shouldn't let these men get away with what they've done. Don't you believe in justice?"

"I do," Cato said. "But I don't want to end up in jail again."

"Don't worry." Joe raked his fingers through his hair. "You're with a brave," he said proudly. "I will protect you."

"All right," Cato said. "After what you've done already, I believe you. What should we do?"

"Saddle Oscar so we can ride to a spot where I can teach you how to be quiet. Then we'll track down the men who took your money."

Cato saddled Oscar and together with Joe and Nice they went back up the road, several miles away from Sparta, until they found a grove of woods that Joe deemed suitable for his lesson. Inside the woods, with the horses watching, Joe began to teach Cato how to walk.

"You must concentrate," he said. "Focus your mind on your steps." He pointed at Cato's feet. "It will be easier if we get you moccasins. You don't know what you're walking on in those boots. You need to learn how to feel the earth as you step. And you need to step on spots that are soft, and yielding, and, most of all, on spots that are quiet."

"I'll try," Cato said. He took several steps gingerly, staring at the ground in order to avoid the leaves.

"That's good," Joe said. "But try to do it without looking at the ground. Try to see what's in front of you without staring at it."

Cato tried again. He tried to sense the ground in front of him just by using his peripheral vision. It was awkward. He found it hard to maintain his balance.

"Right now you walk like a duck," Joe said. "You must practice. It will get easier."

And so they spent another hour and a half as Cato practiced walking in the woods, holding his head up, while avoiding stepping on anything that might make a sound. Finally Joe said, "That will have to do. You're doing much better."

"Thank you."

"We should go now to find those men. Do you have any idea where to find them?"

Cato remembered what Sam had said. "They said they were gonna come back this morning to look for Oscar."

"I doubt they've tried to find him yet," Joe said. He thought for a moment. "They must have been distracted by the fire."

"Or maybe they've been busy spending my money."

"I reckon they'll come looking for him now," Joe said. "Apart from the horse, they'll figure it would be the best way to find you. Let's find a spot near the buggy. That's where they'd start their search. We can stay out of sight and wait to see if anyone comes."

"What will we do if they show up?"

"It depends on who comes. If it's all four of the men you saw last night, it'll be better to follow them and wait until they're not all together. But if it's just one or two of them, we'll capture them and force them to return the money."

"How will we do that?"

"They'll be looking for you and Oscar. We can use Oscar as bait. And as soon as they come near to him, we'll catch them."

"I don't like that idea," Cato said. "I promised Oscar I'd protect him. And now you want to use him as bait."

"They won't hurt him. They have no reason to. Besides, they won't get that far, I promise. You've got to trust me."

"I trust you, Joe, but how are we gonna catch them?" Cato asked. "They have pistols. I had one, but they took it."

"Did you know how to use it?"

"Not really."

"Then it's better that they took it." He pointed to the knife in its sheath at his waist. "I have my knife," he said. "And in my saddlebag I have rope."

"But what about me?" Cato asked. "What do you want me to do?"

"Mostly," Joe said, "I want you to be quiet—so I can surprise them. Do you know how to tie a knot?"

"Yes. I can do that quite well."

"Good. Then when the time comes, you'll come out from your hiding spot and I may ask you to tie a knot."

Cato was more than a little apprehensive about this. But he nodded.

They rode the horses back to the spot where Joe had previously left them. But this time, they tied up Nice and then led Oscar to a spot on the edge of the field opposite the buggy—just about where he had disappeared into the woods the night before.

Joe tied Oscar to a small tree that stood by itself, ten feet away from the main thicket of woods, making him easily visible from the road—despite the dark color of his coat. Cato petted him and told him in a soft voice that they'd be watching over him from close by. Then Joe and Cato hid behind the trees deeper in the woods.

As they waited, Joe tied a knot in a length of rope that he'd brought with him from his saddle pack. He made a loop. "Have you ever roped an animal?" he asked.

"No. Is it hard?"

"It takes practice to land it right. I used to practice on fence posts when I was a boy." Joe nodded toward a nearby clearing. "Go stand over there, about 10 feet away from me."

Cato did as directed. "OK," he said. "Now what?"

"Now this." Joe swung the rope and landed the loop over Cato's head. It slid down his chest and Joe pulled it tighter—but not enough to make Cato fall over. "If I pulled it harder, you'd fall down."

Cato looked down at the rope around his torso. "I believe you." He tried to loosen the loop, but it wouldn't loosen.

"It only gets tighter—not looser." Joe smiled. "That's nice, ain't it?"

"Very nice," Cato said. "Now get it off me."

Joe walked over to Cato and pulled on a particular strand of the knot, which loosened the loop. He let the loop fall to the ground and Cato stepped out of it. He pointed to a tree near the edge of the thicket. "Let's sit beside that tree. We can see the road from there, but they won't see us. When they come, I'm going to climb up there." He pointed to a spot about twenty feet up the tree. "It's easier to hit the target from a higher vantage point."

Cato looked up.

"Also, they won't see me up there."

Cato nodded.

"But I may need you to step out and show yourself if they don't get close enough to the tree."

"Show myself? You want me to be bait, too?"

"Yes. Maybe. It depends on how close they come to the tree once they reach Oscar. If they don't get close enough, or if there's more than one of them, you'll need to draw one of them in close to the tree and distract him."

"By doing what?"

"If you just show yourself, that should be enough. I reckon they'll be very excited to see you again."

"I won't be so excited to see them."

"Don't worry," Joe said. "I'll be up here. And it may not be necessary. If we see them coming, I'll climb up there and judge what's needed. If I want you to show yourself, I'll give you a signal like this." He fluttered his hand down near his waist. "If I don't signal, just stay put and wait till I land the rope."

When Joe had everything prepared, they sat. They watched and waited. An hour went by. No one showed up on the road.

"Maybe they won't come," Cato said.

"Perhaps not," Joe said. "If they don't come before dark, we'll go into town to find them."

"I think it would be better if they came here," Cato said.

"Yes," Joe said. "It would be."

"What day is it?" Cato asked.

"It's Wednesday," Joe said. "Why do you ask?"

"I was just thinking about Jimmy. I wonder what he's doing."

"You said the men who kidnapped him were going to auction him."

"Yes."

Joe shrugged. "Then he must be working on a plantation somewhere."

"Somewhere near Savannah, if Mr. Johnson is right."

"I can track him," Joe said. "I'm very good at tracking. Also, I'm eager to meet this Jimmy."

"You'll like him." Cato smiled. "Not as much as Jack, of course."

Joe raised his chin. "Do not worry. I do not think of anyone else."

"Good," Cato said. "And since we're sitting here waiting, are you going to finally tell me what happened between you and Jack?"

"Do you want to know?"

"Of course. I want to know everything."

"Oh, Cato, you should have seen how his eyes lit up when I told him how I felt. He didn't say anything at first. He just led me into the woods. When we were all alone, he told me he'd been thinking about me ever since we first met. He said he'd thought about other men, too, but he hoped I wouldn't hold that against him. I said I wouldn't. I told him I heard all about what happened between him and you."

"You told him that?"

"Of course."

"What did he say to that?"

"He said, 'Dad blame that Cato. He has a big mouth!'"

"No! He said that?"

"Yes. But then after I explained to him that you were the one who encouraged me to tell him how I felt about him, he changed his tune. He said you were so dad-blamed pretty he couldn't help himself. Then he told me that despite all that, I was making him more aroused than ever, on account of my smooth skin and my stout-heart and my brave and manly ways."

Cato rolled his eyes. "Oh, brother."

"Then he took hold of me and kissed me—and before you know it, he was shucking off his clothes. I couldn't believe how pale and handsome his body is. There was hair on his chest! I never saw a white man naked before."

"Did you get naked, too?"

"Cato, I had my moccasins and leggings off before he even got out of his shirt. I am very quick!"

"I believe it."

"And then we spent a considerable long time lying on the ground kissing."

"Just kissing? That's all?"

"Well ..." Joe blushed. "Jack put himself inside me during that time. He was gentle. But he's very big! It hurt, at first. But I did not mind it."

"You didn't mind it?" Cato laughed.

"No, as a matter of fact, I liked it quite a lot. And I am very limber! I flexed my hips in such a way that he got quite excited. He said I was driving him to distraction. Cato, you know how quiet I am. But once he started saying my name, I couldn't stay quiet. I made many loud sounds. It was a good thing we were so deep in the woods. It wasn't too long before— well, you know, he ... I ... we ..." Joe stopped, seeming unable to continue.

Cato smiled. "Oh, Joe. I'm so happy for you. Jack is a good man. And so are you. I'm so glad that you like each other."

"Yes," Joe said. "It's nice, isn't it?"

They waited another hour. By then it was mid-afternoon. Joe said, "We need to eat something. I'm going to go back to Nice. I have food in my saddlebag. You wait here while I go get it."

"What if they come while you're gone?"

"Don't let them see you. Just stay out of sight. I'll be right back."

Cato nodded.

Nice was tied up a mile away. Joe got up and headed into the woods to find him. Within a minute, he was out of sight. Cato sat and stared through the trees at the road. Now he hoped that no one would come—not while Joe was gone. After thirty minutes had gone by, he began to wonder what was keeping Joe. He had calculated that it would take him no more than half an hour to get to Nice and back again. He worried that Joe had run into a problem on the way.

Then Cato heard a noise. He looked up and saw two men on horseback coming down the road. The men were Pete and Bill, and they were headed straight for the buggy. He looked around. Joe was nowhere in sight.

36

"BOY, I GUESS I DON'T EVEN KNOW YOU"

On Wednesday afternoon, Jimmy was working in the field. He'd had what he knew would be his last lesson in the library that morning. Everything had gone as usual. He'd given no clue that anything about the day was different. He'd paused for a moment when he left the library—taking a last look at Ben Crenshaw and his sister, Bonnie. Ben had raised his eyebrows and waved his hand dismissively before turning back to his atlas. Bonnie had said, "We'll see you tomorrow, Jacob." And then he was gone.

In the field, he worked energetically, to make certain Eppley had no excuse to punish him. Regardless, he paused from time to time to look at his surroundings. He realized he might actually miss the red earth and the mossy trees, which he liked. The climate in Savannah was usually hot and muggy, which he didn't like. But now that it was autumn, the humidity had broken and the air had grown crisp. He basked in that pleasant change.

As he contemplated his escape, he was forced to acknowledge that there were aspects of his experience on the Crenshaw plantation to which he'd grown attached. He was glad to have met Pheby, Little Joe, Isaac, and Poky. He didn't know how he felt about having met Bonnie and Ben Crenshaw, but he couldn't deny that he was glad they'd made efforts to expand his knowledge. He'd learned things from them that had made him reconsider the possibilities of his life. Ben, in particular, had made him realize that sexual fascination had the power to draw him into emotional interactions he'd otherwise never consider. He thought Ben must have felt beguiled in a similar way.

As the sun set, Jimmy girded himself for what was to come. He'd arranged things so that there would be only a brief window of time to say his good-byes. He kept his eye on Poky, who he imagined was feeling a similar mix of wistfulness and excitement. Poky would have only a small amount of time to perform two of the most critical tasks for their escape.

Just before sunset, Isaac would go to the mill to 'balance the accounts' with Lewis in order to get the cider. By habit, Poky was always the first in line to have his load of cotton weighed in the weighing room at the end of the day. That meant Eppley would be occupied for another thirty minutes after Poky left the weighing room. During that time, Poky would run over to the mill to join Isaac and get the jug of cider from Lewis. After Poky arrived at the mill, Isaac would find a way to distract Lewis so that Poky could quietly grab the oars on his way out of the mill with the cider. Poky would have fifteen minutes to hide the oars in the boat, then run to Eppley's house to put the cider and Jimmy's note on the porch, and then get back to his cabin. All this had to be done before Eppley emerged from the weighing room and before Lewis locked the mill.

Since both the mill and Eppley's house could be seen from the door outside the weighing room, Jimmy would make a point of being the last one to go into the weighing room. If he saw that Poky had not completed his tasks by the time he went in, he could try to delay Eppley's departure from the weighing room by pretending to trip and drop his bag in such a way that spilled the contents. That would carry some risk of punishment, but it would be safer than having Eppley discover what Poky was doing.

When sunset came, everything started to go wrong. Poky was first in line at the weighing house, as planned. In order to avert any possibility that Eppley would punish him for having too small a load, Poky had picked an unusually large amount of cotton. He normally brought in just over three hundred pounds. But in his zeal to avoid a problem, he'd overshot the mark. The scale showed he'd picked nearly four hundred pounds. Instead of being pleased, Eppley was outraged.

"So," he said, "now we see what you can do! And what have you been doing all these years? You've been dawdling and dallying, that I can tell you. It's obvious to me now that you've tricked me into thinking you could only manage three hundred pounds. How many days have you left cotton behind that you ought to have picked, that you could easily have picked? And who is going to make up for all those pounds you left behind?"

"Massa Eppley," Poky said, "I don't know how I came to have so much cotton in my bag today. Somebody must have put some cotton in my bag by mistake. Or it could be there was some cotton got stuck in the bottom of the bag from the day before."

"Oh, is that so? And how likely is that?"

"It does get stuck sometimes," Poky said, trying desperately to make it sound plausible.

"I'll tell you what's stuck—it's you. You're stuck with a punishment for your deception. Wait here until I weigh the others. Then I will give you your punishment."

When Jimmy saw what was happening, he asked the other slaves if he could go to the front of the line. He had no choice: since Poky was going to be detained, he'd have to do what Poky was planning to do.

And so, Jimmy had his bag weighed and was dismissed. He went to Poky and whispered, "I'm gonna take care of that matter for you."

Poky whispered back, "OK. You better go quick."

"What about the note?"

"Oh," Poky said. He dug into his pocket. He took out the note and simultaneously spun around and back-handed Jimmy the note so that Eppley couldn't see it.

Jimmy stuffed the note in his pocket, left the weighing room, and ran to the mill, only to find that Lewis was already in the process of locking it up—despite protestations from Uncle Isaac, who was with him.

"I can't wait any longer," Lewis said.

"It won't be but a minute," Isaac was saying. "I know Poky will be here soon."

Jimmy joined the conversation. "Poky's been delayed," he said.

"Don't matter. I got to go now," Lewis said. "I got plans to meet a gal who's comin' up here from Mulberry Grove just to see me."

"I understand," Isaac said. "But me and Poky got to have that cider tonight."

"Well, then," Lewis said, "why don't you take it? Why do we have to wait for Poky?"

Jimmy nodded at Isaac.

"All right," Isaac said. "I'll take it. Let's go on back in there and get it right quick."

Lewis unlocked the door and Isaac scurried inside. Lewis reluctantly followed him back into the mill. Jimmy stayed outside the door and peeked in. He could see Lewis near the back of the mill, bending over the jug he'd promised to give Poky. Isaac was dithering and waving his arms, saying something Jimmy couldn't hear.

Jimmy quickly surveyed the area near the door for the oars. They were latched on a hook about six feet from the door. He stepped inside. Isaac saw him. Jimmy nodded. Isaac instantly fell down on the floor.

"Oh, my leg," Isaac cried. "Owww!"

"What?" Lewis bent over him. "What's the matter with it?"

"I got a crick or somethin.' It just came over me."

"Just like that?"

"Gettin' old, Lewis. Gettin' old. That's what happens."

While this distraction was underway, Jimmy darted up to the oars, unhooked them, and then dashed back out the door. He could see other slaves coming out from the weighing room, but there was no sign of Poky or Eppley.

Breathlessly, Jimmy carried the oars down the slope of the bank, bent beneath the overhang of the mill, and crawled along until he reached the boat, which was bobbing in the water. He placed the oars in the boat, trying not to make any sound. The second one dropped loud enough that Jimmy grimaced. He looked around, then crawled back out from under the overhang, stood, and stepped up to the door of the mill, just as Lewis and Isaac stepped out.

"Where in the world did you get to?" Lewis asked, surprised to see him climbing up the bank.

"Call of nature," Jimmy said. He gestured down toward the river. "Feel better now."

"How come Poky's delayed?" Isaac asked.

"Eppley's fixin' to lay the whip on him 'cause he picked too much cotton."

"Too *much* cotton?" Isaac was shocked. "Well, I'll be damned. That's the first time I heard of a man gettin' whipped for workin' too hard."

"Yes," Jimmy said. "Poky told me to ask you to take the jug over to where you and he were gonna go later tonight, Uncle Isaac."

"Oh, he wants me to take it?"

"Yes. I think you'll have time if you go soon."

"What are y'all talkin' about?" Lewis asked. "You got some kind of get-together happening tonight?"

"Yup," Isaac said. "Me and Poky's gonna celebrate."

"Celebrate what?"

"It's his birthday," Isaac said. "Thirty years old today! But I gotta hurry." And with that he started to dash off in the direction of Eppley's house.

"Wait!" Jimmy shouted.

"What's wrong?"

"Don't forget the note. Poky gave me a note."

"Oh, right." Isaac came back to retrieve the note from Jimmy. He took it and turned and began to run toward Eppley's house again.

Jimmy put his hand on Lewis's shoulder and pulled him around so he wouldn't see where Isaac was headed.

"What's this about a note?" Lewis asked.

"I should've said 'pass.' Poky got a pass because it's his birthday."

"A pass?" Lewis was clearly skeptical. "Crenshaws never did a thing like that before."

In order to distract Lewis, Jimmy said, "I didn't know it was Poky's birthday, did you?"

"No, I didn't," Lewis said. "And I don't know what he's got to celebrate about."

"That's true," Jimmy said.

"Look here," Lewis said. "I was just telling Isaac that I got to lock up and get back home. I'm meetin' a gal tonight."

"Oh," Jimmy said. "Well, let me walk with you, and you can tell me about it."

"First I gotta lock up," Lewis said.

"Right."

Lewis turned and locked the door to the mill. Instantly, Jimmy had his arm back on Lewis's shoulder and began to shepherd him away from the direction of Eppley's house. "So who's this gal?" Jimmy asked.

Jimmy walked Lewis all the way back to his cabin, while Lewis told him about his planned liaison with the slave from Mulberry Grove. After he was done with Lewis, Jimmy ran over to his own cabin. Pheby was there, but Little Joe was not.

"Where's Little Joe?" he asked her.

"He had to go to town earlier," Pheby said. "He's gonna be back soon. Why do you ask?"

"It's too bad he's not here," Jimmy began. "The truth is, I've got something to tell you and I wanted to tell Joe, too."

"Uh-oh." Pheby was immediately wary. "Tell us what?"

"I'm leaving tonight."

"What? You leaving? Tonight?" She covered her mouth with her hand and shook her head furiously.

"I'm afraid so. I'm sorry I couldn't tell you sooner. Me and Uncle Isaac are leaving. And maybe Poky, too."

"Oh, my Lord!" Pheby said. "Are you serious? You talkin' about runnin' away? All of you?"

"Yes. We're gonna do it. We're fixin' to leave after dark."

"Why you didn't tell me before now?"

"I didn't want anyone to know. It's safer that way."

"Oh, Jacob! You mean nobody knows? What about Little Joe?"

"You'll have to tell him."

"You sayin' I'm not gonna see you no more? Just like that? It's too quick. You oughta have gave me some warning." Her eyes were welling up now.

"Who knows?" Jimmy said. "Could be we'll see each other again someday ... after the war."

Pheby threw her arms around Jimmy. "Oh, baby, you gotta be careful. Don't you let nothin' happen to you." Then she sucked in her breath. "And you say, you say Uncle Isaac's going, too? But I've known him my whole life. How can that be? Oh, my Lord. How you all gonna manage it?"

"Don't worry," Jimmy said. "We got a good plan."

"Where you goin' to?"

"I ought not to say," Jimmy said. "The Crenshaws will try to make you tell them. It's better if you don't know."

"You right," she said. "It's better if I don't know. But how'm I gonna say good-bye to you? You know how I feel about you."

"I do."

"No, you don't. Oh, lord. I only wish ... I never did get a chance to kiss you even."

"Come over here, now." Jimmy took her in his arms, leaned her back, and kissed her on the lips. Then he said, "You're such a good friend. I'm sorry to say good-bye to you."

"Oh, Jacob, Jacob. You know you gonna make me fall over, kissin' me like that." She brushed her hands along the sides of her dress. "I reckon you be goin' back to your sweetheart."

"Yes. As soon as I can."

"And she lucky, Jacob. I hope you find her real soon."

"Pheby, I'm not gonna lie to you no more. My sweetheart ... she's not a she."

"What?"

"I never told you. But it's like it was with Elijah. I mean, I'm like him ... and I've always been that way. And like you said, it's not in the regular way of things."

"That can't be! You, too? But you don't seem like that."

"I am, Pheby. I am. And my sweetheart's name is Cato. He's fine, Pheby. He's real fine. You'd like him."

"Oh, my Lord. A man like you! I guess I don't know half what I think I know."

"None of us does, Pheby."

"I've seen so little of the world," Pheby said. "I guess the regular way of things ain't so regular as I thought."

"I can't say," Jimmy said. "I'm not sure how much it's like that in the world. But it's true for me."

"And the feelin' just came on you that way?"

"It did. It does. Ever since I can remember."

"Well, I guess that's how you are."

"And there's one more thing," Jimmy said. "I want you to know my real name. It's Jimmy, not Jacob. Jacob was the name that kidnapper Hogan gave me."

"And you just now sayin'?" She shook her head. "Boy, I guess I don't even know you."

"I'm sorry. I've been trying to keep it a secret because I thought it'd be safer. That's one more thing I don't want the Crenshaws to find out about."

"Oh," Pheby said. "I won't tell them. They won't get nothin' out of me."

"Don't worry. They don't know, so they won't ask about it."

"It's gonna be a sorry thing around here once you all go. Them Crenshaws are gonna be vexed."

Jimmy took in a deep breath. He hadn't considered this. "I hope they won't take it out on anyone else. Oh, Pheby, I hope this wont cause any trouble for you."

"Look here," Pheby said. "Don't you think about it. It's not your fault. It's them. You gotta do what you gotta do. Whatever they do, it won't be anything we ain't seen before. And at least we'll know that for once it's on account of something good happened."

"I suppose."

"But you gotta be careful. You know? That would be worse than anything, if something happened and you got caught."

"We're gonna be careful. Don't worry. We've got a good plan. Poky and Isaac, they know the river. And I know the maps. I know how things are from the maps. The Yankees are right out there—just a few miles away. And, Pheby, you got to know ... freedom, it's the only thing that counts. I can't live like this."

"No," Pheby said, "I guess you can't."

"If anyone asks, just say I've gone to get my portrait painted."

"What?"

"I know it sounds crazy, but just remember it, OK?"

"OK."

They hugged one last time. Then, with pain and hope in his heart, Jimmy pulled away and left the cabin.

37

"YOU'RE A DEAD MAN!"

Cato cautiously peeked around the tree. Pete and Bill, the men who'd robbed him, were almost at the buggy. He turned to go look for Joe. He took careful steps, quiet steps —even though his legs were shaking. The further he got from the edge of the thicket, the faster he stepped. Despite all his practice, he wasn't confident enough to step quietly, and still keep his head up. He was looking at the ground, so he didn't see Joe approach. And since Joe didn't want to startle him, he came up from the side and put his hand over Cato's mouth.

Cato's eyes registered alarm. Joe looked at him meaningfully, then lowered his hand.

"They're here," Cato whispered.

"I know," Joe said. "Let's go back to the tree. You stand below. I'll go up."

They walked quietly back to the edge of the thicket. Joe shimmied up the tree like a squirrel—limber. He leaned down and nodded at Cato. Cato nodded back.

They both watched as Pete and Bill dismounted. Bill climbed into the buggy and began to rummage through it. Pete shielded his eyes with his hand and turned to scan the area. He saw Oscar. He said something and pointed at Oscar. Bill looked where he was pointing and made a face. They spoke back and forth, then Pete began to walk into the field, coming straight toward Oscar. Bill climbed out of the buggy and began to harness his horse to it.

Pete was mumbling to himself as he came up to Oscar. When he noticed that Oscar was tied to a small tree, he stopped and looked around, warily.

Cato glanced up at Joe and saw that he was fluttering his hand down by his waist. Cato took a deep breath, then took a step to the side of the tree, right where Pete could see him. "That's my horse," he said, in a voice loud enough to be heard by Pete but not loud enough to be heard by Bill.

"What the hell!" Pete immediately went for his pistol.

Cato took a step backward.

"Don't move, nigger, or I'll shoot!" Pete spoke in a quiet but firm voice. And then he took a step forward.

Cato took one more step backward.

"I'm warnin' you. I ain't gonna say it again." He lifted the pistol and pointed it at Cato.

Cato raised his hands in the air.

Pete took two more steps toward Cato. He smiled. "For a teacher, you're one stupid nigger." He stood just at the edge of the woods.

Cato saw but didn't hear the sound of the rope as it fell and landed in a perfect ring, encircling Pete's body. He did hear a slight crunch as Joe leapt down to the ground and pulled on the rope. The force of the rope tightening around his arms caused Pete to stumble forward and drop his pistol.

Pete said, "What the hell!" The color drained from his face. He looked at Cato in disbelief.

Joe nodded toward Cato. He held the rope in one hand and lifted the finger of his other hand up to his lips.

Cato caught his meaning and darted to Pete's side, then

clamped his hand over Pete's mouth—just as Joe had done to him a few moments earlier.

Joe picked up the pistol and stuffed it in the back of his pants. Then he pulled a handkerchief out of his pocket and tied it tight around Pete's mouth to gag him. Both Joe and Cato looked back toward the buggy. Bill was preoccupied with harnessing his horse. Joe jerked on the rope. He used it to drag Pete deeper into the thicket. When they reached a tree ten feet inside the woods, he shoved Pete down. He forced him to sit with his back to the tree. Joe quickly wrapped the other end of the rope around the tree and tied it off.

Then Joe ran to a spot further back in the woods. He rummaged on the ground until he came up with another length of rope—one he'd hidden earlier. Then he nodded at Cato and they both returned to the big tree at the edge of the woods. In an instant, Joe scurried up the tree. Cato resumed his position, standing watch below him.

They both looked on as Bill finished hitching his horse to the buggy. They watched as Bill stood waiting beside the buggy. He turned his head, then, looking into the field, he peered toward Oscar. For a moment Bill stayed put without speaking. Then he began to shout.

"Pete! Where the hell'd you go to?" He craned his neck as his eyes swept around the field. "C'mon, Pete. We ain't got time for this!"

After another moment of shifting impatiently on his feet, Bill said, "Aw, hell." He began to walk into the field toward Oscar.

But he didn't stop when he got to Oscar. Instead he kept going, heading right toward the woods, shouting Pete's name. When he got to the spot where he could see Cato, he stopped and bellowed, "You!"

Joe threw the rope—but this time his aim was not perfect. The rope fell on top of Bill's head, but landed askew. Shock registered on Bill's face, but he shook the rope off his head. Seeing this, Cato rushed out of the woods straight toward Bill. He tried to push Bill over, but only succeeded in pushing him back several steps.

Bill pushed back hard. And in a moment, they had their arms around each other, pushing and shoving, writhing around, neither man gaining the advantage. But then Bill fell to the ground. Cato bent down and tried to hold him on the ground, but Bill pushed Cato off with his feet. Cato reeled backward. Bill immediately jumped back up and lunged at Cato. Cato stepped to the side in time to avoid him, but then Bill whirled around. He pulled his pistol from his holster. He charged at Cato and kicked him in the groin. Cato fell down in pain, and Bill stood over him, pointing his gun and shouting "You're a dead man!"

From up in the tree Joe let out a menacing whoop. In the same instant, he leapt to the ground and landed behind Bill. Before Bill could turn, Joe had one arm around Bill's torso and held his knife up to the edge of Bill's throat with the other. "Drop it," Joe said. He let the knife blade touch the skin of Bill's neck. "Or I'll slit your throat."

Breathing hard, Bill dropped the pistol. Cato shook himself off and stood up, then quickly fetched the pistol from the ground. He pointed it at Bill. At that point, Joe stepped aside to retrieve the rope, which had fallen several feet away. Once he had it, he stepped back and dropped the loop of rope over Bill's shoulders, and, as before, when it slid onto his arms, Joe pulled it tight.

He looked Bill in the face. "Why are you men always so ugly?" Joe asked.

"And vicious," Cato added. "He was all set to kill me."

"That's not nice," Joe said. "C'mon." He tugged the rope and pulled Bill into the woods, this time to a tree that faced the tree Pete was tied to. Moments later, Bill was tied in a similar fashion.

Joe took the rag out of Pete's mouth. "Now you can talk to

each other," he said. "But first, I want to know where my friend's money is."

"We ain't got it," Pete said.

Joe slid his knife out of its sheath, leaned down, and placed it against Pete's forehead.

"My God," Bill said. "He's gonna scalp you."

"Hold on," Pete said. "I don't have all of it. We split it up. We each have some."

"Where's yours?" Joe asked.

"In my saddlebag," Pete said.

Joe pulled the knife back. He walked over to Bill and knelt down beside him. This time he simply pointed the knife at Bill's head. "How about you?" he asked. "Where's your share?"

Bill stared at the knife. "In my pocket," he said.

Joe looked at Cato. "You go get the money from the saddlebag. I'll get the money from this one's pocket."

Cato nodded. He left and went back to the road, to Pete's horse which was hitched to the buggy. The horse's saddlebag had three flapped compartments. Two were empty, and inside the third was Cato's purse. When he opened the purse, he found only a few of the many gold coins that had been inside it when it was taken. He drew in a sharp breath, disappointed to find so little of his money remaining. As he started to leave, his eye caught on the rifle scabbard attached to the saddle. There was no rifle in it—but he noticed that the bottom portion of the scabbard was slightly distended. Cato pushed his fingers down into the scabbard, and there he felt a knot of cloth. He pulled on it, and as he wriggled the bundle out of the scabbard, it became apparent that it was full of coins. He unknotted it and quickly counted the coins: it was more than half of the money that had been in his purse originally.

He went back to the thicket. "I found the money," he told Joe. "He put some of it in his saddlebag. But he hid most of it in his rifle scabbard."

"What?" Bill said. "What's he talkin' about, Pete?"

"I was savin' it for later," Pete said. "To give you the rest of your share. No need for Sam and Bobby to know about it. You and me did most of the work anyway."

Joe handed Cato a tied-up handkerchief that held Bill's coins. "Here's what the other one had in his pocket."

"You didn't say nothin' about savin' some for later," Bill said. "You tried to cheat me!"

Joe made a wry face. "You two can fight about the money later. Right now it's time for your punishment."

"What punishment?" Pete asked. "We was just doin' our job."

Joe nodded. "It's not a very nice job, is it? And I don't think your job is supposed to include stealing."

"What're you gonna do?" Bill asked. There was fear in his voice.

"I'm gonna teach you not to ridicule strangers who never did you any harm," Joe said. "You called my friend bad names. That wasn't very nice." He stood and walked back over to Pete. "I'll take this one," he said to Cato. "You take the other one."

"What're you gonna do?" Cato asked.

"Follow my lead," Joe said. "I'm gonna show this man what a pissant miscreant he is." He looked down at Pete. "Let's see if you like the taste of this." Then Joe carefully opened the fly of his leggings, pulled out his penis, aimed it at Pete, and began to shoot a stream of urine onto Pete's face.

"Oh, fuck!" Pete shouted.

"Go on, Cato," Joe said. "I bet the other one wants some, too."

Cato could hardly believe what was happening. But he, too, opened his fly, pulled out his penis, and began to pee straight onto Bill's face. "Jesus Christ!" Bill shouted.

"I believe they like it," Joe said. "This is some top quality piss, gentlemen. Nigger piss and Injun piss—ain't that how you like it? Tastes good, don't it? I'm not sure which one is better for you."

After they finished and buttoned their pants back up, Joe said, "C'mon. Let's go see to the horses." They quickly walked out of the woods. Cato untied Oscar, while Joe went back to the road, where he tied the horses to a fence. When the horses were secured, he went back to the woods. He walked up to Pete and said, "I hope you've got a loud voice, Petey, my boy. Sooner or later somebody'll notice your horses out there. That'll be your chance to yell 'help, help, help, oh help me!' real nice and loud."

"You'll pay for this," Pete said. "You and that nigger."

"Oh, man," Joe said. "You still haven't learned to be nice." He shook his head. "Be careful. So far you got off easy. But if you come after us, I promise you, you'll pay a much higher price." And in a deft move, Joe unsheathed his knife and pretended to swipe it across the man's scalp. Pete flinched and lowered his head.

Joe left the men tied to their trees and went back to Cato and Oscar. "C'mon, let's go get Nice," he said. "And then we've gotta get out of here right quick."

38

"STOP!"

Except for a smattering of moonlight, it was completely dark as Jimmy made his way toward the mill. Jimmy hadn't seen Uncle Isaac since he'd sent him off toward Eppley's house with the jug of cider. Nor had he seen Poky since he left the weighing house where Poky was awaiting punishment. The original plan had been for the three of them to meet at the mill at midnight. Midnight was only an hour away.

When he got to the mill, he crawled under the overhang to a spot from which he could see anyone coming. He could also see Eppley's house. He saw the glow of candlelight coming through the window from inside the house, but there was no sign of anyone moving around inside. The moon was a quarter full, but it hung in the sky behind Eppley's house. Despite the light from the window, most of the porch was in shadow, so Jimmy couldn't tell whether or not the jug of cider was there.

While he waited, he double-checked the boat. It was tied and bobbing in the water just as he'd left it, the oars still lying inside.

Hearing footsteps coming toward him, he scurried as far as he could under the overhang. He saw the feet of someone coming, and although he could only see the approaching figure from the knee down, he knew it wasn't Eppley. It was someone wearing shabby shoes, so he knew it had to be a slave. Jimmy was dressed in his work clothes as well; he'd packed his fancy clothes in the knapsack. He was saving them for Philadelphia.

When the feet were just at the edge of the mill, a head leaned down and peered beneath the overhang, right at Jimmy.

"I figured you'd be here already," Poky said.

"Where's Isaac?" Jimmy asked.

"He's gone to your place to say good-bye. Before that he was at my cabin. He put salve on my back."

"How're you feeling?"

Poky shrugged. "Sore." He bent down fully and scooted under the overhang toward Jimmy with obvious discomfort. "I hope that was the last time."

"Don't worry," Jimmy said. "We're gonna make it out of here. And then we'll be free."

"If nobody catches us," Poky said.

"Did Isaac get the jug over to Eppley's house?"

"He did." Poky nodded. "He left it with the note, on the porch, just like you said. After that he came over to the weighing house. That was when Eppley was whipping me."

"Eppley had no right to do you like that."

Poky gave a bitter laugh. "He said I picked too much. Can you believe that?"

"Forget about him. You won't see him no more. Not after tonight."

Poky looked at the boat. "Did you get the oars?"

Jimmy nodded. "They're in there. Lewis didn't see me take them. Or if he did, he didn't say anything. He had his mind on someone else anyway."

"I know," Poky said. "He told me yesterday he was meetin' his gal tonight."

Jimmy said, "I hope Uncle gets here soon. I'm ready to get goin.'"

Poky peered out from under the overhang. "Here he comes now."

They watched as Uncle Isaac made his way to the mill, carrying his rucksack. They could hear him humming to himself while he came closer. As he was approaching, he tripped and fell face-down on the ground.

Just then, Jimmy heard Eppley's voice calling from the porch of his house. "Sarah, is that you?"

Isaac lifted his head high enough to peer toward the mill.

Jimmy stuck his head out from beneath the overhang so that Isaac could see him. He put his finger to his lips.

Isaac looked back toward Jimmy and nodded.

"C'mon, Sar-ee!" Eppley shouted. "I know you're out there. I got your present." He stumbled down the stairs from his porch. He was tottering in a way that indicated he'd already drunk a good deal of the cider.

Isaac lifted his torso with his arms and tried to crawl toward the mill.

"Is that you, Sar-ee?" Eppley shuffled straight toward the mill. A cloud floated from in front of the moon, which now cast a soft but distinct light on Isaac's body.

Isaac stopped moving. He tried to sink into the ground as much as he could.

But Eppley kept on coming. "I know'd you'd come out to see me," he called. "Come out where I can see you, honey."

Jimmy and Poky scrambled further under the overhang so that Eppley couldn't see them—but once there, they couldn't see Eppley or Isaac either.

"What the hell?" Eppley's voice suddenly turned indignant. "Who is that?"

Poky grabbed Jimmy's arm. But Jimmy again put his finger to his lips. Neither of them moved.

"Turn over so I can see you," Eppley cried.

Jimmy heard the sound of Isaac rolling over in the dirt.

"Isaac!" Eppley shouted. "What in the name of Creation are you doin'? And what's that bundle you got with you?"

"It's OK," Isaac said meekly. "I got a pass."

"Boy, a pass don't mean you can be out here at this time of night lyin' in the dirt next to some bundle."

"I just tripped, is all," Isaac said.

"You tripped? But where're you goin,' old man? That's what I want to know."

"I'm jus' goin' back to my cabin."

"Then what's all this stuff you got with you? What you got in there?"

"Just some things I had over at Poky's."

"What kind of bullshit are you givin' me, Isaac? That don't make no sense."

Eppley usually had a pistol in a holster tied around his waist. But Jimmy had noticed that Eppley wasn't wearing it. Half-drunk, without his pistol, without his whip, Eppley was no match for anyone. Jimmy pulled away from Poky's arm. He put his finger to his lips again. But then he crawled out from under the overhang. He stepped up to face Eppley. "Leave him be," he said firmly.

"You!" Eppley shook his head in disbelief. "What the hell's goin' on here?" he shouted. "What're you two up to? Y'all fixin' to run away?"

"Tain't nothin' like that," Isaac said from the ground. "Go on back to your cabin, Jimmy. I'll explain everything to Massa Eppley. It's just a misunderstandin.'"

"Jimmy?" Eppley lolled his head. "Who in the hell is Jimmy? And what in the name of Christ are you two boys up to? I'm gonna go fetch my whip!"

"You know somethin,'" Jimmy said. "You're not much of a man without your weapons." He walked up to Eppley, and stood just inches away from him.

"What're you doin,' nigger?"

"I'm gonna teach you a lesson, cracker." Before Eppley could react, Jimmy swung his fist and punched Eppley in the face. Eppley stumbled backward and then fell over. Jimmy kicked him in the side. "How do you like that, motherfucker?"

Isaac tried to pull himself up on his knees. "Look over there, Jacob!" he said. "She's on the porch!" He pointed back at Eppley's house.

Suddenly there was a loud clang. Jimmy turned to see a woman on Eppley's porch. She'd rung the big alarm bell that hung from the side of the porch.

"That's Sarah," Isaac said. "That's the gal he's been waitin' on.'"

Jimmy ran toward the porch. He thought if he stopped her before she rang the bell again, it might not be enough to wake the others. But just as he reached the bottom of the porch, she rang the bell again. Then Jimmy heard a scream. He turned and saw Eppley crouching over Isaac, holding a dripping knife.

Jimmy ran back toward them. Eppley stood and turned to face him, wielding the knife. Jimmy stopped ten feet away from Eppley. He looked down at Isaac, who wasn't moving. Then he looked up at Eppley. "What'd you do to him?"

"I kill't him," Eppley spat. "Just like I'm gonna do you." He waved the knife, slicing it through the air. He took a step toward Jimmy.

Jimmy took a step backward. As he did so, he saw something move behind Eppley. Poky climbed out stealthily from beneath the mill. He began to creep up toward Eppley. Jimmy took another step backward. He glanced down at Isaac again. He said, "You had no cause to do that."

"I caught you red-handed," Eppley said. "Y'all runnin' away. I got ... I got every right." He was slurring his words.

Jimmy took a step toward him. "Crenshaws are gonna be mad you killed one of their men."

"Oh, no," Eppley snarled. "Nigger was old ... and, uh ... couldn't work no more." His head lolled to the side. "Waste of good food." Eppley waved the knife erratically. He was tottering from the cider.

Jimmy looked around frantically. Despite the alarm, no one from the house was coming. He glared at Eppley. "You think you can take me?" he asked.

Eppley laughed. "You goin' down, boy. You goin' straight down to hell." He took another step toward Jimmy.

"Look out behind you!" The voice came from Sarah, who was still on the porch.

Eppley turned. But Poky already had his arms around Eppley's torso. He pulled hard, pinning Eppley's arms to his side. Jimmy leapt forward, grabbed Eppley's immobilized wrist, and shook it until the knife fell from his hand. Poky squeezed Eppley hard, pulling him backward. Jimmy picked up the knife and pointed it at Eppley.

Poky began to swing Eppley from side to side, shaking him like a rag doll. Eppley was heavy, but much lighter than a load of cotton. "God damn you!" Poky shouted. It was the first time Jimmy had ever heard Poky swear. His eyes were wild with fury. "What have you done?"

Poky began to whirl Eppley around in a circle, spinning him like a whirligig. "That was my friend!" He spun even faster. "No, sir, sinner. You can't hide!" With a tremendous heave, he flung Eppley high into the air, throwing him as far as he could. Eppley landed face-down with a thud, as his head smashed into a rock. He lay on the ground, not moving.

On the porch, Sarah, clanged the bell wildly.

Poky and Jimmy dashed back over to Isaac. Blood was pooled on his chest. Jimmy bent down and tried to lift him up, but he could see that Isaac was dead. He laid him gently back down.

"Oh, Isaac," Poky said, tears in his eyes. "Oh, uncle!"

Jimmy looked back at Eppley. "I think Eppley's dead, too," he said.

Poky looked back at Eppley. "Oh, lord," he cried. "What've I done?"

"C'mon." Jimmy pulled Poky away from Isaac's body. "We've got to move fast. They're all awake by now."

Jimmy put his hands over Isaac's eyes and closed them. Then he stood, and Poky stood, too. Without speaking, they both ran toward the mill.

Poky scampered down the embankment and climbed into the boat. He picked up one of the oars and began to mount it in its socket on the side of the boat. Meanwhile, Jimmy untied the rope that moored the boat to the mill. Then he leapt into the boat—but he jumped too hard, and the boat lurched and wobbled. Jimmy lost his balance and fell into the middle of the boat.

Poky got the other oar mounted on the side of the boat. With Jimmy lying on the floor of the boat, Poky began to row away from the mill. Jimmy raised himself up and looked back at the shore. He could see a figure coming toward them. It was Ben Crenshaw, his cane in one hand, a pistol in the other. When he reached the embankment, he pointed the pistol above his head, and fired. "Stop!" he shouted. "Stop, Jacob! It isn't safe!"

"He can't catch us," Jimmy said. "Keep rowing."

"But he's gonna shoot us," Poky said.

"He won't."

"Why you think that?"

"Because he ... because I don't think he will."

Poky kept rowing. When they were out in the middle of the river, Jimmy looked back to shore. The boat was rapidly pulling away downstream. Ben was shuffling sideways along the shoreline with his cane, trying to keep pace with them. He shouted something, then stopped and again pointed his pistol in the air. He fired it again. The echo of the shot reverberated in the night air. Poky kept rowing. Sarah continued ringing the bell.

By then several other figures had assembled near the shore.

Jimmy saw Bonnie Crenshaw run to her brother's side. He was still holding the pistol above his head. She pulled Ben's arm down until the pistol was pointed at the ground. She shook her head.

Little Joe, Pheby, and Jane had gathered in a cluster on the shore, twenty yards downstream from the Crenshaws. Little Joe shouted something, but Jimmy couldn't make out what he was saying. Jimmy waved at them. He saw Pheby drop to her knees and clasp her hands together—she was praying.

A few minutes later, the boat reached the boundary of the Crenshaw plantation. Poky kept rowing, strong and steady, despite the pain in his back. But he was sobbing. "I didn't mean to kill him," he whimpered.

"It wasn't your fault," Jimmy said. "You had to do something."

"I oughtn't to've thrown him so hard."

"It was just bad luck how he hit that rock," Jimmy said. "It was an accident."

"Maybe," Poky said. "But that's the trouble. I'm not sure it was. I don't know if I meant to do it or not—and the Lord's gonna know I did it."

"The Lord'll know you didn't mean to," Jimmy said. "I know you. You were trying to protect me. And you had to protect yourself, too. Eppley's the one who did the killing."

Poky was silent. He kept rowing.

Jimmy looked ahead. Poky was facing him, so he couldn't see where they were going without looking over his shoulder. "There's a fork in the river coming up," Jimmy told him.

Poky nodded. "We're gonna take the left fork. It goes around an island. When we come back around to the main channel, we'll be by Mulberry Grove. It won't be long after that we should come to where the patrol boats are."

"Is the left fork the quickest way?"

"No," Poky said. "But it runs along the South Carolina side. Nobody'll be able to see us from the Georgia shore once we get past the fork. At least not till we get back to the main channel."

Jimmy looked around. "Too bad there's no fog."

"Maybe," Poky said. "It's bad now. But it'll be good once we get out to sea. We're gonna need to see them Yankee boats."

"You're right," Jimmy said. "And we're gonna need to be sure the Yankees can see us."

39

"I WOULD MAKE A VERY NICE PET"

After Cato and Joe retrieved Oscar and Nice, they rode along the outskirts of Sparta, turned away from town, then headed east toward Augusta. After they'd ridden twelve miles east, they found a road going south, and turned toward Savannah. After another twenty-four miles, they reached Sandersville, the county seat of Washington County.

Since Cato had recovered most of his money from Pete and Bill, he proposed that they board the horses and stay in a hotel, as had been his custom throughout the journey.

Inside the hotel room, they sat on the bed and talked over everything that had happened to Cato at the hands of the slave patrollers.

"You told them you were a teacher?"

"Yes. That was a mistake," Cato said. "I should've told them I was Spanish. That's what I told a sheriff in Madisonville, and he believed it. I told it to the sheriff in Sparta, too."

Joe reached out and brushed his fingers through Cato's hair, to see how it might part. "You could pretend to be Shawnee," he said. "All you'd have to do is wear clothes like mine. You've got your money now. We can buy you buckskin leggings and moccasins. I could part your hair in the middle, like this, see? Then I could tie it in place with a headband. If you wore a feather in it, the white men wouldn't even think about you, they'd barely see you at all. They'd think 'Injun' when they saw you—and keep going."

"But my hair's not straight like yours."

"They won't see it. They'll see the feather. Most of your hair will be hidden by the band."

"I suppose it might work. I've already been Mr. Velasquez."

"Besides," Joe said, "you'll be riding with me. When they see me and they see you—they'll see us together, as if we're one person."

"That's probably true," Cato said.

The next morning Joe told Cato to wait in their hotel room while he went shopping. At the Sandersville General Store, using Cato's money, he bought the clothes and moccasins. When he came back, he had Cato put the clothes on. Then he told him to lean over the wash basin while he poured water onto his hair, wetting it thoroughly.

"That's cold!" Cato exclaimed.

"Be brave."

Joe parted Cato's hair in the middle and tied it with a green headband. He stood back to admire his work. "It's good you haven't cut your hair for a long time. It hangs down straight now."

"It'll curl right back up when it dries," Cato said. "Into ringlets. I know how it behaves."

Joe shrugged. "The band will hold it in place."

"What about a feather?" Cato asked.

"We have to find one first."

"OK, but where do we look?"

"They fall from the sky. They're a gift. We'll look on the ground." Joe spoke in a tone that implied that this was obvious. "But we must look for one that's suitable for you. It should be from a bird that can fly a long distance. Then you, too, will fly free throughout your journey."

"What kind of feather do you wear?"

"A crow's feather. The crow gives me skill and cunning." He thought for a moment. "I think we should find you a falcon's feather. Falcons are fast—and quiet!"

When they left Sandersville, they rode east toward Sylvania—a two-day journey. Savannah was another two days beyond that. When they stopped to rest on the first day, they ventured into the woods to look for feathers. After careful searching, Joe found one that he deemed suitable. "Here's a falcon feather," he said. He held it up for Cato to admire.

"It's beautiful," Cato said. "I like the stripes."

"And here's one more. I found this yesterday by a stream." Joe pulled out a pale blue feather that he'd tucked into his shirt. "This is from a great blue heron. It will give you patience."

"It's beautiful!" Cato took it in his hand and held it up to his head. "Can I wear them both?"

"Yes, but not at the same time. You'll have to choose between speed and patience—depending on the day."

"Today I want speed," Cato said.

Joe nodded and fastened the falcon's feather into Cato's headband. "Now we must practice walking," he said. "This time with speed."

He began to run noiselessly around in a large circle. Cato ran after him, giggling, despite his effort to run quietly.

"Lalawethika!" Joe called back to him. "Even with your moccasins, you're too loud!"

After their walking practice, they continued riding toward Savannah. In each town they entered, they rode side by side, dressed as Shawnee. And as Joe had predicted, none of the white men they encountered gave them a second look. Oscar and Nice soon learned to keep a side-by-side pace.

As they rode, Cato told Joe much of his history—about his childhood on the Askew plantation; about his father, Augustus;

about his brother, William; about his friend, Erastus Hicks; and about Dorothy, who had married his brother. But most of what he had to say was about Jimmy.

"I'm sure we'll find him," Joe said. "I can track down anybody."

"I believe you," Cato said, recalling how readily Joe had found him in Sparta. "But even if we find him, how can we get him back to the North? Jimmy won't be able to pass as Shawnee —or as Spanish—or as anything."

"He could act as our servant."

"But Shawnee people don't own slaves. Do they?"

"No. Of course not!" Joe shook his head. "But Cherokee people do—a few of them, anyway."

"So we'd have to pretend to be Cherokee?"

"No," Joe said. "It wouldn't matter. To white men we're all the same. None of them will give it much thought."

"I don't think Jimmy would care much for that—he wouldn't want to pretend to be my slave. It would be too strange."

"He could pretend to be my servant, then. People will see how fierce I am and assume I'm the master."

Cato laughed.

"You laugh?!"

"Yes. Because you pretend to be fierce. But I know you're not. Not really."

Joe put a hand on his hip. "That may be. But you must not let anyone else know."

"What about Jack Robinson? I must be sure to let *him* know what you're really like."

"No, you will not!" Joe grinned. "Jack Robinson will have to learn about me through firsthand experience."

Cato smiled. Then he turned serious. "Do you think Jack will be all right?"

"He'd better be. But I have not heard how the Rebs treat prisoners."

"My brother was a prisoner at Camp Douglas in Chicago," Cato said. "He said it was a hellhole."

"If anything happens to Jack, I will go to war against the Rebs myself."

"Then the Rebs better treat him well—or they will regret it."

"I hate this war," Joe said. "I wish these white men would stop fighting one another."

"You remind me of Jimmy," Cato said.

"How so?"

"He doesn't like white men, either."

"I didn't say I don't like white men. Some are bad, yes. But some are good."

"Like Jack."

"Yes. He's a good man."

"How do you know?"

"I can just look at a man and tell what kind of man he is."

"How? What do you look at?"

"It's not something I can describe. It's a matter of spirit."

"You put great store in spiritual things, don't you?"

"Of course," Joe said. "What else matters? Everything else is a dream."

Cato thought for a while. "If everything is a dream, then why are we having this dream?"

"You mean all of us? Or you and I in particular?"

"I mean you and I."

"Oh, that should be obvious," Joe said. "You and I are spirit brothers. Don't you think so?"

"We must be," Cato said. "I've never had a friend like you."

"Nor I like you," Joe said.

"It's strange how something that's terrible, like Jimmy being kidnapped, can lead to something wonderful, like meeting you and meeting Jack."

"Yes," Joe said. "I've noticed this happens in life."

"Me, too."

"Jack really liked you," Joe said. "He told me so."

"What did he say?"

"He said you were like a beautiful butterfly. A butterfly alights on your hand, but it does not stay."

"What? That doesn't sound like Jack at all."

"You're right. He didn't say that. That's what I say. What he said was something else entirely."

"You're teasing me! What did he say?"

"Oh, he said you were dad-blamed sweet."

"Ha!"

"That's his favorite phrase. Everything is dad-blamed this or dad-blamed that. He is funny."

"What did he say about you?"

"He said he'd have to keep his eye on me. He thinks I'm cunning like a cat."

"You see? That's what comes from slinking around quietly in the woods."

"That's all right with me. As long as he wants to pet the cat and have it curl up on his lap."

"He is lucky to have such a nice pet."

"Yes," Joe said. "I would make a very nice pet."

After that they did not speak for many miles. But they continued to bask in the warmth of their friendship as they rode south toward Savannah.

40

"WE'VE GOT TO FIND SOMEWHERE TO HIDE"

By the time Jimmy and Poky passed through the left fork in the river channel, the alarm bell back at the Crenshaw plantation had long since gone silent. Now the only sounds were the sounds of the night. Autumn crickets chirped a mesmerizing chorus that rose and fell in volume. Poky's oars made a soft splash with each dip into the river, then a gentle *whoosh* from the pull of the oar against the water as their rowboat glided downstream. Poky kept up a steady, aggressive pace—enough to form a small backwash behind the boat.

As they moved away from the Crenshaw plantation, Jimmy's clenched fists had gradually relaxed until, without thinking about it, he let his arm loosen and hang over the side of the boat. He dipped the tip of a finger in the river, letting it trail a tiny, soothing wake in the water. From time to time, when the breeze swirled through the trees, he heard the rustling of the strands of Spanish moss that hung from the boughs of the live oaks.

The night was peaceful. But Jimmy was not at peace. He knew that when they rounded the island and entered the main channel the odds were high that patrollers would be waiting for them. He turned to his left, to watch the trees and marshes glide by on the South Carolina shore, then he turned to his right, where the remnants of a rice paddy on the island side slid past him.

"How solid is the ground over there?" he asked Poky, pointing to the Carolina shore.

"More than on the Georgia side. It's all rice fields at the Mulberry Grove plantation on the Georgia side."

"Do you think we could lift the boat out of the water on the Carolina side and carry it between us?"

"This afternoon I dragged more'n four hundred pounds of cotton along the road to the weighing house." Poky took a breath. "And this evenin', I've been rowin' for the better part of an hour." He took another breath. "But even with all that, I know I could hold up one end of this boat and carry it." He took several swallows of breath. "What about you?"

"I only dragged half as much cotton as you. And I haven't rowed a mite. So I believe I could hold up an end of it, too."

"I suppose you're thinkin' about carrying the boat along the Carolina shore ... till we get past the patrollers."

"Wouldn't that be the safest way to do it?"

"Could be we'd run into marshes." Poky took a breath. "Then we'd have to go further inland."

"Can we keep track of where the river is if we lose sight of it?"

Poky sighed, then took another sharp in-breath. "I reckon I could—though I've never set foot on the Carolina side."

"You think the patrollers will be waiting on the main channel when we get back to it?"

"They generally wait there or another mile downstream." He took a breath. "And there could be Reb soldiers watchin' the mouth of the river, too." He swallowed. "Hard to say."

"Once we get close to the main channel, we'd better go real slow. We gotta be sure we see the patrollers before they see us."

"That'll be up to you." Poky turned his head to the side. "I can't see what's comin' up while I'm rowin.'"

"Then let's take it slow."

"You know ... right about now, Massa Ben's gonna be ridin' down the coast ... to sound the alarm."

"You think he'll follow us?"

"He did the last time someone ran off.... That's how he caught Isaac ten years ago."

"Isaac took off down the river?"

Poky nodded.

"He never told me that. What'd he use for a boat?"

"You're sittin' in it."

A picture of Isaac lying dead on the ground flashed in Jimmy's mind and he clenched his fists again. But he said nothing. He didn't want to remind Poky of those moments. Ever since killing Eppley, Poky had been breathing strangely, panting from exertion but also gasping from time to time like a hiccup. Jimmy sensed that he could barely hold himself steady.

Poky glanced at the island side of the shore. "I know this spot. We're getting near the channel." He took a breath. "It's half a mile from here." Talking helped him breathe.

"Then you'd better go even slower."

Poky slowed his pace, until he was taking one measured stroke about every fifteen seconds. The boat glided in almost perfect silence.

"Let's stay close to the shore," Jimmy whispered.

Poky nudged the boat slightly to the left.

Jimmy shaded his eyes with his hands. The quarter moon was drifting in and out of clouds. He could barely see fifteen yards ahead. He knew the patrollers couldn't see any farther than that either—and they wouldn't be expecting to see anyone at any particular moment. But he wanted to see them and for them to not see him at all.

Eventually he saw a bend approaching. "I see the channel," he whispered.

"Anyone there?"

"I can't see 'em. But keep slow—as slow as you can."

Poky slowed even more—to a single stroke every twenty seconds. The boat was barely drifting along. He'd pulled as close to the Carolina shore as he could get and still row with both oars. When they were twenty yards from the point where the fork rejoined the main channel, Jimmy murmured, "We're very close."

Poky nudged the boat toward the shore and pulled in the oars. He reached out, grabbed hold of a sapling that grew out of the bank, and brought the boat to a stop. "Let's rest a moment," he said. He was out of breath and panting.

"How far do you think we can carry the boat on land?" Jimmy asked.

"Depends on how solid the ground is—and how often we stop to rest." Poky took a few breaths, then continued. "I'd say we could go maybe two or three miles in an hour."

"If you feel ready, I think it would be safer to get out of the river now. Once we're in the main channel it'll be harder to stop before they see us."

Just then an owl hooted in the distance and Poky jerked in his seat. Then it hooted again and he relaxed. But being startled seemed to have helped make up his mind. "Let's do it," he said.

As quietly as they could, they climbed out of the boat onto the embankment, then pulled the boat up behind them. Once they were on solid ground, they dragged it behind the nearest trees, then both took an end of the boat to lift it.

"How is it?" Jimmy asked.

"It's heavy, but I can handle it," Poky said. "How is it for you?"

"I can manage," Jimmy said. "You'd better guide the way."

Poky led them, threading his way between the trees. Because of the length and width of the boat, wherever the trees were too thick they had to backtrack and circle around, in order to keep moving forward. Gradually they lost sight of the river.

"Let's stop," Jimmy said, when he realized he couldn't see the river any longer. "You rest a minute. I'll go check the river. We gotta know where they are so we can decide when to go back in the water."

Poky nodded. Jimmy left and scrambled through the underbrush, making his way back toward the river. As soon as he saw the first glimpse of water, he slowed his steps. Then he crept as quietly as he could up to a tree near the water's edge. He stood behind the tree, leaning just enough to peek around it. He saw no one.

But as he turned to go, he heard the sound of voices in the distance. The sound, barely audible, wafted across the water for a moment, then stopped. He turned to look again. This time he leaned farther out, in order to peer all the way down the river. In the distance he saw something bobbing in the water. He heard a muffled laugh. He pulled his head back in, then crept back to where Poky was waiting.

"They're half a mile downstream," he said. "Unless there's someone else out on the river."

"Ain't gonna be nobody but them sittin' out there in the dark," Poky said.

"Then we'd better carry the boat another mile at least," Jimmy said.

Poky nodded. They both picked up an end of the boat and continued through the woods. As they got closer to the spot where Jimmy thought the patrollers were, the land became marshier. The muddy ground forced them to move further inland.

"We're getting too far from the river," Jimmy said at one point.

"Right now, going away from the river means we're going east," Poky said. "But the river turns east, too. Once we find solid ground, we'll have to go south to pick it up again."

As the ground grew more solid, they turned right and headed south. When at last they saw moonlight glinting off the river through the trees, they stopped. Once again, Jimmy crept toward the shore and peeked out from behind a tree. He saw them clearly now. They were in two boats, a hundred yards back up the river. He counted four men, two in each boat. One of the men raised his rifle and pointed it upstream. The other men turned to look upstream, too. After a moment, Jimmy saw what they were staring at. A boat was sailing down the river toward the patrollers.

Jimmy was about to go get Poky when he felt Poky's hand touch his shoulder. Startled, he turned to find Poky looking past him at the boats in the river.

"That's the *Wentworth,*" Poky whispered. "Massa Ben must've gone to Mulberry Grove Plantation to get it."

As the *Wentworth* pulled closer, Jimmy could make out two figures in the sailboat. One, he knew, was Ben Crenshaw. The other man was someone he didn't know.

"Who's that with him?" Jimmy asked.

"Jeremiah Perkins," Poky said. "He's an overseer at Mulberry Grove."

Jimmy and Poky watched as the sailboat drew close to the patrollers' rowboats. Jeremiah Perkins yelled something to the men in the rowboats. A moment later, the man who'd raised his rifle lowered it. Just then, Ben Crenshaw pulled hard on the boom and the sail went slack. The *Wentworth* slowed. A moment later, Perkins dropped an anchor and the sailboat came to a stop ten feet from the rowboats. The men in the patrol boats rowed alongside the *Wentworth*.

Jimmy couldn't make out what they were saying, but he saw the men in the rowboats shake their heads. He realized it would soon be apparent to all of them that he and Poky had taken their boat out of the water. And just then, he saw Ben Crenshaw shield his eyes to peer toward the Carolina shoreline.

"Let's go," Jimmy said. When they got back to their boat, Jimmy asked, "You think they'll come ashore to look?"

"I reckon they will. But they'll split up. Two of 'em'll come on the Carolina side, two on the Georgia side, and two'll keep to the river. That's what I'd do if I was them."

"What should we do?"

"Head east. We've got to find somewhere to hide."

Without further discussion, they each picked up an end of the boat and began to carry it away from the river. Eventually they came to a dry stream bed. They walked along the stream bed until they came to a spot where a tree had fallen parallel to the stream. There they set the boat upside-down, in line with the tree. Then they gathered leaves, twigs and brush, and piled them on top of the tree and the boat.

Once the boat was hidden, they looked for a place to hide themselves. While they were looking, they heard a sound behind them. They quickly ducked into a clump of bushes. The bushes only partially hid them—but it was dark, and the tree canopy blocked most of the moonlight. They huddled, bent down near the ground, and waited.

Eventually they heard men approach. The men weren't talking. They were methodically snaking through the woods, moving from side to side. Jimmy and Poky held their breath. At one point, one of the men came within ten feet of them. Jimmy caught sight of him, just as he turned his head away. Then he kept going.

Jimmy waited until they were gone before he spoke. Then he whispered, "There were two of 'em. Just like you thought."

Poky nodded. "I reckon Massa Ben's still in the river."

"Will he stay put or sail?"

"I don't know," Poky said.

"Let's hope he stays put."

"If he does, he won't stay put for long."

"Should we get back in the river?"

"We can't stay here," Poky said.

"It'll be light before long."

"There are more forks and channels downstream," Poky said. "We'll have to pick one and hope they pick a different one."

"Let's go," Jimmy said.

They went back to the stream bed where they'd hidden their boat, uncovered it, and lifted it up. This time they carried it straight back to the river. At the river's edge they saw no sign of the *Wentworth* or the patrollers. They dropped the boat back in the water and climbed in. Poky took up the oars before Jimmy could get to them. Jimmy wasn't surprised. He'd admitted to Poky earlier that his only previous attempt at rowing had been a disaster.

After a few minutes, the current began to pick up. It carried them along quickly. Soon Jimmy saw a fork in the river ahead of them.

"We're almost to a fork," he said. "Which one should we take?"

"The main channel's on the left," Poky said.

"Let's take that," Jimmy said. "They won't expect us to stay in the main channel."

Poky kept the boat in the main channel. He continued to row hard and steady. Jimmy watched the shoreline flow by. After a few minutes had passed, he noticed that the Spanish moss hanging from the trees was still. "Can you stop the boat a spell?" he asked. "I want to check something."

Poky maneuvered the oars to slow the boat's movement. When they'd slowed to the point of drifting, Jimmy licked his finger and held it up. "The breeze is gone," he said. He looked up and down the shoreline. The leaves on the trees were motionless. "There's no wind. Massa Ben can't sail. That's how he lost his race with the Mulberry Grove men in the first place." Jimmy smiled. "Come on. Let's keep going."

Poky resumed rowing. After another half hour, though, he

finally began to slow down. "I can't go no further," he said. "I'm tuckered out. You're gonna have to take over."

They switched places. Jimmy's last attempt at rowing had been during his effort to cross the Ohio River in April, when he'd made his initial escape. He'd managed to overturn the boat in that undertaking and nearly drowned. And now again, his main problem was understanding how to manipulate the oars to control the boat's direction. He went slowly at first. He put in fifteen minutes of haphazard rowing before he began to learn how to control his strokes to keep the boat from drifting to the right or left. He gradually gained confidence, and began to row harder and faster.

Poky, meanwhile, sat with his eyes closed. He began to list to one side, and Jimmy thought he'd fallen asleep. But just as he was about to lean so far to the side that he might fall over, he jerked. He put out a hand and grabbed the side of the boat to steady himself. He opened his eyes.

"Stay with me," Jimmy said.

Poky nodded.

The current began to pick up even more. Jimmy had to make his strokes long and smooth. But he grew anxious about steering. At the speed they were moving, it would be disastrous if he ran into the river bank. Poky's eyes were fluttering. Jimmy couldn't rely on him to guide them.

Poky again began to lean to the side. And once more, just before he fell over, he jerked, grabbed the side of the boat, and opened his eyes. Then his eyes went wide. "We're there!" he said. "This is the mouth of the river."

Jimmy turned around to look behind him. The river channel had grown very wide, but now he saw it spreading out even wider. He could see a spot coming up where the shoreline disappeared completely. "Is that the ocean?"

"Yes, sir. The Atlantic Ocean," Poky said. "We're almost in it. You're gonna feel the waves pretty soon. Can you handle it?"

Jimmy wasn't sure if he could. "Got no choice," he said.

He kept rowing until they passed the edge of the coastline. Then as they moved out into the open sea, waves began to roll the boat.

"It's not too bad," Poky said. "It's lucky the breeze died down."

Even without the breeze, Jimmy had to fight the steady rolling of the waves while he rowed the boat farther out to sea. After thirty minutes they were out so far that he could barely see the shoreline.

"Do you think we lost them?" Jimmy asked.

"Like you said, the man can't sail without the wind."

Jimmy stopped rowing and let the boat drift. He had no idea how far away the Union blockade might be. He assumed they'd have to row much further north. And even then, there was no way to guess where the Yankee ships would be. He looked at the vastness of the water all around him. He was beginning to grasp how huge the ocean really was.

Despite this, the further they got from the shore, the more optimistic he began to feel. Then—just as he was letting himself dare to think they were safe—a waft of air tickled his face. A moment later, he felt the breeze again. This time it was a gust that blew across his hair.

He held up his finger. There was no doubt about it. The wind was rapidly picking up. He looked at Poky with alarm. Within a matter of moments, the wind had begun to blow steadily. And it was blowing from the west.

41

"I'M ONLY ASKING FOR MR. ROBINSON'S SAKE"

When Cato and Joe reached Savannah, they soon determined that there were only two auction houses left in town. The war had forced the others to close. The first one they went to was locked up. So they made their way to the second one, which was in a granary—and had a small red flag outside to signal its purpose.

Earlier they'd decided it would be better if Joe asked all the questions. Cato had been feeling vulnerable ever since his encounter with the slave patrollers. They both thought it would be less risky for Joe to interact with any white men they encountered—especially men in the business of appraising and selling slaves.

When Joe tried the door of the granary he found it unlocked. He told Cato to wait for him across the street, then he opened the door and went inside.

He entered a room that had chairs set up in front of a small platform. No one was in sight, but he heard sounds coming from a small office built into a corner of the larger space. As he approached, he saw an overweight man in the office who sat at a desk writing.

Joe approached the man. "Excuse me, sir," he began. "Are you the proprietor here?"

"Yes?" The man looked up from his desk and instantly formed a wary expression.

Joe wasn't wearing face paint or his feather—but he knew it was easy to see that he wasn't white. He put on a disarming smile. The man's wariness didn't faze him. "I'm looking for someone who I believe may have done business here some while ago."

"Here? We've had no Injuns in here."

Joe scratched his nose as if he had an itch, then he continued. "The person I'm looking for is a white man named Hogan. Mr. Horace Hogan. He came here to auction a slave, I believe."

The man at the desk raised his eyebrows. "What does a fella like you want with Mr. Hogan?" he asked.

"I want to spit on him and take back the money he made from kidnapping my friend's lover," Joe thought to himself as he smiled even more broadly. But what he said was, "I have an important message for Mr. Hogan from his daughter, Martha. I was sent to find him."

"His daughter?" The man looked skeptical. "Are you saying you have something to do with a white man's daughter?"

"In a manner of speaking, sir. You see, I'm a scout for the Army. I was with the Army at the capture of Munfordville, Kentucky. One of our soldiers, a man named Jack Robinson, is engaged to Mr. Hogan's daughter, Martha. Mr. Robinson hired me to deliver a message to Mr. Hogan. He wants me to tell him that Martha is with child."

Joe had rehearsed some of this speech earlier—but now he faltered, not knowing what more to add. And he had to suppress a giggle as he thought about who Jack had actually had intercourse with.

"You say you're a scout? A scout for which army?"

"Why, the Confederate Army, sir. You don't think I'd be

here otherwise, do you?" Did this man think he was a complete idiot?

"And now you've come here to deliver a message to Horace Hogan?"

"Yes, sir," Joe said. "As I was saying, Mr. Robinson offered to pay me to deliver the message. He's given me half the money already, and he promised I'd get the rest after I speak to Mr. Hogan." Joe smiled again, thinking of what he hoped Mr. Robinson might actually give him when next they met.

"What does this Robinson fellow expect Hogan to do after you find him?"

"He only wishes Mr. Hogan to know that he will soon be a grandfather. And he hopes that Mr. Hogan can come to be with Martha at this time—since Mr. Robinson cannot leave the Army."

The man folded his hands together on top of his desk. "Sounds to me like this Robinson fella expects Hogan to take the daughter off his hands."

"I don't know, sir. But I wonder if you can recall when Mr. Hogan was here. He would have been here to sell a male slave who was about twenty-five years old," Joe said. "And a damn fine-looking slave, from what I hear," he thought, but did not say.

"Twenty-five, you say." The man opened a drawer and took out a ledger. He turned back the pages and scanned the columns. "Well," he said. "Hogan was here—as you say—some time back. He sold a buck named Jacob—ornery fellow. I remember him."

Joe nodded. "Sometimes when fellows are chained up, they tend to get ornery about it," he thought to himself. What he said was, "Do you know where Mr. Hogan went? Did he say something about his plans?"

"Not to me."

"Maybe the man who bought the slave can tell me where Mr. Hogan has gone."

"I doubt that," the man said. "I don't think Hogan spent more'n five minutes talking to Crenshaw. Hogan got his money —and five minutes later he walked out the door."

"I take it, then, that it was Mr. Crenshaw who bought the slave?" Joe's eyes lit up. He was delighted that the man had let the buyer's name slip.

"Yes, yes," the man said, glancing again at his ledger. "Samuel Crenshaw. Hogan got a good price from him. Surprised me how much Crenshaw paid. Anyway ... Crenshaw won't know where Hogan's gone to." The man gave Joe a sour look. "Look here, can't you see I have work to do? I don't have time for all these questions."

"I'm only asking for Mr. Robinson's sake. He told me he'd come himself if he weren't fighting for the 'Cause.'" Joe saw the man perk up at the mention of the 'Cause,' so he dared to ask one more question. "Where can I find Mr. Crenshaw?"

The man blinked several times. "He owns a plantation up river a ways. But he's got a gal he visits here in town. That's where he is most of the time ... her house is next door to the post office." The man waved his hand. "Now, go on about your business and let me get back to my work."

"Yes, sir. Thank you," Joe said. "And may you rot in hell," he thought, but did not say. Instead, he bowed, then turned and left.

When Joe told Cato the news, Cato was so excited, he hugged Joe right on the street.

"The man said the plantation is not far from here?" Cato asked.

"Yes. He said it's just up river a ways."

"And he told you Hogan sold a slave named Jacob?"

"That's what he said. 'A buck named Jacob.'"

"That's got to be Jimmy. He must have used that name to keep Hogan from knowing his real name."

Joe nodded. "But Mr. Crenshaw's right here in town. He has a girlfriend who lives near the post office."

"Why should we bother with Crenshaw?" Cato asked. "All we have to do is find his plantation. I think it would be better if Mr. Crenshaw doesn't know anything about us."

"Yes," Joe said. "You're right."

After they left the granary, they made inquiries at the general store, where they got directions to the Crenshaw plantation. They set off on a road that took them past a line of plantations along the Savannah River: Hermitage, Brampton, Whitehall, Coleraine, Drakies, Mulberry Grove, Richmond Oakgrove—until at last they reached the Crenshaw estate.

From the road, they surveyed the grounds of the plantation. It was evident that something was wrong. Even though it was midday, there were no slaves working in the fields. In fact, they saw no one doing anything at all.

"That's strange," Joe said.

"It's eerie," Cato agreed.

"Look." Joe pointed. "Those must be the slave cabins." He indicated a group of cabins near the main house. "Let's go see who's there."

"Would you mind going by yourself?" Cato asked.

Joe looked surprised."But Jimmy might be in there. Don't you want to see him?"

"I do! Of course, I do. But I don't want our reunion to take place in front of a lot of strangers. I'd rather be alone with him —at least for a few minutes. If you find him, you could bring him back here—to give us some time alone together."

Joe nodded. "I understand," he said. "Wait here. I'll find out what's going on. If Jimmy is there, I'll bring him right back."

When Joe came back twenty minutes later, he was still alone. It was obvious from the look on his face that he didn't have good news.

"Jimmy was here, but ... I'm sorry, Cato, I'm afraid he's already gone." Joe took Cato's arm to steady him. "He and another slave escaped by boat last night. According to the woman I talked to, before they left, they attacked the overseer.

Then a third slave who was planning to go with them was killed. Nobody knows what happened exactly. But right now, none of the owners are here. Crenshaw is in town. His daughter's gone to find him. And his son's gone off to chase the runaways. The overseer is hurt bad. That's why nobody's working."

"Damn it!"

"I'm sorry, Cato."

"Did anyone say where Jimmy was headed?"

"I didn't ask," Joe said. "I think you should talk to them and see what you can find out. None of the white folks are here right now, so you should be safe. I found the cabin where Jimmy was living."

"You're right. I should talk to them."

THEY TIED UP THE HORSES, and Joe led him to Jimmy's cabin. Inside was a young woman named Pheby. She stared at Cato with undisguised curiosity.

"You must be his friend," she said. "You must be Cato. He told me about you."

"I'm pleased to meet you," Cato said. "I've come all the way from Chicago to find him."

"From Chicago! He didn't say where he was from."

"Did he say where he was planning to go?"

Pheby shook her head. "He wouldn't say. He didn't want anyone to know. He figured that was the best way to keep the Crenshaws from finding out about it." She looked at Cato sadly. "I'm sure he'd want *you* to know where he went. But I don't think he ever figured you'd come here."

"Is it possible that someone else here might know where he went?"

"Not from what he told me." Pheby shook her head again. "All I know is he and Poky took off in a boat headin' down the river. Like I told your friend, something terrible happened before they left. Uncle Isaac got killed and our overseer, Eppley, he got punched and knocked down. Hit his head on a rock. He's in a bad way."

"Did Jimmy hit him?"

"Nobody knows. Could've been him or Poky—or even Uncle Isaac, I reckon." Now Pheby began to cry. "Poor old man was just tryin' one last time to get away from here."

Joe reached out to comfort her. Cato was lost in thought and too distraught to know what to do.

After Pheby recovered herself, she said, "Jacob—I mean, Jimmy—told me he and Poky had a plan. He said he knew the maps. He found out that the Yankees were just a few miles up the coast in blockade boats. My husband says the Yankees will take in any slave who gets to them."

"Jimmy had maps?"

"No, but he'd studied them," Pheby said. "The Crenshaws had maps in the library. He studied those."

Cato and Joe thanked Pheby and left the cabin. When they were ten yards away, Pheby opened the door and called out. "I almost forgot!" she said.

Cato ran back to her. "Yes?"

"Jimmy said to tell anyone who asked that he'd gone to get his portrait painted."

"His portrait?"

"That's what he said."

"Oh, Pheby!" Cato was so happy he took her hand and shook it. "Thank you!"

"Does it mean something?"

"Yes," Cato said. "It means everything!"

Cato and Joe made their way back to Oscar and Nice and rode back to town.

Joe asked, "What did that mean, what she said about him getting his portrait painted?"

"It means Jimmy's going to Philadelphia. We have a friend there—Erastus Hicks, a painter. He's the one who gave us all that money. When we first met, he used me as a model for one of his paintings. Jimmy knew if he said he was going to get his portrait painted, nobody but me would know what it meant."

"Are you sure?"

"Absolutely."

"Then I guess you'll have to go to Philadelphia."

"Don't you want to come with me?"

"Well ..." Joe thought about it. "I'd like to meet this Jimmy. And, truly, I'm more than ready to say good-bye to the South. So, yes, I'll come with you for a ways. But then I have to find out what's happening to Jack. I've heard that sometimes the Yankees and Rebs exchange prisoners. He might be freed."

"How will you know?"

"We have to find a newspaper." A troubled look came over Joe's face. "Can you read?" he asked.

"Yes," Cato said. "I can. What about you?"

"I can read some things. But I don't always know all the words. It would be good to have a second opinion."

"All right," Cato said. "We'll find a newspaper—and read it together."

With that in mind, they mounted Oscar and Nice and turned north.

42

"YOU HAVE NO CHANCE!"

Jimmy rowed as hard as he could. He couldn't see where he was going, and there was nowhere in particular for him to aim to go. He only knew he had to go north. The vast emptiness of the ocean made him feel as if he was lost in a dream.

Poky was fast asleep in the back of the boat. He'd been sleeping for an hour, and all throughout that hour the wind had been blowing. Jimmy kept his mind on his rowing, so he wouldn't think too much about how worried he'd been. For an hour he'd been straining to see in the darkness, looking to see if they were being followed. Now the first glimmer of light rose in the east. For the first time, Jimmy could make out the line of the horizon.

Though he was trying to row north, the wind was causing the boat to move further out to sea. He was keenly aware that the wind would help the *Wentworth* move, too, if it was still out there.

He scanned the horizon for a sail. Once or twice he thought he saw one in the distance. But then the vision would vanish—and he realized he was only seeing the crest of a wave. From time to time, he turned his head to face north. Each time, before he turned, he drew up a picture in his mind of a big Union ship sailing toward him, willing it to be there. But then each time he turned, he saw nothing.

Jimmy was glad Poky was asleep, but gazing at him made Jimmy yawn. Sleep, he realized, was contagious. He started to feel as though he'd give anything for a short nap. He found himself staring at Poky, fascinated by the look of contentment on his dreaming face. He didn't know which load had weighed on Poky more, the burden of guilt he felt for having killed Eppley, or the strain of the physical effort he'd expended rowing the boat and carrying it. But now that he was asleep, he looked as if he'd left all his burdens behind.

Jimmy longed to leave his burdens behind, too. He had to stay awake, of course. But considering how far he'd rowed, and how far away from the river they'd traveled, he thought it might be safe for him to rest—just for a moment. There was no doubt that he needed rest. And he reasoned if he didn't rest now, when would he?

He pulled the oars into the boat and let it drift. He scanned the horizon. Since the sun had risen, he could see far into the distance. But there was nothing to see. He could no longer even see the shore.

The boat rose and fell with the waves, which were undulating, mirroring the wind. The waves weren't rolling enough to tip the boat. Instead they rocked it gently with a rhythmic swell and slump. Jimmy felt as if he was in a cradle—as if he were being steadily rocked by a lulling, gentle hand. His eyelids fluttered. His body relaxed. His head lilted lightly to the side. He let his eyes close—just for a moment. The boat swayed up and down in a soothing, comforting pattern. And before he knew it ... he fell asleep.

When he awoke, it was with a start. The boat had lurched upward on the crest of a wave, then slammed back down. The hard slap of the hull on the water woke him, and it woke Poky, too. They looked at each other, both of them coming back to the world at the same instant. And as they remembered where they were, they each turned around to see what was behind them.

Jimmy judged by the changed location of the sun that the boat had turned completely around while he was asleep. He was now facing northeast—and Poky, who was in the back of the boat, was now facing southwest.

When Poky turned to see what was behind him, he saw what Jimmy had seen when he opened his eyes. Off in the distance was a big ship—and there was no doubt that it was a Yankee ship. When Jimmy turned, he saw what Poky had seen when he opened his eyes. The *Wentworth* was heading straight for them. And it was much closer to the rowboat than the Yankee ship.

Jimmy fumbled with the oars, inserting them into the post as fast as he could. He slapped both oars into the water. He had to turn the boat around to aim it toward the Yankee ship.

"Use just one oar to turn!" Poky shouted.

Jimmy pulled on one oar, but he pulled it so hard that the rowboat began to spin, and they went all the way around in a circle until they were back where they started.

"Not so hard!" Poky tried to stand up so they could trade places. But the boat was pitching so forcefully, he fell back in his seat. "Use the other oar to stop us."

Now Jimmy pulled on one oar to start the turn and pulled the other one to stop it. Then he lifted both oars and dipped them in the water at the same time, trying to get them in synch. He pulled hard and fast, but he was sputtering in the water. His strokes were too short. He was staring straight at the *Wentworth* —and he could see that it was gaining on them quickly. He saw a flash of Ben's red hair blowing in the wind. He glared at Poky, imploring him to take over, but Poky just shook his head. The boat was rocking too wildly to let him move.

It took all of Jimmy's concentration to force himself into a steady rhythm. He matched his strokes with his breaths. He took long breaths and made himself pull with long strokes. He plunged the oars deep in the water and pulled them as hard as he could. He tried to remember what Uncle Isaac had told him about the bet Ben Crenshaw had made with the owner of Mulberry Grove. Ben had bet he could sail the *Wentworth* faster than the men could row their boats. Ben had lost that bet—but only because the wind had died down.

Now the wind was blowing steadily, buffeting Jimmy's face, whipping across his eyes. When he looked around, he saw that the wave that had awakened them was typical of what they now faced. The boat was moving, but it was climbing up and falling off the crests of waves with such regularity that it was hard to tell if they were moving forward at all.

As Jimmy flexed his arms, he felt again as if he was in a dream. The harder he rowed, the more he seemed to stay in the same place. He felt as if he was endlessly climbing the same wave—only to find himself shoved back to the trough of the next one. The harder he rowed, the more the *Wentworth* seemed to gain on them. Poky gaped at him, his eyes full of terror. But there was nothing Poky could do either.

Jimmy kept turning around to look toward where they were heading—hoping each time he turned that the Yankee ship would be closer. And it did seem as if the Yankee boat was slowly growing closer. But then when he'd turn back, he'd find that the *Wentworth* was closer still. There was no doubt that the *Wentworth* was approaching them much faster than they were approaching the Yankee ship.

The waves were splashing them so hard that both Jimmy and Poky were soon drenched. Poky leaned over and used his hands cupped together to try to bail water from the bottom of their boat—but he, too, looked as if he was moving in a slow-motion dream. The more water he threw out, the faster he threw it, the more water splashed in from all sides.

Poky couldn't see what was happening behind them while he was bailing water. "How close are they?" he shouted.

"They're close," Jimmy yelled. "And they're getting closer!"

"Let's trade places," Poky yelled back.

"It's too risky. We're rocking too much."

"Maybe if we move slowly, we can do it."

"I don't think we should try," Jimmy shouted. "We'll lose too much time if we fail."

"You're right," Poky said. "But what else can we do?"

As they were debating this, the *Wentworth* bore down upon them. It drew close enough that Jimmy could see inside the sailboat. Ben Crenshaw held the rudder and the mast of the sail. In the front of the boat stood Jeremiah Perkins, with his pistol drawn. He had it pointed at Jimmy.

"Stop," Perkins yelled. "Or I'll shoot!"

"Go to hell!" Jimmy yelled back.

Ben Crenshaw shouted something, but the sound of the waves drowned him out.

"Get down!" Poky shouted. Poky was bent over, facing the bottom of the boat as he bailed the water, but he'd looked back long enough to see the weapon that was pointed at their boat.

Jimmy thought Perkins wouldn't shoot unless he was closer. And since he couldn't bend down and row at the same time, he stayed where he was and kept rowing. Then he saw the bow of the *Wentworth* turn slightly. The sailboat began to head for the side of the rowboat. Ben Crenshaw was aiming to draw alongside them.

"Fool nigger!" Perkins shouted. "You have no chance!"

Jimmy again turned around to see what was happening behind him. The Yankee ship was closer than ever. But it was still not close enough. Adrenaline coursed through his blood. It occurred to him that his life might be over.

He thought of Cato. One moment from their life together sprang into his mind. It was a moment when they were standing alone, out in a field. Jimmy had wanted to show Cato how nimble his hands had become from picking cotton, so he'd plucked a single hair off Cato's chest. He remembered the smile of surprise on Cato's face.

Jimmy carefully pulled the oars in and set them inside the boat. The *Wentworth* was ten yards away. He took one last look at Poky, then he stood and leapt into the water.

43

"THE TREETOP IS VERY NICE"

The trip from Savannah to Philadelphia was more than 730 miles. Cato calculated that it would take them at least three weeks of steady travel by horseback to complete the journey. On each day of their journey, he bought a newspaper in whatever town they slept in. Most of the small-town newspapers were filled with local news, and many of them only covered national events that were of interest to local readers. Joe worried that these local papers might not cover the fate of Jack's seventy-fourth Indiana Infantry.

The newspapers in Raleigh, North Carolina, and Richmond, Virginia, though, were full of national news. To make sure they hadn't missed any news about Jack's regiment, they spent a day in Richmond searching sundry locations for discarded newspapers, to check the news as many days back as possible.

Cato spread the newspapers out in front of them while he read each headline. If an article had to do with the war, he read it aloud. But even though it had been a full month since Jack had been captured at Munfordville, they found no news about a prisoner exchange for Jack's regiment.

Joe was grateful to Cato for spending so much time on this

task. Even though it added time to their journey, Cato had no qualms about doing it. He was thankful that Joe was willing to make the journey with him, and he was as interested as Joe was in finding out about Jack's fate. He was also glad that they continued to make progress north without encountering anyone who questioned his race.

Joe's steady confidence helped Cato maintain his poise whenever they had to interact with white Southerners. Cato continued to dress to look as if he was Joe's Shawnee brother. Joe taught him various Shawnee phrases he could use in conversation whenever he felt he was under the suspicious gaze of a white man. They'd grown so close that anyone who saw them talking together assumed they were old friends chatting in an obscure tongue.

Cato, in turn, taught Joe how to read any English words he didn't recognize. They argued about the limitations of language. For Cato, reading was the gateway to all knowledge. Joe, on the other hand, believed that knowledge was best learned from nature. Whenever they stopped to rest, Joe habitually spent a few minutes surveying their surroundings, examining plants and observing animals. He would then hold forth on their qualities and virtues—explaining to Cato how to use his imagination to inhabit other life forms.

"You and I look very big to this squirrel," he might say. Or, "That bird who's watching us lumber through the woods must think we're very clumsy creatures." On one occasion he said, "I wish I could see the treetop as well as a bird." And then he proceeded to climb the tree as high as he could. And when he came back down he proclaimed, with great satisfaction, "The treetop is very nice."

One day when a thunderstorm broke, they took shelter in an abandoned barn. The barn was just a shell, with no windows or doors. They sat in an open doorway, staring out at the rain. A large puddle had formed in a gulley near the door. Joe was fascinated by how the puddle mirrored and distorted the appearance of the sky and trees. From time to time he ventured out to stare at his reflection in the puddle as it was pummeled by raindrops, then he'd dance around and laugh at how the distortions made him look. During these escapades, Cato, Oscar, and Nice watched him from inside the barn, happily dry, but entranced by his antics.

Joe loved to slosh through puddles in his bare feet. He thought it great fun to splash the horses, who soon learned to give him wide berth whenever he commenced his game. He didn't go so far as to splash Cato, but Cato could see that were he to show any indication of joining him, they'd both be soaked from head to toe in no time. As it was, they made frequent use of the towels they carried in their saddlebags—each drying the other's back after they rode in the rain.

Joe liked to perform various tricks while riding Nice. Sometimes he'd ask Cato to carry both saddles on Oscar's back so he could ride bareback on Nice. On such occasions he'd race ahead, then gallop back while doing his tricks. Sometimes he'd turn around on Nice's back and ride facing backward. Sometimes he'd crouch on his knees on top of Nice and try as best he could to stand up. Sometimes he'd take a running jump, fling himself onto Nice's back, cling to his neck, and whisper in his ear to urge him forward. During these times Cato and Oscar would saunter along, while Cato watched Joe's antics and Oscar did his best to stay out of Nice's way.

They also passed the time during their journey by stopping to collect rocks. Whenever they passed a forgotten mine or an abandoned quarry, or any likely spot with an outcropping of rocks, they'd dismount and tie up the horses. Then they'd wander about picking up interesting stones.

They discarded most of what they found. They only kept those special gems they deemed worthy enough to be hauled along in the saddlebag as part of their small collection. They found a piece of obsidian, several pieces of rose quartz, and a pretty piece of sandstone. They also kept a piece of pyrite, known as fool's gold, to remind themselves not to be fooled by it. Still, they spoke thoughtfully about how they might one day find a piece of real gold or some precious stone. In Joe's mind the treasure hunt was an affirmation of the great gifts that lay upon the earth waiting to be discovered. And though Cato privately doubted that anything much would come of these efforts, he eagerly acquiesced to the adventure, and often outmaneuvered Joe when they spied a likely stone on the ground, by being the first one to grab it up.

During one of these maneuvers, Cato stubbed his moccasined foot on a rock. Joe took him to a tree and sat him down. "You must be careful where you step," he said. "A moccasin is not so hard as a boot." He gently removed Cato's moccasin and massaged his foot. Cato was startled by how good it felt. As Joe rubbed, Cato grew ever more relaxed, while a titillating feeling traveled up his leg. He contemplated how that particular physical intimacy was a fitting expression of what they'd come to feel between them—something that verged on but did not cross over into erotic desire. Sometimes they looked at each other with a tinge of longing. But it was understood between them that Cato was longing for Jimmy and Joe was longing for Jack. The only concession they made to whatever latent feelings they had came at night, when they fell into the habit of kissing each other sweetly on the lips just before going to sleep.

Joe would say, "Sleep deep, Lalawethika."

Cato, in turn, would say, "Sleep without woe, Joe Crow," and then they'd gently kiss and fall asleep, sometimes waking the next morning to find themselves cuddled together.

Despite their various side adventures, they continued to make steady progress north. They daydreamed about what they would do to celebrate as soon as they crossed the border from Virginia to Maryland, which would put them back in Union territory. Joe considered painting his face white. "White symbolizes a rite of passage," he said. "But, mostly, I think it would be nice to be white in the North."

"Maybe I should paint my face white, too." Cato laughed. "People would think we're crazy."

"Perhaps we are," Joe said.

"But as soon as we get to Philadelphia," Cato said, "I have to go back to my regular self. I want to be sure Jimmy can recognize me."

"How do you think Jimmy will get there?" Joe asked—a question he'd been reluctant to ask. "He could be traveling by boat or by land, or both."

"I don't know how he'll do it," Cato said. "But I know he'll get there, sooner or later!"

If Jimmy were rescued by the Union Navy, there was no way to know how long it would take him to get to Philadelphia. But Cato was certain Jimmy would succeed. He'd banished all doubt from his thoughts. He knew he'd hardly be able to get through each day if he allowed himself to ruminate on all the challenges Jimmy might face. Instead he pictured his reunion with Jimmy again and again—each morning when he awoke, each night before he went to sleep, and many times throughout the day. In this picture he and Jimmy were safe and overjoyed.

He also frequently turned his thoughts to Erastus. He pondered what he could say to his friend to console him. He imagined how calamitous it would be to lose something that gave life meaning. For Cato, it would be like losing Jimmy. If Cato were ever to lose Jimmy completely—in the way that Erastus had lost the use of his hand—he would wonder what there was left to live for.

He also often thought about Sammy, Jimmy's younger brother, who'd been saved from being sold to strangers when Erastus had redeemed him as payment for one of his paintings. Erastus had brought Sammy to live with him in Philadelphia. He was only a child, and Cato wondered how he was adjusting to his new life in the North. It had been half a year since he'd seen him, but half a year was a long time in the life of a child. He wondered if the boy had grown too big for Cato still to be able to pick him up.

Cato imagined it was more likely than not that he'd have to stay in Philadelphia for some time while he waited for Jimmy. He was sure Jimmy would come to him as quickly as he could, but he also knew it wouldn't be easy—since there were many obstacles in Jimmy's path. Yet he was confident that Jimmy would prevail. He told himself that Jimmy would swim all the way to the North if he had to.

44

"WHAT'S A CONTRABAND?"

Jimmy was disoriented. He could piece together only fragments of what had happened. He remembered the first blast of icy cold when he broke the surface of the water—it had made him think of the sensation he'd felt when Hogan's crony Jonah had forced him into the barrel of cold water to clean him up. That memory had dissolved into the memory of the moment he plunged into the Ohio River, flailing to reach the shore, in his desperate effort to reach his first taste of freedom. He struggled to focus, to pull himself out of the past and into the present.

He'd acted so abruptly, there hadn't been time to wonder why he'd chosen to die rather than be captured. He couldn't deny that he'd made the choice, jumping into the ocean when he didn't know how to swim. Yet his leap felt involuntary—as if his body had decided to seek freedom in death against the wishes of his soul. But then his soul had reminded him, after he'd stopped flailing about wildly and water had begun to fill his lungs, that it was not only the end of his life, but also the shattering of Cato's. And just when that realization washed over him, he'd discovered he had no more air—and that he hadn't the strength to move. After that, he'd felt himself begin to sink into the deep.

It was Poky who had guided him to salvation. It was Poky who'd leapt in after him, Poky who'd swum down and pulled his head up and out of the water just in the nick of time. And it was Poky who'd decided that since he couldn't hoist Jimmy back into the rowboat on his own, going to the *Wentworth* was the only way Jimmy could be saved. Poky hadn't hesitated.

Jimmy dimly recalled how hands had come down from the *Wentworth*—from both Ben Crenshaw and Jeremiah Perkins—and had hauled him up. He remembered the force of Ben's hands pushing down frantically on his chest. He recalled the whoosh of air that had come from Ben's lips when they pressed against his own. He recollected, too, the confounding feel of the resuscitating kiss—the kiss Jimmy had once denied him, the kiss Ben had dreamed of—and he remembered, also, the water he'd spit back into Ben's face.

But then he recalled how after that there'd been a great commotion. He'd lain on the floor of the *Wentworth* in a daze while Ben and Jeremiah had scrambled madly to maneuver the rudder and the sail. He remembered how they'd begun shouting and how Poky had then lifted him and cradled him in his arms. It had been then that he'd first been able to see over the deck of the boat, and it had been then that he'd first seen the looming Union ship as it bore down upon them.

Then, without warning, Poky had let his head drop. And the next thing Jimmy could remember was the sound of gunfire. The first shot had exploded in his ears from close at hand. It had come from Jeremiah Perkins's pistol. The second shot had come from afar, and was followed by a sharp cry right beside him. In the next instant Jimmy had watched as Jeremiah Perkins landed on the deck at his side, blood oozing from his shoulder.

Then there'd been more shouting. Jimmy had heard the distinctive clomp of Ben's wooden leg when he clambered toward the tiller. Then he remembered the moment when Poky had shouted, "Watch out!" and covered him with his body—just as another shot was discharged from somewhere in the distance.

Then it had grown quiet. Nothing had happened for a long time, until at last Poky had rolled off him. And then there'd been hands that had hauled him out of the *Wentworth* and onto another boat.

Twenty minutes later he'd been hoisted up the side of a huge vessel. More hands had taken him and set him down on the vessel's deck, which was where he now lay with his eyes closed as he recalled in wonderment all the circumstances of his rescue.

JIMMY'S EYES were still closed when from somewhere close by a steam whistle blew and the boat began to move. He opened his eyes. A uniformed Navy officer stood over him. He lay on the deck and listened as Poky told the man everything that had happened.

When Poky finished, he heard the officer turn to Ben and say, "Mr. Crenshaw, we are seizing your property, your boat, and your slaves, as contraband." Then the officer spoke to two of his men. "Take the prisoner to the brig."

Two soldiers led Ben Crenshaw away.

The officer spoke to another soldier, who was leaning over Jeremiah Perkins as he wrapped a bandage around his shoulder. "And take that one to the brig, too, as soon as you've got him patched up."

Jimmy propped himself up on his elbows to survey the ship. Smoke rose from a giant smokestack in the center of the boat. In front of it, inside the pilot house, stood a black man calmly turning the steering wheel. Covered paddle-wheels flanked both sides of the boat, churning and splashing, driving the boat forward at a fair clip. A Union flag flapped noisily in the breeze, atop a tall pole in front of the main smokestack.

The officer knelt down and spoke directly to Jimmy. "Can you stand up?"

Jimmy rolled onto his stomach. He tested the strength in his legs. He raised himself onto his knees. The officer reached out his hand and helped him stand.

"You're aboard the *USS Planter*," the officer said. "This is a United States federal vessel. I'm going to take you to the contraband camp at Port Royal in South Carolina. You can take refuge there."

"What's a contraband?"

"It means you're a contraband of war. Don't worry. It means you won't be sent back to your owner."

"But I don't have an owner."

"You don't?" The man cocked his head, looked at Jeremiah Perkins, then back at Jimmy. "But this fellow Crenshaw just told me he was your owner."

"He's not. I was free. Then I was kidnapped. The man who sold me to Crenshaw didn't own me."

"Well, there's nothing I can do about that." The man pursed his lips. But then he smiled. "Look here, we're taking you to Port Royal. That's where all the contraband slaves live. You'll be free there."

"But I need to get to Philadelphia," Jimmy said.

"Philadelphia?" The man scratched his head. "What does a boy like you have to do with Philadelphia?"

"That's where my people live."

"Oh, for goodness sake ... I can't take you there. This is not a passenger ship. This is a supply ship for the United States Army."

"Is there another ship going north?"

"I doubt it. Look here, you're lucky to be alive. They said you almost drowned."

"I was trying to escape from those men." Jimmy pointed

toward Jeremiah Perkins. "That one pointed a gun at me."

"Did he?" The man looked back at Perkins again. "Well, he doesn't have a gun anymore. We took it away. So there's nothing to worry about. You'll be safe here. Now why don't you and your friend go on and get something to eat." He looked up at one of the soldiers standing nearby. "Wilkins, take these contrabands to the galley and give them some food."

"Yes, sir," Wilkins said.

Wilkins led Jimmy and Poky into a cabin, where he spoke to the cook. Twenty minutes later the cook handed them both plates piled with cornbread and bacon. They sat and ate without speaking.

When they finished eating, Jimmy finally spoke. "Thank you for saving me," he said to Poky.

Poky shrugged. "I pulled you over there. But Massa Ben got you to breathin' again."

Jimmy nodded. "And now he's locked up."

"I wonder what they'll do to him," Poky said.

"He's not a soldier," Jimmy said. "What with his leg and all. They ought not to keep him."

"Maybe they'll put him in the camp with us," Poky offered.

"I don't know. I don't know what's going to happen to us, either."

"The man said we're free now."

Jimmy scowled. "Free to go to some camp. But I've got to get to Philadelphia."

"How're you gonna do that?"

"I don't know." Then he asked, "Did you notice the pilot?"

Poky nodded. "Dark-skinned fella."

"I'm gonna talk to him," Jimmy said. "Maybe he can tell me what's what."

Later, when Jimmy spoke to the pilot, what he learned amazed him. He recounted all the details of his conversation with the pilot to Poky.

"The pilot's name is Robert Smalls," Jimmy began. "He used

to be a slave. But he knew how to pilot a boat, so when the war broke out, the Rebs assigned him to be a pilot for the Confederate Navy. One night last May, he stole this ship we're on, the *Planter,* right out from under the Rebs. He broke into the cabin, put on the captain's hat and jacket, fired up the engine, then sailed out to a channel island where he'd told his wife and children he'd meet them. Then they all sailed right out to sea. He took down the Rebel flag, put up a white sheet, and went straight over to a Yankee ship. Right there, the Union Navy took command of the *Planter.* Then the Navy gave the boat to the Army and they made him the pilot. They're down here to protect a Yankee fort that's on an island off the coast near Savannah. That's how they came to see us."

"And now he's free?" Poky asked.

"He's free. Back in August he was sent to Washington. He met with President Lincoln."

"He met Abe Lincoln?"

"That's what he said. He said he went there to get permission from the Secretary of War to arm the freed slaves at Port Royal, so they could protect themselves from Rebel raids. In three weeks he's going to New York City, to a meeting at Shiloh Church to raise money for all the freed slaves that are living at Port Royal. The Yankees are taking us to Port Royal now. But Mr. Smalls said he'd take me with him to New York City."

"I guess that'll leave me all alone, then," Poky said. He smiled wanly. "But you're gonna get your wish to see your sweetheart." Poky's feeble smile faded. "Did you find out what they're fixin' to do with Massa Ben?"

Jimmy shook his head. "Mr. Smalls didn't know about that. He said they might take him to a prison camp."

"Even though he's not a soldier no more?"

"He's not a soldier, but that overseer, Perkins, fired shots at the Yankees. That's what got them in trouble."

"I'm gonna to try to see him," Poky said. "I got to tell him what happened. I got to tell him what I did to Eppley. He's got to know you had nothin' to do with it."

"What does it matter now?"

"It matters to me," Poky said. "I want Massa Ben to know I didn't mean to kill Eppley. It was an accident."

Jimmy shook his head. "I don't think you ought to say anything about it. You don't know what the law is. You could get in trouble with the Yankees."

"But if I did kill him, then I ought to go by the law."

"No, Poky. That's not right. You should keep quiet. It won't do any good to get yourself in trouble. It won't bring back Eppley. It won't make anything better."

"I got to do right by the Lord," Poky said.

Jimmy shuddered. He had no use for the Lord. But he knew how troubled Poky was feeling. He said, "The Lord can't blame you, Poky. Like you said, it was an accident. Look here, hadn't Eppley just killed Uncle Isaac? And wasn't he waving a knife? The man was drunk and fixin' to kill us. You had to do somethin' to protect us, didn't you? No—the Lord can't blame you for that!"

"I was angry."

"Of course you were," Jimmy said. "So was I. I'd have done just what you did, too."

"Would you?"

"Believe it." Jimmy thought for a moment. Then he said, "I'll go talk to Massa Ben. I'll explain what happened. It's better if I talk to him."

Poky nodded. And that was all they said about it.

THE NEXT MORNING, Jimmy asked the captain if he could speak to Ben Crenshaw.

"What do you want with him?" the captain asked.

"I want to thank him," Jimmy said. "I almost drowned, but he saved my life. I never had the chance to thank him."

"Very well," the captain said. "But don't tell him where we're taking you. We don't want the Rebels to know that information."

"He's not in the Army anymore," Jimmy said. "He lost his leg."

"That's as may be," the captain said. "But he and his crony fired at a United States vessel. That's an act of war."

"I saw who did it. It wasn't Massa Ben. It was the other man, Perkins. You ought not to hold Ben Crenshaw responsible for it."

"It's not up to me," the captain said. We'll have to sort that out in a hearing."

WHEN JIMMY DID SEE BEN, he was alone in the brig—locked in a cell behind bars.

"Where's Mr. Perkins?" Jimmy asked.

"They took him out to change the dressing on his wound."

"I came to thank you," Jimmy said. "For saving me."

Ben sneered. "It seems I saved you and lost you in one stroke," he said with a trace of bitterness. "But at least I finally did some good." Then a wistful look washed over his face. "I only wish I'd saved Elijah, too."

"You couldn't help that."

"That's not true," Ben said. "I could have stopped him from coming with me. I was selfish."

"But you told me you loved him," Jimmy said.

"I did."

"And that he loved you."

"He did."

"So why wouldn't he come with you?"

"I should have stopped him—even though he wanted to come."

"Like you tried to stop us from escaping? You can't stop people from doing what matters to them."

"I wasn't trying to stop you. I was trying to look out for you. I was worried something would happen to you if I didn't."

"You mean you came after us to protect us?"

"Yes," Ben said. "That was my purpose. But I didn't tell Perkins. I couldn't. He wouldn't have helped me if he'd known —and I needed his help. With my leg as it is, I couldn't have sailed by myself."

"Why would you want to protect us?"

"It should be obvious," Ben said. "You know how I feel about you."

"Yes, you've made that clear—in more ways than one."

"For all the good it's done me."

"You kissed me on the boat."

"I had to. I had to get you to breathe again."

"It felt strange."

"It felt strange to me, too."

They stood staring at each other for a long moment.

Then Jimmy asked, "What are they going to do to you now?"

"The captain said there'll be a preliminary hearing to decide what to do with us."

"I told the captain you didn't shoot at them. I told him it was Perkins who fired the pistol."

"Thank you."

"I'll them that at the hearing, too."

"Thank you."

"Look here ... you saved me. Maybe I can save you, too."

"Yes," Ben said. "I would be grateful for that. I can't leave my sister alone."

"Your father is there."

"Sometimes."

"Little Joe is there."

"Yes," Ben said. "I take comfort in knowing that."

"What happened to Eppley," Jimmy began. "It was an accident. He fell. He was drunk. He hit his head. It wasn't anything we did."

"I believe you," Ben said. "I mean about him being drunk. I hope by now he's slept it off."

"What do you mean?" Jimmy asked, surprised. "Are you saying he's still alive?"

"Yes, of course." Ben was puzzled. "Why? Did you think he wasn't?"

Jimmy hid his astonishment. "I couldn't tell," he said. "It all happened so fast."

"He was just passed out—from drink I reckon," Ben said.

"You should get rid of him," Jimmy said. "He's evil. He killed Uncle Isaac. You're responsible for what he does."

"Me?"

"Who else?"

Ben's eyes flashed. "My father, that's who! I've tried to convince him to fire Eppley for years. But he won't do it."

"You've asked your father to fire him?"

"Of course," Ben said. "I ... you didn't think it was my decision, did you?"

"I did."

"Well, it isn't. My father controls everything."

"I didn't know that."

"My father doesn't trust me to do anything. I'm quite a disappointment to him. Even when I lost my leg in battle, it wasn't enough for him. All he cares about is when I'm going to marry."

Understanding dawned on Jimmy's face. He hadn't considered how Ben's inclinations would diminish his power. "Your father's a fool," he said. "He ought to be proud of you. You have more talent for music than any man I've met. Until you played for me, I never knew music could sound like that—like something from heaven."

"My father cares nothing for music. All he cares about is that woman he's got in town."

Jimmy shook his head. "I don't understand white men. They have so little feeling for what matters in life."

"We're not all without feeling."

"I don't mean you. I know *you* have feelings. I heard them in your music." Jimmy put his hands on the bars of the cell. "I appreciate what you've done for me. You taught me to read. I'm grateful for that."

"I only wish I'd met you in another world, Jacob. Maybe then I could have had a chance. I hope your life will be happier than mine."

"Why shouldn't you find happiness? You have money. You have a beautiful home. You have education. You have talent. You're a handsome man." Jimmy counted out these blessings on his fingers. "You ought to be able to find a friend—I mean someone like Elijah ... only white."

Ben winced. "I'm afraid I don't care for white men any more than you do." His face softened. "But I take your point."

"I've learned to care for one white man more than I ever thought I could," Jimmy said. "It might happen to you, too."

Ben smiled almost shyly. Then his expression grew wistful. "I reckon you're going back to him now ... to your friend."

"Yes," Jimmy said. "I am."

"I wish you well," Ben said. "You must believe me. I really do."

Jimmy nodded. "Thank you," he said. He stepped up to the bars of the cell and reached his hand in. "Come closer."

Ben stepped closer to the bars. Jimmy reached through them to put his hand around the back of Ben's head. He pulled Ben's face to his, and then he leaned in and kissed him on the lips. Ben's eyes rolled back in his head—and he moaned.

And then Jimmy left. There was nothing more to say between them.

45

"YOU SHOULD ALWAYS TELL ME THE TRUTH!"

As soon as they crossed into Maryland, a weight lifted from Cato's shoulders. Being back in a state where slavery was illegal let him relax. For the first time in days, he was able to give all his attention to the scenery, since they no longer had to watch out for patrollers.

Joe had painted a white lightning bolt on his forehead to help them travel as quickly as possible. Cato had been wearing his falcon feather for a similar reason, but upon crossing the border, he shed his Shawnee persona. Now that he was back in the North, he wanted to return to his normal clothes and manners. He took off his headband and let his curly hair unfurl. He would no longer pretend to be Shawnee or white. He knew Jimmy had strong feelings about this. He didn't want to take any chance that Jimmy might see him acting like anyone other than who he really was.

He also wanted to restore his normal character as much as he could before he saw Erastus. He assumed that in the midst of his personal upheaval, his friend would be reassured to see the Cato he knew and recognized.

When they arrived in Philadelphia, Cato and Joe spent their

first night in a hotel. Cato wanted to wait until the next morning to go to Erastus's house. He wanted to be rested and to look his best. He'd obtained Erastus's address from Walter McNish. The hotel they stayed at was within walking distance of that address, so in the morning, they left Oscar and Nice stabled at a livery and walked the half-mile to the street where Erastus lived.

Cato wore his best clothes. He'd insisted that Joe dress up as well. The night before, he'd gone so far as to buy Joe a suit and tie and new shoes to wear. He was very strict with Joe. There would be no face paint, no feather in his hair—nothing to call any attention to themselves as they made their way to Erastus's house.

Cato was surprised at how different Joe looked in his new clothes. He was still handsome, but in a transformed way—like a familiar painting put in a new frame. At first, Joe walked in his new shoes as if they were a pair of leg irons—making an exaggerated show of how uncomfortable he found them. But Cato knew he was teasing. By the time they got to the front of Erastus's house, he'd stopped clomping along and was walking with his usual grace.

They rang the bell at the front door. When the door opened, Giovanni Frazza, Erastus's friend and lover, stood before them. It took Mr. Frazza a moment to recognize Cato. When he did, his expression fluttered between a smile and a wary uneasiness. He stepped out of the house and gently closed the door behind him.

"It's good to see you again," he said cordially. "Erastus will be quite happy to see you. I understand from Mr. McNish that you heard what happened to Erastus."

"Yes." Cato nodded. "Did Mr. McNish tell you what happened to Jimmy?"

"Yes, how awful," Mr. Frazza said. "Have you found him?"

"We missed him in Savannah by just a day," Cato said. "But he left word that he was coming here."

"Oh, well, I reckon it will be quite a reunion, then," Mr. Frazza said.

Suddenly remembering Joe, Cato introduced him. "Mr. Frazza, this is my friend Joe Bird. I wouldn't have been able to find Jimmy without his help. Joe, this is Erastus's dear friend from Chicago, Mr. Frazza."

Joe and Mr. Frazza shook hands. But before either of them could speak, the door burst open. Sammy ran out and threw himself into Cato's arms.

"Cato! Cato! I saw you from the window," he said, his voice bubbling.

"Sammy!" Cato tried to scoop him up, but the boy had grown too big. Instead, he hugged and kissed him. "Look how big you are!" he said. He turned to Joe. "Sammy, this is my friend, Joe Bird." He lifted an eyebrow. "He's Shawnee."

"You're Shawnee?" Sammy looked incredulously at Joe. "You're an Indian?"

Joe winked and nodded. "Yes. But this is not how I usually dress. Cato wouldn't let me wear any of my feathers." Joe made a sour face. "He's very fussy."

Sammy laughed and looked at Cato. "He can be like that sometimes." Then he looked past Cato to the street. "Where's Jimmy?"

"He's not here yet," Cato said. "We're hoping to meet him here."

"Is he coming soon?"

"I hope so," Cato said.

"Hooray!" Sammy said. "I haven't seen him for a long time. He missed my birthday."

"How old are you now?" Cato asked.

"Fourteen and a half," Sammy beamed. But then abruptly, he grew grave. "Cato," he said. "Erastus had a bad accident."

"Yes," Cato said, nodding. "I heard about it."

"He lost part of his hand. He can't paint with it now."

"That's what I heard."

"But I'm still learning to paint. I told him that as soon as I know how to paint really good, then all he has to do is to tell me what he wants to paint and I'll paint it for him."

"I hadn't thought of that," Cato said. "That's a good plan. Is he giving you lessons?"

"Yes, of course," Sammy said proudly. "I paint every day. I have my own brushes and everything!"

"Sammy is doing very well with his lessons," Mr. Frazza added. "His progress is one of the few things that has raised Erastus's spirits in recent days."

"Will it be all right if we visit him?" Cato asked.

"Yes, yes," Mr. Frazza said. "Of course. I just wanted to make sure you were aware of the situation. Come in." They stepped into the house through the door that Sammy had left open. "You can wait there in the library." Mr. Frazza pointed to a doorway off the front hall. "I'll go and let Erastus know you're here."

"Thank you."

Cato and Joe entered the library, which was ornately decorated and furnished. The dominant color in the library was dark red: the bindings of most of the books were red leather, the velvet drapery adorning the windows was a deep Indian red, and the Oriental carpet on the floor was woven in an intricate red and cream design. Cato and Joe sat across from each other in matching red leather wingback chairs. Sammy sat on the carpet at Cato's feet.

"Erastus has quite a lot of books," Joe said, looking around the room.

"He has 653," Sammy said. He puffed out his chest. "I counted them." Then he turned to speak to Cato. "Erastus told me he taught you how to read."

"That's right," Cato said. "He did. What about you?"

"I learned to read in school," Sammy said. "I go to the Friends' Select School for Boys."

Cato stared at Sammy with fascination. The boy had lost his

child-like appearance. His face had lengthened and narrowed. A trace of fuzz showed above his upper lip, and his voice had deepened. Sammy and Jimmy weren't brothers by blood—and yet he was growing handsome, as if he'd inherited Jimmy's good looks. Cato sighed as he thought of Jimmy. "That's wonderful, Sammy," he said. "What are you learning?"

Sammy ticked the subjects off on his fingers. "History, science, mathematics, music, and English," he said. "Also, we learn how to be peaceful." He gave Cato a wry look. "It's harder than you think."

"I believe you," Cato said. "I never had the chance to go to school."

"But you know so much," Sammy said. "How did you learn everything?"

"From reading."

Just then Joe got up and walked to a framed drawing on the wall near a window. He turned to look back at Cato. "Is this you?"

Cato stood and joined him to look at the drawing. "Yes," he said. "Erastus drew that sketch of me in Chicago."

"It's really a good drawing!" Joe said. "You look quite different with no clothes on."

Sammy tittered.

"It's a classic nude," Cato said.

"Ah," Joe said. "Does that mean everything is drawn to proportion?"

"Erastus believes in poetic license," Cato said. "He says it's a way to express the truth of something."

"I see," Joe said. "Well, that's quite a lot of truth."

The door opened behind them, and there was Erastus, smiling, with his right arm in a sling. Cato quickly saw that his thumb and two of his fingers were gone from his right hand. Erastus noticed Cato's eyes as they registered his hand—and his smile disappeared. His eyes were watery and full of emotion.

Cato ran up to him and they embraced. Cato whispered in his ear, "I've missed you."

"It's a cliché to say so, but you are very much a sight for sore eyes," Erastus said.

"Are your eyes sore?"

"Yes, my dear," Erastus said. "They are. Since I last saw you, I've seen things I wish I hadn't."

"And yet," Cato said, looking deep into his eyes, "I still see the light within them."

"Do you?"

"Back in the corner," Cato said.

Erastus now let his eyes well up with tears. Cato kissed him on the mouth.

Sammy, Joe, and Mr. Frazza stood aside, their heads lowered in honor of the private moment between Cato and Erastus.

Then Cato turned and pulled Joe toward him. "Erastus, this is someone very special—Joe Bird, a Shawnee scout, capable of tracking anyone or anything, and my dear friend. He's guided me back to you." Then he spoke to Joe. "Joe, this, as you know, is my wise friend and mentor, Erastus Hicks."

Joe used his left hand to shake Erastus's left hand. "Cato's told me a lot about you," Joe said. He reached inside his shirt and removed a feather he'd hidden there. "This is for you." He handed it to Erastus. "I chose this especially for you. It's a dove's feather. It symbolizes love, gentleness, and kindness. Cato told me these are the qualities you are known for."

"I'm gratified," Erastus said. "It's a lovely gift. Thank you."

"Erastus, I must warn you. Joe is a living Whitman poem."

"I am?" Joe asked. "What's that?"

"It means," Cato said, "that like the poet Walt Whitman, you love the natural world so much that you make others feel the same way."

"That's good, then," Joe said.

"In that case, I'm doubly pleased to meet you," Erastus said. He looked at Cato. "I've heard from Dorothy."

"Did she tell you that I wrote her?" Cato asked.

"Yes," Erastus said. "She said she'd been reluctant to tell me about Jimmy's misfortune, because she didn't want to upset me —but she did, because of something even more surprising. She got a letter from Jimmy."

"From Jimmy!"

"Yes," Erastus said. "It seems he found a man in Savannah who could write to her on his behalf. He told her he was planning to come here—so that she could let you know where to meet him."

"I knew it!" Cato exclaimed. "He told his cabin-mate in Savannah that he was going to get his portrait painted. I knew right away that meant he was coming here."

"I wondered how you knew to come here. I've been watching and waiting for Jimmy," Erastus said, "but there's been no sign of him yet."

"He escaped by boat—to the Union blockade," Cato said. "I'm not sure how he's going to get from there to here."

"There's a Union shipyard here," Mr. Frazza said. "Boats come and go to and from the South all the time. I know because the wives tell me bits and pieces about their sailor husbands."

"Giovanni has opened a shop here," Erastus said. "Mr. Frazza is a hair cutter and purveyor of perfumes," he added for Joe's benefit.

Sammy showed his confusion. "I don't understand. Why did Jimmy have to escape? Why is he back in the South?"

"He was kidnapped," Erastus said. "Some men took him from Chicago. And I'm afraid they sold him back into slavery in Savannah."

"What?!" Sammy's face showed his anger.

"I didn't tell you," Erastus said to the boy. "I'm sorry, but I didn't want you to worry."

"How could you keep that from me?" Sammy was livid. "I'm not a little boy."

"You're right," Erastus said. "I should have told you. I only found out a few days ago, and I didn't know what I should do or say about it. I keep forgetting how much you've grown." He looked at Sammy plaintively. "You must forgive me, Sammy. I'm sorry."

"You should always tell me the truth—especially if it concerns my brother!"

"I see that now," Erastus said meekly.

Sammy turned to Cato. "But you're certain he's escaped, right, from Savannah?"

"Yes," Cato said. "In a boat, about three weeks ago. We've just come from Savannah."

"How did you find out where the kidnappers took him?" Erastus asked.

"It was partly luck," Cato said, looking at Joe. "It was luck that I met Joe Bird, because it turns out he can track anyone. I was following the trail of the man who kidnapped him—a man named Hogan—when I met Joe, who generously offered to help me."

"But what if something has happened to Jimmy since he got away?" Sammy asked. "You don't know what happened to him after he escaped, do you?"

"No." Cato shook his head. "But I know that your brother is resourceful and brave and he can handle just about anything."

"There's no point in worrying about him, Sammy," Erastus said. "We must focus on what we do know. And the one good thing that has come from all of this is that it has brought us together with Cato again."

"Yes," Cato said. "And I am very glad to be here with all of you."

46

"THEY WERE JUST STRANGE"

The proposed hearing to consider the fate of Ben Crenshaw and Jeremiah Perkins did not come to pass. Someone in the military command had ascertained that the Mulberry Grove plantation, where Jeremiah Perkins was an overseer, was a storied location in American history. At one time it had been owned by General Nathanial Greene, to whom the British surrendered at the end of the American Revolution. George Washington himself had called at Mulberry Grove to give his condolences to Mrs. Greene upon the death of her husband. Many years later, Eli Whitney had been a guest at Mulberry Grove when he invented the cotton gin.

No one in Washington wanted to see any headlines about anyone associated with the former home of a Revolutionary War hero—or reminders about George Washington or Eli Whitney's associations with a Southern plantation. Both Mr. Perkins and Mr. Crenshaw were civilians. Although Mr. Perkins had fired shots, no one but him had been injured. And so, word came down from the military command that the men should be released. The confiscation of Mr. Crenshaw's slave property was deemed a sufficient disciplinary action. His boat was returned to him—to allow him to return to his family.

When Jimmy and Poky disembarked at Port Royal, so did Mr. Robert Smalls. Mr. Smalls kept his word to Jimmy. Three weeks after they arrived, he took Jimmy with him to New York City. They traveled in the company of Reverend Mansfield French, who was an organizer of the "Port Royal Experiment," as it was known.

Jimmy went with Smalls to a meeting at the Shiloh Church in New York on October 2. When Smalls walked into the church the crowd went wild. He was presented with a gold medal, embossed with a picture of the *Planter* sneaking out on its way from Fort Sumter to the blockaders.

On September 22, just days before Jimmy and Smalls arrived in New York, President Lincoln had issued an Emancipation Proclamation, which was set to take effect in only three months' time, on January 1, 1863. It would unconditionally free all the country's slaves.

As a result, when the Shiloh Church choir sang "There's a Better Time a-Coming," everyone in the congregation was on their feet and clapping with unalloyed joy.

By an act of Congress, Smalls had been given a financial reward for his heroic deed. He'd also earned money as a pilot for the Union Army. Having money, and knowing what it was like to have nothing, Smalls generously gave Jimmy the money he needed to buy a train ticket from New York to Philadelphia. And so, after Jimmy paid his respects to Mr. Smalls and his family, he boarded a train to Philadelphia.

But Jimmy did not know where in Philadelphia Erastus Hicks lived. And when he got there late one Friday morning, he was unsure how to go about learning that information.

Initially, he spent the morning asking random strangers on the street if they knew Hicks—which led to encounters that ranged from polite to hostile, but yielded no results. It wasn't until the afternoon that he hit upon the idea of looking for a Quaker meeting house. He knew the Quakers were abolitionists, and assumed they would be sympathetic to the plight of a runaway slave. He also knew that Erastus was a Quaker. It stood to reason that someone at the meeting house might know him.

His inquiries led him in mid-afternoon to the Race Street Meetinghouse at Cherry and Fifteenth streets. Jimmy studied a plaque outside the building. He was startled to discover he could read it. He couldn't wait to show Cato what he could do. The plaque said the building was the site of the yearly meeting of a sect of Quakers founded by Elias Hicks in 1827. Jimmy reasoned that Erastus Hicks might be a descendant of Elias Hicks.

But the Race Street Meetinghouse was locked. A sign announced that worship services were on Wednesdays and Sundays.

Jimmy stood in the pleasant open courtyard in front of the building, unsure what to do next. He noticed a woman in modest attire trimming the shrubs on one side of the building.

He approached the woman and asked her if she knew Erastus Hicks.

"Mr. Hicks," she said. "Why, of course I know him. He's one of the leaders of our community."

Jimmy's voice bubbled with excitement. "Do you know where he lives?" Jimmy asked. "I've come to visit him."

"You wish to visit Mr. Hicks?" The woman looked skeptical about this idea.

"Actually," Jimmy said, thinking it might reassure her, "I've come to visit a boy named Sammy. He lives with Mr. Hicks."

"You mean Mr. Hicks's ward, Samuel?"

"Yes," he said. "That's him!"

She looked at Jimmy closely. "Is he a relative of yours?"

"Yes," Jimmy said. "He's my brother. I'm from Chicago. I've come to visit him."

The woman digested this, then decided—after looking Jimmy in the eye—that she would trust him. "Samuel is a student at the Friends Select School. The school is two blocks from here, at Cherry and Seventeenth Street."

"Do you know Sammy?"

"I do indeed," the woman said. "The boy comes here every Wednesday for our worship meeting," she said. "We have two colored students in our school," she said proudly. "And he's a very proper young man."

Jimmy grinned so wide it made his jaw hurt. "Do you think he's at school now?"

The woman glanced at the sky to gauge the time of day. "Well, I reckon he ought to be," she said. "If you hurry you'll catch him before he leaves school for the day."

Jimmy walked the two blocks down Cherry Street to the Friends Select School as quickly as he could without calling too much attention to himself. Then he stood outside the two-story building, taking it in. He counted eight windows on the first floor, and eight more on the second. He watched the windows for signs of children. Eventually, he noticed a man inside the building walk up to one of the windows on the second floor. The man opened the window—and Jimmy heard a peal of children's laughter from inside.

Jimmy waited on the lawn for the school to let out. He was overjoyed to think he might see Sammy, and he reasoned that he could learn everything he wanted to know about Cato from Sammy.

He'd sent his letter to Dorothy with the explicit hope that she'd find a way to let Cato know where he was going, so that Cato could meet him in Philadelphia. It was a plan that made a great deal of sense logically, but nevertheless it was a plan that worried him emotionally.

His relationship with Erastus was fraught with resentment. He'd never been able to let go of the jealousy he felt about Erastus's alliance with Cato. He knew that Erastus had pursued a romantic relationship with Cato during the period when they were alone together in Chicago—before Jimmy found them. And he believed that Cato, despite what he'd said, had been tempted by it. When given the choice, Cato had been absolute in his desire to part ways with Erastus in order to be with Jimmy. But Jimmy had wondered from time to time if Cato ever regretted forgoing the privileges of the life Erastus had offered him.

He couldn't fault Erastus for his behavior, which had been honorable in every respect. Erastus had given them a large amount of money, and he'd made it clear that the gift was intended for both of them. He'd blessed their relationship. Jimmy knew that he did all of this out of love, and he could hardly be ungrateful. And yet he dreaded meeting Erastus again. Just the thought of it dredged up feelings of rivalry he could not shake—even now when he was on the verge of finding Cato again. He was so excited to see Cato, so anxious to find out what he'd been doing and how he'd been feeling—and yet, he could not dislodge his nagging jealousy. He hated himself for it.

He found himself wondering if Cato and Erastus had spent time together again in his absence, and if so, if they might have rekindled the feelings that they'd nearly consummated in Chicago. He took some comfort from the fact that Erastus was living with his lover, Mr. Frazza—and that Mr. Frazza would hardly stand by while Cato and Erastus revived their romantic friendship.

As a result of these concerns—despite how much he missed him, despite how eager he was to see him again—Jimmy found himself hoping that Cato had not yet arrived in Philadelphia. How much better it would be, he thought, if he arrived before Cato. That way there would be no time for any new little intimacies to develop between Cato and Erastus.

Jimmy's rumination ended as soon as he saw Sammy emerge

from the front door of the Friends Select school. He was surprised by how much Sammy had grown in the months since he'd last seen him. The changes weren't just physical. Sammy carried himself with less abandon—and more poise—as he wended his way among the other students. His poise quickly gave way to exuberance, though, when he saw Jimmy standing on the lawn. At first, he tilted his head from side to side, uncertain if he could believe his eyes. Then he launched into an all-out sprint toward Jimmy, throwing himself, at the end, into Jimmy's arms.

"Cato told me you'd be here soon," Sammy said. "But I didn't think you'd come to see me at school."

"Is Cato here in Philadelphia?" Jimmy asked.

"Of course he is," Sammy said. "Haven't you seen him yet?"

"No, not yet."

"Then how did you know where I was?"

"I didn't know where Erastus lived," Jimmy said. "So I asked a Quaker lady at the Race Street Meetinghouse if she knew him. She told me you were in school here. So I came to see you first thing."

"Oh, boy! Cato and Erastus will be surprised."

"When did Cato get here?"

"He came a week ago," Sammy said. "And he brought a new friend with him—an Indian, named Joe."

"A new friend?"

"Yes," Sammy said. "Joe helped Cato track you down. He's really funny. You'll like him. Cato and Joe went all the way to Savannah to find you. But they said you escaped before they got there. Nobody even told me you got kidnapped. But now here you are! I'm so glad to see you."

"I'm glad to see you, too."

"Wait a minute! Did anyone tell you about what happened to Erastus?"

"No," Jimmy said. "What happened? Is he all right?"

"He had a bad accident," Sammy said. "Last month, he went to the battlefield as a nurse—to help the Union soldiers. But while he was there he got hit in the hand by a stray shot. And, well, he lost three of his fingers on his right hand, and, well ... the worst part is, now he can't paint anymore."

"Oh, no," Jimmy said. "That's terrible. He loves to paint. Can't he paint with his other hand?"

"That's what I thought," Sammy said. "But he says it's too hard. He says he can't control the brush the way he likes. He's very sad about it. I tried to cheer him up. I told him I'd paint whatever he wants. Of course, I'm not as good as him. But I'm going to be."

"And now you're in school, too."

"Yes! Jimmy, you won't believe what's happened! I've learned how to read."

"That's wonderful!"

"And I've learned a lot of things." Sammy's voice grew serious. "I'm not just a little kid anymore."

"No," Jimmy said. "I can see that. And you won't believe what's happened to me! I had some reading lessons, too."

"You did?" Sammy was shocked. "I thought you were kidnapped."

"I was," Jimmy said. "It was a peculiar thing. The people who bought me wanted to teach me things. They thought I was an experiment."

"What? Were they white folks?"

"Yes," Jimmy said. "In Georgia."

Sammy shook his head. "That's strange. Were they Quakers?"

"No," Jimmy said. "They were just strange."

"Well, come on," Sammy said. "Don't you want to go home and see Cato?" He started to walk away.

"Wait a minute," Jimmy said. "The truth is, I'd like to see him alone. I don't want to see him with everyone else around."

"Oh," Sammy giggled. "I forgot. You and Cato are like that. I suppose you want to be all lovey-dovey."

"Well," Jimmy said. "You know I love him, right?"

"I know."

"And we haven't seen each other in months."

"It's OK," Sammy said. "I understand. What do you want me to do?"

"Can you tell him where to meet me?"

"All right. What should I tell him?"

"Tell him to meet me here."

"Here? At the school?"

"This seems as good a place as any," Jimmy said, looking around. "Tell him to meet me at that tree—the one next to the wall." He pointed to a brick wall that ran along the left side of the property.

"OK," Sammy said. "I'll tell him."

"And just tell Cato," Jimmy said. "Don't tell the others that I'm here."

"But he might not be alone," Sammy said.

"You can make up a reason to get him alone if you have to," Jimmy said. "Can't you?"

"I guess so."

"Then go on and do it. OK?" Jimmy looked at the sky. "It's gonna get dark soon."

"All right," Sammy said. "But then you'll come home with him, won't you? You're not going away again?"

"No. No, I'm not. Don't worry," Jimmy said. "I'll come to see you soon. I just want to spend a little time with Cato alone."

"OK," Sammy said. "I guess that's all right then. I'll go get him. I'll see you later."

"OK. Bye."

As soon as Sammy left, Jimmy made his way to the tree near the wall. When he got there, he found he was trembling with anticipation—he was so eager to see Cato. And yet, he was also anxious about it. Cato had spent a week with Erastus. And now there was some new friend Jimmy had never heard of before. He didn't know what to make of that, and he couldn't ask Sammy what he really wanted to know. The only way he could be sure what Cato was feeling was to see him in person.

And so, he stood between the tree and the wall, his back against the tree, alone with his private thoughts. And he waited.

47

"HOW DO I LOOK?"

Sammy was not so grown-up that he couldn't still skip. So skip he did. He skipped and ran and—despite his grown-up size—when he saw Cato sitting alone in the library, he jumped onto Cato's lap. He was so excited he couldn't speak.

"What's happened?" Cato didn't know if something wonderful or horrible had befallen Sammy.

"Jimmy!" Sammy stuttered. He took a deep breath, then spit it out. "I saw him! He's here!"

"He's here? He's where? Where, Sammy, where?"

"Down at my school. He's waiting for you there. He told me to come and tell you. He wants to see you alone."

"Oh, Sammy!" Cato picked up the boy and whirled him out of the wingback chair and onto Erastus's expensive carpet, where they rolled around like children playing in the mud. Cato was beside himself. He could hardly breathe. He spun onto his back and waved his hands in the air. Then he turned to face Sammy. "Where's your school?"

"It's not far. You can be there in fifteen minutes."

"Oh, God!" Cato stood up. He ran his hand through his hair, which was mussed from rolling on the floor. "How do I look?"

Sammy stood up, too. "Brother, you look like a crazy person."

"I guess it doesn't matter, does it?"

"I don't reckon it does."

"OK. Sammy, I'm going to go there now. How do I get there?" Sammy gave him the directions. "Now, Sammy, wait for me here. I'll be back soon."

"You? Just you?"

"No. I mean, we ... we'll be back soon—both of us. Oh, I can hardly believe it!"

"Don't forget what I told you," Sammy said. "He's standing back by the wall, the wall at the side of the building. The building is red. I mean, it's almost pink. It's pinkish-red."

"Yes. The wall at the side of the pinkish-red building."

"He's standing by a tree," Sammy added.

"Sammy?"

"What?"

"How does he look?"

Sammy laughed. "Less cuckoo than you, I reckon."

"Good. I think."

Cato left the house and began to walk toward the school. But he could no longer feel his body. He moved like a ghost, like a spirit floating above the ground. And though his eyes could see where he was going, none of the physical objects in the world around him registered in his mind. His mind was entirely filled with a vision of Jimmy.

He could see Jimmy from head to toe. He pictured Jimmy's hand reaching around, touching him on the backside—and he instantly felt himself get aroused. He tried to adjust his pants. He could hardly walk down the street in the state he was in.

And yet, he didn't care. Gone were the cigar, the spectacles, and the Bible. Gone, too, was the Spanish surname. Gone were the feather, the wig, and the top hat. Gone, the imperious air, the patrician aspect. Gone was the purse and the box of matches. Gone was any pretense of propriety.

He was nothing but a rabbit. He was Jimmy's gentle, prancing rabbit. He started to move faster. He bounded. He leapt. He thought if he moved fast enough no one could see him. No one would see the happy hopping rabbit with tears in his eyes.

48

"I'VE BEEN DREAMING..."

Jimmy slid his back down the trunk of the tree until he was sitting on the ground. The sun was low in the sky, but it shone a brilliant red spotlight on everything around him. He looked up at the tree above him. The leaves were a fiery orange. He felt a waft of air on his face that was neither warm nor cool. It was a perfectly even temperature. It was autumn. He was aware that the sun was setting earlier each day, which also meant that the day and night were more in balance.

He reflected on what Sammy had told him. Cato had traveled all the way from Chicago to Savannah to find him. He began to consider what that must have been like for Cato. As he thought about it, he watched a squirrel climb out on a high branch above him. The squirrel paused, wagged its tail, then jumped in a stupendous leap that spanned the seven-foot gap between the tree Jimmy sat beneath and the thin branch of the next tree along the wall. The squirrel was fifty feet above the ground.

Jimmy marveled at the creature's daring. It must have

understood the danger of falling from such a height. And yet it jumped, because it was the most natural thing for it to do.

In that moment he was struck by how much Cato's journey was like the squirrel's leap. It was the action of someone for whom great risk was nothing, because it was part of the path that nature compelled him to follow. And, thinking about this comparison, Jimmy was overwhelmed by the force of Cato's love for him. He flushed with self-reproach as he recalled the jealousy he'd felt moments before.

In the protective space of the Friends School courtyard in Philadelphia, his anxieties melted. He was in the North. He was free. He was about to be reunited with the man he most loved in all the world. And as he basked in the abiding comfort of those realizations, he found himself able to wonder why he'd ever had doubts.

An insight swept over him. It wasn't Cato that he'd doubted. He doubted himself. Some part of him had doubted that he was good enough for Cato. And as he admitted the truth of this insecurity to himself, he realized why it should be so. How could it be otherwise? There were so many reasons a man enslaved might doubt his own worth.

He saw, then, the sweep of his life, from his childhood in slavery in Tennessee—to his adulthood working as a free man on the docks of the Chicago River—to his kidnapping and re-enslavement in Georgia—to his escape and subsequent near-death on the open sea. It had been the great trial of his soul—the struggle to break through his degradation and reach the essential truth of his own goodness. It was nothing for a man born to wealth and privilege to feel self-worth—to love the world, to love himself. But for a poor slave to learn to do so was an enormous achievement.

And as he felt the rush of this kind and forgiving view of himself, kindness and forgiveness coursed through his body. In that moment, sitting beneath that tree, with that gentle breeze on his face, with the red light of the sun illuminating the trees in the courtyard of the Quaker school, he understood for the first time in his life the thrill of freedom from judgment. In that moment he saw all the people in the world undivided—not sheep, not goats, not saints, not sinners, not good, not evil, not master, not slave. Not in any category subject to appraisal—but as souls in a drama that could not be without meaning.

He saw how meaning in his life—being someone born into abasement—might come from experiences that had nothing to do with wealth or social esteem. The joy he felt in this moment, he realized, was a triumph over the evils he'd known. For in this moment, joy was surging through him. His joy made him believe, not in God, but in a grand force of goodness in the world. He glimpsed a new version of himself—a version of himself that had emerged from the prison of hate. Forgiveness was opening his heart.

In this moment of idealism, he looked around. He thought to himself, "I will remember this moment the rest of my life." He looked at the grass planted in the lawn that ran through the courtyard—the grass beneath the tree, so green and lush.

He lay down on his back and stared at the sky—at the clouds, at the same amorphous shapes he'd watched in the meadow where Ben Crenshaw had first approached him. The clouds were bright pink—free and floating. The sky was filled with gradations of warm colors. He rolled onto his stomach, then buried his face in the lawn. He smelled the grass. He let his eyes focus on an ant making its way between the blades, zigzagging, climbing up and over obstacles that were so minute in Jimmy's eyes—and yet so substantial in the eyes of the ant. The ant was carrying some tiny thing—its own version of picking cotton. Jimmy let himself breathe—slowly, in and out.

And then he felt the touch of a hand on his back. His whole body shivered. He rolled over. Cato stood above him—backlit by the fiery sky. Jimmy leapt to his feet.

Neither of them could speak. And yet sounds came from their throats. They threw their arms around each other. They moved as a unit, without thinking, sidling along the wall, moving along the edge of the school building, until they were in a passageway out of sight from any other human being. And then they began to kiss. The kiss became unrestrained devouring—with their lips fastened together, their tongues probing to the limits of their reach. Tears dropped from their eyes. The salty fluid ran down their noses and cheeks in tickling little rivulets of rapture. Their arms pulled their bodies together with such zeal that they became like a single thing—like an orb rotating with the celestial majesty of the stars. They turned round and round in a circle—for there was no other way for the force of the gravity between them to show itself, except in centripetal momentum. They whirled in an ecstatic trance—marveling at the power of their love, at the ache and glee of their passion.

They could each feel the arousal in the other. And yet, in their public circumstance, they knew they'd have to wait. But they also now were certain that the force that drove them toward fusion could not be stopped. It was enough to fill their imaginations—to enable them to foresee all that was yet to occur between them—which in that moment felt eternal and unbounded.

"Cato," Jimmy cried, at last.

"Jimmy!"

"I've been dreaming ... I've been waiting ... I've been hoping ... I've been wanting you so bad. Oh, baby, sweet man, my gentle rabbit, my very own Cato! I love you so much."

"Do you?"

Jimmy laughed. "You know I do."

"How much?" Cato giggled.

"Oh, Cato! I love you all to pieces!"

~

THE END

About the Series Logo

Prior to the publication of Unmentionables in 2010, there was no written account of the lives of gay African American slaves in any history books or primary documents. Nor had the story of gay slaves ever been told in fiction. The publication of Unmentionables marked the first time that these characters, who had previously been expunged from history, were the subject of an historical fiction novel.

The logo reflects the love between slaves that society refused to acknowledge. These slaves were people who had been deemed "unmentionable" by historians and writers.

ALSO BY DAVID GREENE

The Winkler Case

When insurance salesman Elliot Blake makes a house call at the home of fight promoter Walt Winkler, it's handsome boxer Vito Vellucci who comes to the door. In this gay re-imagining of the classic noir novel *Double Indemnity*, obsessive desire unfolds in an unexpected direction.

Detonate

Ride from Niagara Falls to New York City on a speeding train with biracial, bisexual private eye, Tyrone King, and fellow passenger, Sarah, as they race to stop terrorists from blowing up the Statue of Liberty.

ACKNOWLEDGMENTS

I'm grateful to editor Teja Watson for her help with this book. Her insights and suggestions truly brought the story to life!

Thank you, too, to Karl Koch, who designed the cover, and to Michael Banning, who amended Homer's painting to make the figures in the boat look like two slaves might have looked.

My deepest thanks to David Melnick for his help with the text and for his early encouragement, which helped me commit to writing this book.

Finally, thank you to all the *Unmentionables* fans who asked that I write a sequel. I hope you enjoyed it.